A Rose

From

The

Executioner

A Novel

By

Edward Izzi

A ROSE FROM THE EXECUTIONER

AUTHOR'S DISCLAIMER

This book, "A Rose from the Executioner" is a complete work of fiction. All names, characters, businesses, places, events, references and incidents are either the products of the author's imagination or are used in a fictitious manner in order to tell the story. Any references to real life characters or incidents are used purely as a fictitious means of reciting a narrative, for enjoyment purposes only.

Author makes no claims of any real-life inferences or actual events, other than to recite a fabricated story with a fictitious plot. Any resemblance to actual persons, living or dead, or actual events is purely coincidental or used for entertainment purposes.

ABOUT THE AUTHOR

Edward Izzi is a native of Detroit, Michigan, and is a Certified Public Accountant, with a successful accounting firm in suburban Chicago, Illinois. He is the father of four grown children, and one "incredible" granddaughter. He has written many stories over the years, including the thriller "Of Bread & Wine" in 2018.

He currently lives in Chicago, Illinois.

For my father, Mario Izzi
...the strongest man I know.

PREFACE

It was a warm, late Sunday afternoon as the elderly man finished planting his spring flower garden. He had just planted several flats of begonias, petunias and geraniums around his house and yard, and was returning his gardening tools to his backyard shed. Although it was hard work, the old man enjoyed his gardening and landscaping the park-like setting around his Chicago residence. He had just rotor-tilled a small patch of ground towards the end of his backyard yesterday, as he was cultivating it to be a vegetable garden this season. He figured he would run to the garden store and buy several tomato and pepper plants tomorrow morning. The old man was very proud of his residence on West Argyle Street in Chicago's Albany Park neighborhood, and his plush lawn and his decorative flower garden was meticulously kept. He often received compliments from his neighbors about how beautiful his flowers and green lawn looked surrounding his yellow bricked, bungalow home.

As the sun was starting to set later that Sunday evening, he washed up and went into the kitchen to warm up some leftovers from earlier that day. That afternoon, he had Sunday dinner at the home of a good friend down the block. Angela Pecorino, an older Italian 'lady-friend' whom he had known for many years, had sent him home with some freshly cooked mostaccioli and home-made meat balls. Although the 79-year-old man lived alone, he had many friends around the neighborhood. He had never married and had no close family or relatives who lived nearby.

Since his retirement working at the Archdiocese of Chicago several years ago, his main activity was his volunteer work with the sick children at Lurie Children's Hospital three days a week. He was well liked at the hospital, as he wheeled the sick children from the children's ward to various departments around the facility. His volunteer work at Lurie and his community involvement with his church, Our Lady of Mercy Parish, kept him quite busy indeed, and left him with very little idle time.

After the elderly man finished his dinner, he went into the family room to watch some television for a few hours or so, and then slowly walked upstairs to wash up before going to bed. His back was hurting from the day's work around the house. It was just after 11:30pm.

The old man had just settled into his comfortable bed when he heard some loud noises coming from the basement. As he listened intently, it sounded as though there was someone downstairs. He got out of bed, wearing only his pajamas, and tried to quietly walk out of his bedroom. The elderly man lightly tip-toed out of the second floor, down the stairs, and across the family room. He slowly opened the door to his basement. He turned on the light and gingerly walked down each stair, realizing that he had no weapon, no bat, or sharp utensil to use to protect himself. He looked around his basement and saw nothing. He paused for several moments. The noises that he had heard seemed to be gone, as there was only a long, dead silence. He walked across the basement floor and began to climb back up the stairs after closing the basement lights.

As he climbed to the top of the stairs, he suddenly froze. He immediately felt a cold, sharp knife up against his throat. The old man's heart started beating heavily, as though it were ready to jump out of his body. Someone had grabbed him from behind, and he was feeling the strength of a stranger's left arm across his chest and the old man was unable to move.

He began to scream, yelling "Help" at the top of his lungs.

There was no one around to hear him. The intruder only whispered into the old man's left ear, the last final words that he would ever hear:

"May Jesus grant you mercy, Father Marquardt."

CHAPTER ONE

I was sitting at my desk eating my Subway sandwich at the Sixteenth District in Jefferson Park. It had been a slow Monday morning that day, and I was finishing up some prior case paper work when I got a phone call at 12:53pm.

"Detective Dorian speaking."

I was trying to answer my desk phone with my mouth still full from the last bite of my turkey sandwich.

"Phil? It's Tommy Morton, from the Seventeenth District," said the voice on the other line.

"What's up Tommy? How's it going?"

"Great Phil. Except we got a victim here at 4215 West Argyle, and we don't have any spare detectives to come over and help us. Can you come over?" he politely asked.

"I don't know, Tommy. I just finished my lunch and I'm not sure if I'm in the mood for any dead bodies' right now," I kiddingly responded.

"Can you get here quick? We could use your expertise." He sounded too serious for my liking that day.

"Ok Tommy. I'll be right over."

I dusted the breadcrumbs off myself at my desk and grabbed my suit coat. I figured this was probably some alley gang-banger caught up in a drug deal gone south. We had been seeing a lot of those lately, and some of the detectives in our unit have been helping over in the Seventh District in the Englewood neighborhood on the south side of Chicago, where the drug wars and the gang member bodies keep piling up daily. I jumped into my Crown Victoria police car and sped over to the Albany Park neighborhood. With the sirens on, I was at the West Argyle address in less than ten minutes. Detective Tom Morton was anxiously awaiting my arrival at the driveway of the home. The patrolmen had already posted the crime scene tape around the house, and there was a Chicago EMT Unit and several more police cars parked in front of the crime scene.

"Hey Tommy, what do we got?" I said as we shook hands.

He was staring at my stomach as I approached him, and I was just waiting for him to make a smart-ass comment about how many Dunkin' Donuts I must be eating.

"Hey Phil, sorry to bug you on this call. You have a little more experience on these kinds of murders than anyone in our department. "

"What kind of murder?" I innocently asked.

"Come with me downstairs."

I followed Detective Morton inside the house and down the stairs to the basement, where there were several other patrolmen and a couple of guys from the Chicago Fire Department. I had been on the force for over twenty-five years, and I have seen more than my share of dead bodies and horrific murder scenes. I seemed to be getting the reputation of being the 'Detective Stabler' (Law & Order: SVU) within the precinct. But this one really took me by surprise, and I was sorry I had even taken the call after enjoying my footlong Subway sandwich.

In the middle of the basement, was a body of a naked old man, probably in his eighties, hanging from his neck by a rope tied up from the rafters. He had several stab wounds across his torso, and his neck had been slit open. His hands were tied together, and his genitals had been cut off and mutilated. The old man's eyes had been gauged out and bleeding. A sharp, long broomstick was impaled into his body, and crammed inside of him from behind. Judging from all the blood and the position of the body, it looked as though he had

11

been killed first before being hung up and filleted like a porterhouse steak.

There was pool of blood everywhere around the body, but there was one thing left under his feet that really made me raise my eyebrows. Beneath the victim, next to all the blood, was a long-stemmed red rose.

Tommy kept shaking his head, as I kept staring at the dead corpse in total amazement.

"Nobody kills like this anymore," observed Detective Morton.

I continued to study the victim, trying to process the whole murder scene. I hadn't seen a murder like this since that dead body we found over at the Admiral Theater on West Lawrence ten years ago. That victim turned out to be the strip club owner, who was all 'mobbed up', and there wasn't any doubt that it was a Mafia hit. But this murder was different. The killer was definitely very angry with his victim and made an extra effort to take out every ounce of his anger, using a knife into the victim's body. The killer was also trying to make a statement.

"Who is this guy?" I asked Detective Morton.

"His name is John Marquardt; he's 79 years old. According to the neighbors, he was the nicest old man on the block. Helped all the neighborhood ladies shovel their snow with his snow blower every winter. Always planted beautiful tulips and flowers in and around his house and passed out candy to all the neighborhood kids. Nobody has anything bad to say about him, and everyone on the street is in shock," he explained.

I continued to stare at the hanging dead body, still dripping blood onto the basement floor.

"Who called this in?" I asked.

"The Polish cleaning lady came in here this morning and found him like this. The guy apparently lives alone, and it looks like he's been dead for several hours. We put the time of death somewhere around midnight."

I kept staring at the body, then walked around the basement, looking for any obvious clues. Morton was looking around with me as he asked, "What do you think about the red rose, Phil?"

"It's interesting," I thought out loud, "definitely Murder 101."

He looked at me with that dumb look on his face that most of the detectives from his precinct usually have. The detectives over at the Seventeenth District weren't the sharpest pencils in the box.

"Tommy, the murderer left a calling card," I explained. "Are there any rose bushes around the house?"

"Nope. The old man planted every other flower that you can think of. He obviously loved flowers, but for some reason, no roses. "

"Interesting," I mumbled again.

I thought that it was odd that the murderer would go out of his way to plant a red rose next to the victim's body. But why? He obviously was trying to say something. This homicide had a lot of symbolism. Some psychotic murderers get off on trying to make a valiant statement when they kill. Some use objects, some leave the murder weapon, and others leave notes. But a red, long stemmed rose? I kept turning it my head over and over. A red rose is the symbol of love, of romance, and of deep spirituality. In early Christian times, it became associated with the virtue of the Virgin Mary.

But what does that have to do with a 79-year old man who helped old ladies and passed out candy to little kids? Something was going on here, I was just having a hard time putting my finger on it. Why did the killer bother to hang his victim? Why the mutilated genitals and the impalement? Why didn't the murderer just simply cut his victim's throat and be done with it?

There were too many unanswered questions, and it was obvious that the murderer had more than just anger issues.

"Has CSI gotten here to lift any prints yet?" I was referring to the Crime Scene Investigation Unit, who usually show up to take prints and pictures.

"They just got here. So far, it looks as though everything was wiped clean," replied Morton.

"Looks like this guy is a professional. Maybe this was a mob hit?" asked another patrolman.

"Yes, except why would the Mafia be putting a hit on a 79-year-old man who loved to plant flowers?" I asked. It just didn't make any damn sense.

"Anything else we know about this old man?" I asked Tommy.

"We called it in. This guy used to work for the Archdiocese of Chicago."

"The Archdiocese of Chicago? Really?" I was surprised, for some odd reason.

"Apparently, he was in the administration office for a long time. He was an ex-priest for many years prior to that."

"An ex-priest? Who the hell would want to kill an old, ex-priest?" I asked.

"Don't know," Tommy replied.

"Was he defrocked?" I asked.

"As far as we know, he wasn't. We've got a call into the Archdiocese. So far, all we could confirm was his identity and that he worked in their office for many years."

"Very interesting," I answered.

I walked up to the dead victim and after acquiring an evidence bag and putting on a set of gloves, I put the red rose into the evidence bag for the crime lab. I also wanted to study it, along with the other evidence gathered at the crime scene. When I got back to my office, I decided to make a phone call to the Archdiocese of Chicago and see how far I could get through the ranks in getting someone to give me some information on the victim.

I left a message for a Monsignor Joseph Kilbane, who was the Administrative Chief of Staff to the Cardinal. I then went online, and I found an abused victim's website, which listed and categorized every single Catholic priest, nun, bishop or other clergy who was ever accused of any sexual inappropriate behavior over the last fifty years. But the victim's name wasn't on the list. So, I then decided to drive over to the Archdiocese of Chicago office at 835 North Rush Street.

There was a middle aged, gray haired lady standing guard at the front desk, who obviously didn't like Chicago coppers. She gave me quite a dirty look when I showed her my star.

"Monsignor Kilbane is very busy today. You can leave me your name and he will try to call you back."

"Excuse me ma'am. This is urgent. It's regarding the murder investigation of John Marquardt."

She looked at me with a shocked look on her face. She then walked back to his office and Monsignor Kilbane then appeared. We exchanged greetings and he brought me over to his lavish office within the Archdiocese's primary headquarters. I gave him my card and told him about John Marquardt's murder today, and how we were trying to do a thorough murder investigation. He had no reaction when I said that Marquardt was dead.

"Can you tell me a little about John Marquardt and why he left the priesthood?" I asked him. He looked at me and thought for a moment.

"From what I recall, he voluntarily left due to personal reasons over thirty years ago. He used to be a parish diocesan priest, and he was assigned as pastor to several area parishes within the Chicagoland area. He couldn't fulfill his duties any longer and needed to be a caregiver for his mother, which he did for several years. When his mother passed away, Cardinal Brody put him on staff, and he worked here at the office for many years. He just recently retired," the Monsignor calmly explained.

"So, he voluntarily left the priesthood? There were never any complaints about any inappropriate behavior while he was a priest?" I asked.

"None. He was the nicest old man with a heart of gold. Everyone here at the office loved him. He did some volunteer work at Chicago Lurie Children's Hospital a few days a week as well," he mentioned.

"And he wasn't defrocked or ever accused of anything inappropriate?" I pressured.

I could tell Kilbane was starting to get a little aggravated with me.

"Look, Detective. Whatever it is that you're looking for, you're not going to find any dirt on John Marquardt. He was a well-respected former priest and a wonderful man. He will be mourned and missed by many," he curtly answered.

He then rose from his desk and began escorting me out of his office.

"Please excuse me, Detective. I have a very busy schedule today."

We shook hands and mentioned that I would probably be contacting him again soon with any more questions. He gave me the 'good luck with that' look on his face and retrieved back to his office.

I thought it was unusual that the Monsignor wasn't shocked, nor did he ask any questions regarding the circumstances of Marquardt's murder. Usually, when a friend or colleague is killed, people usually want to hear all the details and ponder the situation as to whom, what and where. But Kilbane didn't ask me anything at all. He didn't even look surprised.

I went back to my office and started writing up my investigation report. I had a feeling that, unless CSI can come up with any DNA evidence at the crime scene, or find any witnesses, or come up with any clues or suspects, this murder investigation was going to remain open for a very long time. Whoever this murderer is, he is no amateur.

Getting a 'collar' on this murder was going to be very difficult. The red rose in the plastic bag was still sitting on the corner of my desk, and I had neglected to submit it to CSI for testing. It was still fresh and hadn't displayed any discoloration or wilting yet. I would send it off later, I thought to myself. As I continued to stare at the fresh, long stemmed red rose, I kept repeating to myself the same observation that Tommy Morton mentioned out loud at the crime scene:

Nobody kills like this anymore.

CHAPTER TWO

The valet from Trattoria Pagliacci on North Halsted opened the door of the black CTS Cadillac as Monsignor Kilbane handed him the keys. The traffic last December on that cold winter's evening was hectic, as it was only a week before Christmas and everyone in Chicago was out finishing their Christmas shopping.

Monsignor Kilbane was almost a half hour late for his dinner meeting with his longtime friend, whom he had known for many years and was hoping he hadn't missed him. Anthony "Little Tony" DiMatteo and the Monsignor had been lifelong friends since their childhood, as they both grew up in the Bridgeport neighborhood two blocks away from Mayor Daley's home. They always kept in touch and the Monsignor was involved in many DiMatteo family occasions, including baptisms, first communions, and confirmations. He even officiated over the wedding of DiMatteo's oldest daughter a few years ago. The two close neighborhood friends went to the Nativity of Our Lord Catholic School together, had been the best of friends since the second grade. Their friendship never seemed to get in the way of their two very separate and completely different professions.

Monsignor Joseph Kilbane was from a devoutly Irish Catholic family in Bridgeport. He was involved in some local gangs as a kid and got into some trouble with Tony as a teenager, before his family's pastor, Fr. Patrick O'Malley interceded. The priest became his role model, and he graduated from DeLaSalle High School, in the upper part of his class. He then attended Notre Dame University, graduating magna cum laude, before attending Mundelein Seminary. He was ordained a priest in 1981 and had risen throughout the ranks of the Archdiocese of Chicago, from being an associate pastor of several Chicago parishes to becoming the administrative chief of staff and the second most powerful cleric in Chicago. Being the "Assistant Cardinal" within the Archdiocese required the business savvy of a corporate CFO, and Kilbane keenly oversaw all the fiscal and financial functions of the third largest diocese in the United States.

"Little Tony" DiMatteo took a different path in life. He was a juvenile delinquent and had a 'rap sheet' by the time he was 13 years old. Despite his family being upper middle class and financially comfortable in the Bridgeport neighborhood, he chose to continuously get into trouble and hang around the wrong crowd. He was involved in several local robberies and was implicated in some local gang beatings and auto thefts. He was kicked out of Richards High School in the tenth grade for beating up and critically injuring one of his Math instructors. He then spent several years in the juvenile court system and ended up doing four years in Statesville for armed robbery and attempted murder.

But it wasn't until he joined the family business, that "Little Tony" gained his callous, ruthless reputation. The DiMatteo Tomato Company was a second-generation food distribution entity, handling the sales and shipment of produce to grocery stores all over the country from their giant warehouse on South Ashland Avenue. The DiMatteo's were also infamous for their other family businesses; the largest bookmaking and loan sharking operation in the city. They also supplied a majority of the video poker games and slot machines throughout Chicagoland. Little Tony was well known and recognized by 'Mob watchers' and the FBI as being "The Capo" of all the Chicago crime organizations.

DiMatteo ran a very successful operation from both sides of the law, having a vast array of 'drivers', or enforcers, who installed machines, made collections, and administrated "accounts receivables." His drivers were Teamsters during the day, making deliveries of food and other produce to various grocery stores throughout the city. After hours, he had a select group of 'enforcers' of fifty or more men, who effectively did "whatever was necessary" to collect on all his receivables, both on and off the books. He had vast business interests, including investments in two Chicago area casinos, several restaurants, and various real estate developments throughout the city and suburbs. Chicago Crain's had recently estimated his net worth to be in the billions.

Little Tony liked this restaurant for the great food and ambiance, and he knew the chef-owner extremely well. He was always guaranteed the utmost discretion and privacy to conduct his meetings and private affairs, using the small VIP room located in the back of the restaurant. He never had to worry about the press, the feds, or any "wise-guy wannabee's" interrupting him while he was there, as there was a separate entrance from the side of the building going directly to his private booth and table. Monsignor Kilbane had never been at this restaurant before, and it took him several minutes for him to find his way around to Little Tony's private dining room.

"Father Joe!" Little Tony excitedly exclaimed, as the two greeted and kissed each other on the cheek.

"You look great Tony. You're never going to get old."

At 63 years old, Little Tony was still fit and trim at five feet, five inches tall. Although his black raven hair had turned completely white over the years, he was still quite healthy for his age. He maintained a rigorous fitness schedule that included weight lifting and cardio five times a week. Little Tony arrived at his warehouse at four-thirty every morning and worked out in his personal gym in excess of two hours every day.

"I wish I had your life!" Tony jokingly said. "Fr. Joe", as Tony and his family liked to call him, was closer to six feet tall, average build, and his circular, wire rimmed glasses were his trade mark. Although he was the same age as Little Tony, the pressures of his pastoral career had accelerated his years, and he looked much older for his age. He had some health and heart issues in the past, and his facial wrinkles and balding hair was beginning to reveal the difficult stresses of his job running the Archdiocese of Chicago.

The Monsignor ordered a Manhattan cocktail, while Little Tony was on his third Crown Royal on the Rocks.

They continued to make small talk for almost an hour, and it wasn't until their entrée's had arrived before Fr. Joe finally 'broke the ice' to address the purpose for their meeting.

"Tony, I need your help," the Monsignor started as Little Tony listened intently. "The Archdiocese is broke." he exclaimed. DiMatteo looked at him a little startled, as he was grasping the spoon to begin twirling his linguini and clam sauce.

"Are you looking for a juice loan, Father?" he jokingly asked.

"Frankly...no. I wish it were that easy." The Monsignor then began to explain in detail his dilemma:

"The Chicago Archdiocese has paid out over $200 million dollars in lawsuit settlements to abused recipients who were the victims of pedophile priests over the last twenty years. It has been the policy of the Archdiocese to pay these lawsuits from the church's assets, rather than the weekly collections donated by parish parishioners. Because of the cost of these excessive lawsuits, we have exhausted most all our liquid assets and investments, and we can no longer make any more claims on our liability insurance coverage for such malicious settlements. We have even taken excessive, unsecured loans from the Vatican. We are now being forced to sell off assets." Monsignor Kilbane took a break as he was sampling several bites of his chicken cacciatore.

"So, the Archdiocese is having a garage sale?" Tony jokingly asked with his mouth full. He was having a difficult time believing that the Archdiocese of Chicago was close to being broke.

"We cannot take out any more loans and leverage our churches and parishes and put the burden of these lawsuits on our parishioners in Chicago. We now have to find an alternative means to raising more money for the Archdiocese or we could end up like Boston, or Portland and other dioceses and be faced with a bankruptcy." Kilbane explained.

"Doesn't sound like a bad option?" DiMatteo observed.

"Well, technically, it is a bad option. The Archdiocese issued some bonds twenty years ago that were publicly traded and are now coming due. A Chapter Eleven would not effectively absolve all the church's liabilities due to these excessive lawsuits, along with these bond redemptions. And with all our real estate, all the land, churches and schools owned by the Archdiocese, any bankruptcy trustee would require us to sell it all off in a bankruptcy at "fire sale" prices. We've talked to several law firms and concluded that any bankruptcy or reorganization would not be a good option for the Archdiocese," said the Monsignor.

"Then the church doesn't have too many alternatives," Little Tony stated. He was enjoying his linguini so much at that point that he was barely paying attention to the conversation.

"Well," Kilbane continued. "We do have one option…." He was trying to make eye contact with Tony in between his pasta twirling and his fourth Crown

Royal. DiMatteo stopped feeding his face just long enough make the Monsignor think he was interested in the conversation.

"And what option is that, Joe?" as he took another long sip of his drink.

"Many, many years ago, starting back in the 1970's, the Archdiocese of Chicago started taking out and paying the premiums on life insurance policies that it took out on our defrocked and pedophile priests. We now have over $200 million dollars in life insurance policies on the lives of these old priests that are still around. Some of them are for five million dollars or more. Cardinal Brody and his successors had the intuition to realize the potential avalanche of lawsuits that was going to someday occur. The problem is, most of these term life policies expire when these insured ex-priests surpass the age of 80 years old. Quite frankly, although we have collected on a few insurance policies, we have many septuagenarian ex-priests who are close to attaining that age. I figure we have over seventy-five percent of these old ex-priests still around, and many of them are in good health." Kilbane was explaining, noticing that his chicken cacciatore was starting to get cold.

Little Tony had just finished polishing off his linguini and was starting to dip his bread in the clam sauce. He quickly put his head back into his 'dog dish', not taking a whole lot of interest in the Archdiocese's financial problems. Several moments went by, as the two of them continued to eat in silence. Finally, Monsignor Kilbane said something that made Little Tony almost choke on his food.

"Tony, I need a *hit man*." he softly said, making sure no one was around.

Little Tony DiMatteo stopped eating and looked at him intently, originally thinking that the Monsignor was joking. He stared at him for about three seconds, and then started to laugh at what he thought was a very stupid joke.

"Tony, I'm serious. I need a hit man." Fr. Joe said again.

DiMatteo put his fork and bread down and looked at him again, wondering what was in his drink.

"Joe, are you fucking nuts? What the 'fon-goole' are you going to do with a hit man?" he asked.

"We don't have many other options, Tony. We've been paying on these life insurance policies for years, and we can't even collect on their cash surrender values anymore because we have used them to pay the outstanding premiums. Within the next three to five years, because of the age of these pedophile priests, most of these policies will expire." The Monsignor explained, trying to convince Little Tony that he wasn't crazy.

DiMatteo wiped off his mouth with his napkin and smirked at Kilbane.

"Joe, do you remember when we were kids at Nativity School back in Bridgeport?"

"Yes, I fondly remember."

"Do you remember that crazy idea you had back in the eighth grade? To sneak into the girl's locker room while the girls were taking showers after gym class?" he reminded Fr. Joe.

"Yes," Kilbane softly laughed. "We would have pulled it off if you didn't chicken out."

DiMatteo took another long sip of his Crown Royal.

"Well, you haven't had another crazy idea like that again until now." Tony continued his lecture.

"Are you out of your fucking mind? Do you think you're going to get a hit man to take out all these old

23

pedophile priests and collect on these insurance policies without the coppers getting wise? You're going to have every goddamn detective in the Chicago Police Department banging on the Cardinal's front door."

"Would you rather we put up a 'For Sale' sign up in front of Holy Name Cathedral? Because that may be our next option." Kilbane retorted.

"Look Joe, you're a damned priest. What ever happened to that 'Thou Shall Not Kill' commandment? Do you really want that on your conscience? I mean, come on, Joe. I'm a hood! I'm going to Hell anyways, so I'm going to enjoy myself while I'm here. But you? You're a fucking priest." Little Tony was preaching to the Monsignor.

"Tony, I have seen firsthand what these pedophile priests have done to these abused children over the years. Do you know how many screwed up people there are out there who have turned to drugs, alcohol, and even suicide because of all these sick pedophile priests that the Archdiocese has protected over the years? No thanks to the Vatican! These sick, old ex-priests, who have raped and molested all of these children over the years, are now living their comfortable lives in peace, while their tormented victims are having a hard time living day to day, their innocence and young souls stolen from them at a very early age," Kilbane angrily defended himself.

Monsignor Joseph Francis Kilbane never made any secret of his contempt for pedophiles, and has always been very outspoken about the subject, especially those sexual deviants who entered the priesthood.

"I don't feel one bit of sympathy for any of these old, sick bastards." Kilbane continued. "The Archdiocese has been carrying and protecting them long enough. It's time to start eliminating these psychotic sons of a bitches. These are old, ex-priests who are going to rot in hell anyways. I'm just suggesting that we send them there a little sooner. We can use the insurance money to pay off their victims. The Roman Catholic Church should have never, ever protected these pedophiles."

Fr. Joe was starting to raise his voice, trying to get his point across. Little Tony looked at Kilbane intently, as he was starting to feel the effects of his fourth drink.

"Oh, so now you're an executioner, huh, Joe? When did you become so judgmental? " he asked.

Little Tony was starting to wonder if they were both role switching, with Kilbane playing the Mafia hood and DiMatteo pretending to be Father Flanagan. There were several more minutes of silence as the Monsignor continued to finish eating his meal.

"Look Tony, you're right. This is a crazy idea. I'm just so damned frustrated. Most of our problems within the Archdiocese are concerning the despicable sins that were created by these monsters. We should be using our money to feed the homeless and hungry families in the city, funding foster homes and city-wide food banks, not wasting our resources to pay off all these pedophile rape victims," he valiantly said.

By now, Little Tony had practically licked off his pasta dish and was swirling around the ice cubes in his Crown Royal. "Let's pretend we didn't have this conversation," Tony said. "Besides, I don't think the Archdiocese can afford my services," he said with tongue in cheek.

Fr. Joe started to broadly smile, taking the last few bites of his chicken entree'.

"Really? And what is the going rate for knocking off an old ex-priest?" the Monsignor jokingly asked.

"Fifty-percent, Joe. If we're gonna start slicing up little old priests for the insurance money, I want half of the action." Little Tony was grinning, knowing that his priest friend would never take such a deal. Kilbane started to laugh.

"For fifty percent, I'll knock them off myself!" The whole conversation between the two of them was turning into a dialog of humor and laughter, as they were both joking at the very thought of Fr. Joe's ridiculously absurd request.

"And how would you do that? Stab them with a sharp crucifix?" Tony was amused by Joe's retort.

"No, I wouldn't have to work that hard." Fr. Joe smiled.

"Since most of these old guys are in their seventies, I would kidnap them and take them to a strip club, and then watch them die of heart attacks!" The two of them started laughing hysterically.

"Come on, Joe. That wouldn't work. Do you know how much Viagra you would need? And what about the ones that don't like girls? Now you really have a problem!" he jokingly added. The laughter between the two of them continued for several minutes, as their waiter finally brought them their check.

Little Tony peeled off a couple of one hundred-dollar bills from his wade of currency and placed them inside the waiter's billfold, without even looking at the bill. They both got up and acquired their coats, and then Little Tony began walking toward the restaurant's side door exit.

"Merry Christmas, Joe. I'll tell Santa to put that sharp crucifix under your tree!" DiMatteo joked.

"You do that, Tony. Don't forget the Viagra!" they both laughed as he added, "Merry Christmas, my friend."

The two men kissed each other on the cheek, and then the 'Capo' got into his shiny, black Maserati and drove away on North Halsted Street. Monsignor Kilbane handed his ticket to the valet, feeling embarrassed of the favor he had requested from his old friend.

He was grateful for Little Tony's discretion and loyalty, and assumed that his crazy, foolish idea of hiring a hit man would never be brought up again.

Or so he thought.

CHAPTER THREE

It was a beautiful, sunny Saturday afternoon as Paulie Russo arrived at St. Rosalia Church for altar boy duty. His bicycle was making a squeaking noise and the chain needed some oil, as he pulled out the kickstand of his almost new Schwinn ride, with the shiny chrome monkey bars and white banana seat. He locked the front Wheel onto the bike rack, and then entered the church sacristy from the side entrance door. His friend, Joey Campisi, had already arrived early to serve Saturday afternoon mass on that warm summer day in 1964. Joey had brought along his transistor radio, and Paulie could hear the new Beatles song "Can't Buy Me Love" playing loudly in the background. He was putting his black cassock on when Paulie walked in the door.

"What's up, Paulie?" as Joey shut off his radio.

"Hey Joey. What's up with the gym shoes?" Paulie asked his best friend right away.

They both knew Fr. Marquardt's strict rules about the altar boy dress code and wearing gym shoes while serving mass was strictly forbidden. Fr. Marquardt was the church pastor, and he ran a tight ship when it came to the rules and regulations regarding the altar boys and serving mass.

"I was at baseball practice and I forgot to bring my other shoes," Joey explained.

"He's gonna send you home!" Paulie said right away, as he fumbled through the closet, looking for a black cassock that would fit him.

"He can't. He's not gonna find another altar boy ten minutes before mass. Besides, these are new gym shoes. And they're cool!" Joey answered.

He started preparing the water and wine cruets and went into the sacristy cupboard to get the red wine that was used for mass. Paulie noticed Joey grabbing a different bottle of wine, which was loosely corked in a dark, green wine bottle.

'Where did you get that bottle of wine? It looks different," Paulie asked.

"It's my Nonno's. I told him we needed some wine for mass today, so he sent me over here with a bottle of his homemade wine. He figured Fr. Marquardt would enjoy it," Joey casually answered, now knowing that he was breaking all of the pastor's rules that Saturday afternoon.

"Fr. Marquardt won't even notice the difference," he sarcastically reasoned.

"Yeah, right!" Paulie answered.

They both started laughing loudly and giggling at the thought of the priest saying mass using his grandfather's Italian, homemade wine. They both figured the pastor would enjoy the change in mass wine and might even ask Joey's grandfather for more.

The boys were both fully dressed and ready when Fr. Marquardt arrived from the rectory, as the five o'clock Saturday mass was about to start in ten minutes. As he entered the church sacristy, his eyes were immediately fixated on Joey Campisi's shoes.

"Are those shoes appropriate for Holy Mass, Mr. Campisi?" the pastor asked.

"I'm sorry Father, but I was at baseball practice today and I forgot my black Sunday shoes" Joey apologized. Fr. Marquardt began putting on his holy vestments, including a purple chasuble, as there were people beginning to enter inside the church.

29

"You will need to remember this when you come to confession this week," he reprimanded. The two boys were in the fifth grade together at the grade school, and more than familiar with Fr. Marquardt's strict rules and regulations.

Fr. Marquardt was the parish pastor and school principal and ran St. Rosalia Parish with an iron fist. The deacon and the others had also arrived, and within several minutes, the mass was about to start. The entrance hymn started playing, as the altar boys lined up with the others to the begin Saturday afternoon mass.

St. Rosalia was a beautiful, old Chicago Catholic church, with high domed ceilings, gold painted trim and antiquated, stained glass windows. The white, Carrera marble altar looked majestic, beneath the magnificently large, life-like crucifix suspended high above from the wooden rafters. The old church was located a few blocks away from Halsted and Taylor streets, and although most of the parishioners were Italian families, there were Irish Catholics from neighborhood who came to worship at the parish as well. The church was the center of the Italian community back in the Fifties and Sixties. Most all the children in the neighborhood went to St. Rosalia grade school to receive a "better" education.

Back in those days, the families in the neighborhood dutifully trusted the nuns and the diocesan priests who ran and operated the local, community Catholic school. No questions were ever asked as to how or why their children were being taught and at times, severely disciplined. Many of the Italian families wished to stay in the good graces of the local Catholic school, as there was a waiting list for the neighborhood children to be enrolled. The nearby public grade school, located several blocks away, was beginning to become integrated, and many of the neighborhood parents resented the compulsory integration that Mayor Daley was forcing upon them at the time.

Almost everyone in the neighborhood had 'racist' views regarding the public school education of the Negro children with the neighborhood white kids, and practically all the parents didn't want their children going to school with them.

The Saturday mass continued uneventfully, as Fr. Marquardt preached to his flock about faithfully following "God's Holy Commandments", and to not be dissuaded by the 'modern, adulterous evils' that lurked rabidly within the community. As he received the gifts of bread and wine, Paulie and Joey stood side by side next to the mass celebrant. The Saturday mass was more than half way through, when Fr. Marquardt grasped the cruet filled with wine. He poured the wine into the gold chalice, looked up to the church rafters and the large crucifix hanging above, and gave thanks. Father Marquardt then took a drink of the homemade wine from the gold chalice.

Paulie and Joey looked at each other, both trying hard to keep from laughing, as Fr. Marquardt had a cringing, distorted look on his face after taking a gulp of the red wine. Paulie was biting his lip so hard to keep from laughing out loud, and he could taste the blood in his mouth. The celebrating priest angrily looked over to the deviant altar boys, who were trying very hard to keep a straight face and look in another direction.

Fr. Marquardt calmly finished blessing the bread and wine, and gave communion to each of the worshippers, with Paulie holding the gold platted paten. When the dispensing of communion was finished, and the closing blessings were made, the priest declared the mass over. Fr. Marquardt then darted a dirty look of revenge to both of his altar boys. As the closing hymn was played, Paulie and Joey followed Fr. Marquardt as they processioned out of the church and into the sacristy. The priest then stood outside and greeted all the parishioners, as Paulie and

Jocy hurriedly disrobed their cassocks and tried to bolt out of the front door of the church.

"We're in so much trouble!" Paulie nervously said.

As the boys were trying to leave, Fr. Marquardt grabbed them both by the arm and ordered them both back into the sacristy. When the church had emptied, Fr. Marquardt angrily entered the back room, ready to do war with his two belligerent altar boys. He was foaming at the mouth.

"Which one of you two decided to switch the mass wine with that undrinkable garbage?" he demanded.

Both the boys stood there with their heads down, not willing to 'spill the beans'. Paulie and Joey were the best of friends since kindergarten, and they had gotten in trouble together many times before. They once planted a pack of cigarettes inside the desk of one of the other bigger boys in class and got the kid who was bullying Paulie to get a detention without Sister Jean ever suspecting the truth. They were loyal friends, who had each other's backs, and their allegiance to each other was without question. Paulie and Joey had previously made a pact to one another that they would never 'rat' on each other, no matter what the consequence was.

"Would any of you two care to talk?" the pastor demanded.

Both boys stood there in the middle of the sacristy, in silence. Fr. Marquardt then went into his cabinet drawer and pulled out a long, two-foot paddle with several drilled holes. Holding the paddle in his hand, he demanded an answer.

"If neither one of you talks, I promise that the punishment that you'll both receive will be far more painful together than the agony you'll receive alone," Marquardt demanded. He was trying hard to coax an answer out of the boys. They both continued to stand there in silence.

"The mass is a very holy ritual, and you two boys have totally disrespected the Lord," he lectured. Both the boys stood in silence, staring at the floor for several longer minutes.

"Okay boys, have it your way. Both of you remove your pants." Paulie and Joey both began to remove their trousers.

Suddenly, Joey Campisi spoke up. "It was me, Father. It was me. I'm sorry. It was my grandfather's wine. I'm sorry," as Joey started crying profusely, confessing to the harmless prank.

More long minutes of silence as Fr. John Marquardt stared at the two young boys, holding the paddle in his hand.

Marquardt was a smaller man, balding, and in his late thirties. He had an intimidating presence about him and wore his black cassock and his dangling gold cross as if they were sacred vestments directly from Rome. He was the typical, Catholic school discipline-arian, who believed that children should be only seen and never heard. He often wore his reading glasses on the tip of his noise, and he had this piercing look of anger that he made with his icy cold blue eyes, often instilling fear into any young boy or girl who had broken any one his many school rules.

The total disrespect that the two young altar boys had demonstrated was far more insulting to the pastor than the actual innocent trick during the mass itself. It was an 'unholy' deed that the young altar boy participated in, and he needed to be severally punished.

"Leave us alone, Mr. Russo," as he ordered Paulie to leave the sacristy and the church. Paulie looked over to his friend, as tears were streaming down Joey's face. As he left the side door of the sacristy, he could hear Fr. Marquardt locking the door behind him.

Paulie quickly walked to his bicycle and was ready to ride away back to his house as quickly as possible. But there was something inside of the little boy that made him stay behind and wait for his best friend. He walked back over to the sacristy door, holding his Schwinn bike and tried to listen to what was going on inside.

There were no "whacks", no "whipping" noises, and no slaps of the paddle against Joey's bare bottom. But he could hear Joey screaming and crying loudly, with such a horrifying, eerie sound. It was as though his best friend were being tortured. The sounds and the agonizing noises coming from Joey in that sacristy room were ghastly, earth shattering screams of horror, screams that Paulie would never be able to put out of his mind.

A good hour had passed, as Paulie faithfully waited by the sacristy door for his friend. Finally, Joey had appeared out of the church's front door, walking slowly toward his bicycle securely locked in the bike rack. His hair was disheveled, and his face was drenched with tears.

"Joey, what happened?" Paulie demanded. Joey was silent. It was as though he couldn't talk. He only unlocked his bike and slowly walked along side of his bicycle, all four blocks to his house. Paulie couldn't understand why Joey wasn't riding his bike, choosing to walk it home instead. Paulie decided to walk his bike along with him and they continued to walk with their bikes together in silence. After several unanswered questions, Paulie just figured that whatever had happened, it was far too painful for Joey to talk about.

As the two approached Joey's house, Paulie loudly said, "See you tomorrow, okay?" Joey looked at his best friend and nodded, then turned and walked towards the front door, dropping his bicycle on the front lawn.

As Joey was climbing the steps of the front porch to go inside, Paulie saw something on his best friend that he would never, ever, forget.

The back of Joey's trousers was completely drenched with blood.

CHAPTER FOUR

It was a cloudy Thursday morning in March
1982, as Fr. John Marquardt arrived at Cardinal
Brody's Chicago mansion on North State Street. His
Eminence requested a meeting with Father Marquardt
last week to discuss "some issues" which had transpired
since his being the pastor at Guardian Angels Parish on
the near north side. He had been the pastor there since
1978, and after several transfers between difference
parishes around the Archdiocese of Chicago, was hoping
he could remain at Guardian Angels Church for several
more years until possibly, his retirement.

He was aware of John Cardinal Brody's health
and legal issues. The Cardinal had recently been
diagnosed with late stage four lung cancer. It had been
announced in the press that his health was quickly
deteriorating, and that he refused further
chemotherapy treatments. There had also been
newspaper reports in the Chicago Sun Times about the
Cardinal's illicit activities and corrupt business affairs.

Various charges and preparations for legal
indictments into the Cardinal's financial transgressions
were no secret to Chicago's Catholics. There had been
various allegations of the Cardinal diverting millions of
dollars from the various financial funds and church
coffers to fund the opulent life style of his married
Winnetka girlfriend, Mrs. Katherine Giudice, which
included jewelry, cars, lavish vacations, mink furs and
a luxury home in Boca Raton, Florida. To say that
corruption within the Archdiocese of Chicago was
widespread was an understatement. Everyone within
the diocese knew that, if the Cardinal's current health

problems didn't kill him, the pending indictments from the Justice Department would.

Fr. Marquardt parked his yellow, 1980 Ford Fairmont within the adjacent parking lot and walked down North State Street to the entrance of the massive, red bricked Chicago mansion. Its neatly manicured lawns, landscaped bushes and oak trees complimented the black, wrought ironed fences surrounding its beautiful, park-like setting.

He entered the ornate mansion, and after checking in with several of the Cardinal's associates, entered the immense, lavish office of Cardinal John D. Brody. His Eminence was in a Wheel chair, wearing a light fleece blanket around his shoulders as Fr. Marquardt knelt to kiss the Cardinal's right hand.

"Please sit down, Father," His Eminence ordered as he wheeled himself behind his decorative, massive oak desk. He coughed several times, clearing his throat, and then wiping his mouth with a white handkerchief. There clearly wasn't any doubt that the Cardinal was not in the best of health.

"Father, I called you in here to discuss some issues which have arisen from your parish," His Eminence began. "Reports and accusations that, according to your previous records, you are no stranger to."

The pastor sat motionless as the Cardinal began to articulate, "We have several complaints from parents within the Guardian Angels School that you have been, quite frankly, behaving inappropriately with their children," the Cardinal coughed several more times as he continued. "Inappropriate behavior that, to be direct, you have been reprimanded and treated for in the past."

"Your Eminence, I can explain…"

"There is nothing to explain!" the Cardinal screamed. Cardinal Brody was well known for his explosive, domineering temper.

"You're touching and even possibly, raping small boys within your school needs no explanation, Father." Cardinal Brody was uttering his contemptuous words to the shamed priest, while keeping from grinding his teeth.

"The Church bears no forgiveness for deviants such as yourself who have taken such liberties of sexual misconduct upon these young children," the Cardinal loudly reprimanded.

"This is the fifth assignment which we have had to make because of your inappropriate, sexual behavior. You have been in extensive counseling for these deviant, sexual acts in years past, but your misconduct seems to continue. We have paid and sponsored for your therapy sessions and brief sabbaticals, hoping that, through extensive prayer and therapy, you may realize and change this disgraceful behavior," Brody said.

Father Marquardt was defenseless, feeling shameful that some of his current 'inappropriate episodes' that had apparently, reached the desk of the Chicago Cardinal.

"As is the policy of this Diocese, we will not pass judgement on you for your current sins, Father. But we cannot allow you to continue to be a pastor within our diocese schools and have these various accusations continue to come across my desk."

The Archdiocese of Chicago, through the direction of the Vatican Church, discretely dealt with these "inappropriate transgressions" at that time. It had been the policy of the Vatican Church since 1962, to 'swear to secrecy" the diocese administrators who had to deal with these various episodes that were occurring with many of their pedophile priests. The church was steadfast in dealing with these issues 'internally' and to 'take care of their own.' Many various dioceses across the country were committed to taking responsibility in getting the counselling and help that these various priests needed in order to serve the Catholic communities that they were assigned to.

Father Marquardt sat there silently, knowing that he would have to brace himself for whatever penance Cardinal Brody would have to, again, strongly recommend.

"We cannot allow you to continue as a priest within our diocese any longer. And judging from your current conduct and your deviant sexual behavior in years past, I do not feel that you can serve the Lord as a Catholic priest," Brody said. There were several moments of silence, and Fr. Marquardt tried to put his head around the Cardinal's statement.

"Are you asking me to leave the priesthood?" Fr. John asked.

"I am not asking. I'm demanding," Brody sternly answered.

Marquardt began to turn three shades of red. Here he was being judged by the most corrupt, most dishonest Cardinal to ever serve the City of Chicago in recent years. He was being asked to leave the priesthood, the only life he has ever known for the last twenty-three years. Since his ordination in 1959, Fr. John Marquardt had always relished his life as a Catholic priest. He enjoyed being the center of the Catholic communities which he served, and the respect that he was given while administrating his pastoral duties.

But he had spent a considerable amount of time in 'intense prayer and counseling' to control his sexual demons, but to no avail. He had hoped that some of these 'inappropriate transgressions would remain discrete and unreported, as many of them did. After being reprimanded and warned for a fifth time by the Chicago Archdiocese, he knew deep down that he had no alternative. He would either voluntarily leave the priesthood or go through the laicization process of being 'defrocked.'

"Perhaps, Your Eminence, you could give me another chance and transfer me to another diocese where...."

"No, Marquardt! You have run out of second chances," he loudly retorted.

"You are a pedophile, Fr. Marquardt. Shame on you for continuing this hideous behavior and shame on us for not realizing it sooner."

"You have spent a considerable amount of time in therapy, to no avail. We cannot allow you to serve the Lord in either our diocese or in another. We have discussed this with the Vatican, and it is their recommendation that we demand your resignation as Pastor of the Guardian Angels Parish and to respect-fully ask, that you abandon your ministry here as a Catholic priest."

Fr. Marquardt sat in his chair, stunned, as though a bolt of white lightning had impaled his whole body. Several minutes had passed, as his Eminence started shuffling some papers across his desk, taking time to wipe his mouth with each of his heavy coughs. The priest was motionless, not knowing what to say or do in retaliation to the Cardinal's strong recommend-ations.

Cardinal Brody then continued, "As been the policy of our Archdiocese, when there have been priests who have broken their vows and shamed the Catholic Church with their inappropriate behaviors, they are asked to resign and abandon their ministries, along with signing several legal documents and policies."

"What documents?" the scorned priest asked.

Cardinal Brody laid the documents in front of Fr. Marquardt on top of his desk. He explained to the priest that these were legal waiver documents, allowing the Archdiocese to take complete control of any legal defenses from any potential lawsuits that may incur in the future against the Archdiocese. The last document was an application for a term life insurance policy for five million dollars, underwritten by the Great Lakes Life Insurance Company.

Fr. Marquardt read the documents thoroughly, signing the legal waivers with apprehension. He thought for a moment of hiring an attorney but knew it would only cause more friction between himself and the Archdiocese. When he got to the life insurance application, he questioned the Cardinal.

"Why is it necessary for the Archdiocese to take out a life insurance policy on my life?" he asked.

"In case the Archdiocese is sued for any of your inappropriate actions which you so recklessly performed," he sternly answered.

"Consider this life insurance policy as part of your penance as a pedophile, Father."

The priest was speechless. It had been the recent policy of the last several years for Cardinal Brody to require all the defrocked priests who had left the priesthood to apply for a large life insurance policy, with the Archdiocese of Chicago as the beneficiary. This was to insure the diocese reimbursement of any potential lawsuits which may be incurred from the malicious actions performed by any of their defrocked priests. This became the policy of the Archdiocese of Chicago at that time, and until recently, was continued by each of the Cardinal's successors.

When the documents were signed, the former priest sat in his chair, his eyes filled with tears. Cardinal Brody continued coughing profusely, while pulling out another folder from his credenza.

"It says in your file that you have a Bachelor of Science in Business Administration, with a major in accounting degree from Loyola University. Is this correct?" he asked.

"Yes, Your Eminence."

The Cardinal thought for a few moments. "I will talk to my administrative chief of staff about bringing you into our Archdiocese office. Our accounting department could use your assistance." There were several more coughs between sentences, as the Cardinal continued to speak.

"We will not report your circumstances to the authorities, and we will use complete discretion if asked regarding your situation or condition for your depart-ure," the Cardinal slowly said.

"We will give you a severance package and assist you in finding housing. You have twenty-four hours to pack your personal belongings and leave your parish rectory."

"And..." Brody continued, "You will go back into therapy."

Marquardt looked at the Cardinal, at least grateful that he was not being completely thrown out on the street. John Marquardt mentally took inventory of the many young boys he had sexually abused and molested over the years within the various parishes in Chicago. He knew that he was at the mercy of the Archdiocese of Chicago to keep his dark secrets away from any state or federal prosecutors.

Yet still, Marquardt was bitter. Here he was, being judged and thrown out of the Catholic ministry by a man, whom the Chicago Sun-Times called "the most corrupted Cardinal the City of Chicago has ever had." He was accused of crimes against the church that no one before him would ever consider in his sacred position as Cardinal of the Chicago Archdiocese.

Yet Marquardt was in no position to 'lawyer-up' and play hard-ball with the crooked Cardinal and his diocese. He knew that the cards were stacked against him and his so-called demons and knew that he would be spending the rest of his life in jail if the Archdiocese turned him over to the authorities.

The Vatican and the Catholic Church had dealt with the problems of pedophile priests for centuries and was not about to let any outside state or federal authority impede upon their jurisdiction. Like the sovereign state of the Vatican, the malicious affairs of its bishops and priests were beyond the reproach of any federal or state laws prohibiting such deviant behavior.

According to the Vatican, the laws of God were far higher than any insignificant criminal laws of the State of Illinois, or the United States for that matter. The church will always take care of their own.

This has always been the philosophy of the Vatican and the Catholic Church, and Marquardt's circumstances would fall within that philosophy.

"You are to speak to no one, regarding these circumstances or this arrangement. Do you under-stand?"

The now former priest nodded his head in agreement. He then got up, knelt and kissed the Cardinal's ring, and thanked him for all he had done. He then exited the Cardinal's mansion and drove away in his yellow, Ford Fairmont.

John Marquardt was now about to begin his new life as a layman and former priest.

CHAPTER FIVE

It was almost six o'clock that evening, and I was staying late to finish up some reports and to follow up on some phone calls on that homicide on West Argyle this morning. Commander Callahan, who was the head of our Sixteenth District, had asked me to head up the investigation since he figured the detectives over at the Seventeenth weren't that experienced enough to handle these kinds of homicides. The Chicago Police Superintendent Ryan felt this murder investigation was way too messy and far too complicated for the Seventeenth District to screw up. Some of those detectives were morons and didn't know the difference between a box of Cracker Jacks and a Happy Meal.

I had just gotten off the phone when a reporter nemesis of mine entered my office and decided to honor me with his presence.

"Hey Phil...what's up?"

His name was Charles "Chaz" Rizzo, and he was an investigative reporter from WDRV-8 Eyewitness News. He was a shorter, stocky guy who tried to intimidate everyone, especially within the Chicago Police Department. He was a well-dressed, arrogant bastard, who pushed himself around on everyone with his press badge, as though he were an over-sized linebacker for the Chicago Bears. He reported mostly on "syndicate crime" investigations, as he was their so called "Mafia reporter". Whenever there was a story that WDRV-8 News suspected was "mobbed up", Rizzo was all over it.

"Who let you in here?" I replied.

I had enough verbal sparring matches with Rizzo in the past to skip all the kind pleasantries. He started to laugh that little girl giggle of his, and then made himself comfortable in front of my desk.

"Come on, Philly! You get a mob hit on West Argyle and you don't call me? Shame on you! We go back too far!"

"A mob hit? What the hell are you talking about, Rizzo?"

"Come on Phil. You know what I'm talking about. That old man hanging in his basement this morning. You're not going to play stupid with me now, are you?"

I couldn't tell if Chaz came over to fish out information or to volunteer details. As much of a scumbag that Rizzo was, he was pretty good at investigating crime scenes and enlightening me with new information.

"Look Chaz, we haven't classified it as a homicide or a mob hit or anything right now. For all we know, this could be a suicide." That was a ridiculous statement, but I was trying to get a reaction out of him and find out what he knows.

"A suicide? Really?" He laughed that girly laugh of his that always manages to get on my nerves.

"Hmmmm....let's see. The old man stabs himself several times, impales himself with a sharp broomstick, cuts his own throat, and then cuts off his balls after gouging out his own eyeballs."

"And...oh yeah...then he hangs himself. Yep, sounds like a suicide to me," as he pretended to spit in his right hand and made some obscene stroking gestures.

"Stop jagging me, Phil."

I now realized that this reporter bastard had the whole crime scene memorized. Rizzo was turning this into a contest to see how fast I could throw him out of my office. I glared at him for about five seconds.

"If there was a party on West Argyle, I don't recall sending you an invitation. We didn't put out a press release and didn't call you guys for a reason. We're not sure what we have here." I was fumbling with my automatic lead pencil, trying to get it to work.

"So where are you getting your info?" I asked, knowing he was going pull me into that verbal chess game of his that he always pulls me into.

Rizzo looked at me and smiled, with that 'I know something you don't' look on his face.

"Come on Philly don't play coy with me here. You have a 79-year-old ex-priest murdered, gutted and sliced up like a pig! You've got no prints, no weapon, and no evidence except a red, long-stemmed rose."

This son-of-a-bitch had more information than I thought. He probably came straight over here from the Seventeenth District. I would bet money that those moronic detectives were probably chirping to him like mindless, little parakeets.

"Ok, Mister-Know-It-All reporter. What's your theory?" I asked, knowing I was going to get his opinion anyways.

"This is a mob hit, Philly. Bet the farm." Rizzo was smiling from ear to ear, knowing that he had his next feature story for tomorrow night's six o'clock news.

"A mob hit by whom? Dion O'Banion? Is the 'Flower Shop Gangster' still around?" I sarcastically asked.

"Nice guess, Philly. It's probably a mob henchman with Catholic priest issues." Rizzo was fumbling with his car keys on my desk.

"Maybe this killer had his pants pulled down when he was an altar boy," he said. I could tell Rizzo was amusing himself, trying to pump information out of me at the same time.

"But why an old ex-priest?" I asked out loud, hoping Rizzo had some constructive ideas.

"I went to the Archdiocese office this afternoon," I began to tell Rizzo.

"I talked to a Monsignor Kilbane. He says this old man was a model Catholic layman, and even did volunteer work at Lurie Children's Hospital. This Marquardt guy wasn't defrocked and isn't listed anywhere as a pedophile." I reasoned.

Rizzo looked at me, deep in thought. He pulled out a pack of Marlboro Lights, and put a cigarette in his mouth without lighting it, as he glared at the "No Smoking" sign hanging on the other side of the office.

"How do you know, Phil?" he asked, looking at me straight in the eye.

"Know what?"

"How do you know?" he asked again. There was a five second pause as I was without an answer.

"How do you know that he wasn't a pedophile?" Rizzo asked me again, pretending to take a long drag from his unlit cigarette. A few silent moments went by, as I pondered Rizzo's question.

"What do you remember about Cardinal Brody?" he asked, blowing fake smoke circles into the air.

"Seriously? That he was one of our more corrupt Chicago Cardinals," I tried to recall, only that he died in the early eighties. My background on Chicago Catholic history wasn't the greatest, and I knew I was going to get a short history lesson from my buddy Rizzo.

"'Corrupt' is a very mild word for Cardinal John Brody. He was a thief, an adulterer, and a crooked, ruthless criminal who followed his orders from the Vatican without question. One of those Vatican orders was to keep a 'cloak of silence' in the diocese regarding pedophile and homosexual priests. And Brody did just that. If you notice, that registry of pedophile priests on the internet doesn't have any Chicago names from the last fifty years, until recently. That wasn't by accident. Brody made them 'quietly' go away, paid some of them off, and kept the complaints quiet, never involving the authorities." Rizzo was fumbling inside of his coat pockets as he continued the history tutorial.

"The attorney general's office had Brody's indictments prepared and ready to be delivered when he died in April 1983. After his death, the investigation into the Archdiocese and Cardinal Brody died with him."

I sat at my desk, digesting what Chaz was saying. Was it possible that Marquardt was a pedophile priest who was pushed out of the church by Cardinal Brody? If that were true, that would create motive, but by whom? Why kill an old former priest now, after all these years? There were too many missing puzzle pieces before coming to any conclusions.

"Chaz, you still haven't come up with a good motive here. Why would a professional killer, or even the Mafia, butcher up an old, former priest? And let's say he was a pedophile. Why would someone take him out now? His alleged crimes probably occurred over fifty years ago. If this guy was a pedophile monster, I'm sure the authorities would have gotten involved by now. Your theory just doesn't add up."

Rizzo just took another fake drag from his unlit cigarette. I was starting to wish he would just light it up already.

"Philly, you're not getting it. Cardinal Brody was very, very good at making pedophile priests disappear."

Rizzo totally had my attention, and he was a treasure chest of information on the Archdiocese.

Besides chasing mob hoodlums on the six o'clock news, he had done a few feature stories on the Chicago Archdiocese when some of the pedophile priest lawsuits started coming into light, thanks to the help of the Chicago Sun-Times.

"He defrocked them, he relocated them, and he put them into new careers. It was like a 'Witness Protection Program' for defrocked priests. And this policy continued well after Brody was gone. The Archdiocese of Chicago did this for many defrocked priests up until around 2002. It wasn't until after all that shit hit the fan in Boston with Cardinal Law that the Chicago Archdiocese started turning these guys over to the authorities," Rizzo lectured.

I listened intently and scribbled down a few notes. All the information and the history lesson made a lot of sense, but it still didn't explain a motive for the murder.

"I get it, Riz. That would explain the victim's past. But it still falls way short on a motive for the murder."

"If I were a gambling man," Rizzo began stating again, knowing that he had my full attention, "I would put my money on the theory that this killer is a professional, probably an abused pedophile victim, who had it out for this old ex-priest, big time."

"Really? That sounds like quite a stretch," I said.

"But let's say you're right. How do you suppose we get a list of Marquardt's pedophile victims? From the Archdiocese of Chicago? Fifty years or more after the fact? Unless there are recent civil lawsuits against the former priest, the Illinois statute of limitations is 18 years old plus 20 years. So, anything prior to the 1980's had already long expired on these cases."

I knew that trying to get into the Archdiocese's office on Rush Street and attempt to acquire any old information on any past child abuse cases would be next to impossible.

"What do you know about the Cardinal's Administrative Chief of Staff?" Now I was the one fishing for information.

"Monsignor Kilbane?" he asked. "Good luck with that guy! You've got a better chance of catching the Cardinal walking out of a whore house than getting anything out of him. Kilbane runs that office with an iron fist. Nothing goes in or out of the Archdiocese of Chicago without him knowing about it. He will throw so many brick walls in front of you, and he will make it impossible for you to get any information." he said.

"And if your subpoenas and warrants manage to get past his desk, you've got their hot shot, LaSalle Street lawyers to deal with."

"Yeah..." I was starting to concede. "I imagine the Archdiocese is pretty lawyered up."

"Are you kidding? Herzog, Cohen and Schwartz. They've been their lawyers for years, and these guys are the 'disciples of darkness'. They will quash every single subpoena the prosecutor's office throws at them. Unless you can make a direct connection between any crime and the Archdiocese, you won't get anywhere." he stated.

"They will stall and mess with you, big time. It took us over a year of legal hassles and court appearances just to get what little information we could get on Cardinal Brody. If it wasn't for the AG's office, we would still be standing outside their front door, with our 'schlongs' in our hands."

Rizzo was starting to make my night, as he probably could sense the frustration on my face with this homicide investigation. Chaz Rizzo then got up from the chair and gathered his car keys.

"Ok Riz....you've got my attention. So where do you suggest I start?" I asked, feeling like a little high school boy, looking for advice on his first date.

He looked at me and made that girly laugh of his, making me cringe. He was walking towards the door to exit my office before turning around.

"Follow the money, Amigo." I looked at him, totally confused.

"What?"

"Follow the money!" he said again. I could hear him giggling to himself as he closed my office door behind him.

Follow the money? What the hell was he talking about? What was Rizzo referring to? He wasn't making any sense. What would money have to do with this homicide? Did Marquardt have a large personal estate? Are there heirs to his money that could make them murder suspects?

Maybe this old man had a lot of cash stashed in the house somewhere, and we were so consumed with the murder that we didn't think that this could have been a robbery too. Maybe there is an angry nephew or another relative somewhere that we need to investigate. Maybe there is an estranged family member who knows that the old ex-priest was loaded up in cash.

I always hated it when the media knew more about a pending investigation that the coppers did. Rizzo obviously had one up on me already. Not only did I need to quickly solve this homicide, but I had to compete with Rizzo and WDRV-8 News as well. I was getting a migraine headache and feeling totally frustrated.

And this investigation had barely even started.

CHAPTER SIX

The line of people at Starbucks was almost to the door as Olivia Laurent arrived for her usual morning cappuccino, for which she preferred grande, extra wet. It was a beautiful Friday spring morning in downtown Detroit, as the temperature was starting to climb to 78 degrees without the heat index. She was suffering from an intense migraine headache first thing that morning and was skeptical as to whether a fresh cup of her usual cappuccino was going to do her any good.

The young, business executive had just gotten off the bus from her downtown Jefferson Street condo to her office at the Great Lakes Life Insurance Company, where she was the chief financial officer. Olivia grabbed her coffee that morning and walked over to her office on the thirty-sixth floor of the Renaissance Center across the street.

She was a beautiful, smart, well-educated brunette, who received her accounting CPA certificate after graduating from Albion College. She went on to get her law degree from Wayne State University, with the hope of having a career in taxation law and forensic accounting. She instead took a temporary job while in law school as an insurance adjuster with the life insurance company and climbed the corporate ladder over the last twenty years to her present, executive position within the corporation.

Her law and accounting degrees became valuable tools for which she utilized in her career, as she was able to apply her forensic accounting

52

techniques, along with her excellent understanding of the law, to various life insurance claims. She was considered quite an asset to the insurance company and signed off on any and all life insurance claims which the Great Lakes Life Insurance Company was liable for. She had just settled into her office when her associate brought in some documents and some insurance claims to review.

"Good morning, Olivia," greeted her associate.

Cindy Jankowski was a sharp, heads-up claims accountant whom had been with the insurance company for several years. Olivia considered her "the extra pair of eyes and ears" within the company. She had been assembling some recent life insurance claims and brought this claim from Chicago to her attention.

"Olivia, did you have a chance to review this claim?" she asked, while putting the several files and documents on her desk.

"Which claim, Cindy?"

"The one about the 79-year-old man in Chicago who was violently murdered last week. The Archdiocese of Chicago is the beneficiary of a five-million-dollar insurance policy which was taken out on the deceased back in 1982."

Cindy had attached a copy of a small newspaper article from the Chicago Sun-Times. They had done a small, three paragraph article regarding the homicide on West Argyle, in which the victim was found violently murdered and mutilated, with the Chicago Police Department having no suspects or witnesses.

"So, what? I hear everyone is killing everybody in Chicago these days. What else is new?" Olivia sarcastically said. She should have probably gotten herself a glass of tomato juice and some aspirin to soothe her throbbing morning headache, or perhaps, her hangover. She had gone out with some girlfriends to Detroit's Greek Town for dinner and drinks the night before and didn't get home until one o'clock in the morning.

"Cindy, do you have any aspirin?"

Cindy noticed her bloodshot eyes upon closer inspection, and realized that her usual Starbucks grande cappuccino, extra wet wasn't going to do the trick. She quickly went to her office and brought back two Excedrin aspirin for her boss a few minutes later, along with a small cup of water.

"How late were you out last night?" Cindy asked, as Olivia swallowed the two Excedrin.

"Until one in the morning. I'm getting too old for this shit," Olivia replied.

She had just celebrated her birthday last week, and although she looked phenomenal, was starting to feel the effects of her ripe-old age of forty-two years old. She followed a vegan diet, watched her waistline, and invaded the local gym and Zumba classes four nights a week. Other than her periodic cravings for cheese fries and her usual margaritas, Olivia lived a healthy lifestyle.

She was also single. Although she had her fair share of past relationships, she had never married and had no children. She had given up on her biological clock, realizing that her lucrative, corporate career was far more rewarding than all that over-rated hype regarding kids, marriage and motherhood.

Olivia rustled a few of the papers and files concerning the Chicago insurance claim, paying more attention to her throbbing headache than to Cindy.

"What about this claim?" Olivia asked again. Cindy looked at her and smiled.

"This is a five-million-dollar life insurance claim on a 79-year old ex-priest from Chicago" she said.

"The Archdiocese of Chicago has made a claim regarding the policy and has attached the insured's death certificate. When I saw the cause of death on the certificate, I went on the internet and found the article regarding this man's murder. I've attached the newspaper clipping from the Chicago Sun-Times."

Olivia looked through the insurance claim, read the death certificate and the news clipping.

"It says this man was mutilated, with several stab wounds, knife insertions, and blunt trauma to his face and body, and was impaled among other things," she read out loud.

"Wow. When they kill someone in Chicago, they don't screw around," Olivia chuckled.

"Who made this insurance claim?"

"It was signed by a Monsignor Joseph Kilbane, who is the administrative chief of staff at the Archdiocese," Cindy answered.

Olivia just shook her head. "Amazing," she said to herself.

Olivia continued to scan through the files and paper work. It was the general policy of the Great Lakes Life Insurance Company to investigate and review any insurance claims where a violent death or a homicide of an insured was involved, invoking a review period of up to 120 days.

"Why did our company allow the Archdiocese of Chicago to take out such a pricey insurance policy on an ex-priest thirty-five plus years ago? Have there been similar claims?" Olivia asked.

"We had another claim two years ago regarding another ex-priest in Chicago for two million dollars, but that one wasn't a homicide. The Chicago Archdiocese was the beneficiary of that policy as well."

"Interesting," Olivia observed out loud. "I would imagine we are not the only insurance company underwriting these policies for these Chicago ex-priests. I'm sure there have been other claims."

Olivia pensively sat at her desk and contemplated her company's options before paying out on this life insurance claim.

"Let's invoke the full review period on this claim and do some homework. Find me the name of the detective who is handling this case for the Chicago Police Department," she requested.

"Phillip Dorian," Cindy quickly said.

"Who?"

"Detective Phillip Dorian of the Sixteenth District. I'm way ahead of you, boss," Cindy smiled.

Olivia looked at her and smiled, knowing that her Thursday night drinking binges with the girls had to come to an end.

"And of course, you have his number, correct?"

Cindy reached across Olivia's desk and opened the file containing the Chicago Police Department information on the detective.

"It's right here, boss." Cindy said, knowing that she was running circles around her corporate CFO today.

"Stop calling me boss!" Olivia jokingly reprimanded her associate. She opened and read through all the files and work papers, noting that it was still an open investigation.

"We can't go any further on this claim until the Chicago P.D. closes this case, one way or the other. I will give this detective a call this morning and see where this homicide case stands," Olivia stated.

She thanked her diligent associate for all her detailed hard work on this insurance claim, and Olivia started to do some research on her own.

She went on her computer, to find out whatever other information she could find on a 79-year-old John Marquardt. She looked up his obituary, from the Belmont Funeral Home in Chicago, finding nothing unusual. She then went on the Chicago Archdiocese web site and found nothing on him either. Olivia then looked up and researched the all sex abuse victim web sites, including the internet site where a directory of defrocked priests over the last sixty years were chronologically listed. But Marquardt's name wasn't listed anywhere. Olivia couldn't find anything negative on him or why he was no longer a priest. So, what was the motive of murdering and mutilating this victim? She just couldn't figure it out.

She called Detective Dorian at the Chicago Police Department and left him a message to return her call.

I had just arrived back at the Sixteenth District after grabbing lunch and doing some leg work on some other investigations. Our department had been inundated with some robbery and rape cases over the last week, so my attention had been diverted away from the Marquardt murder, as that homicide was still an open investigation. Outside of what little information I could get out of Rizzo and going back to the crime scene a few times, I had made very little progress on that case. As I settled at my desk, I noticed a message from the dispatcher to return a call from an Olivia Laurent of the Great Lakes Insurance Company. The phone number started with a '313' area code, so I knew right away she was calling from Detroit.

"Ms. Laurent, this is Detective Dorian returning your call," as a soft, female voice answered the phone.

"Oh, thank you so much for calling me back, Detective. We have an open life insurance claim relating to a recent homicide case which we understand you're investigating," she said.

It didn't click in my head right away, as to why a life insurance company would be calling me.

"Which case ma'am?"

"The Marquardt murder case. We have an insurance claim which was made by the Archdiocese of Chicago," she answered.

Suddenly, I felt like I was standing in front of a slot machine in Las Vegas, with all the bells and whistles loudly going off, spinning triple sevens and making 'ding-ding-ding' noises.

This is what that son-of-a-bitch Rizzo was alluding to. 'Follow the money' he had said a few times, but I just didn't get it. I didn't understand what the hell he was talking about. But now, the very break that I needed in this homicide case had now just fallen right into my lap. There were several moments of silence as the puzzle pieces were starting to magically fit together.

"Hello?" said the female voice from the other end.

"Yes, I'm sorry. Did you say the Archdiocese of Chicago?" I asked, making sure I wasn't hearing things.

"Yes, I did. I was hoping you could share some information with us regarding this investigation" she replied.

The Archdiocese of Chicago had a life insurance policy on John Marquardt, a former priest and now, murder victim. I was trying to put my head around it. Rizzo's phrase 'Follow the money' kept going around and around in my head.

"I'm sorry Ms. Laurent. I'm not at liberty to openly talk about this case right now. But could I call you back later?" I politely asked.

"Absolutely, Detective. We're not going to be paying out on this claim anytime soon right now. We will need more information regarding the circumstances of the insured's death, so take your time."

"Thank you," and I abruptly hung up the phone.

I quickly looked up the number and made my next phone call. It was a rare occasion when I was dialing this bastard's phone number rather than him dialing mine.

"Hello?"

"You son-of-a-bitch! You knew there was a life insurance policy on that ex-priest, didn't you?" I was so annoyed with this asshole reporter.

"Hey Philly! What's up?" I was not in the mood for Rizzo's unusually cheerful voice.

"How did you know there was a life insurance policy?"

Chaz Rizzo started laughing his girly laugh, playing his little 'cat and mouse' game with my temper.

"Philly, Philly, Philly! You want way too much information!"

"Fuck you, Rizzo! How about if I haul your ass down here and throw you in the can for obstructing a homicide investigation?" I loudly replied. My temperature was starting to boil.

"Hmmm, now that sounds like a stretch. But you know, Philly, I do love it when you talk dirty me."

"Dammit Rizzo! Get your ass over here! You've got some explaining to do," as I hung up the phone. I was so infuriated with him.

It wasn't more than thirty minutes before Chaz Rizzo casually walked into my office, wearing that cocky grin of his.

"Hey Phil, nice weather we're having," as he sat down in front of my desk and put that unlit cigarette back in his mouth.

"Cut the bullshit, Rizzo. I need to know what you know. You knew there was a policy on this Marquardt guy and you said nothing," I sternly said. He just looked at me and smiled.

"Phil, you surprise me. When I said, 'follow the money', what the hell did you think I was talking about? I'm shocked that it took you this long to figure it out," he gleefully replied.

"So how did you know, Chaz?"

The reporter started fumbling again with his unlit cigarette, as though he was waiting for me to give him the permission to light it up.

"Come on, Detective. You know a reporter can't reveal his sources of information."

"You're pushing my buttons, Rizzo. Cut the bullshit!" I said loudly, making sure that he knew I was serious about throwing him in jail.

Chaz made himself comfortable and crossed his legs, showing off his fancy alligator stripped socks and his high end, wing-tipped black shoes. When it came to make a fashion statement, Chaz Rizzo 'dressed to the nine's'. He wore his expensive apparel as though he were posing for a photo shoot with GQ magazine. He was wearing a dark, Canali pin-striped suit, crisp white shirt and a complimentary blue stripped tie. It didn't take a genius to figure out that he kept his charge accounts at all the high-end, men's clothing stores on Michigan Avenue.

"So just tell me, Rizzo. How did you know about the life insurance policy on this guy?"

"Truthfully, Phil. I didn't know. I was just guessing that at the time of the murder," he replied.

"Don't mess with me, Chaz," I loudly warned him.

"Relax, Phil. We interviewed a former priest while we were doing that 'Cardinal Brody' piece last year. He had explained to us that allowing the Archdiocese to take out a policy on him was part of his 'penance', in case there were any tentative lawsuits filed against them. I really didn't think anything more about it until this murder case," Rizzo said.

"Do you know if Cardinal Brody took out policies on all of his former priests?" I eagerly asked.

"I'm not sure. The ex-priest we interviewed wouldn't go on record, but he did mention that he thought many of the priests who left the priesthood, especially those who were defrocked during the '70's and '80's, had large life insurance policies taken out on them. They were threatened and 'bullied' into taking out these policies, or they would be facing the threat of criminal prosecution. It was a way for the Archdiocese to 'cover their asses' financially in case there were any liable suits down the road."

Rizzo was a treasure chest of information regarding the Chicago Archdiocese, and I was realizing that I was going to need his expertise if I were going to solve this case. I scribbled down a few notes while he was talking, and then started to contemplate my last phone call to the life insurance company.

"Chaz, you do realize how this homicide looks so far, don't you?" I calmly asked.

"Of course. The Archdiocese hired a Mob hit-man to kill an ex-priest for the insurance money. Are you surprised?" Rizzo was amusing himself and annoying me again with that girlish giggle of his. He was chewing on his unlit Marlboro Light cigarette as though it were a toothpick.

"But do you think that is even possible?" I asked him.

"Personally, Phil? No, I don't. I don't think Kilbane, Cardinal Markowitz, or anyone else at the Archdiocese is that goddamn stupid. Even though they have a history of breaking most of the Ten Commandments, I don't believe the 'Thou Shall Not Commit Murder for the Insurance' is one of them," Chaz said.

"But the Archdiocese is all too happy to collect on this old priest's life insurance policy," I quickly interjected. Rizzo sat there and thought about it for a several long seconds.

"Is there a law against taking out an insurance policy on a former employee, such as a former priest, and then collecting years later?" Chaz asked.

I rattled that question in my head a few times, knowing that there was no easy answer.

"Maybe it's time to pay another visit to Monsignor Kilbane," I suggested to myself out loud, as Chaz sat in front of my desk, nodding his head with a smile.

"Good luck with that," he said, as there were some moments of silence.

"May I go now, Detective?" he innocently asked.

"Sure, Riz," I replied. "Go out and enjoy this beautiful day," I suggested as we both stood up from my desk, before throwing in one last reprimand.

"But don't go far. I'm going to need more of your help on this homicide case, Mr. Rizzo."

He just looked at me and smiled, knowing that he still had one up on me.

"Anything for you, Detective," as he left my office, closing the door behind him.

I knew Chaz Rizzo was licking his chops for another exclusive "Channel 8"news story. I also knew that I couldn't trust him as far as I could throw him. But he always seemed to have more information than I did when it came to these messy homicides, and I knew that I had to keep him around if I wanted to solve this case. But I kept asking myself same the question:

Who would kill for the Archdiocese?

CHAPTER SEVEN

The morning dawn was peeking across the cloudless sky that cold winter morning before Christmas, as Little Tony pulled his Maserati into his South Ashland parking lot. It was just after five in the morning, and he was late for his early morning workout, which he did religiously five days a week. He had a large exercise room in the DiMatteo Tomato Distribution plant, which he and several of his employees would meet each day to do weights and cardio machine workouts. Tony was very health conscience and was a firm believer in living a healthy lifestyle. He encouraged his employees to take advantage of the company exercise room, which was filled with several Precor elliptical and treadmill machines, along with a large weight room and some stationary bicycles. He hired a trainer to come to the warehouse plant on that day, as he and several other employees were preparing for their private spinning class, which started at 5:15am.

As Tony came out of the adjacent locker room, which was complete with a private sauna and showers, several of his employees were already on their stationary bikes, ready for class. One of his employees there was Salvatore Marrocco, his financial controller and trusted colleague. Sal was an older, heavy-set man in his late sixties, with over dyed jet-black hair and a moustache.

He was very well educated, with an MBA degree from Northwestern University and a law degree from the University of Chicago. Although his corporate title was that of chief financial officer, he was better known as the 'Consigliere' of the DiMatteo Family. Little Tony consulted him daily regarding all business matters within the company, and topics 'outside' of the DiMatteo Tomato business. Marrocco was quite valuable to Little Tony and was well paid for his diverse business knowledge, his understanding of the criminal and civil laws, and his well versed 'street smarts'.

"What's up Sal?" he said as he climbed onto one of the free spinning cycles next to him.

"How was your dinner last night with the Monsignor?" the Consigliere asked, as he usually spoke with a very deep, raspy voice.

Little Tony started to chuckle to himself as he contemplated his dinner meeting with Monsignor Kilbane at the Trattoria Pagliacci the night before.

"You're laughing, so you must have had a good time," Sal observed.

Tony was still laughing to himself as he began peddling his stationary bike, with the trainer yelling out instructions.

"That Fr. Joe is still fucking crazy after all of these years." Tony laughed.

"Why? What happened?"

"You're not going to believe this!" Tony said, as he was accelerating his peddling, his head down facing the floor.

"I think Fr. Joe wants to become one of us!"

Sal looked at Little Tony with a confused look on his face. He had also gotten to know Monsignor Kilbane very well through his relationship with the DiMatteo Family, and knowing his affiliations with the Archdiocese, was bewildered by his bosses' comment.

"What are you talking about?"

"I think the Monsignor has been watching too many 'wise-guy' movies."

Sal was still perplexed by his comments but decided to play along.

"You're probably right, Tony. The last time I saw the Monsignor was at your daughter's wedding. He was at the bar doing a very bad 'Joe Pesce' imitation after sucking down three or four Manhattans."

"I remember that," observed Tony as he was adjusting the speed of his spinning bike.

"He should stick to 'DeNiro'. He does him a lot better!"

They were both laughing as they were accelerating and decelerating their stationary bikes. They continued to make small talk until the forty-five-minute spinning class was finally over. Tony grabbed a towel after his workout and followed his 'consigliere' into the locker room. While they were both getting dressed, Sal decided to press his boss for more details.

"So which movie has the Monsignor been watching these days?"

"I think he's got 'Casino' of the fucking brain," Tony said loudly, making sure there was no one else in the locker room.

Sal laughed as he pressed Little Tony further, "So what did he want?"

Marrocco was more than aware of Tony's dinner date with the Monsignor the night before. When Monsignor Kilbane personally called to invite Little Tony out for dinner, Sal became suspicious. He knew that Fr. Joe was looking for more than just a 'soup kitchen' donation. Whatever the matter was, the Consigliere knew it had to be serious enough for Kilbane to insist on meeting with Little Tony alone.

"That crazy bastard wants me to loan him out a 'hit man'!" Tony said, knowing that there was no one else within earshot of his comment.

The 'Capo' knew he could completely trust his faithful advisor with anything and had no issues with Sal Marrocco's ability to be discrete and keep their conversations confidential.

Marrocco stopped buttoning his shirt and gazed at Tony, completely confused.

"What the hell is Kilbane going to do with a 'hit man'?"

"That's what I asked him. Some bullshit about taking out some pedophile ex-priests with large insurance policies. I guess the new story now is that the Archdiocese is broke."

Salvatore Marrocco became frozen, as he blankly gazed at Little Tony, completely speechless.

Marrocco had grown up on Taylor and Halsted Streets, and went to catholic school as a young boy at St. Rosalia's Parish. He was barely in the second grade when his mother forced him to serve as an altar boy for Saturday afternoon masses. He had suppressed many of his childhood memories during his time at St. Rosalia's Catholic School, as his family moved away to the western suburbs when he was ten years old. He had suffered nightmares as a young boy, and was often medicated as a teenager, struggling to cope with the horrendous experiences he had suffered through during his time at St. Rosalia's, and especially, his time as a young altar boy serving mass. He was still struggling to remember the abusive pastor's name, for which it had taken him decades to forget.

As he slowly sat down in front of his locker, Tony looked at him, noticing that he was in some sort of a trance.

"Are you okay?"

Sal quickly looked at Tony and shook himself back to reality.

"Oh yeah, I'm fine," he replied. "I hope you told him 'No'. We don't need to get involved in that shit."

"Of course," replied Tony. "Besides, I told him the Archdiocese couldn't afford our services."

Marrocco looked at Little Tony and shook his head. "I think your Monsignor friend is losing it."

"I'm starting to think you're right," replied Tony.

"Maybe Fr. Joe had too many Manhattan's last night," Sal suggested.

Tony thought about it for a few seconds. "No, not really. I was the one gulping down the Crown Royals," he remembered.

"Anyways, I reminded Fr. Joe of one of His Ten Commandments and squashed his big 'wise-guy' idea!"

"Was he really serious?" Sal asked, still perplexed by the subject of their conversation.

"Oh yeah. He was fucking serious. I told him it was a 'whack-job' idea and that he should stick to running the Archdiocese, saying masses and hearing confessions."

Sal walked over to the sink with his shaving kit and began silently shaving his heavy beard. He was still thinking about his grammar school days in the old neighborhood, and especially, his memories as an altar boy. He started thinking about all the times he was attacked and assaulted in the church sacristy after Saturday afternoon masses, and how ashamed he was to mention anything about it to anyone.

He thought about his poor tormented mother, Elsa. *'God Rest Her Soul',* he thought to himself. She used to beg her son to tell her what was wrong, as he used to recluse himself in his bedroom after school for weeks at a time. Little Salvatore finally told his mother that he didn't want to be an altar boy anymore, for which she finally gave in. Sal was an only child, and his loving mother, Elsa, selflessly doted on him.

When the young boy started having nightmares, his mother realized that something was terribly wrong with her son. She blamed the school for the 'bullying' that she assumed was going on and faulted his dropping grades on the school nuns. She presumed their inability to properly teach her young son was the reason for his unexplainable depression and failing grades. When they finally moved away from Taylor Street, young Salvatore never looked back.

As a young teenager, he went to St. Fabian High School in Oak Park, where he continued to struggle with his studies as a freshman. He became suspicious and angry with the Jesuit clerics, who oversaw instructing the high school students. He had experienced some physical and emotional abuse at St. Fabian in the form of corporal punishment, when he and his high school friends didn't always 'follow the rules'.

His high school counselor, Mr. Thomas Saunders, a layman, realized Sal's deep depression problems and assisted him in getting help with his classes. His study habits and academics significantly improved, and he graduated in the upper third of his class.

But Sal Marrocco grew up with a very tainted view of the Roman Catholic Church. He married and raised his three children outside of the Catholic faith, never allowing any of them to make any of the holy sacraments. He struggled throughout his life to hide his hatred and distain for Roman Catholic priests. He still believed in a 'divine being' and organized religion but was very anti-Catholic. Over the years, he learned to restrain his personal opinions and religious viewpoints upon others.

The Consigliere at that moment, had tears in his eyes, as he struggled to focus on the mirror and continued shaving without cutting himself. He then walked to his locker and slowly put on his trousers and his crisp white shirt, blue sweater and gold cufflinks. He was careful to wear his gold Rolex watch that he just received as an early Christmas gift from his wife. He made sure he didn't forget to put back on his gold, 18-carat red cross ring that he always wore. He was still trying to remember the name of that monstrous pastor from St. Rosalia's Church who had stolen his innocent soul when he was a child.

"Aren't you done getting dressed, Sal? We've got a busy day today. We've got a ton of bad debts that we need to review before the year end," Little Tony said.

Marrocco was aware of the year end duties that awaited his controllership position that day. He tried to stay focused, struggling to put his past childhood nightmares behind him. It had taken him a lifetime to forget the terrifying incidents he experienced as a young altar boy at St. Rosalia's Church.

It took him many years to control the emotional flashbacks he experienced, remembering the pastor pulling his pants down, beating and punishing him with a thick paddle for dropping the container of communion hosts on the floor during holy mass. He could still remember being sexually accosted in the sacristy after mass and threatened by the pastor that he would instantly burn in Hell if he had ever mentioned anything to anyone. It took him years to forget as a little boy, how he would hide his blood-stained underwear away from his mother, so she wouldn't get suspicious. He remembered crying and screaming in the middle of the night, afraid he would be condemned to a burning fire of death, if anyone ever found out what that evil priest had been doing to him.

Sal Marrocco walked out of the company locker room and took the long stroll to the other side of the distribution warehouse, as his upstairs office was located on the opposite end. As he unlocked his office door, he broke into a cold sweat. The wicked face of the priest who had abused him as a little boy, his evil eyes casting down on him as he mentally struggled to escape his fury, suddenly appeared before him. The pastor's icy cold blue eyes were radiating fire as he loudly screamed for help, before the priest's hand covered his mouth.

He could still feel his head being pushed up against the cinder block wall of the church sacristy, feeling excruciating pain encompass his whole body as blood dripped onto the marble floor. The immoral image of his face, wearing his holy vestments, flashed before his eyes as the name, which took him years to forget, finally came back to haunt him. A name, which he now swore with a deep vengeance, he would never, ever forget again:

Fr. John Marquardt.

CHAPTER EIGHT

It was a bright, sunny spring morning, as the sun's reflection from the lawn's morning dew blinded my eyesight. The neatly manicured lawn and the park-like setting of the Cardinal's mansion was breath-taking, as I parked my Crown Victoria police car at the nearest illegal parking space. As I started climbing up the grand entranceway, I began chuckling to myself, wondering what these great walls of the Cardinal's mansion would have to say, if they were ever subpoenaed and forced to talk.

When I entered the office, I approached the old, frumpy receptionist, remembering that she didn't like coppers. I asked her in a well-mannered tone of voice, if I could possibly have a short, pleasant visit with Monsignor Kilbane.

"The Monsignor is very busy today. You will have to make an appointment if you wish to see him."

"The Chicago Police Department doesn't make appointments, ma'am," as I showed her my star, still trying very hard to be polite.

The old women gave me a dirty look for about three seconds. She probably thought that I had a lot of nerve questioning her sentinel duties, as she aggressively guarded the main gates to the Monsignor's office.

"I will let him know that you are here," she growled.

"Thank you," I politely answered with one of my fake smiles.

I sat myself down on one of their plush, velvet oak chairs and waited, noticing the ornate décor of the general reception area. I would have to remember all this elaborate opulence the next time I was at Sunday mass, I thought to myself. It was probably more than fifteen minutes before the Monsignor came out of his office to greet me.

"Hello, Detective," he said in a very cold, monotone voice, letting me know through his body language that I was more than disturbing him.

"Good Morning, Monsignor Kilbane," as I extended my hand and showed him my star again.

"Would you mind if I asked you a few more questions?"

"I have a very busy day today, Detective. I can only spare you a few minutes."

"That's very kind of you, Monsignor," as I was trying hard not to sound sarcastic, even though I knew this guy thought he was doing me a huge favor.

We walked into to his very extravagant office and I sat myself at one of the chairs, in front of his antique, wood carved, Maplewood desk.

"Since I'm a Catholic, may I call you Father?"

"Of course."

I took out a small note pad from my dark suit jacket and crossed my legs, trying to make myself comfortable.

"Is there any information you would care to tell me, regarding our investigation into the murder of John Marquardt?"

"Nothing that I can think of," he replied.

"Then I will get right to the point, Father. We have gotten word from the Great Lakes Life Insurance Company that there was a five-million-dollar insurance policy taken out on the life of John Marquardt back in 1982, naming your Archdiocese as the beneficiary. Are you aware of this?"

Kilbane started to change skin colors, as the few hairs he had combed across his bald scalp started to reflect his perspiration.

"Yes Detective. That is correct."

"Is this standard procedure?"

"What do you mean?"

"Does the Archdiocese go around insuring all of their former priests for five-million-dollar life insurance policies?"

The Monsignor looked directly in my eyes, never flinching for a second as he answered my questions.

"John Marquardt was employed by the Archdiocese in our accounting department. His life insurance premiums were one of his employment package benefits, taken directly from his salary."

"Really?" as I smiled. "And he named the Archdiocese as a beneficiary to his life insurance policy?"

"Of course, Detective. As a matter of fact, he did," Kilbane boldly answered.

He then pulled out one of his desk drawers and retrieved a thick, yellowed manila folder. He fumbled across a few papers before showing me a copy of the life insurance application, dated March 20, 1982, signed by John Marquardt. There was a highlighted section of the application where the named beneficiary was handwritten: *Archdiocese of Chicago.* I read through the actual application, noticing that it had been notarized by an outside party.

"Could I have a copy of this, Father?"

"Of course, Detective."

He dialed his receptionist's front telephone, and within several seconds my favorite secretary came in to make a copy of Marquardt's insurance application, still wearing one of her dirty looks. She came back moments later with a copy, which I folded and placed in my pocket.

"Why would Marquardt name the Archdiocese as his beneficiary?"

"Well, Detective, I don't know if you're aware. Besides administering to our churches and schools within the City of Chicago, we are involved philanthropically within the community as well. We fund food banks, child care services, adoption services, and many other needy organizations within the city."

I looked at him for a moment. It was as though his answers to my questions were very well scripted.

"And Marquardt never asked to change or amend the beneficiary of his life insurance policy?"

"Of course not. Why would he? Mr. Marquardt was aware of our philanthropic activities."

"Of course, he was," I couldn't hide my sarcasm any longer. "Your Archdiocese also funds the pension plans for old and retired priests, correct Father?"

"That is correct."

"And I imagine, this five-million-dollar insurance policy is going to help pay for a lot of pensions and a lot of needy soup kitchens, correct?" I retorted.

"How did you know about the life insurance policy, Detective?"

I broadly smiled as I answered his question. "We got a phone call from the Great Lakes Life Insurance Company. Seems they're a little suspicious, being that John Marquardt was brutally murdered and all."

Monsignor Kilbane looked at me sternly. His circular wired glasses appeared to be showing condensation as he was starting to vent out steam.

"I'm sorry, Monsignor Kilbane. I'm just having a very hard time understanding all of this. Why would a former priest, who decides to leave the priesthood in 1982 to take care of his sick mother, subsidize and pay the premiums of a five-million-dollar life insurance policy, through his employment here at the Archdiocese, and leave all of that money to the Archdiocese of Chicago when he dies?"

Kilbane looked like he was beginning to get very aggravated. "What's your point, Detective Dorian? I have a very busy day here and you're taking up a lot of my time," he replied as he was fumbling with his letter opener, holding it at one point as though it were a dagger.

"It just doesn't make any sense to me, Father," I continued. "Do all of your former priests sign up for high dollar insurance policies when they leave the priesthood?"

Kilbane knew at that point that I was interrogating him about these various life insurance policies.

"Some do, yes..."

"Five million bucks worth?" I retorted.

"John had no family, and he wanted to leave something substantial to the Catholic community, I'm sure."

"But five million dollars' worth?" I asked him again. I was trying so hard to push his buttons.

Kilbane just sat there in silence, as he knew he was inches away from hearing the Miranda warning and being hauled down to the district office for questioning.

"Father, I heard you grew up in Mayor Daley's old neighborhood," I blankly asked him.

"Yes."

"Well, I know for a fact that you guys from Bridgeport are all connected to one another, isn't that right?"

"Connected?"

"Well, yes, you know, connected."

The priest looked at me, pretending not to know what I was talking about.

"I've heard through the grapevine that you and 'Little Tony' DiMatteo are pallies," I mentioned this, wanting to let him to know that I had done my homework on him.

"We went to grade school together, at Nativity of Our Lord in Bridgeport," he said.

"Of course, you did. I also heard through the grapevine that you're the family's priest, and that you even married off Little Tony's daughter."

Monsignor Kilbane looked directly in my eyes, looking as though he was ready to jump over his desk and wrap his hands around my throat.

"Is there a law against presiding over a wedding? They asked me to marry them and I was honored."

"I'll bet you were. You and Little Tony have a nice, cozy little friendship going on, isn't that right?"

"What are you insinuating, Detective?" Kilbane angrily asked.

"You know, Father. It's kind of strange that when I was here last week to tell you about Marquardt's murder, that you weren't shocked or surprised. You didn't even flinch. Especially, since that old man was employed here at your diocese for so many years. I thought it was unusual that you didn't ask me any questions as to how or why he was murdered."

The Monsignor didn't say a word. He just sat there, stone-faced, making sure he didn't say anything that would incriminate him. His eyes continued to lock into mine, as though we were in a silly, staring contest.

"You know," I continued, "That murder had all the signs of a mob-hit. Did you know that? That old man was cut up and sliced up pretty good. Now why would a nice, do-gooder, former accountant from the Archdiocese of Chicago, who volunteers at the Children's Hospital three times a week, suffer such a gruesome, violent death? It was as though somebody wanted revenge. It was though the murderer wanted to make a violent statement by killing and mutilating this old former priest, Father. Doesn't all of this sound peculiar to you?" I mentioned in detail, trying to study the Monsignor's reaction.

"I did read about it, Detective Dorian," he responded. I could tell he was struggling to remain calm, as his forehead was beginning to perspire.

"Was the former Father Marquardt a pedophile priest, Monsignor?" I interrogated him.

"I wouldn't know the answer to that, Detective," he quickly responded.

"You're not aware of any pending pedophile lawsuits, where Father Marquardt was involved?"

"No, I am not," he quickly answered.

"I imagine, Monsignor, that the Archdiocese could really use five million bucks right about now, don't you agree? With all the pedophile lawsuits going on and all?"

Kilbane was starting to turn colors again, as the perspiration was now starting to drip from his forehead.

"I think our little visit here is over, Detective. I will put you in touch with our attorneys."

"Of course, you will, Father. You do that. I hear your high-priced attorneys are very good at quashing subpoenas from the D.A.'s office," I was starting to get angry, as we both rose up from our chairs.

"Just think what your diocese can do with five million bucks?" I kept asking him, as I was going to do my best to rattle him and to bait him into losing his temper.

"With all of the pedophile lawsuits the Archdiocese is on the hook for, and with all of the many victims of the all those pedophile priests your Archdiocese has protected over the years..."

"Goodbye Detective. We're done here," he sternly warned as his face was starting to turn red. I just kept pushing the envelope, waiting to see if he would crack.

"Boy-oh-boy, Father. Five million bucks sure comes in handy, especially when you have all of those pending lawsuits going on," I kept pressing him.

Kilbane looked like he could be easily flustered and coaxed into losing his hot, Irish temper. I had read somewhere that he ran around with a few of the tougher kids in the Bridgeport area, including DiMatteo. All the guys that I knew from that neighborhood hit first and asked questions later. The Monsignor looked like he wasn't in bad shape and had probably spent more than his share of his younger days at the gym.

Monsignor Kilbane just stood up and walked around from his large, antique desk, and approached me, within inches of my face. I wondered for a second if he had the balls to punch an on-duty police officer. I pulled the right side of my suit coat behind my gun, so that my Glock 17 sidearm was well displayed. Kilbane just stood in front of me, glaring at me for about five seconds without saying a word. I'm sure he was trying very hard not to say any of the 'f-bombs' that were probably going through his head at that moment.

"You need to leave, right now, Detective," he warned me again.

"I'm sure you'll be needing this when you talk to your attorneys," as I pulled out one of my cards and placed it on his desk.

"This conversation is far from over, Father," I stated.

I walked out of his office and tapped my hand on the secretary's desk, letting her know that I would be back soon. Chaz Rizzo had warned me about Kilbane. He was one 'tough cookie'. I realized that after leaving the Cardinal's mansion that it was going to take more than a coincidence or some circumstantial evidence to get Monsignor Kilbane down to the Sixteenth District for questioning. Judging by the Monsignor's friendship with DiMatteo, it would make sense if the Archdiocese solicited the homicide of an ex-priest, all cashed up in life insurance.

But 'Little Tony' DiMatteo enjoys keeping a low profile, and I was certain he wouldn't be stupid enough to let himself get involved in a 'murder for hire' plot of a former priest for the insurance money. And like Rizzo said, although the Archdiocese has probably broken a majority of the 'Lord's Commandments', he didn't a think murder-for-hire scheme was one of them.

So, if Kilbane and DiMatteo had nothing to do with this murder, who does that leave? Maybe somebody, who has nothing to gain, randomly kills and mutilates a little old ex-priest for shits and giggles, and now the Chicago Archdiocese is coincidently, enjoying a nice little windfall in the form of a five-million-dollar life insurance policy?

It just doesn't make any sense.

CHAPTER NINE

The evening sun was beginning to set as Monsignor Kilbane was alone in his office that early evening. The rest of the Cardinal's staff had gone home, and he was alone at his desk thinking about his unexpected morning visit with Detective Dorian earlier that day.

He had known about the murder and killing of John Marquardt for some time now and presumed that Little Tony was involved in his death. He asked himself at first, how Little Tony would have known that the pedophile and former priest was the first one on his 'hit list'. Monsignor Kilbane had previously pulled out the Archdiocese's files and records on the former priest.

There were over twenty complaints and incidents of sexual molesting allegations against Marquardt, starting from 1963 until his 'retirement' in 1982, that the Archdiocese was aware of. Many of these reported incidents had occurred while he was the pastor at St. Rosalia's Parish on Taylor Street. Although the former priest was never 'defrocked', the rumors of his sexual deviances with small boys were no secret to the surrounding community.

Kilbane presumed that, because of the vicious rumors amongst the Italians and Irish who lived in that neighborhood at the time, Marquardt's perverted actions and malicious reputation would have put him first on any list of pedophile priests who deserved to die for their evil sins. Little Tony and the DiMatteo Family were always very involved within the Chicagoland Italian community, and it wouldn't have taken a genius to figure out that John Marquardt's name was the first one on his 'wish' list.

The Monsignor was thinking about the questions and comments that the Detective brought up this morning and began to wonder: How much did Dorian know? By the statements that were made by him, it sounded as though he was suspicious that Marquardt's murder was a 'mob-style hit'. Meaning that, because of his longtime relationship with Little Tony, the Chicago Police Department was already apprehensive to this killing being a 'murder-for-hire,' plot, all to the benefit of the Archdiocese of Chicago.

But Fr. Joe also knew that Little Tony and his team of 'hit men' were professionals, and that they would never attempt such a murder unless they were 'one hundred percent' sure that they would never get convicted. He was confident that Little Tony had well planned this 'hit' on Marquardt, and knowingly didn't get him involved in order to keep him ignorant of any of the details. In this way, the Monsignor thought, he was not an accessory to the crime. Little Tony was very 'street smart' and very thorough when it came to performing these 'hits'. His silence kept Kilbane from being a participant in the murder.

Kilbane decided that evening, regardless of Detective Dorian's questions and insinuations that he wasn't going to worry about the Chicago Police Department. If they hadn't made an arrest by now, due to the lack of evidence either at the crime scene or elsewhere, it wasn't going to happen.

Kilbane needed to get in touch with Little Tony. He didn't want to make a direct call to him, even though he had his direct cell phone number. There were always suspicions that his telephones were 'bugged'. His mode of communication to Little Tony in the past was for his administrative assistant to make a telephone call from her cell phone to his daughter, Gianna, on one of several 'burner' phones that she was provided. These 'burner' phones were opened and closed on other people's names and accounts and were typically switched off and disconnected after two or three months of cellular service.

She in turn, would communicate the message to the Consigliere, Sal Marrocco, who would then relay the message directly to Little Tony. This was a long and arduous process, but it always assisted the two of them in keeping their private meetings even more discrete.

Kilbane had met Marrocco on several occasions. Their last encounter was at DiMatteo's daughter's wedding, which the Monsignor presided over. He remembered being impressed with Marrocco's intellect and 'street smarts', knowing that as the DiMatteo Family Consigliere, he was well aware of all of Little Tony's personal and business affairs. He also admired the 18-karat gold, ruby red cross ring that Marrocco was wearing that evening, along with his gold, diamond-clad, Rolex watch.

Kilbane had Ms. Palella, his administrative assistant, call Gianna earlier that afternoon, and was awaiting the details as to when and where he and Tony were meeting. He needed to know the specific details of Little Tony's fees, and how much they would be, seeing that he had taken it upon himself to carry out this 'hit'.

That evening, the Monsignor went into the Archdiocese safe, which was located in the basement of the mansion. He brought with him a black satchel bag and the combination, which only he and the Cardinal had. After spinning the tumblers to the combination lock, he opened the safe.

There were large stacks of cash inside, spindled in dominations of $10,000 each. It was not unusual for the safe to have in excess of one million dollars or more in cash and currency. There were also over one hundred gold and silver 'bars', several bags of gold and silver coins, and some 'private' documents filed separately, locked in a safe deposit box within the safe.

There was also a large, red ledger book, which recorded all the deposits and withdrawals of cash and currency within the safe. Kilbane opened the ledger book and recorded the withdrawal of $50,000 dollars in cash that evening. He marked down the withdrawal as a 'Deposit for services –NB". The initials "NB" stood for "Nativity Bridgeport", which was the acronym Kilbane decided to use for the payoff of Little Tony for his 'murder for hire' services. He hoped that the 'fifty large' would be enough to thank Tony for his services, and to let him know that there would be more cash available when the insurance paid out on Marquardt's life insurance claim.

He put the five large stacks of cash in the black satchel. He was sure he would see Little Tony either the next evening or soon thereafter, and he wanted to have the black bag ready for their private encounter. He closed the safe and returned to his office. Before leaving, he took his expensive 18-karat gold, ruby red cross ring off, which he never wore in public, and placed it in his small jewelry box on his credenza. He then shut off the lights and locked his office door.

The valet eagerly took the Monsignor's car keys the next evening, as he pulled his black Cadillac sedan in front of Trattoria Pagliacci on North Halsted. It was a warm spring evening, and he took a few minutes to close the sunroof and windows of his car, in case it would rain. He grabbed his black satchel, located on the floor the back seat, and proceeded to find Little Tony in his private room within the restaurant.

"Father Joe!"

"Hey Tony," as they excitedly greeted each other with a kiss on the cheek.

Little Tony immediately fixated his eyes on the black satchel that Father Joe brought with to accompany them at their dinner. The two of them sat down, as Tony was finishing his first Crown Royal while the Monsignor ordered his first Manhattan. The two made small talk as usual, as they continued to drink down their cocktails and ordered entrée's. Little Tony was discussing his excitement of being a first-time grandfather, with his daughter Gianna pregnant with their first child. The Monsignor, as usual, discussed the frustrations of running the Archdiocese of Chicago.

Neither one of them discussed the contents of the black satchel nor the reason for their visit until Tony DiMatteo finally brought up the subject after they had both finished their dinners.

"So, Joe," began Little Tony, "What did you need to discuss?"

Monsignor Kilbane looked at Little Tony, perplexed at first, wondering why Tony was playing so coy.

"Well," the Monsignor began.

"I wanted to thank you for your services, and I brought with me a small token of my appreciation."

Father Joe then passed the black satchel over to Little Tony, making sure none of the servers or the wait staff were around in the room.

Little Tony opened the bag and displayed a shocked look on his face when he realized that his friend had enclosed $50,000 in cash in bundled currency, all neatly stacked inside the satchel.

"Joe? What the fuck is this?"

"Tony, now, don't get upset. It's a small deposit until we receive the proceeds. As soon as the Chicago Police Department completes their investigation, I am sure we will have the insurance proceeds by then..."

Little Tony just looked at Father Joe with a bewildered look on his face.

"What?"

"It's a small deposit, Tony."

"Deposit for what?"

"It's a deposit, Tony, for your services....you know...."

Little Tony looked even more confused, thinking that his intermittent amnesia, which only he only saved for federal agents, was starting to catch up with him.

"Joe, what the fuck are you talking about?"

Monsignor Kilbane was starting to get even more confused with Little Tony's reaction. He looked around the room, making sure no one was around.

"Come on, Tony? You know! The hit?"

"What hit?" he whispered loudly. "What are you fucking talking about?"

85

Father Joe looked at him, now thinking that Little Tony was now losing his mind.

"Marquardt!" he whispered back.

Little Tony sat there for a moment, thinking. They were both silent, as Tony was taking inventory of all his recent activities and didn't recall ever making or ordering such a hit on anyone named Marquardt.

"Look Joe...whatever you're talking about, I had nothing to do with it!"

"What?" Now the Monsignor was even more confused. They both sat there silent, as Tony continued to try and figure out who Fr. Joe was talking about.

Suddenly, Little Tony burst out laughing, at the Monsignor's expense.

"Wait! Are you talking about that old man that got murdered in Albany Park not too long ago?" He remembered reading about it in the papers.

"Yes....John Marquardt," the Monsignor answered. "It was your hit, correct?"

Little Tony started laughing even louder.

"Joe, I think you're goddamn losing it."

A few more moments passed by until Little Tony could control his laughter.

"Joe, I would just love to take your money," as his laughter calmed down. "But that wasn't *our* hit!" Little Tony explained.

"Huh? What do you mean it 'wasn't your hit'?"

"We didn't do it, Joe. We didn't order any such hit. It wasn't ours, Joe."

Monsignor Kilbane had a confused and shocked look on his face. He was speechless.

"As a matter of fact," Tony explained. "I told Sal your idea when you asked me a few months ago and we both thought you were fucking nuts!"

The Monsignor was still in shock, not knowing what to think.

"Joe, I told you that this was a crazy idea and that we didn't want to get involved."

"Well," said the Monsignor, at a loss for words. "If you didn't do this, who the hell did?"

Little Tony took another long sip from his fourth Crown Royal on the Rocks.

"Beats the shit out of me, Joe. Besides, why would we make such a hit with all the heat from the 'coppers' and detectives lurking and snooping around? Aren't the 'coppers' sniffing around your place right now?"

"Yes, and they know about the life insurance policies."

"Good luck with that, Joe," Little Tony started smirking, twirling his ice cubes around.

"At least you can say with a good conscience that you had nothing to do with this."

"Well, I've got a Detective Dorian from the Chicago P.D. creeping around," Fr. Joe replied.

"Who? Dorian?" Little Tony perked up.

"Yes. Do you know him?"

"Yeah, he brought me and a few of my guys down to the station once on a potential homicide charge a few years back. He's a pussy!" he remarked.

Monsignor Kilbane was still perplexed and confused.

"If you don't know anything about this, Tony, who else would take him out?"

Little Tony finished his drink and called the waiter to bring him the check.

"Frankly, Father Joe, I don't know, and I really don't give a fuck."

He passed the black satchel back to the Monsignor, then stuffed a few hundred-dollar bills into the waiter's billfold.

"Until this murder is solved, Joe, there is going to be a lot of heat coming down on the Archdiocese.

You had better call your attorneys and watch your back. These 'coppers' have a way of coming out of the woodwork."

The Monsignor just sat there, not knowing what to say.

"I'm going to have Gianna drop those burner phones, so don't try to contact me."

With that, Little Tony quickly rose from the table and gave his friend a quick peck on the cheek.

"Take care, Joe. I'll call you when the baby is born."

He then quickly left the restaurant through the side exit, leaving the Monsignor sitting there, holding his black satchel bag...alone.

Monsignor Joseph Kilbane kept turning the facts of this murder over and over in his head: Did Marquardt have that many enemies that someone else had him killed? Who else would murder him? He didn't know what to say or think, as a cold chill began to run through his body and his hands started shaking. The only thing Fr. Joe could think of, was that if this killer was out there, and this homicide was unsolved, he could possibly, be the only suspect in this murder case. He had better 'lawyer-up', he thought to himself.

The Monsignor took a few moments to gather his thoughts. He didn't know if his hands were still shaking out of nervousness, or from the three Manhattans he had gulped down during dinner. He pulled out a ten spot to the valet and climbed into his Cadillac, placing the black satchel bag in the backseat of his car. He then began to drive towards his luxury townhouse in Lincoln Park.

The lights and the oncoming traffic seemed a little blurry as he was driving. He was having difficulty distinguishing his immediate surroundings, and especially, driving on the right lane. He didn't notice, until it was too late, that he had run the stop sign at the intersection of Aberdeen and Halsted Streets.

Within seconds, he heard a siren and saw bright, blue flashing lights in his rear-view mirror.

CHAPTER TEN

The library at St. Peter Chanel High School on the west side of Chicago was jammed with students on that warm, spring day in May 1966. It was final exams week, and the boys were grouped together, sitting at various long, wooden tables within the library as several Marist priests were keenly patrolling the crowded study hall. Scott DeSantis and his best friend, Stephan Walker, were studying for their sophomore chemistry finals, and were passing notes to each other back and forth when the keen-eyed monitors weren't looking.

Scotty and Steve went to St. Veronica's Grade School together, lived close by, and had known each other since the second grade. They were trying to be unnoticed and discrete as the two boys pushed pieces of paper back and forth to each other, trying hard to control their laughter.

The subjects of their notes were humorous and unmemorable, ranging from John Romeo's ugly, over-weight prom date that prior Saturday night to Tom Keegan's brand spanking new, 1966 Mustang convertible. Scotty was just passing another note to Steve when Father Senopoli pounded his fist on the table, covering the unread note with his hand.

"Are you two boys done horsing around?" Father Senopoli said sternly, as he crumpled the unread note with his hand. He was completely uninterested in what the two boys were gossiping about, as their behavior was disturbing the other students trying to study.

"Yes Father," Scotty said. He was keeping a straight face, trying very hard to control his laughter by biting his lower lip.

Fr. Lucas Senopoli was the Dean of Students at the all-boys high school and wasn't afraid to grab any student by the hair and pound their heads against the wall to get his point across. His methods of discipline went beyond the definitions of corporal punishment. Fr. Senopoli's violent procedures in controlling his students in those days would raise the eyebrows of many parents and outsiders even then.

Two weeks prior, three boys were caught smoking in the men's bathroom, and he made each student eat and swallow a whole pack of cigarettes before administering 'swirlies' by dunking their heads into the men's room toilets. Senopoli kept a "rider's crop" in his desk drawer and wasn't afraid to harshly whip the bear ass of any boy who was caught breaking one of the high schools' many rules.

After Fr. Senopoli walked away, Scotty and Steve started laughing and giggling again, and Scotty continued to pass more notes to Steve while the monitors weren't looking. As the two boys continued to entertain themselves and disregard their studies, Fr. Senopoli was standing behind a shelf of books targeting the two boys. As the study hall was starting to conclude, the Dean of Students approached the two sophomores.

"Mr. DeSantis and Mr. Walker follow me to my office please," Fr. Senopoli calmly said.

The two students began to shudder, as they followed him down the long, darkened hallway and into his office, which was in the far rear of the school. This location of his office turned out to be an advantage for Fr. Senopoli, as his private area was void of outside noise and located remotely away from the school classrooms and the student cafeteria.

Once the boys entered his office, Fr. Senopoli exploded:

"Which one of you would care to tell me what is so important that you needed to pass notes back and forth?" as he grabbed both boys by their black ties, pushing them both up against the wall.

Steve started saying, "Nothing Father. We were laughing about the prom last week and..."

He shoved the boys even harder.

"What about your exams?" he asked with intense intimidation.

"Why aren't you both taking your final exams more seriously, instead of mocking your teachers and this institution?" he remanded in a very loud, angry voice.

"But we were not..." Scotty started to say.

"Shut up! Both of you!" Senopoli screamed.

He walked over to his desk and pulled out his 'rider's crop.' On the corner of his desk was also one of those new, Polaroid cameras that takes instantaneous black and white pictures. He then demanded both boys to remove their trousers. As they removed their pants and underwear, Father Senopoli took several pictures of the two boys standing side by side up against the bare office wall.

"These pictures are for your disciplinary school records," Senopoli remarked.

Scotty and Steve had never been in trouble with the Dean of Students before. They had heard about his 'rider's crop' bare-ass whippings and his 'pictures' from the other students over the past two years, but neither boy had ever been in his office or experienced his excessive corporal punishment. For some odd reason, Fr. Senopoli seemed to target most of his disciplinary actions and corporal punishment on the school's freshmen and sophomores.

He then demanded Stephan to bend over his desk. As the young boy followed his orders, Stephan started crying.

"I'm sorry Father. Please don't hit me with that. I promise we won't do it again. I promise I won't ever disrespect you. I promise, Father. Please don't hit me," Stephan begged.

Senopoli only became more enraged, as he cracked the whipping device against the top of his desk a few times.

"Take your punishment like a man, Mr. Walker. You should have thought of this while you were horsing around in the library."

Fr. Senopoli grabbed Walker by the hair, and forcibly pushed him down, bent over across his desk. He then began whipping the boy as hard as he could, placing his left hand over his body to keep him still. Steve began crying and screaming with pain, as the lashes seemed to come down on his bare buttocks harder and harder. Scotty DeSantis trembled as he watched his best friend get whipped and abused by the Dean of Students, as he was hitting Steve's bare bottom with all his force and with all his rage.

Senopoli must have whipped the boy more than a dozen times. When the beating concluded, Stephan's face was drenched with tears. He painfully grasped his underwear and his trousers, and slowly began to dress himself. As he was struggling to get dressed Scotty noticed the blood and red whipping marks on Steve's bare buttocks.

"Now it's your turn Mr. DeSantis," as he demanded Scotty to bend over his desk.

At that point, a combination of fear and hatred came over Scotty. He did something on that afternoon that no one in the history of St. Peter Chanel High School had ever done. As the boy was beginning to bend over his desk, he suddenly stood up and grabbed the rider's crop away from Father Senopoli.

"Fuck you! You're not hitting me with that thing!"

He pushed the office door open and bolted out of his office with Senopoli's whipping device in his hand. He was struggling to pull up his trousers, as he began running and screaming down the hallway.

"Come back here, you little bastard!" screamed Father Senopoli, as he ran out of his office chasing after the sophomore.

The open commotion and Scotty's screaming for help down the hallway alerted the attention of several teachers, who peered out of their classrooms to see what was going on. One of them was Fr. Gabriel Swann, who was in the middle of administering his trigonometry finals to his eleventh-grade students.

Fr. Gabriel was a large, burly man, in excess of six feet, five inches tall, and well over three hundred pounds. He was one of the more popular Marist priests at St. Peter Chanel, as he seemed to have a good reputation and was well loved by his students. He was a great math instructor and spent a tremendous amount of time tutoring students after school. "Father Gabe" was involved in the schools' drama club, student government, and monitored many of the other student high school activities. He was also the head football coach.

As Fr. Gabriel stepped out into the hallway, Scotty ran into his arms, screaming and crying for the priest's help, still grasping the whipping device in his hand.

"Help me Fr. Gabe, please...." Scotty was crying uncontrollably as Senopoli caught up with the young boy. As he tried to reach for Scott, Fr. Gabriel grabbed his arm.

"What the hell is going on here?" Gabriel demanded.

"This little bastard ran away with my rider's crop!" Fr. Senopoli screamed. Scotty started crying uncontrollably.

"He beat the hell out of Stevie Walker and he wants to beat me up too," Scotty explained between sobs.

Fr. Gabe sternly looked at Fr. Senopoli. Everyone on the staff of the high school was aware of Fr. Senopoli's extreme acts of corporal punishment. Fr. Gabriel had voiced his disapproval of their Dean of Students' excessive actions of abuse on many occasions in the past but seemed to always fall on the deaf ears of their aging principal, Fr. William Ouellette.

As Fr. Gabriel stood between Senopoli and the boy, he boldly ordered, "I think it's time that we have a meeting in the principal's office tomorrow, Father." Fr. Gabriel glared at Senopoli, the two locking eyes on one another with total contempt.

"Scott, go to your locker and get your things. Return here with your parents first thing tomorrow morning. We will meet at the principal's office."

Scott let go of Fr. Gabriel and quickly walked to his locker, picking up his books and notepads to catch the bus home.

The two Marist priests just stood there, alone in the middle of the hallway, glaring at one another. As the two priests were beginning their standoff, Fr. Gabriel saw Stephan Walker slowly walking toward his locker. He could tell that the boy was in an extreme amount of pain and was walking with a limp, trying to cover up the pain on his buttocks as he slowly walked. He was still whimpering from the beating.

"What the hell did you do to that boy?" Fr. Gabriel demanded.

"They were both misbehaving in study hall. They were passing notes to one another...."

"Are you kidding me? You beat up a student with that damn whip for passing notes?" Fr. Gabriel screamed. His eyes were filled with rage and anger, as he stood toe to toe with Fr. Senopoli, his face within centimeters of his.

"I have sat back and watched you physically and emotionally abuse these boys for years. I am waiting for the day when one of these boys grabs that rider's crop of yours and whips the living hell out you," he screamed at the Dean of Students.

"Maybe you would like the first opportunity," Fr. Senopoli angrily replied.

"I think the Lord would forgive me for taking one good crack at you," Gabriel loudly remarked.

The two priests were screaming and taunting each other in the middle of the hallway, as the teachers and students began leaving their classrooms and gathered to watch the two priests getting ready to go at it. Before there were any blows taken or any punches thrown, the English teacher, Mr. Robert Kelly, interceded in between them.

"We don't need to have these students watch the two of you fight like teenagers," Kelly said, as he pushed himself between the two of them.

Fr. Gabriel gave one last dirty look to Fr. Senopoli, as the both returned to their respective corners, Gabriel's classroom and Senopoli's office. They both knew there would be quite a standoff in the principal's office tomorrow morning.

Scotty DeSantis and his father had arrived at the principal's office just after 7:30am the next morning. Scotty's father, Mario DeSantis, owned and operated a local bar and pizzeria near Grand Avenue and Noble Streets.

He was an old school Italian who had arrived from Cassino, Italy as a young boy, and had worked in the restaurant business all his life. He was a well-built, stocky man at five feet, eight inches tall, and had a look of fury on his face as Father Ouellette welcomed the two of them into his office.

After refusing any coffee or water from the principal's receptionist, the two of them sat in silence in the adjacent conference room as they waited patiently for Fr. Senopoli and Fr. Swann to arrive.

As the Dean of Students arrived in the conference room, the elder DeSantis could barely contain his look of rage. Mario DeSantis only glared at Fr. Senopoli when he extended his hand out to greet him. He openly refused to shake his hand.

Fr. Ouellette walked into the conference room and took his place at the head of the table, with his morning coffee.

"I believe there was an incident yesterday afternoon, gentlemen, which has brought all of us here this morning," Fr. Ouellette started the meeting.

"Would you care to enlighten us as to what happened in the library yesterday, Mr. DeSantis?"

The principal directed his first question to Scotty. He nervously recounted the library incident whcre he was passing handwritten notes to his friend, Steve. He also recited the events which occurred in the Dean of Student's office, and how Steve was mercilessly whipped by Fr. Senopoli.

At that moment, Fr. Swann entered the conference room along with Monsignor Patrick Kelly, who was an associate from the Chicago Archdiocese and the Cardinal's office. The Monsignor was carrying a red photo album and Senopoli's 'rider's crop' along with him. The Dean of Students glared viciously at Fr. Gabriel, recognizing the red photo album immediately.

"I'm sorry we're late, Father Ouellette. I asked Monsignor Kelly to join us at this meeting this morning," Fr. Gabe said.

As the two of them sat down at thc other end of the conference table, the principal asked Scotty to recite the events from the day before again, in front of Monsignor Kelly, from the Library to Senopoli's office. As they all sat around the conference table, Fr. Gabriel took charge of the meeting.

"As you well know, Father Ouellette, I have complained to you on many occasions regarding the harsh and somewhat 'violent' corporal punishment actions which Fr. Senopoli has administered to our students in the past. I have also heard many students complain about the whipping sessions that the Dean of Students has aggressively incorporated in disciplining the students here at St. Peter's," Swann recited, sounding almost like a prosecutor from the "Perry Mason" show.

"But something has recently come to my attention over the last twenty-four hours that prompted me to ask Monsignor Kelly from the Archdiocese to join us here this morning," Fr. Gabriel continued.

He was focusing on the red photo album and the whipping device placed at the end of the conference table, which was now in the possession of Monsignor Kelly.

Mr. DeSantis sat silently with his son, as Father Ouellette listened intently to Fr. Gabriel. The old, aged principal, well into his eighties, seemed to be totally clueless to the harsh beatings that his Dean of Students was so liberally prescribing to the students. He also had no idea what was inside of that red photo album.

"We cannot allow you to harshly beat up and assault any more students, Fr. Senopoli, at either this institution or any other school within our Archdiocese," Monsignor Kelly explained.

"Needless to say, this will not go on," he sternly insisted.

There were several moments of silence in the room, as the Dean of Students realized that this "Principal's meeting" was turning into a civil trial, with himself as the defendant. He only glared at Fr. Gabriel in total silence, steaming with total anger and contempt. He figured out that Fr. Swann must have gotten permission to go into his office when he wasn't there. He probably rummaged through his office until he found the proof the he was looking for. The "red photo album" confirmed the suspicions Fr. Swann had long suspected.

"Father Senopoli, we are going to play a game this morning," Monsignor Kelly stated.

"We are going to call it, 'Let's Make A Deal'".

"I am going to ask you to sign your letter of resignation, effective immediately. I will in turn, keep this 'red photo album' for safekeeping at the Cardinal's office, and we can end any other discussions regarding your harsh methods of discipline at St. Peter Chanel High School right here and now," the Monsignor proposed.

Fr. Lucas Senopoli began turning several shades of red while Monsignor Kelly was still speaking.

"Or..." the Monsignor continued. "I can turn over this red photo album to Mr. DeSantis here, for him to do whatever he wishes."

There was a look of shock and confusion around the table, as Father Gabriel gleefully stared down at the Dean of Students. Fr. Senopoli was appalled and livid over the Monsignor's proposal. He started to angrily voice his opinion.

"I do not appreciate the means or your methods in demanding my dismissal here...."

Fr. Gabriel stood up and angrily pounded his open hand on the conference table, startling everyone in the room.

"You've lost your right to say anything here, Lucas," he angrily screamed. "A thousand deaths into the burning halls of Hell wouldn't be good enough for you, you son of a bitch! And this 'red photo album' only proves it."

There were several moments of silence as everyone quietly focused on Fr. Senopoli. He then stood up from the conference table.

"I will honor your wishes and leave St. Peter's this afternoon." Fr. Senopoli said as he began walking towards the exit door. At that moment, Mario DeSantis stood up and walked towards the disgraced priest, blocking the exit.

"Sit back down Father. You and I haven't squared up yet," the boy's father said.

As Fr. Senopoli begrudgingly sat back down at the table, Mario DeSantis took over the floor.

"I want everyone to leave this room, except Fr. Swann," he directed. "I want him to witness what I am going to say."

Scotty, Fr. Ouellette and Kelly slowly exited the conference room, with the Monsignor taking the red photo album and the Dean's rider's crop with him. When the door was closed behind them, DeSantis glared at Fr. Senopoli with total contempt as he began speaking:

"If what's in that red photo album is what I think it is, you and I have a problem, Father," DeSantis began.

"There had better not be any photos of my son in that album. Because if there are, no angel from Hell will protect you from the fucking beating that I'm going to give you right here and now," he threatened.

Fr. Gabe interjected, "There are no photos of your son, Mr. DeSantis. Although he did take some pictures yesterday, they are not in that album and are in my possession."

DeSantis angrily stared down at Senopoli.

"You sick fuck! It's a good thing you didn't touch my kid with that whip yesterday," he continued.

"I would have immediately come here, gauged out your eye balls and skull fucked you, you sick bastard."

Fr. Senopoli started turning several shades of red, as Mario DeSantis continued to berate the former Dean of Students.

"In all the years at this school, I'm surprised no one has taken that rider's crop and shoved it up your ass".

Senopoli sat there silently as DeSantis delivered his poignant statement.

"Pray to God that I never, ever see you again, Father. Because if I ever do, may the Lord have mercy on your soul."

With that, Scott's father rose up from the conference table and left the room with Fr. Gabe, leaving Fr. Senopoli to sit there at the conference room table, alone. As they all walked out of the principal's office, Fr. Gabriel smiled at Scotty as he put his arm around him.

"I've been looking forward to this day for many, many years," the burly priest said.

"You have no idea what a wonderful service you have done for this school," Fr. Gabe gleamed.

At that moment, they all shook hands outside of the Principal's office and everyone went in their own directions. Scotty had another final exam to study for, while his father had to go to back to work and Fr. Gabe had a final math exam to administrate.

Although Fr. Senopoli never set foot at St. Peter Chanel High School again after that faithful morning in May 1966, he was unfortunately, only reprimanded by the Archdiocese of Chicago. After a brief sabbatical and some 'very intense therapy', Fr. Senopoli was reassigned as the assistant principal to Marist High School on the south side for several years, and then to

Notre Dame High School in 1975. In both instances, his abusive methods of corporal punishment and his "red photo albums" caught up with him, and Cardinal Brody quietly forced him to resign and leave the priesthood in 1979.

No assault or child pornography charges were ever brought up against him.

CHAPTER ELEVEN

The elderly man was pulling into the alley of his modest, Jefferson Park bungalow where his garage was located on that bright, Friday afternoon. It was the beginning of the Memorial Day weekend, and the old man was looking forward to the bocce ball tournament at the Mazzini Verdi Club which was starting at seven o'clock that evening. He needed to get himself cleaned up and ready before his friend from the club came over to pick him up.

At the age of 78 years old, Lucas Senopoli did his very best to stay active. With the onset of diabetes and two heart valve stints that were installed a few years ago, he struggled to remain active and in good health. He walked five miles every day with his golden retriever, Rocco, around the local neighborhood, and always tried very hard to stay energetic. Since leaving the priesthood in 1979, he worked for the maintenance crew for the Archdiocese of Chicago, doing mechanical repairs and landscaping for its various churches and schools. He had enjoyed his work until his recent retirement. Mr. Senopoli lived alone, and he preferred it that way, as he kept to himself and didn't socialize very much. He didn't have many friends, other than those he had made at the Mazzini Verde Club. Most considered him a loner, and he enjoyed his privacy.

Senopoli unloaded the groceries from his 2007 Buick, and walked from the back door of the garage, through his back yard and entered his house. His modest, red brick bungalow was tidy and well kept, as he did his own maintenance and landscaping. He had just planted some flowers along the front of the house, and the scent of the freshly cut lawn reminded him of the grass clippings that needed to put out for garbage pickup next week.

Although he enjoyed being in his home, he was beginning to get despondent over Jefferson Park area. There had been a significant number of Latinos that were starting to move onto his street on North Menard Avenue.

The annual Cinco de Mayo celebrations were fast becoming a major holiday on his block, and he was beginning to realize that he was very much a minority in his own neighborhood.

Very few people knew about Lucas Senopoli's past as a Catholic priest. It had been many years since Cardinal Brody had forced his resignation to leave the priesthood. Although he was grateful to have a job working for the diocese, he was always bitter about his pension and social security package, as he strained to live on his minimal retirement income.

He was forced into leaving his job after turning 75 years old a few years ago and didn't appreciate having to pay all the insurance premiums that he was required to pay in order to keep his employment. He tried several times to stop paying the required five-million-dollar whole life insurance policy which he was obligated to pay every quarter but was told by the Archdiocese that his position would be terminated if he did so.

Senopoli was on a very strict budget since his retirement, and the $2,400 in monthly income from his pension and social security didn't go very far. After paying his utility bills, prescriptions, insurance and taxes, there sometimes wasn't much left for groceries. The old man had to save and cut corners wherever he could. He had a large container in his garage for plastic and aluminum cans, which he cashed in at the local Jewel grocery store every month.

He was grateful for the New Hope Food Bank, where he would pick up some packages of pasta and cans of tomato sauce when his cupboards were bare. St. Malachy, his neighborhood parish, had a 'soup and salad' dinner every Friday, which he frequently attended, along with the Knights of Columbus Spaghetti Dinners once a month. There was a goodwill store in his neighborhood, where he would occasionally buy whatever clothing he could afford.

But Lucas Senopoli was a tormented soul, and his biggest problems were not his finances. The former priest was in constant battle with his inner demons and spent a tremendous amount of time coping with his manic depression. He was a life-long insomniac, and often woke up in a cold sweat most every evening, battling the evil spirits that fermented inside of his brain for so many years.

He was often wide awake by 2:00am and was frequently seen walking Rocco around the neighborhood in the middle of the night, trying to escape his horrifying nightmares.

The local police knew of his bad sleeping habits, and Senopoli took his evening walks as though he were running away from his nocturnal demons. He always regretted his decision to enter the priesthood as a young man, and only entered the seminary as a vehicle for hiding his immoral, sexual deviances. He had been in and out of psychiatric therapy almost all his adult life and would often negate taking the high dosage of Lexapro which he was prescribed but could barely afford. When his sexual 'urges' became uncontrollable, he had a large collection of illegal 'kiddy porn' magazines, which he kept in a double locked, wooden truck in his bedroom.

The old man was in his kitchen putting his groceries away that afternoon, when realized he had forgotten a grocery bag of vegetables from his car. He walked back to the garage and grabbed the last bag of groceries, located in the back seat. He closed the car door and walked towards the garage exit.

But hiding behind the garage door, a stranger was lurking. The former priest suddenly felt a hand cover his mouth and a sharp blade rubbing up against his throat. He tried to scream and began to gag as he dropped the bag of groceries onto the garage floor. As he began to struggle, the assailant pushed the aged man up against the garage wall, his sharp knife still touching his throat. Struggling for air, the elderly man was starting to turn blue. As he inserted the pointed dagger into his victims' throat, he whispered these final words into the old pedophile's left ear:

"May Jesus grant you mercy, Father Senopoli."

CHAPTER TWELVE

Throngs of people were beginning to gather inside of St. Peregrine Church in the Portage Park neighborhood, as Chicago Police Department Sergeant Paul Russo arrived on that cold, Saturday morning in January for his best friend's funeral. Joseph Campisi had committed suicide that prior Tuesday evening by standing in front of the Big Timber Westbound train at the Western Avenue train station.

It was the rush hour going home, and Russo couldn't understand why any of the bystanders didn't rush to stop Joey Campisi from calmly walking onto the railroad tracks in front of an oncoming train that early evening. Witnesses said that at 5:56 pm Tuesday night, he parked his car at the nearby park-ing lot, and then leisurely walked past the train depot onto the railroad tracks. As the Metra train began feverishly sounding its horns, he only stood still, looking away towards the other direction as he was hit by the force of the train head-on. His body was instantly dismembered and dragged over twenty feet across the tracks, as bystanders and passengers looked on in horror. Several Chicago EMT ambulances were called to the scene, as two older witnesses fainted at the sight of Campisi's decapitated and mutilated body scattered all over the railroad tracks.

As everyone filed past the closed casket, all his friends and family were still in shock as to why the 61-year-old construction worker, who was divorced with three grown children, would so tragically, and yet so publicly, end his own life. But Russo, having been on the Chicago Police Intelligence Unit over at the Old Maxwell Street Station for over thirty years, had seen more than his share of tragic suicides and needless

105

deaths. He was extremely close to his lifelong friend since their days at St. Rosalia's Catholic School and Notre Dame High School on the north side of Chicago.

Sergeant Russo was aware of Joey Campisi's enduring, horrific demons that embattled him his whole life, and was afraid a tragedy like this would happen. Campisi was a full-time alcoholic and part-time drug user. He took whatever he could take, and whatever was available to him, to alleviate his mental anguish and help ease his inner pain.

As he knelt before the casket at the vestibule of the church, Russo began crying uncontrollably, remembering all the horrendous incidents of Joey's childhood that eventually, put him over the edge. He remembered the incident at St. Rosalia's church as altar boys, when they thought they were going to be punished for switching the mass wine at Fr. Marquardt's mass and Joey instead, being raped and molested by the priest that day. Although he eventually figured out what had happened to his best friend on that day in 1964, Joey Campisi absolutely never, ever talked about it.

Ever.

Sgt. Russo remembered having drinks at their local watering hole, the Glenwood Lounge in Wicker Park, where they usually met on Friday nights. He remembered bringing up the altar boy incident to him, asking him what had happened almost fifty years earlier. Joey turned red and became extremely violent, almost attacking Russo outside for bringing it up. He totally denied that the molestation ever happened.

There was another incident at Notre Dame High School. Fr. Lucas Senopoli, the head principal at the time, maliciously whipped young Joey with his 'rider crop' for smoking in the bathroom, until he drew blood across his buttocks. The young freshman then witnessed him masturbating under his desk while Joey, standing there naked, was forced to watch. Paul had only found out about it because Joey had confessed the incident to him while they were both inebriated during a high school football party. Russo knew that his best friend had endured childhood experiences that no young boy should ever have to endure.

He had helplessly watched Joey become an alcoholic, leaving his wife and children home alone and without money while he went to the bar almost every night after work until one o'clock in the morning. He remembered getting phone calls from his wife, Suzanne, pleading with him to 'fish Joey' out of the bar and to bring him home in one piece.

Joey had several DUI offenses and was without a driver's license for a few years until hiring a high-priced lawyer to retrieve it back for him. His alcoholism and cocaine use contributed to the failure of his marriage and the destruction of his family.

And yet, Joey Campisi would never admit that he had an alcohol or drug abuse problem. Russo pleaded with him many times to get help. He once waited for Joey to come out of the bar one night and purposely arrested him, locking him up in a jail cell over the weekend until he agreed to get help for his problem.

His former wife, who was still totally devoted to him, only ended the marriage to force him to realize his drug and alcohol problem, and to get the psychological therapy he needed to overcome his addictions. Suzanne would call Russo at all hours of the night, begging to know why Joey was so mentally tortured and so emotionally demonized. Russo, out of loyalty to his best friend, said very little to his former wife, fearing that she would turn that information against him in a divorce. Because Sgt. Russo was probably the only person in the world who knew about Joey's child molestations as a kid, he was limited as to how much he could help his best friend.

He thought about recommending Joey to file a lawsuit against the Archdiocese of Chicago, but after talking to an attorney, realized that the statute of limitations had already passed on Campisi's ability to successfully file. He tried bringing him to a precinct psychiatrist who came highly recommended, specializing in drug and alcohol patients, but to no avail. Joey always refused to get any help, and Paul was sure that his best friend's child molestations were the root of all his psychological and emotional problems.

Sergeant Russo put on the white gloves and stood next to the casket, as the pallbearer to his best friend. Joey's forever loving wife, along with his three children, followed the casket to the front of the church, as the canter sang the "Ave Maria" in a loud, glorious tenor voice. The traditional song seemed to reverberate from the magnificent walls of St. Peregrine Church, with its ornate stained-glass windows, containing its holy sounds for all those who came to witness the ascension of his lifelong friend.

As the priest presided over the funeral mass, Russo's mind was elsewhere. At that moment, Russo was having 'survivor's remorse', wondering why his best friend Joey was chosen to suffer the mental anguish and consequences of his childhood sexual abuse and why he was spared. He sat there in total contempt, vehemently blaming the Catholic Church and its hypocritical doctrines for the death of his best friend.

Why, he asked himself, did it take the Catholic Church so long to publicly recognize the molesting and raping of so many young children for so many, many years? Why were these pedophile priests allowed to teach so many children the gospel for so long, then privately dehumanize them behind closed doors? Why were these monsters relocated from church to church, raping and taking advantage of so many children at such a young, vulnerable age? So many children like Joey Campisi, who grew up alone and isolated, with no one to understand their inner torment. Why did Joey grow up to be a drunk, with DUI's on his record and a cocaine drug habit? Why did Joey have to suffer an untimely death in front of an on-coming train?

Those were good questions for all the evil, satanic priests like Fr. Marquardt, Fr. Senopoli, and every other priest who hid behind their holy vestments to practice their sexual deviances.

At that moment, Sergeant Russo's rage was beginning to overcome him right there in the middle of his best friend's funeral mass. Russo wanted revenge. He could taste it in his mouth. Above all the drug dealers, all the rapists, all the murderers and gang bangers he ever pushed through the jails of his precinct, at that moment, he hated all Catholic priests the most.

He wanted revenge, not just on the priests who destroyed his best friends' life, but on all the Catholic priests who stood there at the pulpit, preaching the gospel out of one side of their mouths, and then breaking the Lord's Commandments and preying on God's children when no one was looking.

As an experienced police officer and intelligence detective, Sergeant Paul Russo had a reputation that preceded him throughout the Chicago Police Department. At five feet, nine inches tall, he was well built and more than fit for his 61-year-old body. He ran five miles every morning and could still run a seven-minute mile during any 5-K race. He was a widower and kept a good relationship with his 31-year-old daughter, Arianna, who was an accountant at a Chicago Loop CPA firm. Although he had many friends within the City of Chicago, Russo had more than his share of enemies. His volatile temper and hard, suspicious demeanor made him a difficult person to work with, and a very hard person to get close to. Although Paul Russo was well beyond the age of retiring from the police department, he chose to stay on the Intelligence Special Task force for a few more years, until he could figure out what to do with his spare time and his excess anger.

He intuitively understood the 'in's and out's' of any crime scene and knew how to stage the 'perfect murder' if he had to. He was always the first person to arrive at a crime scene and had an experienced staff of loyal intelligence detectives to assist him in solving many of the heinous crimes and murders that occurred within the city. He also had developed a reputation for taking the 'law into his own hands'. He had appeared before the supervisory and police disciplinary committee several times, and his district commander was more that aware of his explosive temper and quick trigger finger. There had been several murderous outlaws and drug pushers who haplessly 'disappeared' within his precinct, who had skirted the judicial system on a technicality, then becoming victims of "Russo's Law."

As the funeral mass concluded, Paul Russo carried his best friends' casket out of St. Peregrine Church on Melvina Street and onto the long, black hearse waiting at the bottom of the church's steps. He grieved all alone in his car, following the funeral procession, passing Joey's house in the Portage Park neighborhood, and then onto Queen of Heaven Cemetery in Hillside. When the parade of cars finally arrived at the cemetery, the funeral hearse pulled up in front of the many aisles of neatly arranged marble crypts, each row named after an obscure saint.

Russo assisted the other pallbearers, carrying the coffin to Joey's final resting place. There was an open marble crypt at the seventh row on top, whose stone slab had already been removed, awaiting the arrival of his best friend's body. The priest mumbled a few more prayers, as each of the gatherers placed a red rose on top of the dark brown, silver trimmed casket. All the mourners, including Joey's family, stood silent as the special fork lift lifted the casket, with two undertakers alongside of it, and slowly pushed Joseph Campisi's body into the empty marble crypt, high up on the seventh row.

As Paul Russo watched his best friend become forever entombed, he said the Lord's Prayer to himself, wishing eternal rest for his soul. As his face was soaked in tears, he silently waited for the rest of the mourners to leave, until he was the very last one facing Joey's gravesite...alone.

He solemnly stood there, with one hand in his coat pocket and holding the last red rose with the other. He placed it on the ground beneath Joey's crypt, then loudly said goodbye to the tomb of his best friend.

He then swore a thousand deaths to the two priests who put him there.

CHAPTER THIRTEEN

SENOPOLI DISCOVERED

It had been a very busy day at the Sixteenth District. It was the Friday before the long, Memorial Day weekend, and all the detectives were trying to finish and wrap up their pending cases before the holiday. It was about 4:00pm in the afternoon, and I kept looking at the clock, hoping that the end of my shift at six o'clock would come quickly.

Being divorced, I didn't have to rush home to anyone except my yellow lab, Ginger. But I was looking forward to having dinner with my daughter, her husband and my little granddaughter at 7:30pm, and I was hoping nothing would come up that would make me cancel that.

I was sitting at my desk working on some files when my desk phone went off. I decided to let it ring three or four times before answering. Usually when my desk phone goes off after four o'clock, it meant I should cancel my evening plans and be ready to work the extra night shift.

"Detective Dorian speaking." I was trying sound pleasant, like I had nothing else better to do before the holiday weekend.

"Phil? It's Tommy Morton...from the Seventeenth"

"Hey Tommy, did you find another dead body hanging around?" I was kidding.

"Phil, you better come over here," said a very serious voice on the other line.

"What's up?"

"Another murder, same as the one on Argyle a few weeks ago. We definitely have a problem here."

Morton's voice was so serious he was almost quivering on the phone. I had never heard him so shaken up before, as this one must have really spooked him.

"Oh shit. Where at?"

"5027 North Menard. You may want to get here as soon as you can."

"I'll be right there," I responded.

As I threw on my suit coat and grabbed my gun, a thousand thoughts were going through my mind. I was almost afraid to run over to the crime scene, as I texted my daughter and canceled our dinner plans. When I got there, Detective Morton was standing in front of the address, and he had motioned me to enter through the alley, where there was crime scene tape and two Chicago EMT Units already at the crime scene. Two more police cars had followed behind me as I parked on the adjunct street closest to the alley.

"Hey Tommy, what do we got?" I said as we shook hands.

He just shook his head and pointed over to the garage. Morton was usually a talkative, friendly guy. For him to be speechless, the sight of this murder had to be bad.

I walked over toward the garage, which had been taped off and the garage door was closed to block off the crime scene. I opened the gate and entered the garage from the backyard. There were several others, including patrolmen and a few paramedics standing around as I entered the darkened garage. In the middle of the garage, was another body of a naked old man, hanging from his neck by a rope tied up from the rafters above.

Morton was right. This murder was identical to the Marquardt killing two weeks ago. The victim had several stab wounds across his torso, and his neck had been slit open. His hands were also tied together, and his genitals had been cut off and mutilated. The old man's eyes, like Marquardt's, had been gauged out and bleeding. There was also a sharp, long broomstick impaled into his body, and crammed inside of him, like the previous murder. An empty, plastic grocery bag,

113

with strewn vegetables, was scattered across the concrete floor.

Blood was splattered everywhere, especially on the parked car in the garage. I presumed that the killer used the hood of the car as his "work bench" to do his cutting and slicing. This crime scene looked like it was 'painted in blood' and was far more gruesome than the Marquardt murder two weeks ago. And like the Marquardt murder, beneath the victims' dangling feet, amidst a pool of blood, was a long-stemmed red rose.

I stared at the body and tried to absorb the bloody crime scene. I just couldn't believe it. How was this killer able to duplicate the same murder within the garage of his victim on a Friday afternoon before the holiday weekend, without any clues or anyone noticing?

"Congratulations," I said to Detective Morton as he followed me into the garage.

"We officially now have a serial killer," I announced. Morton just looked at me, clearly shaken.

"And let me guess..."I added. "This guy was a former priest too?"

"His name is Lucas Senopoli. He's 78 years old and lives alone. He's a retired maintenance worker with the Archdiocese of Chicago. His friend, James Rubino, found him like this about an hour ago. They were supposed to go to some bocce ball tournament together at some club somewhere on Belmont Avenue." Morton replied.

"And yes, Phil, we verified it. This guy was a former priest," he added.

"Any priors on this guy?"

"Nope, not even a parking ticket. A model citizen. Only difference from the other murder victim is that this guy pretty much kept to himself," Morton stated.

I continued to stare at the hanging dead corpse, trying to process this whole murder scene. I started to think out loud, as I began talking to myself:

*What the hell was going on? What has sparked
this recent motivation to start killing former priests in
Chicagoland? Especially those former priests who never
had any sex-related priors?*

"How long has he been dead?" I asked.

"A few hours now. We figure the time of death
was approximately 2:00 in the afternoon?" Morton
replied.

I looked around the garage, trying to avoid all
the splattered blood. I didn't want to ruin another
Brook Brothers suit coat, especially since this one was a
larger size. I borrowed one of the patrolman's
flashlights, and took a quick scan of the dark, one car
garage. For a second, I was sort of hoping that the killer
might have been stupid enough to leave his murder
weapon behind.

"Did anybody see or hear anything? Has anyone
talked to any of the neighbors?"

"We have a few patrolmen on the street talking
to a few of them now. Seems most of his neighbors are
Latino, so I called the precinct and they are sending
over a Spanish-speaking policeman."

"Great." I replied.

I continued to gaze around the garage. There
had to be some clue here somewhere. Some sort of left-
over artifact or something that we could possibly lift a
DNA sample from. Looking under the car, adjacent to a
puddle of blood, I found a cigarette butt. I pulled out
some plastic gloves that I kept in my pocket, and
reached under the car, putting the potential evidence
sample in a crime scene evidence bag.

"Was the victim a smoker?" I asked. "This
cigarette brand is a Marlboro Light."

"Not sure," replied Morton, who was starting to
look a little nauseated.

"When we search through the house, we'll see if
we can find any cigarettes or ash trays."

"Have one of your patrolmen scour the
neighborhood and around the house. Start looking for
more clues" I ordered him, whose face color was starting
to turn a melancholy green.

115

"Have someone go through the house with a fine-tooth comb. Find out any clues of anyone who might want to hurt him," I requested.

"Looks like we have a serial killer on the loose," said one of the patrolmen. I then noticed a nauseous Detective Morton run out the garage and out into the alley. I asked one of the patrolmen to follow the detective outside and check on him, knowing that he was probably throwing up somewhere.

I walked outside of the garage and started looking around the house, trying to notice anything obvious. No sooner did I walk around to the front yard, that I saw my buddy, Chaz Rizzo and the Channel 8 News Truck.

There was a camera man filming while he was interviewing one of the neighbors. I decided to walk over and unload on him.

"Rizzo? What the hell are you doing here?" I demanded. This reporter bastard didn't miss a trick. He abruptly ended the street interview with the neighbor and walked over towards me with his microphone, the camera man still filming and pointing his camera at my direction.

"Shut that damn camera off!" I yelled. Chaz motioned to his camera crew to cut out the filming and to wait by the news truck, while he walked over towards me, smiling as usual.

"Hey Philly, looks like we've got a serial killer on our hands, huh? " Rizzo proclaimed.

"What's the definition again? A person who kills more than one victim in more than one location in a very short period?"

"Knock it off, Chaz! We don't know what we have here, and I certainly don't need you broadcasting that right now."

"Come on Philly! Same kind of victim, same kind of murder scene, same red rose? Cut the bullshit!"

"No, Rizzo! You cut the bullshit! We don't need the press out here stirring things up while we're trying to figure out what the hell is going on. We don't know what we have right now, and I certainly don't need you making any assumptions and stirring up the public," I sternly replied.

I was feeling frustrated, and I was starting to unload my temper on my favorite news reporter. I was so tempted to hit this son of a bitch, until I realized that I might need this jerk to give me a hand in solving these murders.

"I didn't mention anything yet about a serial killer, Phil. We're still trying to report the facts of this homicide."

"Well, I would really appreciate it if you would hold off a bit until we know what is going on," I replied in a calmer voice.

"I understand the victim is also a former priest," he interjected.

"We haven't confirmed that yet," I lied, not wanting to volunteer any information.

"We have," he said. "This guy was the Dean of Students at St. Peter Chanel High School back in the '60's. He was also the principal at Notre Dame High School until he left the priesthood in 1979." I glared at him, and for almost ten seconds I was speechless.

"Where did you get your information from?" I immediately knew that I had just asked him a very dumb question. This damn news reporter always had a reliable resource for everything.

"One of the guys at the news station remembered him when he was in high school. Says he was one of those old school disciplinarians."

"Old school?"

"Yeah, you know. Back in the days when the priests and nuns used to crack around their students like fucking baseballs," Chaz replied.

I took out my notepad and I started scribbling down some notes, while Chaz was being motioned by his camera crew. Seemed the Channel Eight newsroom was blowing up his cell phone.

"Look Phil, I gotta take this call. It's the newsroom. Help me out here, please? We gotta make a living here too. Let me interview a few of these 'cops' so that we can get the exclusive on this story. I will call you later and let you know what else we find out. Deal?"

Chaz Rizzo extended his hand as a peace offering, which I firmly grabbed.

"Do not mention the words 'serial killer' until we know what the hell we have here," I sternly warned.

He looked at me and smiled, nodding his head. He then rushed off to his news truck while I returned to the crime scene, trying to figure out what other evidence we could find.

I accompanied one of the patrolmen inside of the house and walked upstairs to the bedroom. Usually, if there is any relevant information to investigate at a residential crime scene, it's usually starts in the bedroom. I scoured through his dresser drawers and whatever documents were on his roll top desk. I didn't find anything significant, other than the verification that he used to be a Catholic priest and that he retired working for the Archdiocese.

I looked around, noticing a large, wooden trunk with two padlocks, one was a keyed lock, and the other was a standard combination lock. I asked one of the policemen to bring up some bolt cutters to cut the locks. When the locks were cut, and the trunk opened, its contents made me sick to my stomach.

Neatly stacked, were over one hundred child pornography magazines. They were all from foreign countries, including German, Swedish, Japanese, and some other foreign languages that I didn't recognize. The victim obviously acquired them on the black market somewhere. I called up a few of the patrolmen to secure the trunk, dusted it for prints, and then brought it down to the station. I also found an Apple computer in one of the bedrooms and seized that as well. I now realized that our former priest and current victim, like Marquardt, was also a pedophile.

I exited the house and within minutes, my cell phone was ringing. It was an unfamiliar number with a '312' area code.

"Dorian here."

"Detective Dorian? This is Sergeant Hansen from the Eighteenth. I understand that you're still investigating that murder in Albany Park from a few weeks ago?"

"Yes," I replied. I couldn't understand why the Eighteenth District would be calling me on my cell phone.

"Well, we're holding someone here you may want to talk to. We just picked him up last night on a DUI."

"Really? Who?" I inquired. There was a five second pause on the phone before his response.

"He's a Catholic priest. His name is Joseph Kilbane and says he works for the Archdiocese. The district commander knew you were working on this case and the word was out that you've been leaning heavy on this guy. We've kept him here because he refused to 'blow', and the arresting officer pulled him over with a suitcase full of cash," the Sergeant continued.

"We've impounded his car and we're getting a warrant to search his vehicle for whatever else we can find."

I couldn't believe what I was hearing, as I was having another one of those 'Las Vegas Jackpot' moments.

"Where did you pick him up?" I asked.

"On North Halsted, near Webster Street. The arresting officer caught him last night swerving onto oncoming traffic and blowing off a stop sign," replied Hansen.

"Has he been cooperative?" I asked, already knowing the answer to my question

"Are you kidding? He's all 'lawyered up.' We're waiting for his attorney to get here now," he answered. I wasn't surprised.

"Thanks Sergeant. I'll be right there."

I walked over to Tommy Morton and apologized, letting him know that I had an emergency at the Eighteenth District.

"Call me later, Tommy. Let me know what else you find."

I then jumped into my 'Crown Vic' and sped over to the Eighteenth at 1160 North Larrabee, putting my lights and sirens on. I was smiling to myself, praying that this might lead to a break in this case. Maybe the Monsignor's arrest will get him to finally 'crack open' and start telling me what he *really* knows, and how he might be involved in these two murders.

I said a 'Hail Mary' to myself, knowing I would need all the prayers I could get.

CHAPTER FOURTEEN

I was tempted to double park my police car as I pulled up in front of the Eighteenth District, but thought better of it, knowing that I might be there the rest of the evening. I patiently waited for another police patrol car to pull out before grabbing the adjacent parking place.

I was excited and smirking to myself, just waiting to see what the Monsignor looked like in handcuffs. I checked in with the desk sergeant and proceeded upstairs to meet Sergeant Hansen and his associate, Detective Michael Savarino. We shook hands, then continued towards the interrogation room where they had been holding Monsignor Kilbane throughout most of the day.

As we were walking through the hallway, Detective Savarino was debriefing me on some of the new details since arresting the Monsignor.

"You do know who this guy is, right?" I asked the Detective.

"Well....yeah," he responded. "He works for the Archdiocese."

"No...do you *really* know who this guy is?" I asked them again. They were both silent as I continued to educate them.

"You've arrested the most powerful Catholic priest in the Chicago Archdiocese, after the Cardinal."

"That would explain his silence, and his choice of lawyers," Savarino replied. "Other than asking to use the bathroom and giving him a glass of water, he has been unresponsive. We're still waiting for his attorney to show up," said Officer Hansen.

"Who is his attorney?"

"A Jewish guy by the name of David Herzog. He's part of a big law firm in the Monadnock Building on West Jackson Street, where all the criminal attorneys are," Savarino responded.

"Is he any good?"

"He bills out at $650 an hour. They call him the 'Prince of Fucking Darkness' over at the DA's office. This guy will cut your balls off and hand them back to you in a styrofoam cup."

"No kidding?" I chuckled. "And who says the Catholics and the Jews don't get along."

"Any word from the Cardinal or the Archdiocese?" I asked.

"Not a peep. I think the Archdiocese is laying low and playing it cool until they hear from their attorney. They haven't even tried to contact Kilbane," replied Hansen.

"Does anyone know where he was drinking at, and where he was coming from?"

"No. We asked him that, and he didn't respond to the either us or the arresting officer," Savarino replied.

"I wonder why he was driving drunk with a suitcase full of cash. He had to be coming from somewhere," I thought out loud.

"He lives close by in Lincoln Park from where he was picked up. And he was driving south on Halsted, correct?" I asked.

"Yes."

"Can we find out how many Italian restaurants are in the immediate area of Webster and Halsted?" I asked Savarino.

I had a hunch, and I was guessing that the Monsignor and whomever he was meeting had a penchant for Italian food.

I went on one of my phone app's, and found three restaurants in the immediate area, the closest being Trattoria Pagliacci at 2701 North Halsted. I decided to run over there during the dinner rush hour and ask a few questions.

"Before we interview the Monsignor, I'm going to run out and do some homework. I should be back in an hour."

As I was pulling up the Trattoria Pagliacci, I got a call from Detective Morton.

"Hey Phil, found something in the victims house that you might be interested in. Seems this guy had a five-million-dollar life insurance policy with the Great Lakes Life Insurance Company. From the documentation here, looks like Senopoli was paying the premiums on this policy. Take a guess who the named beneficiaries are?"

"Hmmm...let me guess? The Archdiocese of Chicago?" I answered.

"Bingo!"

I was smiling from ear to ear. "Great job, Tommy. Thanks for the info. Let me know what else you find," as I hung up the phone.

I parked my car and went inside the restaurant. I interviewed a few of the waiters and the valets, who all recognized a man wearing a cleric's collar having dinner with a gray-haired man who drove off in a Maserati. The one valet even remembered a guy looking like Kilbane taking the time to put the suitcase in the back seat of his Cadillac. It was over ninety minutes later when I returned to the Eighteenth District.

"Let's go talk to Kilbane," I said, as Savarino and Hansen jumped from their desks and led me over to the interrogation room. I looked behind the one-way glass and saw the Monsignor sitting there with his attorney, a bald older man with wire glasses and a couple of diamond rings on his fingers.

Detective Savarino and I walked into the interrogation room, where the two of them were waiting.

"Good evening, Father. It's so nice to see you again." I proclaimed with a smile.

"I understand you were out partying last night, Father. What was the occasion?" His little Jewish attorney stood up, shook my hand and gave me his card.

"My name is David Herzog, and I represent Monsignor Kilbane. I have advised him not answer any questions at this time."

"Not even why he was drunk, swerving down Halsted Street with fifty large in cash?" Savarino asked.

"Give us your best offer, Detectives. Otherwise we will wait for the arraignment and post bail, if necessary."

"Oh, I see," I said. "Is this the way you want to play it?" I asked.

"Let me give you the '4-1-1' and what we have on your client, Counselor. Right now, we have him on a D.U.I. charge. We all know he can post bail, go to driving school and take the bus for six months. That isn't the problem," I explained.

"The real problem here is that there have been two murders of two old former priests over the last two weeks. We discovered one of them this afternoon. We know that both former priests had high dollar life insurance policies attached to their heads, with the Archdiocese as the beneficiaries to both of those policies. Now we all know we don't have enough on your boy, here, to call him a murderer," I pointed out.

"But seeing that he had dinner and drinks with Little Tony DiMatteo at the Trattoria Pagliacci last night, then gets pulled over with a boatload of cash, makes me feel a little uneasy."

Monsignor Kilbane looked at his attorney, as the beads of sweat started dripping off his forehead.

"How do you know he was at that restaurant?" asked Herzog.

"Even the Chicago P.D. knows how much Little Tony loves his linguini with clam sauce," I smiled.

"The waiters and the valets 'I-D'd the both of you last night. One waiter saw you taking a black bag from Little Tony before you both left." The two of them sat there, silent.

"We even have a valet recalling the Monsignor carefully unloading a black suitcase out of the back seat of his Cadillac when he arrived last night." I was trying hard to push the Monsignor into blowing up. So far, he was doing a good job of playing it cool.

"We have two similar murders. Two similar victims with two similar backgrounds. Both victims carrying life insurance policies, with the Archdiocese as the beneficiary to both policies. Both were employees of the Archdiocese, and we can safely say, seeing that we found a trunk full of 'chicken porn' at one of the crime scenes, that either one, if not both victims were probably pedophiles," I was driving my point home.

"Now, either your boy here starts talking, or we are going to do our best to charge him as an accessory to two homicides. And seeing that he was out partying last night with Little Tony, and since these two murders both look like mob hits, we're going to grab him and bring him down here too, so that we can have a real house party."

"You don't have shit, Detective. You know damn well you can't make any of that stick. The District Attorney will be all over your ass! Monsignor Kilbane is a very important man and an integral part of the Chicago Catholic community. There is no law against driving around with a suitcase full of cash!"

"Maybe you can explain that to the Treasury Department, Counselor. Because that will be my next phone call if your boy doesn't start talking!"

"Maybe he won it at a card game, Detective? Maybe he won it at the casino? Maybe he just likes to drive around with a lot of money in the back seat of his car? Either way, the Monsignor didn't break any laws, other than maybe, having too many cocktails last night. And as far as Little Tony is concerned, they were meeting regarding the prospective baptism of Little Tony's new grandchild. They have been lifelong friends for years, and they both grew up in Bridgeport."

"And in regard to the DUI charge, my client didn't blow on a breathalyzer, and your friends here didn't get a blood sample last night," Herzog replied, earning every bit of his $650 an hour retainer fee.

"Unless you have some definitive evidence against my client, you don't have anything. I must insist that you release Monsignor Kilbane immediately, or I will have the district attorney down here so fast it will make your heads spin!"

I looked at Savarino as he shook his head. In all the commotion of trying to get a search warrant on Kilbane's vehicle, they neglected to get a blood sample to test the content of his alcohol level.

"The arresting officer said the Monsignor's eyes were dilated, and he couldn't pass the sobriety test," Savarino replied.

"You know that isn't enough to make a DUI charge stick, Detective. And as far as the Treasury Department is concerned, we're not worried," Herzog replied with a smirk on his face.

I was pissed. Here I thought I could, at the very least, get some information out of Kilbane regarding these two murders. Yet here he is now, walking out of the Eighteenth District as free as a bird without breathing or mentioning a single syllable regarding any of the murders.

"Would the two of you care to hear my theory?" I made direct eye contact with the Monsignor.

"Well no, not really," the attorney responded.

"My theory is," I continued, "that the good Monsignor here, was at the restaurant last night trying to make a payoff to Little Tony for a murder that the DiMatteo Family didn't commit."

Monsignor Kilbane started turning three different shades of red, as his black shirt was drenched with perspiration. I could tell, by Kilbane's reaction, that I hit a nerve. The attorney only sat there smiling, knowing damn well that I didn't have any evidence or proof to back up my theory.

"Sounds like a stretch, Detective. But let me know how that works out for you," Herzog replied.

They then both stood up from the table and proceeded to leave the interrogation room.

"Have a good evening, gentlemen," as the two of them casually walked out of the Eighteenth District.

There was a part of me that wanted to tackle the Monsignor down and beat the shit out of him until he started talking. Judging by his reaction, I had a good hunch that my theory was correct. Kilbane must have thought that Little Tony had put the hit on Marquardt and was at the restaurant last night to give him either all or part of his 'hit fees'. For whatever reason, seeing

127

that Kilbane had left the restaurant with a black bag full of cash, Little Tony didn't take the money.

The only reason I could think of was that, Little Tony didn't commit the murder, and didn't want to take the credit for it. If the DiMatteo Family was looking to collect their fees on a 'hit', they would not be passing a black bag full of cash back and forth in a public restaurant. So, if Kilbane was trying to solicit or buy a 'hit' from Little Tony, the mobster wanted no part of it. So maybe, Monsignor Kilbane is responsible for soliciting a homicide? Good luck trying to prove up that theory, as Little Tony would never 'rat out' his childhood friend.

All of this only puts me back to square one.

CHAPTER FIFTEEN

It was a bright, hot Saturday morning, and none of the detectives were in the Sixteenth District as I was getting settled at my desk. I had picked up an extra wet cappuccino from the Starbucks down the street and was debating about whether I should attack that stale, sesame seed bagel left over from yesterday in the precinct kitchen. My thought was to throw it into the toaster, drench it with some cream cheese, and pretend it was from a fresh batch at Dunkin' Donuts.

It was the Memorial Day holiday weekend, and I figured I had better put in the overtime into trying to solve these 'Pedophile Priest Murders', as I wasn't making any progress on this case. Commander Callahan barged into my office, just as I was just starting to enjoy my bagel and cream cheese breakfast.

"How's it going with the 'Pedophile Priest Murders'?" he asked. He had heard how frustrated I was in the lack of progress with this case.

"Not well, Chief. Monsignor Kilbane got picked up on a DUI charge Thursday night over at the Eighteenth, and I was hoping we could get him to talk and get some information out of him. I was hoping he would help us crack open this case, but we ended up empty handed, "I said, and I was sure he could sense the frustration in my voice.

"Well, I'm getting some heat from Police Superintendent Ryan on this case, especially since your buddy from Channel Eight News broadcasted this as their feature story last night. Did you see it?"

"No." I kind of figured Chaz Rizzo was going to splash this all over the news last night.

"Said something to the effect of 'the police are refusing to call the murderer in these crimes a 'Serial

Killer'. Did you tell him that?" he asked, with a half-hearted smile on his face.

"What an idiot! No. I told him not to use those words at all. I told him that I didn't want to start a city-wide panic."

I knew I couldn't trust that son-of-a-bitch Rizzo. This wasn't the first time he's thrown me under the bus. I had just realized that I had broken my own cardinal rule in doing investigative police work: *Never trust a news reporter.*

I regretted not hauling Rizzo's ass in when I had the chance. Now I knew I was going to catch some heat from Callahan and the Superintendent, and I was going to start feeling the pressure to solve these murders.

"Well," Callahan said. "The Superintendent is worried that we can't handle this case by ourselves, and he wants to reassign this over to the Intelligence Unit at the Twenty-First."

Great. A reassignment of this case would look 'just wonderful' to my superiors. Two double murders in three weeks and the 'Ivory Tower' wants to pull me off this case and send it over to the 'hot shots' at the Intelligence Unit.

"Maybe you're in over your head, Dorian. We're obviously dealing with a 'professional murderer' here, and maybe we should send this case over to the guys at the Twenty-First. They're more experienced at 'collaring' these kinds of murders," the Commander said.

"Honestly Chief, I think I can make some progress here. We picked up a cigarette butt at the crime scene and sent that over to the lab for DNA testing. We also bagged the two red roses that were left by the killer." I pleaded. I didn't tell him that the DNA results turned up negative.

Callahan looked at me a little perturbed. "Two sliced up old priests in three weeks and the only clue you have is a goddamned cigarette butt and some old wilted flowers?" he replied.

130

"I've been working day and night on this case, Chief. We know these victims were both pedophiles and both had high end life insurance policies benefitting the Chicago Archdiocese. If we keep leaning on the..."

"Stop it, Dorian!" I could hear Callahan starting to lose his famous, Irish temper.

"Why are you leaning on the Monsignor? Unless you have any definitive evidence putting him at the crime scene, you're going nowhere with him. He's too insulated by the Archdiocese, and they will throw every high-priced attorney they can find to keep him clean and far away from these murders. You're wasting your time on this guy!" he angrily exclaimed.

"Really? This guy has a meeting with Little Tony the other night and gets pulled over with fifty large in his brief case. The Archdiocese is about to collect over ten million dollars in life insurance proceeds from these two murdered ex-priests and we can't even stick him with a parking ticket?" I was starting to raise my voice at my boss.

"I'm telling you, Chief. Kilbane knows something. Why would he have that kind of money in his car after meeting DiMatteo at a restaurant?"

"Maybe it's his first communion money, I don't know. There could be a thousand and one reasons why he would be driving around with that kind of cash. Maybe he was looking to invest it with Little Tony? Who knows? Either way, he's not your boy, Phil. Move on."

I didn't understand why Callahan was trying so hard to discourage me from going after Kilbane. I was beginning to wonder if the Chicago P.D. was getting some pressure from the Archdiocese. I knew where Callahan was going with this whole conversation, and I needed to do some quick thinking to keep these high-profile murder cases on my desk.

"Look Chief, maybe I could use some assistance," I suggested. "If I could have a few more detectives that would be a big help. I'm working day and night on these cases," I said.

"Oh yeah, Phil, I see how hard you're working," as Callahan was eye-balling the stale, half-eaten bagel on my desk.

"I can't spare you any detectives from our precinct right now. We're running thin as it is and have way too many burglary and rape cases that we haven't been able to put any time into," Callahan replied.

I thought for a moment and had an idea. There have been times in the past when other districts have loaned out detectives and officers from other districts to assist each other in solving homicide cases, especially high-profile cases like these.

"Maybe you could contact the Seventeenth District? Have them send over Tommy Morton. He's very thorough and knows a little bit about these cases," I suggested.

"I will see what I can do. Let me get the Superintendent on the phone and ask him," he replied. "Either way, you obviously need some help in solving these cases."

I figured getting some help and a 'fresh set of eyes' on these murders would be a big help and save me from doing some of the required 'leg work' that needed to be done. I had worked with Morton before, and he was an easy-going guy.

I was busy on the phone trying to talk to the crimes labs, getting more information regarding the evidence from that North Menard crime scene, when I got a written message from the sergeant at the front desk: Call Detective Russo at Intelligence.

Just beautiful. The last thing I wanted to deal with was a big headed, arrogant detective from the Intelligence Unit at the Twenty-First.

I had worked with Detective Sergeant Paul Russo a few years ago on another homicide case. He was a mean, tough son-of-a-bitch in his early sixties, who never learned the meaning of the words "case unsolved".

There was a rumor going around the Chicago Police Department regarding a phenomenon called "Russo's Law". He had a reputation for getting the rapists, the drug pushers and the murderers off the streets and especially in his precinct, one way or another.

He was very "old school" in his investigative methods, and the word was out that he wasn't afraid to go as far as torturing his alleged suspects in order to get a confession. There is a caged area is in the basement of the Twenty First District. It is located far away from the monitoring cameras and the other police departments located there, where Russo has been known to administer his brand of justice.

His methods often include physically beating up his suspects, water boarding them, mentally abusing and sometimes breaking their fingers and inflicting deep cuts on his victims. He'd been known to brutally beat up and bruise many of his suspects who 'tried to escape'. I had heard that he once planted evidence to get a conviction on a 'collar' that he was convinced had committed some multiple homicides he was investigating.

Russo was known to 'take the law into his own hands' when he had to, and his closed minded, old school mentality made him plenty of enemies within the city. He wasn't a 'dirty cop', or a 'cop on the take' that I had ever heard.

But there had been a few suspects who got off on a technicality a few years ago that suddenly, disappeared off the face of the earth. These were life-time convicts with rap sheets a mile long, who were probably guilty as hell. But someone, somewhere dropped the ball or couldn't get the evidence that was needed to make the conviction stick.

These were all intelligence cases that came out of the Twenty-First District, which coincidentally, were overseen by Russo. I had gotten a visit from Internal Affairs a few years ago, asking me questions about Russo and whether he was ever inclined to 'fix a case' and make his collars disappear. Although they were probably 'barking up the right tree', I didn't 'rat him out'. I spoke very highly of him to Internal Affairs. Russo later called me to 'thank me' for my esteemed words, and he dodged another suspension from the police disciplinary committee. I was mildly shocked that the 'Ivory Tower' hadn't forced him to retire yet.

"Hey Dorian, I hear you're in over your head," Detective Russo replied when I returned his call.

"Don't believe all the rumors you hear, Russo. We've got a few leads," I lied, trying not to let this old bastard intimidate me on his first try.

"Why haven't you retired?" I half-jokingly asked him, trying to keep the conversation light.

"And do what? I tried planting tomatoes last summer, but they all died on me."

"Try playing bocce ball," I replied.

"I did. I ended up getting into a fight with the old guys and got thrown out of the Mazzini-Verde Club. I figured I better stay on the job here since I can't do anything else," Russo answered.

"I hear stamp collecting is a great hobby," I snickered, trying to imagine him holding a stamp and a magnifying glass. "The guys at the Twenty-First must feel really honored to still have you," I sarcastically said.

"Yeah....right," he mumbled. "You're still a smart-ass, Dorian."

There was a five second silence on the phone, as I realized this conversation was about to get frosty.

"The Ivory Tower called us in on those Pedophile Priest Murders," Russo said, trying to imply that I didn't know what I was doing.

"I didn't ask to get the Intelligence Unit involved," I replied.

I was hoping Detective Russo would back off and just give me some friendly advice instead of muscling in on my investigations.

"Well, the Superintendent has other ideas. These cases are starting to get some very unpopular publicity, and the word is out that a serial killer may be involved."

"Don't believe everything you hear from Chaz Rizzo on Channel Eight News," I curtly answered. "I'm making some progress here and..."

"Look Phil, I don't think you understand. Ryan asked us to take this case over from your district."

"What?" So much for Commander Callaghan putting in a good word for me.

"The problem is, we're swamped. All the gang bangers are still killing each other down here and in Englewood. I told Ryan we didn't have any spare detectives to work on this case, so I talked him into letting me come up there and assist you on these homicides," he interjected.

"I feel honored, Detective. But I'm not sure that you can...."

"Have you ever dealt with a serial killer before?" he asked me, point blank.

"Well, no...I haven't. I've dealt with some pretty messy homicides before, though," I sheepishly replied.

"It's a whole different ball game, kid. You're gonna need my expertise. Besides, we're set up a little better down here at the Twenty-First than you guys are. I can help you get direct access to our IT techs that you guys normally wouldn't have. The only reason why we're not taking these cases away from you and your district is because we're too damned busy down here," Russo matter-of-factly stated.

"Oh, I see. So now you're doing us a huge favor here, huh, Russo?" I was starting to lose my temper and felt myself starting to count to ten. There was a long silence on the phone.

"Look Dorian. Let's not turn this into a pissing match. We're all on the same team here, and the 'Ivory Tower' wants this killer off the streets and in custody before someone else is killed. Do you get it?"

I thought for a moment and realized that my bruised ego was no match for Detective Russo and his Intelligence Unit at the Twenty-First District. I had better start acting more gracious and more open minded to Russo assisting me on these cases, before I got my ass got thrown off them all together.

"Okay, Detective. I'll play ball. But let's make sure we work together on this case. I don't need you going 'cowboy' on me or 'back dooring' me when I'm not looking. Let's have each other's backs here, okay?" I politely asked.

I was trying to set some rules in this investigation, knowing full well that Russo wasn't going to obey any of them. I wanted to especially let him know that 'Russo's Law' didn't apply here. I was not about to let him take control of this investigation and 'bully' around any suspects. But I knew that trying to take control of Detective Paul Russo was going to be like the little Taco Bell dog trying to keep Godzilla on a short leash.

"And besides, Russo," I interjected, "you owe me, big time." There was a long silence on the phone, as he was probably taking inventory in his head. I'm sure he was remembering the last time we had worked together on a homicide, how I became a character witness and ended up bullshitting Internal Affairs on his behalf.

"Okay, Dorian. It's a deal," as he abruptly hung up the phone. I was suddenly listening to a dial tone.

At that moment, I knew these murder investigations were about to get out of control.

CHAPTER SIXTEEN

The wet snow was beginning to accumulate on West Division Street on that cold, evening last February, as the sounds of the City of Chicago snow plows were noisily pushing the snow off the streets. A grey haired, middle aged man parked his late model Cadillac SUV on the corner of West Division and Ashland Avenues, making sure that he was at the right location. He was instructed to come to a meeting at the old church on the corner at 9:00pm, and he looked at the address which he had scribbled on the back of a matchbook cover he had placed in his over coat pocket.

930 West Division Street, he verified, making sure he was at the right location. The old, brown stone church, which looked to be abandoned, had only a few flickering lights visible from the antiquated stained-glass windows. It was dark, and except for only a few cars parked along Division Street, looked to be totally vacant and desolate.

He had heard about this 'secret society' through a friend of a friend, who was a Grand Knight of the Knights of Columbus. That person had heard and investigated their existence in Chicago and anonymously, sent the candidate's contact information to a gentlemen who called himself 'Brother Aaron'.

He walked over to the green parking box, acquired a parking receipt and placed it on the passenger side of his vehicle. The man then, in his black, wing tipped shoes, and formal black tie and tuxedo, gingerly crossed the street in the wet snow.

He carefully approached the side entrance of the old brownstone church, where he was instructed to enter. Bang loudly on the old, wooden door three times,

137

he was instructed, in succession of three loud knocks each:

    Knock...Knock...Knock;
    Knock...Knock...Knock;
    Knock...Knock...Knock.

At that moment, a man with a red, pointed hat and mask covering his head and face opened the door for the well-dressed gentlemen.

"Welcome," was all the door sentry said, as 'Brother Jebidiah' handed him a folded red hat and mask from behind the old wooden door. The door sentry was careful to hand the red mask to the candidate without viewing his identity, which was required to be worn and pulled over his head before entering the old church. The visitor was aware of the secrecy of this elite society, and anticipated receiving a mask, which was always required to be worn. Anonymity was a major element of membership in this secret sect, as it is imperative that no one knows the identity of the other members.

The "Societa' Crocifisso Della Rosa" or the "Society of the Rose Crucifix," which it is commonly called, is a secret, ancient order established in the 15th Century in Florence, Italy. It was originally established in conjunction with the Roman Catholic Church to uphold the strict standards and moral codes of Pope Clement VII, who was the head of the Catholic Church and ruler of Italy's Papal States from 1523 to 1534. He was a prominent member of Florence's Medici family, and believed that the Lord's Ten Commandments applied to all of God's children, except himself. He fathered a child outside of wedlock, and when it became publicly known that he was an adulterer, he vehemently sought revenge against his enemies within the Vatican.

He established the secret society as a means of enforcing the strict moral laws and edicts of the Catholic Church during the Renaissance. The secret society was a means of imposing his version of justice, against all those Cardinals and Bishops whom he considered his enemies.

Pope Clement VII enlisted a "secret army" of red-hooded soldiers who could quickly inflict righteousness, as he saw fit. He imposed his underground army on those within the Roman Curia whom he felt were not upholding 'his ethical regulations' of the Roman Catholic Church. The society's methods of upholding 'integrity' included various means of beatings, painful torture, and very often, slow, heinous executions within the dark, hidden catacombs buried deep beneath the ancient floors of St. Peter's Basilica.

This clandestine society has flourished, in secret, over the last five hundred years, initially in Italy, and then throughout Western Europe and North America. Its' manifesto throughout the years has been simple: Inflict and enforce justice to those who break the moral laws and ethical codes of the Roman Catholic Church.

There are unsupported rumors that a local order of this secret society is in several cities within the United States, Canada and Western Europe. Each society is only allowed twelve ordained members, along with their grand master.

As the 'visitor' entered the old church, there was a long wooden table of eleven red-hooded men, each wearing hoods over their heads and faces and black formal tuxedos, complete with white shirts and black bowties. Each member had a nametag, which bore a biblical name that each brother was referred to.

All the church pews had been removed, and a life-size, red wooden crucifix made of Rosewood, with a likeness of Jesus, was suspended high over the white marble altar. Except for the oversized cross and white marble altar, the old church was empty and barren.

The 'Grand Master', or 'Brother Ezekiel' as he was referred to, was sitting at the head of the church, wearing his red hood, a long red cape, and dressed in a formal black tuxedo.

"Welcome, pilgrim," addressed the Grand Master to the visitor as he cautiously, entered the old brownstone church. All the hooded men were looking squarely at him, as the sentry escorted him to the front of the abandoned church.

At that moment, his society sponsor, 'Brother Aaron' as he was referred to (whom he did not know his real name or identity) stood up from the long, mahogany table of hooded brothers, and approached the Grand Master at the altar.

"You are now in the presence of our Divine Lord and you are now within the sacred walls of the Rose Crucifix," said the Grand Master to the visitor and his sponsor, standing beside him.

"For what reason do you approach these hallowed halls of the Rose Crucifix?" demanded the Grand Master, in a loud baritone voice.

The visitor was given a list of responses from his secret society sponsor, for which he had memorized for that evening. He had waited over eighteen months to be 'referred' and recommended to be a part of this formal, clandestine society.

This process included extensive background checks, written 'anonymous' referrals and recommendations, and a formal commendation from his society sponsor. He also had to wait for the death of one society member, before he could be enrolled and initiated.

"To faithfully serve the Lord and uphold all of his sacred commandments," replied the visitor, as his sponsor stood next to the candidate with his hand placed on his left shoulder.

"And why do you wish to be a Brother of the Rose Crucifix?" asked the Grand Knight.

The visiting candidate thought about his answer for a moment, and then freely spoke with his sponsor's hand still gripping his shoulder.

"To seek out those who have shamed and betrayed our Lord Jesus and have violently broken His holy, sacred commandments in the Lord's name," the candidate replied.

The Grand Knight then instructed the sponsor to assist the applicant in removing his coat, his tuxedo and clothing. He could feel the cold, frosty air of the drafty church onto his half naked body, as he was stripped down to his white underwear. Then, two more hooded members approached the altar, bowed their heads, and then walked up to each side of the altar to light the torches with a match. They then turned around and stood erect beside the Grand Knight, still sitting at his chair at the head of the church.

Then Brother Ezekiel asked the sponsor, "Brother Aaron, what name has this pilgrim chosen as a member of our holy brotherhood of the Rose Crucifix?"

"Barabbas," his secret society sponsor, Brother Aaron quickly answered.

It was the requirement of the brotherhood's secret society to take a name of an individual from the Bible, who was not a saint or an evangelist, as a replacement name to all the brothers within the secret society. His sponsor, Brother Aaron, was a well-respected member of the secret society, and suggested this name to the new applicant.

"Oh Brother Barabbas," the Grand Knight commenced, "thou shall be witness to the eternal laws of the church and an omnipotent disciple of thy holy name of the Lord, and his faithful servant, his Holiness, the Pope. That thy brother and thy servant, Barabbas, be an instrument to thy power and possess thy wisdom to uphold His commandments and blessed sacraments, to keep them holy, and to keep them discrete and surreptitious from all those outside of this holy Society of the Rose Crucifix."

"We humbly adore and worship thee and thy unspeakable truths and perfections," the Grand Knight proclaimed.

He then continued, "We bless and invoke thee to this sacred holy society, and thou will faithfully enforce, at all costs, the sacred commandments of thy Holy Name and our Lord, Jesus."

The Grand Knight then rose from his chair, asked the candidate to recite the sacred vow. His sponsor, Brother Aaron, reached into his tuxedo jacket pocket and unfolded the white sheet of paper with the society's holy oath, and handed it to the candidate:

"I, Brother Barabbas," he recited, "Do hereby promise and declare that I will, when opportunity presents, make and wage relentless war, secretly against all heretics and demons, as I am directed to do to extirpate them from the face of the earth. That I will spare neither age, sex, or condition, and that I will hang, burn, waste, boil, flay, strangle, and bury alive these infamous heretics, rip up the stomachs and wombs of their women, and crush their infants' heads against the walls in order to annihilate their execrable race. That I will, when the same cannot be done openly, will secretly use the strangulation cord, the steel of the poniard of the leaden bullet, regardless of the honor, rank, dignity, or authority of that person or persons, whatever may be their condition in life, public or private. That I at any time may be directed so to do by any agent of the Pope or superior of our brotherhood of the Society of the Rose Crucifix and Holy Father of the Society of Jesus."

The Grand Knight then handed a gold handled, sable brush to the hooded brother standing beside him and dipped the brush into a small container containing lighter fluid. He then brushed the words "ROSE" and a cross onto Barabbas's chest with the dipped solution. Another knight, 'Brother Ephraim' took a candle and lit it from one of the two standing torches burning alongside of the altar. Three other hooded knights approached the altar, genuflected, and approached the candidate.

As the candle was placed against the candidate's chest, a quick fire erupted, burning the word "ROSE" onto his chest for about three seconds. The new candidate started to scream with pain, as two of the red hooded knights held both of his arms, and the other two quickly put out the flame. The quick flame left a burn mark on Barabbas's chest, with the word ROSE and a cross burned onto his skin.

The Grand Knight then took a silver dagger, which was placed on the top of the altar, and held it high underneath the red, rosewood crucifix.

"Oh, great and almighty Lord, I beseech thee to accept our new brother, Barabbas, as your humble servant and devoted apostle of thy superior principles and unwavering scruples. That thy servant shall obey and defend these morals and sacred commandments and destroy those demons that bring harm to your children, in God's name we pray," said the Grand Master.

"Thy blood shall be drawn, and thou shall offer as the ultimate sacrifice to thy goodness and sacred mysteries to our Divine Master and Holy Father."

The Grand Knight then took the silver dagger and made a small cut onto Barabbas's right forearm, immediately drawing blood. He then took the droplets of his blood from the dagger and watched the blood drip into a golden chalice. Another hooded member, 'Brother Reuben' quickly placed a large bandage over the new candidate's wound and assisted him in getting dressed, while the Grand Master poured previously blessed, holy red wine from a cruet into the gold cup.

At that moment, all the red hooded members rose from the table and lined up in front of the altar. Each brother took a sip of the blood tainted wine, genuflected, and made the sign of the cross. When all the society members finished, they escorted Barabbas to the middle of the church, and began to make a large circle around him, each holding a lighted candle. The Grand Knight then approached the new member and placed an 18-carat gold, ruby ring with a red cross onto his right ring finger.

"We welcome thee, oh Brother Barabbas, to this Society of the Rose Crucifix. May you always be honored as a sacred brother of the Red Cross until your very last breath," proclaimed the Grand Knight.

"Wear this holy ring as a sign and testament of your devout loyalty to the brotherhood of our Society of the Rose Crucifix."

At that moment, each hooded society member approached 'Barabbas', introduced themselves by their society name, and kissed his newly adorned sacred ring.

With that, Brother Barabbas was given a black name tag with his society name on it, pinned onto his tuxedo jacket by his sponsor, Brother Aaron.

"Congratulations," each of the members of the secret society said, welcoming their new brother into their secret holy order with an embrace and a handshake.

Barabbas was delighted to finally, become a part of the secret society he had heard and read so much about. He was more than willing to participate and do his part in upholding their lofty, religious ideals and policies. He also knew that, as a secret member of the Rose Crucifix, that it was his sacred duty to seek out and destroy those 'demons' that have sinned and violated any and all of God's children.

He can now seek revenge and extinguish those demons that have taken the sacred oaths of chastity, obedience, and celibacy as servants of the Lord, and have broken those sacred vows. He firmly believed, as did so many other members of this secret society for over the last five hundred years, that they would immediately be absolved by God for any atrociously heinous crimes that were committed in the name of the Rose Crucifix.

As a member of the society, he now had a religious license to murder and annihilate anyone who had ever preyed and sexually abused any of God's children, anytime during the past or present. As a brother of this so-called 'holy' secret society, he was now a part of a very large order of fraternity brothers; those red hooded members who now advocate and uphold their only true current manifesto:

To murder and destroy any and all pedophile priests.

CHAPTER SEVENTEEN

The traffic was starting to build up on North Milwaukee Avenue, as I exited the Starbucks drive-thru and made my way to the Sixteenth District. It was after the Memorial Day Holiday weekend, and I couldn't recall the last time I had a good night's sleep since the occurrence of these Pedophile Priest Murders. I was hoping the extra shot of expresso in my cappuccino would help me stay alert while I 'slayed whatever dragons' came across my desk on that early Tuesday morning.

I couldn't have been at my desk more than a half-hour when I received an unexpected visitor. It was my favorite detective from the Intelligence Unit.

"What's up Dorian?" Detective Paul Russo loudly remarked, as he was closing my office door behind him and making himself comfortable at the chair in front of my desk.

I looked at him coldly, knowing that he was going to do his best to make sure I didn't have a very good morning.

"Am I the only one who can't sleep anymore?" I curtly asked him, making sure that he knew I wasn't pleased with his surprise visit.

"Sleeping is overrated," he said with a smile, as he was watching me absorb my Starbucks coffee and the generous spread of strawberry creamed cheese on my sesame seed bagel.

"You need to start watching your diet, Dorian. Your stomach is starting to fall over your desk," as I inadvertently spilled some coffee on my white shirt.

"Thanks Paul," I rudely replied, acknowledging my penchant for extra shot cappuccinos and stale bagels from Dunkin' Donuts.

"To what do I have this pleasure, so early in the morning? It isn't even 8:00 o'clock yet."

"I've been up since 4:30 this morning, Dorian. I've already done my five-mile run along the Lakefront," Russo replied, fidgeting with a small paperweight on my desk that was gifted to me from the Sears Tower.

While he was toying with objects on my desk, I noticed that Russo was still wearing his wedding ban, even though he has been a widower for several years. I also couldn't help but notice a shiny gold ring on his right hand. I didn't get a good look at it, as it was extremely sparkly, reflecting off the bright, florescent lights from my office.

"Where are you at with this case, Dorian?"

"Didn't I talk to you on last Saturday? I'm still waiting on the lab results of that cigarette butt we recovered at one of the crime scenes," I answered defensively.

"No other clues?"

"No, Detective."

"What have you got on that Monsignor 'what's-his-name'?

"Kilbane?"

"Yeah, that's it. What else do you have on him?" Russo inquired.

"Not much. He was pulled over the other night with fifty large in his briefcase. He was coming from a meeting with Little Tony at a nearby restaurant. The detectives at the   Eighteenth had him on a DUI but had to let him go because they forgot get some bloodwork done on him." I explained.

"Forgot to get bloodwork? How the hell can you forget to get bloodwork on a DUI?" he asked.

"They were so excited to find him with the fifty-large in his Cadillac that they forgot to push the bloodwork on the DUI charge, and his high-priced lawyer got him released."

"Those guys at the Eighteenth are getting very sloppy. They messed up a few collars for us at Intelligence that we had to clean up," Russo replied, as if his Intelligence Unit were the only guys in Chicago who knew how to do proper investigations and police work.

Russo continued to fumble around with the paperweight on my desk, while I unabashedly finished my bagel and coffee. I didn't want to confess to him that I was at a dead end with these investigations. I didn't want to admit it, but it was as though these gruesome crimes had been executed almost perfectly, and I was beginning to wonder if they could ever be solved. It was as though we were dealing with a professional murderer, who was meticulous in performing these executions of both pedophile ex-priests.

"I heard you recovered a red rose at both crime scenes," Russo commented.

"How did you know about the flowers?" I asked him.

"I have ways of finding these things out," he replied in his usual cocky tone of voice.

Except for Detective Morton and a few others within the department, not many people knew about the recovered red roses at each crime scene. I did not mention it in my initial police report. I know that Chaz Rizzo from Channel Eight news didn't report it either, and not many others referred to them. I was a little suspicious at first, wondering how the hell he knew about those red roses, but I then dismissed it. I figured he and the super cops over at Intelligence seemed to acquire whatever information was available regarding both bloody crime scenes.

"So, what's our next move, Phil?"

"I was going to try to get a subpoena and a search warrant on the Archdiocese office on Rush Street, but Commander Callahan is telling me to lay off the Monsignor," I replied with frustration.

"Why is he saying that? Until you find any evidence telling you otherwise, he's definitely your main suspect."

147

"And how the hell am I going to prove that, especially if I can't get into his office?"

"What is it that you're looking for?" he demanded to know.

"I need a list of all the defrocked and retired priests in the Chicagoland area over the last fifty years, and I need to know how many of them have had life insurance policies taken on them by the Archdiocese."

Detective Russo looked at me, thinking about what I had just said, as if he had a better answer.

"You've got two choices, Dorian. You're either gonna have to go over Callahan's head and get those subpoenas, or you may have to go the long way around."

"Long way around?"

"Yeah. I can call IT and get a list of all the church parishes in the Chicago Archdiocese, and then run a list of all the priests and clergy that have been assigned to each parish over the last fifty years. We can then run a detailed report on any or all the clergy who have either passed away, retired, or resigned their positions as Catholic priests," Russo suggested.

"That's gonna take forever," I replied.

"Not really. I can get my IT guys to start researching this right away. In the meantime, you keep pushing for that subpoena."

I thought about both options and realized that my subpoena option was going to really put me in hot water with Commander Callahan.

"Are you trying to get me pushed back into doing a night beat on the streets? Callahan will have me 'wearing blues' and writing parking tickets at Grant Park if I go against him on this one," I retorted. I didn't need any more trouble from the Commander.

"I'll vouch for you, Dorian. We can go around his head if we have to."

I didn't understand at that moment why Russo was insisting on pushing so hard on the Archdiocese and going against my District Commander and against his orders. I also couldn't figure out why my Commander was trying to persuade me away from further investigating Monsignor Kilbane.

Detective Russo was only adding to my frustrations.

"Let me get back to my Unit, Phil. I'll let you know what I find out."

With that, Detective Paul Russo was out of my office, leaving me with more thwarting clues in this case than assistance. I had a fleeting thought that Russo's investigative expertise was going to do more harm than good in these murder cases and didn't quite understand his reasoning.

It was as though he had come into my office to 'fish out' information, just to get me even more irritated in trying to solve these murders.

A few more hours went by and it was past lunchtime when I got a call from the front desk sergeant.

"Detective Dorian, you have a visitor downstairs. She's from an insurance company."

At that moment, I was too busy unwrapping my turkey, ham and cheese submarine sandwich with extra mayo from the Subway down the street. One of the guys at the precinct went out to grab some sandwiches, as I could feel my stomach churning from all the stress these murder investigations were prompting. My pleasant little visit from Detective Russo this morning wasn't helping either.

"Send her up," I replied, not paying much attention. I was too busy assaulting my lunch.

Several moments later, there was a knock at my office door. My back was facing the entrance, and I didn't even bother looking up from my dog dish when I yelled out, "Come in."

My Subway sandwich was all spread out across my credenza, as I had papers strewn everywhere on my desk top. My computer screens were both occupied with police data, and I was too immersed in both investigations to even notice the women who had just walked into my office.

"Hello Detective," came a soft voice from out of nowhere. I turned around and looked up over my computer screens, which were temporarily blocking the view of my office entrance.

There stood a stunning, beautiful brunette with long, curly dark brown hair, beautiful brown eyes and a very shapely figure, probably no more than five feet, five inches tall. She was wearing a light beige jacket, matching skirt and a light blue blouse, which complimented her semi-dark complexion. She was wearing light red lipstick, and a stunning smile. She looked like one of those classy, Hollywood actresses that you often see posing for one of those glamour magazines, displayed next to the cashier at the supermarket. She was drop-dead gorgeous.

I was trying hard not to choke on the last bite of my sandwich, and I nervously replied something that sounded like a gurgled 'Hello'.

"I'm Olivia Laurent, from the Great Lakes Life Insurance Company," she announced, as she walked over to my desk to extend her hand.

I nervously wiped my mouth and looked for a napkin to wipe off the greasy mayonnaise on my hands. I then stood up, noticing the large morning coffee stain on my white shirt and tie.

"I'm Phil Dorian," I nervously replied, accepting her hand and hoping that I wasn't embarrassing myself, with crumbs and sandwich debris splattered across my black trousers.

"I know who you are, Detective," she laughed, shaking my hand.

"I'm so sorry to interrupt your lunch. Did I catch you at a bad time?"

"Oh, no, of course not," I nervously answered, still trying to dust myself off and make myself look presentable.

"We just received another life insurance claim from the Chicago Archdiocese at our office, so my superiors asked me to fly down to Chicago and do a little investigating," she stated, as she was enjoying the surprise assault on my office.

"Oh," I managed to say, as I was still entranced with her beauty and classy good looks.

"I hope I can help," I mumbled, immediately thinking how stupid and nervous I must have sounded.

"I hope you can too," she smiled. "May I sit down?"

"Oh...yes....of course....please. Sit down," I sheepishly said. At that moment, I must have looked like an anxious, high school freshman. I was so nervous, I felt very uncomfortable sitting down at my own desk. She sat at the only chair in my office, and made herself comfortable, crossing her tanned, shapely legs while fumbling through her purse to find her business card. She politely handed it to me, peeking around my computer screens. I immediately noticed that her left hand was without a wedding ban.

"So, how can I help you? Did you just arrive here from the Motor City?" I asked, as I was reading her business card at the same time. I noticed that she was a chief financial officer at the Great Lakes Life Insurance Company, with their home office in Detroit, Michigan.

"Yes, I just flew in from Midway, and rented a car to come here to your precinct. Chicago is such a lovely city," she mentioned. "I had both GPS systems going on my cell phone and in the car, but I still managed to get lost."

"Chicago is an easy city to travel in, as long as you don't get caught up in all the traffic," I replied, as my schoolboy jitters were starting to settle down.

"Yes, I did catch quite a bit of it going downtown to my hotel."

"Where are you staying?" as if it was any of my business.

"The Sheridan on Wacker Drive," she replied. "What a beautiful hotel. Chicago is such a gorgeous city. Every time I come here, I always notice a new skyscraper."

"Indeed," I responded, still trying very hard not to stare.

She then reached into her large purse, pulled out a manila folder, and began fumbling through some papers and reviewing some of her notes.

"I understand there has been another homicide of an ex-priest in your city," she casually mentioned.

"Yes, there has. We've been racking our brains, trying to find some new leads in these two murders, but so far, it has been very frustrating," I retorted.

Even though she was from the life insurance company, I didn't want to come across too forthcoming on the details of these investigations.

"There are rumors floating around that there may be a serial killer responsible for both of these murders," she mentioned. I wasn't sure how much information she really had, or how much homework she had done on the facts of both murder cases.

"We really don't know what we have right now, Ms. Laurent."

"Please, call me Olivia."

"Ok, Olivia...and you can call me Phil," I replied. I didn't know any more if this was really was a business conference or a 'meet-and-greet' encounter, compliments of Match.com.

"We're just not sure what we have right now, Olivia. Even though both murders are very similar, we're not sure what the motive is or who might be involved," I continued.

"Well, judging by the quick life insurance claims that were just made by the Chicago Archdiocese I have a difficult time believing that they're not involved," Olivia responded.

"We can't assume that. We really just don't know."

Olivia gazed at me, with a rather puzzled look on her face. "I am hoping we can solve these cases soon, Detective. There is pressure on our company from everyone to settle these claims, one way or the other," she mentioned, giving me the impression that our investigation into these murders was not progressing to her satisfaction.

"Nobody wants to solve these cases more than I do," I curtly replied.

We both sat there rather nervously, as there were several moments of uncomfortable silence. I was nervously glancing at my computer screen several times during our conversation, just to keep myself from staring at her.

"Are you busy this evening, Detective? Perhaps we could meet for dinner and drinks after work downtown later," she suggested, "We could discuss the details of this investigation when you're not as preoccupied," she smiled.

I was thrown off balance again, not remembering the last time a women asked me out for a date, even if it was only for business.

"I will check my schedule, but I'm sure there won't be a problem," as I didn't want to sound too eager.

"That sounds great, Olivia," I responded.

"My cell phone is on my business card. Please call me later and confirm, and we can decide where to meet and what time," she suggested.

It had been several years since my divorce, and I forgot what going on a 'date' was really like. I hadn't done a lot of dating or 'bar-hopping' since my breakup and messy divorce. Up until now, I wasn't too motivated to go out there and get my heart mutilated and stepped on again.

"I look forward to seeing you later, Detective," as she rose up and grasped my hand again, "It was a pleasure meeting you."

"The pleasure was mine, "as I stood up and returned the pleasantry, hoping I didn't sound or look too nervous or uneasy.

At that moment, she gracefully opened my door and left my office. I could see her from my office glass window, strolling past the other detective's desks. They were all too eager to take notice, as she quickly exited out of the front precinct door.

I was both apprehensive and excited to meet up with Olivia later that evening, hoping that our business dinner date would end up being "more pleasure" and "less business."

Although she had walked out of my office at that moment, I had no idea that Ms. Olivia Laurent was walking into my life.

CHAPTER EIGHTEEN

A black Maserati was speeding south bound on the Dan Ryan expressway on that sunny, Tuesday afternoon. Little Tony DiMatteo had just finished a lunch meeting with some business associates at Gene and Georgetti's Steakhouse on North Franklin Street and was in a hurry to get back to his warehouse on South Ashland Avenue. The afternoon traffic was light in the left lane, as DiMatteo was struggling to keep his eyes on the road. With his daily, 5:00 am workout routines, and after three of his 'Crown Royal on the Rocks' cocktails, DiMatteo was a more than a little tired. He was drowsy and was struggling to keep his car under control. But he needed to quickly return to his office, attend to some business, and to take one of his usual 'power naps' in the late afternoon.

As he was driving, he wasn't paying much attention to his speedometer. The needle was climbing past ninety-five miles an hour, as he was taking the expressway curve a little too fast past the South Archer Avenue exit. He didn't notice the Chicago Police squad car, parked on the far left side of the Dan Ryan expressway, whom he had driven past. The patrolman clocked his speed, then put on his sirens and began to follow the speeding, black Maserati. His radar gun recorded the car's rate of speed going faster than 97 miles an hour.

Little Tony was struggling to stay awake, and loudly turned on his radio. There was a Four Seasons song playing on a Sirius XM oldies station as he was turning up the volume. He didn't notice the police squad car that was chasing after him until the cop car

155

pulled up right next to him on the I-94 expressway and, blowing his sirens loudly, ordered him to pull over.

"Good Afternoon Officer, nice weather we're having," Little Tony politely said as he rolled down his window.

"Driver's License, Registration and Proof of Insurance, please," the unamused patrolman answered, shining a flashlight on Little Tony's eyes and around the front and back seats of the sports car. Tony's eyes were dilated, and the distinct smell of alcohol was more than evident as he was fumbling with his wallet and the papers in his car's glovebox. He finally, after some delayed searching, retrieved the requested identification.

"Have you been drinking, sir?"

"I had a cocktail, but I'm fine. Why are you asking?"

"Sir, step out of the car, please."

"No, officer, I am not going to step out of my car," Tony loudly replied, always remembering his attorney's advice when getting pulled over after having too many drinks.

DiMatteo knew that he shouldn't cooperate with the officer, knowing he was going to get asked to blow into a breathalyzer machine. The patrolman angrily took the driver's identification and typed in the information into his squad car computer, along with the driver's license plate number. It was then that the Chicago police officer suddenly realized whom he had just pulled over.

Tony DiMatteo was then forcibly arrested and brought to the Seventh District.

It was almost 4:00 in the afternoon, and I was looking at my clock, counting out the minutes until I got off from my shift at 6:00pm. I had just received a return text from Olivia, and we had made some plans to get together at 7:30pm at the Dover's Catch, an upscale restaurant on West Wacker Drive near her hotel.

"Detective Dorian," as I answered my ringing desk phone.

"Phil, it's Commander Robertson over at the Seventh District. We're holding someone here at the station that you may want to talk to. Are you still working on those 'Pedophile Priest Murder' cases?"

"Yeah, why?" I curiously asked.

"We've got Little Tony down here on a DUI," the Commander replied. "He was pretending to be Mario Andretti and was racing his Maserati down the Dan Ryan when he got pulled over. We've heard through the grapevine that our little buddy here may know something about what's going on. We thought you might want to come down here and have a little 'chit-chat' with him."

"Tony DiMatteo?" I verified, making sure they had the right Tony.

"Yep, that's the one. We've got him in a holding room."

I couldn't believe what I was hearing. "Has he 'lawyered up' yet?"

"No, not yet. He's too busy entertaining everyone in the precinct with his smart-ass comments. If he wasn't who he was, we would have already thrown him in the shithouse by now," the Commander replied, tongue in cheek.

I wasn't surprised that the 'Capo' of all the crime families in Chicagoland was getting the royal treatment at the Seventh District.

"Thanks Commander, I'll be right down."

I couldn't believe it. Little Tony and his buddy Kilbane, were both getting bad habits of drinking and driving after one too many cocktails.

I had the pleasure of picking up and holding DiMatteo a few years ago on a suspected homicide charge. We had found a dead body in the trunk of a car in Jefferson Park, and it was more than evident by the victim's identification that it was a mob hit. He had three bullet holes in his head, a gun, and over five grand in his coat pocket. The victim had several currency exchanges in the city and had gotten behind on some juice payments that he was into Little Tony and his boys for. DiMatteo wasn't a pleasant 'boy scout' on that day either, and he 'alibied' his way out of getting pinched. In that homicide case, we had uncooperative witnesses, couldn't tie out any of the DNA evidence, and ballistics traced the bullets to an unregistered gun. I had spent several months trying to get a collar on that case, and it was never solved.

But the "Capo dei Capi" was way too smart to be speeding down the Dan Ryan 'all juiced up'. I just didn't understand it, and I couldn't put my head around all this sudden stupidity. I jumped into my Crown Vic, turned on my sirens, and raced down to the Seventh District on West 63rd Street. That afternoon, I certainly wasn't about to look this 'gift horse in the mouth'.

"Thanks for coming down, Detective," Sergeant Charles Anderson said, as he guided me to the holding room where they were keeping DiMatteo. He was an older, overweight police officer who had probably made more than his share of social visits to the donut shop. I could tell he was having a hard time walking and getting around, as he was painfully, escorting me around the precinct office.

"This son-of-a-bitch is one, cocky bastard," he commented. "I'm hoping this won't be a waste of time for you, Detective. Maybe you can get some information out of him. We're all surprised he hasn't called one of his high-priced lawyers yet."

"Don't worry, Sergeant…that's coming. I'm sure he's on his way over. Let's hear what he has to say before his lawyer shuts him up," I advised. I opened the door to the holding room with the desk sergeant behind me, expecting to make a formal introduction.

Little Tony DiMatteo was comfortably sitting on a chair at the table, and his face seemed to light up when I walked into the room.

"Well, well. If it isn't Detective Philip 'Fucking' Dorian," he arrogantly said, broadly smiling from ear to ear.

"It's always a pleasure to see you too, Tony. I heard you were doing a 'stand-up routine' here at the Seventh and I didn't want to miss the show," I amusingly replied.

I already knew from experience who I was dealing with, and I had to make sure that I brought along my 'A-Game' for this visit. Little Tony was a cocky, arrogant, mega-rich Mafioso who knew criminal law better than most law school professors. I knew before this meeting that he was probably going to 'toy' with me and the other officers, until he got tired and bored. At that point, he'll probably call one of his 'over-priced' attorneys to come over to the police station and 'fish him out'.

"I heard you were racing in the Daytona 500 down the Dan Ryan this afternoon," I quickly said, hoping he would give me a straight answer.

"Yeah, I was drag racing some little old lady down on the expressway in a '59 Edsel," he sarcastically replied.

"What I can't figure out, Tony, is where this new habit is coming from?" I asked him point blank. "You guys are way too smart for this kind of shit. You and your priest pally seem to be juicing and driving an awful lot these days. We picked up your buddy Kilbane last week on a DUI as well."

"What? I've got nothing to do with Kilbane, so go fuck yourself, Dorian."

"Is that why you had dinner with him at your favorite little 'trattoria' there on North Halsted last Thursday night?"

Little Tony became deep in thought, trying to remember his activities from the prior week.

"Last Thursday night? Last Thursday night? What the fuck was I doing last Thursday night?" as Tony was scratching his head.

"How in the hell am I supposed to remember what I did last Thursday night, Dorian? I can't even remember what I had for breakfast this morning."

"Judging from your girlish figure, Tony, it was probably a grapefruit and a granola bar," I answered.

From what I remembered in the past, this Chicago mobster was always in shape, and 'dressed to the nines'. He was wearing a grey sport coat and black collared shirt, sporting several diamond rings and an oversized, gold Rolex watch. For a sixty-something, grey-haired hood, DiMatteo always looked impeccable and was very fit and trim.

"I see you're still having your half-a-dozen jelly donuts in the morning, Dorian. How's that working for you?"

"Just fine, Tony, not that it's any of your damn business," I replied.

Little Tony just started shaking his head. "My arteries start to harden every time I stare at that huge 'panza' of yours, Dorian," he answered. "My trainer comes to my gym at 5:00 am every morning. Why don't you get your fat ass out of bed and come over and start working out?"

Little Tony DiMatteo felt qualified to pass out health and fitness information, as he was puffing out his chest, sucking in his stomach, and doing his best 'Jack LaLane' imitation.

"Thanks for the invite, Tony. But we don't want the neighborhood donut shop to go out of business," I bantered back, as I didn't need to hear him taking any more shots at my size forty-four waist.

"So, where were you last Thursday night?" I asked him again.

"Hmmm....,"he answered. "Let me see...." as he silently thought for a moment.

"Oh yeah, I remember now, Dorian," as he was blurting out another cocky answer at my expense.

"I was fucking your wife."

I angrily looked at him silently for about ten seconds, knowing that I couldn't get away with taking a hard swing at that this little son-of-a-bitch and get away with it.

"Wrong answer, Tony. The waiters and the valet at the 'Pagliacci' remember you having dinner with Monsignor Kilbane last Thursday night. We pulled him over with a suitcase full of cash," as I continued to interrogate him.

"And just for the record, Tony, I'm divorced."

Little Tony just rolled his eyes in the air, looking like he was starting to get bored with this whole conversation.

"I don't know what you're talking about," he quickly replied.

"The waiter remembered Kilbane walking in and out of the restaurant with the same black briefcase, and he saw the two of you passing the briefcase back and forth at the table," I said, as Tony was still struggling to remember.

"Again, Dorian, I don't know what you're talking about," he repeated.

"You're well recognized at that restaurant, Tony. They said you've been there many times, and that you even have your own private booth and meeting room," as I was trying hard to squeeze it out of him.

"That has nothing to do with me, Dorian. What Kilbane does and how much money he carries around isn't my fucking problem."

"Well, he obviously thought he owed you some dough, Tony. So, he brought along some retainer money that night, to the tune of fifty large in cash, to tide you and your boys over until the insurance company settled the claim on the murder of those two ex-priests, am I right?" I started to push it, hoping I could get a reaction out of him.

Little Tony started to look nervous, as the sweat was starting to bead on his forehead in the precinct office's warm, somewhat uncomfortable, interrogation room.

"I don't know anything about any old priest murders," he angrily replied.

"They were mob hits, Tony. Both victims were sliced up and filleted like porterhouse steaks. Only you guys have that kind of culinary talent."

"Then maybe you should call the Butchers Local 1546, Dorian. I hear they have a lot of unemployed butchers walking around," he arrogantly countered back.

"Go fuck yourself. You can't put those murders on us. We had nothing to do with them."

"Hmmm, I don't know, Tony. The Archdiocese is the beneficiary of both of those life insurance policies, and there are rumors swirling around town about the Cardinal being broke. Seeing that you and the

Monsignor are so tight, he probably enlisted you for your services," I said.

Little Tony started to laugh. "If Kilbane was hiring us for our services, he would need a lot more than fifty large," he jokingly replied.

"Exactly. That's why he was trying to bring you a deposit, Tony. My theory is, for whatever reason, you refused to accept his money. Maybe he didn't bring enough cash, or maybe..."

"We had nothing to do with those murders, Dorian. I want my lawyer!"

I sternly looked at DiMatteo and made a demand.

"Give up Kilbane, Tony, and you can walk out of here. We'll call it a professional courtesy. Tell us why you were having dinner with Kilbane last Thursday night. We all know Kilbane knows something, and he was probably trying to drag you and your family into this," I continued to push, thankful that I had gotten this far with him. Judging from his reaction, I could tell he knew a lot more than what he was letting on.

"Fuck off, Dorian."

"Rat him out, Tony. Eventually, we will figure out that Kilbane hired either you or one of your boys for these hits. At that point, all of you will go down for these Pedophile Priest Murders."

"Yeah, good luck with that one," DiMatteo replied.

"Or..." I continued to push, "when the evidence left at the crime scenes comes back from CSI with the DNA results, we will be able to tie you directly to these homicides," I was bluffing, but trying to get him to feel very nervous.

Little Tony started to laugh again, not feeling fazed by any of this dialog.

"This conversation is putting me to sleep, Dorian. Let me know when my lawyer shows up." He smugly looked at me, giving me his usual 'go fuck yourself' smile of his.

"I hope your lawyer brings you some bail money, Tony. You're going to need lots of it, and you're going to be here for a while," I replied, motioning the detectives looking on from the one-way glass window that I my interview with Mr. Anthony DiMatteo was over.

"Do you really think I give a shit about a DUI charge, Dorian? I'll just have to give more hours to my chauffer," he cynically replied, as two officers came into the interrogation room to book him and bring him downstairs to lock-up.

"Your problems are far bigger than this DUI charge, Tony. Let me know when you're ready to talk," I replied.

"In the meantime," as I stood up from the table and put my around DiMatteo's shoulder, "you and I are going to be reeeeally good friends again, just like before. Right Tony?"

"Fuuuuuck youuuuuu," he said in his snarky Joe Pesce tone of voice, as the two precinct officers took him away.

I sat in the interrogation room alone by myself for a few minutes, knowing that the other detectives on the other side of the one-way glass window were no longer there, observing my interrogation.

I was very deep in thought. I didn't know where these homicide investigations were going, what direction they were headed, or how much further I could go. Until the crime lab comes up with any hard evidence, or if any other investigative clues turn up anything significant, I felt like I was at a dead end with these cases.

But if I was certain about anything, I knew I was right about one fact: Monsignor Kilbane was probably trying to hire out the DiMatteo Family. Little Tony and the Monsignor had a very close, life-long relationship, and the 'Mob Boss' was the most obvious choice if Kilbane was trying to get someone involved to accomplish these 'Pedophile Priest Murders'. If I hadn't achieved anything else that afternoon, I realized that I had accomplished one thing:

I had planted a seed into Little Tony DiMatteo's brain.

CHAPTER NINETEEN

DOVER CATCH

I was nervously pulling into the parking garage on North Dearborn Avenue, as I was more than thirty minutes late for my business meeting with Olivia Laurent, the executive from the Great Lakes Insurance Company. I had to drive my car several floors up the parking structure, as I texted Olivia on my way to let her know that I would be late for our get together that evening.

The interrogation session with Little Tony at the Seventh District had made my being on time difficult that early evening. In between battling all the traffic on I-94, then running home to clean up and change at my loft in the West Loop, trying to make this meeting with Olivia was very stressful. It was already past 8:00pm, and I was hoping that Olivia would be very understanding.

The sun was starting to set behind me as I walked through the all the shuffling people and the bustling traffic of Chicago. I couldn't help but notice the grandeur of the Merchandise Mart across the Chicago River, casting its long shadow onto the newly renovated river walk. It was a warm summer evening, and you could feel all the excitement in the air as everyone was ready to start another wonderful Chicago summer. It had been a long winter, I thought to myself, and it seemed like everyone was looking so forward to the long summer days and the wonderful, warm summertime evenings in the city.

I noticed a beautiful brunette sitting alone at a table near the window, as I entered the Dover Catch Restaurant at 35 West Wacker Drive. It was a very upscale restaurant that faced the Chicago Riverwalk and the magnificent Merchandise Mart across the river. I was greeted by the hostess, and she casually brought me to our table.

"I'm sorry I'm late, Olivia. We had an interrogation of a suspect at the Seventh District on the south side, and I wasn't sure I was going to make it here this evening," I apologized, as she rose from her table and extended her hand.

"I'm glad you could make it, Detective," she smiled, as we both sat down and made ourselves comfortable.

"I was just admiring the beauty of your city," as she was gazing at the Chicago River across from West Wacker Drive.

"What is that beautiful, old large building across the way?" she inquisitively asked.

"Oh, that's the Merchandise Mart. It was built by Marshall Field in 1930 and was the largest building in the world at the time it was constructed. It has over four million square feet of retail space and was owned by the Kennedy Family for over half a century until it was sold twenty years ago," I explained, trying to impress her with my architectural knowledge. I only knew so much about it because I remember having to do a book report on it when I was a freshman in high school.

"How interesting!" she exclaimed. "You live in such a beautiful city. I always enjoy coming here. It is such a sharp contrast from Detroit," Olivia observed, while taking a drink from her ice water.

The waiter came to our table and we ordered drinks and appetizers, as we were starting to settle in and get comfortable with one another and the conversation.

"There is no better place in the Midwest than Chicago in the summertime," I mentioned, trying to look in another direction other than stare at my beautiful dinner companion that evening. She was wearing a light red blouse and a short, dark skirt. Her black, high heeled shoes seemed to compliment her matching Coach Leather handbag as well.

Her shoulder length, dark brown hair easily complimented her olive, dark skin. A gold necklace with a religious medal reflected the summer rays of the early evening sunset, as it gleamed against her tanned, sensuously dark skin. She had very light, hazel brown eyes that almost looked green in the summer sunlight. Her beautiful, iconic features looked like a cross between a very suggestive Jennifer Lopez and a very sensual Courtney Cox. I could smell her sweet-scented perfume in the air as I was sitting there at the table. I began to wonder if she ever got tired of looking so classy and so damned gorgeous. My mind began to speculate on how many ex-husbands, boyfriends and broken hearts she had left back in the Motor City.

"So how is the investigation going?" she asked, as she was taking a long sip of her Pinot Noir glass of wine.

"It's been frustrating, Olivia. We have two unsolved murders of two pedophile ex-priests in the last three weeks, and it's starting to look like we have a serial killer on our hands. We haven't been able to lift a lot of evidence or DNA results from the crime scenes, and so far, we have no witnesses or any real murder suspects."

"Not even the Archdiocese, that Monsignor what's-his-name?"

"Kilbane?" I answered.

"Yes. Isn't he the assistant to the Cardinal? He's the one who signed the life insurance claims."

"Yes, he is indeed. He is a very powerful, Chicago clergyman, second only to the Cardinal. Monsignor Kilbane is extremely arrogant and very well connected here in town, and he certainly isn't cooperating with our investigation. But the Archdiocese of Chicago is well shielded and extremely protected legally and politically. Even if we could find any evidence that linked them to these murders, trying to prove it will be extremely difficult," I explained, keeping my Courvoisier cognac very close to my lips.

"Well, considering the amount of these life insurance claims, they would definitely have a motive," Olivia said. "I read somewhere that the Chicago Archdiocese is having cash flow problems and is faced with selling off valuable assets and real estate just to settle all of these sexual abuse claims."

"I've heard that too. They have already sold off some valuable, lakefront land in Wisconsin that they've owned for decades, which was used as a campground for children years ago," I recalled, doing some research on the real estate transactions of the Archdiocese the other day.

"Well, considering that these child abuse claims have climbed to a staggering $200 million in lawsuit settlements, it would make sense that the Archdiocese could use the money," she replied, enjoying her glass of satin red wine.

I could tell that Olivia had done her homework on these murder investigations and was well versed on the facts of these homicides.

"Our company is starting to feel a lot of pressure to settle these life insurance claims. We have received some correspondence from the Archdiocese's legal counsel, inquiring about their status."

"I'm not surprised," I answered.

"Have you thought about getting a list of abused victims who have filed claims against the Archdiocese?"

"We have Intelligence at the Twenty-First District helping us on this investigation as well, and I know they are referencing such lists as potential suspects," I replied, rattling the ice cubes of my empty drink glass. The waiter then arrived at our table to take our orders. I had ordered a Chilean Seabass entrée, while Olivia requested a shrimp and seafood salad.

"I understand eating fish is a healthy alternative when watching your weight," I exclaimed, feeling self-conscience about my over-sized waistline.

I was trying hard to change the subject, as I was feeling uncomfortable answering her rapid-fire questions regarding the Pedophile Priest Murder investigations.

"Yes, it is. I seldom eat red meat anymore. I eat a lot of fish and vegetables, and I try to get to the gym two or three times a week when I can," she replied.

"I wish I had the time. The pressures of this job and my divorce several years ago hasn't helped my weight, and I've gained a significant amount over the past few years," I said as I was making an excuse, taking another gulp of my second cognac and buttering up a third slice of freshly baked bread.

"It's hard, especially at our age. It seems like we work harder and enjoy our lives less as we get older. Our health and our waistlines seem to always take a toll," Olivia replied, although by observing her youthful, fit and trim figure, had nothing to be ashamed of.

"When were you divorced?"

"Several years ago. My ex-wife decided she didn't want to be married to a Chicago cop anymore. My daughter is the only good thing that came out of our twenty-five-year marriage."

"I'm sorry to hear this," she replied, sounding very empathetic.

There were a few moments of silence, as our dinner entrees arrived at our table. I was feeling generous and cut off a piece of my Chilean Sea Bass and shared it with her, placing it on her dinner plate. She looked at me, her eyes looking surprised and almost adoring, as she thanked me. Sharing my dinner entrée was a habit I had learned from being married for so many years. These days, I still feel guilty if I don't do it whenever I'm dining out with a friend.

There was something wonderfully comfortable about Olivia. She was easy to talk to, extremely intelligent, and a very interesting lady.

She began telling me about her background and her career, explaining that she had earned both a law and accounting degrees, but chose to continue her career as the chief financial officer at the Great Lakes Life Insurance Company.

"So how is it that a beautiful lady like you isn't married?" I pursued my questioning, feeling ambitious after my second Cognac.

"I've had lots of prospects and have had more than my share of boyfriends. But I get very nervous when the subject of marriage comes up, and after a few bad relationships, I've concluded that I would be far better off alone," she explained, ordering another glass of Pinot Noir.

"I'm very lucky to have my daughter, and my seven-year-old granddaughter," I proclaimed. "She does a great job at looking after me. A day doesn't go by that she doesn't call or text me several times a day."

"You are lucky indeed," she observed. "I would give anything to have a son or a daughter."

She looked out the window, staring at the Chicago River across the way, observing all the hurried people walking across Wacker Drive. She then took a breath and made a long, deep sigh. "I guess everything comes with a price."

We sat there and finished our dinner, making more small talk about the vast differences between living in Detroit and Chicago. I discovered that she was a huge Detroit Red Wings fan and had season tickets for hockey games that she very often attended, first at the Joe Louis Arena in prior years, and now at the Little Caesars' Arena.

"We're rivals," I jokingly said. "I go to about a dozen or more Blackhawks games every year."

"There is nothing greater than the Detroit – Chicago Rivalry," she laughed, as she went on to talk about what a huge hockey family she had come from. Her three older brothers were all hockey players, and she spent most of her childhood in local hockey rinks, rooting on her brothers and their hockey teams. Olivia and her brothers followed the Red Wings religiously and revered to the likes of such older players as Gordy Howe, Alex Delvecchio, Chris Chielios and Pavel Datsyuk. I had to reprimand her a few times though, letting her know that Chelios was really a Chicago Blackhawk, disguised as a Red Wing. We both laughed, and I had to pinch myself, realizing that I had found a beautiful woman who was as much of a hockey fan as I was.

After paying the dinner check, we exited the restaurant and crossed Wacker Drive, walking down the concrete stairwell onto the Chicago Riverwalk down below. Olivia marveled at all the river walk restaurants and cafés, the sidewalk music with all its musicians, playing their version of any song for a nominal donation. We walked together, very closely, and I was tempted several times to grasp her hand while we wandered together along the river walk.

By then it was almost 10:30pm. Olivia apologized, explaining that she had to catch an early flight back to Detroit at 7:00am and had to be at Midway Airport very early the next morning. I walked her back to the Chicago Sheridan, strolling through the revolving doors and into the hotel lobby. We both stopped short of the escalator in the middle of the hotel.

"I had a wonderful evening, Phil. Thank you so much for dinner and for showing me around town."

"I've showed you nothing. There is still so much more to see. When are you coming back to Chicago?" I asked, trying not to sound too anxious.

"That all depends on how quickly your police department can catch this serial killer," she quickly answered. "I'm hoping that we won't have to hire our own private investigators, if your department doesn't make any progress with these cases," she casually said, in a very cold tone of voice.

I was shocked. What? Private investigators?

That's all I needed. More people looking over my shoulder. She never mentioned anything at all about the possibility of getting more investigators involved in these homicide cases.

My expression quickly changed, from casually relaxed to almost shocked. I must have displayed a disillusioned, disenchanted look on my face as I was staring at her, totally speechless. Olivia must have noticed my quick change of moods, and I expected her to wave me farewell and quickly, jump onto the escalator to her hotel room.

But she instead, grasped my hand and gave me a long, wet kiss on the cheek.

"I just know you're going to get your man, Detective," she said seductively, in a Jessica Rabbit tone of voice. She then turned and hoped onto the escalator, retiring to her waiting hotel room. I stood there and just watched her go up the moving stairway, hoping she would turn around and give me a final wave goodnight. But Olivia Laurent never looked back.

My head was spinning. I had never felt so elated, so anxious, and yet so confused, all at the same time. It was as though she was trying to get as close as she could to me, maybe even mentally seducing me, without ever lifting her baby finger. She was giving me signals that maybe, she was personally interested, and that conceivably, wanted to get close to me. A close intimate relationship, perhaps?

But she was also putting out some different signals that evening, and I was totally confused and conflicted. I was beginning to realize that settling these insurance claims might be her only goal in all of this. I was anticipating the possibility of a personal connection with her, but realized that maybe, she just wasn't interested. I had falsely gotten my hopes up that evening, and I was now feeling somewhat dejected.

I strolled out of the hotel lobby and onto West Wacker Drive, wondering if I was ever going to hear from her again.

CHAPTER TWENTY

It was a bright, warm, sunny morning as worshippers were walking up the steps of Holy Name Cathedral for the early six o'clock mass. The early weekday service was popular among working Roman Catholics and commuters who worked in the Chicago Loop and was heavily attended. Monsignor Joseph Kilbane had arrived early that morning and entered the cathedral from the side door entrance. He greeted a few parishioners as he entered the sacristy and began putting on his green chasuble and holy vestments.

It was his turn that Wednesday morning, as he dressed and prepared the cruets that he needed to recite the early, weekday service. He was on a revolving schedule at the Archdiocese with other priests for saying the early morning gospel and hearing confessions on that day at Holy Name. The Sunday church bulletin always advertised the name of the assigned priest who would be saying the daily masses and confessions during that week. Fr. Joe enjoyed offering his time and saying mass when his turn came up, as he found solace in this distraction from his stressful, administrative duties at the Archdiocese of Chicago.

The holy mass went quickly that weekday morning, as he recited a quick homily and dispensed communion to the eighty or so worshippers who attended that day. As was his usual routine after mass, he took off his vestments and walked over to the confessional in the rear of the cathedral. For the next hour, he was expected to offer his time and to hear confessions from the various parishioners who had attended services that morning. He had brought a

175

prayer book along with him, as he usually did, to keep himself occupied in between acts of contrition.

He had already heard the confessions of several people that morning, when another well-dressed gentleman entered the confessional. As he entered the enclosed private chamber, the Monsignor was only greeted with several moments of silence.

"Recite your trespasses before the Lord," the Monsignor began, breaking the extended void. There were only more silent moments, as Kilbane tried to see who the man was that had entered his confessional. It was dark in the ornate, private room, where there were no lights available inside of the cathedral's private chamber.

"Confess your sins, please," the Monsignor requested again.

"I got your fucking sins right here!" said a brash, familiar voice.

"You mother-fucker! I'll confess my sins to you, you fucking son-of-a-bitch!" as more vulgarity came from the other side of the small, private room.

"My sins are that I've allowed you to be my friend for too fucking long, you sick, fucking bastard!"

Fr. Joe immediately knew who it was.

"Please! You are in the House of the Lord!" as he tried to calm down his childhood friend, not expecting him to arrive unannounced to Holy Name Cathedral and to loudly invade his private confessional.

"You mother-fucking asshole! Do you have any idea how much heat you've put on us? Do you have any fucking idea? And there I was, having dinner with you, listening to your crazy, fucking bullshit!"

The Monsignor was completely stunned and surprised to hear the angry voice of Little Tony DiMatteo. He was especially shocked at his coming into his confessional and to begin verbally cussing him out. He had not heard from Tony since their dinner together at the Trattoria Pagliacci a few weeks ago, and he did not try to contact him.

Although he had been pulled over for a DUI that evening, he had been released by the police the next day and he had not thought much more of the incident since.

"Tony," Fr. Joe sternly replied, "this is not the place."

"Fuck you, Joe. This is the only place. Thanks to you and your bright, wild-ass fucking ideas, I can't even be seen with you anymore."

"What happened, Tony?"

"What happened? I'll tell you what happened! The coppers are on to you and your brilliant fucking ideas. And now, you've dragged me into this too."

"What are you talking about?"

"What am I talking about?" Tony replied.

"They picked me up on a DUI charge yesterday, and they said they pulled you over last week as well. Now I've got Detective Fucking Dorian up my ass, and he's saying that they busted you with the suitcase full of goddamn cash," Tony angrily explained.

"And what's worse, Detective 'Fucking Columbo' started taking smart pills. Somehow, he figured out that you've been shopping around for a mobbed-up butcher for the insurance money. He now knows that you were trying to pay me off while we were having dinner at the restaurant the other night, you asshole!" Tony continued to loudly cuss, as the other worshippers sitting in the last pews of cathedral were noisily being disrupted.

"Tony, please! Keep your voice down," the Monsignor loudly begged.

177

"We didn't even 'ace' these fucking priests and now we're taking the fucking heat for it," Tony begrudgingly complained.

"I've got an unmarked cop car sitting at the end of my street, following me around all fucking day. I can't even shit and wipe my ass without the fucking cops watching me!"

"Your voice, Tony," the Monsignor warned him again.

"Fuck you, Joe!" Tony very loudly whispered, "Is this quiet enough?"

"I told you this was a stupid idea," he continued, "and now I've got all these fucking coppers and detectives up my ass, thanks to you!" Tony irately whispered.

The Monsignor was totally shocked and embarrassed. He peeked out of his confessional chamber for a moment and counted the number parishioners who were witnessing the loud, Shakespearian poetry that was coming out of Little Tony's mouth.

"This is not the place, Tony. Let's go into the sacristy where we can talk, please."

"Fuck you, Joe! I can't even be seen with you anymore. And I don't want to be seen with you, you sick, fuck-ball!" Tony angrily replied.

"I'm fucking done with you, Joe. Stay the fuck away from me! If you're too stupid to keep these fucking coppers away from you, don't send them over to me! I've got enough of my own fucking problems."

With that, Little Tony angrily stormed out of the confessional. He slammed the chamber door so loud that the noise reverberated from the stained-glass windows of the landmark cathedral. Several worshippers were staring at the angry 'Capo dei Capi' as he loudly exited Holy Name Cathedral. He walked down the church steps to his black Mercedes parked on North Wabash, where his chauffer was waiting.

"Get me the fuck out of here," he ordered his driver, as the vehicle sped off into the busy morning traffic, going eastbound on Chicago Avenue towards the city.

The Monsignor gathered his prayer book and quickly, walked out of the confessional chamber and over to the front door of the cathedral. Several parishioners were still staring at the rear of the church, witnessing the confessional drama as Kilbane went looking for Little Tony. He wanted to confront him face to face and to rationally, calm him down. He wanted to reassure his childhood friend that, somehow, the Lord will find a way and prayerfully, the truth in all of this will come out. It always does, Fr. Joe thought to himself.

But deep down in his soul, Monsignor Kilbane was horrified. The fact that the police were now suspicious of his soliciting a "murder for hire" plot for the life insurance money was sobering. Kilbane was trying very hard not to panic and not to have a total meltdown. He confidently knew that, no matter how angry Tony was at him, and no matter how hard his juvenile friend was pushed, that Little Tony would never, ever, 'rat' him out.

Not to anyone. Ever.

Despite his suggestion to Little Tony of hiring a hitman for the insurance money several months ago, the reality was that, neither the Monsignor nor Little Tony had anything to do with these murders. Although Fr. Joe was pleased that the Archdiocese was the intended beneficiary of these life insurance policies, he was extremely fearful and suspicious. It seemed in his mind that, somehow, someone was killing these pedophile ex-priests and trying to put the blame on the Archdiocese and especially, himself.

179

But why? And by whom? Was he being framed? Why would he be blamed for these 'Pedophile Priest Murders' that neither he nor Little Tony had committed?

Someone else had to know of his intended plan to 'hire out' the murder deaths of these pedophile ex-priests. But who else would carry out these plans? Who else would know of his evil intentions? Who else would have heard him discussing his malevolent plans to DiMatteo that evening? Did Little Tony mention this to someone within the DiMatteo Family and perversely, carry out his plans? There were too many questions going through his head, and Monsignor Joseph Kilbane didn't have the answers to any of them.

He opened the old, antiquated walnut doors and walked down the steps of Holy Name Cathedral, looking both ways on North Wabash Street for his friend. But Little Tony had abruptly left and disappeared. He was nowhere to be found. Monsignor Kilbane then walked back inside of the Cathedral and, still grasping his prayer book, kneeled in the last pew at the rear of the church and prayed. He prayed for the Lord's forgiveness. He prayed for the Lord's understanding.

But most of all, he prayed for the truth.

CHAPTER TWENTY-ONE

The beautiful, sharply dressed brunette wearing a white, Anne Klein business suit had just left Starbucks on Jefferson Avenue and was casually walking across the street to work and begin her day. Olivia Laurent arrived at her office at the Great Lakes Life Insurance Company on the thirty-sixth floor of the Renaissance Center, as it glistened off the bright sunrays of that early June morning. She settled at her desk with her grande, extra-wet cappuccino, and shuffled through her desk files and the current matters at hand. It was almost 10:30am when her administrative assistant, Ginette, paged her on her desk phone:

"Olivia, you have a visitor from Chicago. He says he would like a few minutes of your time."

Olivia thought immediately of Detective Philip Dorian. Her hands began perspiring, and her heart started to pound out of her chest. She hadn't seen or heard from Philip since her dinner date with him last week and had hoped for several seconds that he would just magically appear in the reception area of her insurance company.

"Who is it?" she inquired.

"His name is James Gleason, and he's an attorney."

An attorney coming here all the way from Chicago? Why? This seemed unusual, and she was curious as to why she would be receiving such an unexpected visit.

181

"Shall I send him in?" Ginette asked.

"No, I will be right out."

Olivia walked out of her office and over to the reception room, where she greeted her unexpected visitor. He was a tall, portly older man, well dressed in a dark blue, pinstriped three-piece suit, complete with a bright blue handkerchief and a pocket watch. He looked to be in his much later years, bald with an over-sized, red Irish nose that could probably compete with W.C. Fields.

"Ms. Laurent? I'm James Gleason, and I'm the attorney for the family of Mr. John Marquardt," the well-dressed attorney announced as he handed her his business card.

"Pleased to meet you, Mr. Gleason. What can I do for you?" Olivia curtly asked, uncomfortable with this sudden visit from a strange Chicago attorney that she had never met, nor expected at her office.

"I'm sorry to barge in on you unexpectedly like this, but may we go somewhere in private to talk?"

"Certainly."

The Chicago attorney followed Olivia into her office, as the conference room on her floor was already occupied with another meeting. The gentleman had brought along a dark brown briefcase and sat in front of Olivia's desk with his case on his lap. As his hands were placed over his briefcase, Olivia noticed a shiny gold ring on his right hand, with several red rubies in the shape of a red cross.

They exchanged a few pleasantries regarding his unpleasant drive to Detroit from Chicago that morning, and he explained that his office was on West Wacker Drive. Mr. Gleason was the founding partner of his law firm, which was established back in 1985, and concentrated on personal injury and liability cases.

"So again, Mr. Gleason, what can I do for you today?"

"As I've mentioned, I'm here on behalf of the Marquardt family. As you may know, the former Fr. Marquardt was violently murdered in his home last month, from what has been reported in the media lately, as a serial killer. We understand that there was a five-million-dollar life insurance policy written against Marquardt's life at the time of his resignation from his pastoral duties by the Archdiocese back in 1982. Our firm has now discovered that the Archdiocese was the beneficiary to this very large life insurance policy. The family of John Marquardt is in the process of filing a lawsuit claim against the Archdiocese for any proceeds that may be distributed to them," Gleason carefully explained.

"I'm not at liberty to discuss this life insurance claim with you, Mr. Gleason, as I'm sure you're aware."

"I understand Ms. Laurent. I've anticipated your unwillingness to discuss this matter with me, and I fully understand," the attorney replied, then asked in the same breath, "Would you be at liberty to discuss with me your progress on this insurance claim?"

Olivia just laughed, not knowing whether she should entertain or insulted by such a blatant, out-of-line question.

"No, I cannot discuss that with you either, Mr. Gleason," she sarcastically repeated.

The Chicago counselor was not astonished by Olivia's reaction nor her reluctance to discuss this matter with him. He only looked at her with a satirical look on his face.

"Have you been following the progress of these "Pedophile Priest Murders" in Chicago?

"Yes, Mr. Gleason, I have."

"Correct me if I am wrong, Ms. Laurent. Since an arrest has not been made in these 'Pedophile Priest Murders, that there is a very good possibility that the Archdiocese's claim to these life insurance proceeds could be approved, notwithstanding any other evidence or arrests made in these murder cases, correct?" Gleason asked.

"Yes. That is correct Mr. Gleason."

"And with the high dollar amount of this life insurance policy, your company would more than likely hire your own private investigators to examine the validity of this claim or any other related life insurance claims concerning these recent murders, correct?" Gleason asked.

"That typically would be correct. But we have not hired a 'P.I.' to investigate these murders yet, Mr. Gleason. We have been reassured by the Chicago Police Department that so far, they have these homicide investigations under control," Olivia stated matter-of-factly.

Gleason laughed to himself and smiled, as he continued to bring his point home.

"I can assure you, Ms. Laurent, that the Chicago P.D. does not have these 'Pedophile Priest Murders' under control," the Chicago attorney blatantly stated.

"But I understand that the FBI is also involved in these investigations," Olivia replied.

"Yes, they are, but the progress of these murder cases has been very slow, and they have not uncovered any evidence leading to an arrest."

"Ok," Olivia replied, "But I don't understand where you're going with any of this, Mr. Gleason," Olivia impatiently said, as she was starting to become angry with this fishing expedition.

"What does your client's lawsuits have to do with us? We cannot approve of any claims until the evidence has been uncovered and we decide whether these insurance monies can be rightfully claimed by the Archdiocese. The Chicago Police Department hasn't completed their investigation into this or the other related homicide. We have no idea what the Chicago P.D. is going to uncover in this or on any of the other murders'," she bluntly replied in a very snarky voice.

The old, Chicago attorney just sat at his chair in front of Olivia's desk and smiled.

"Will your insurance company be hiring a private investigator to examine my client's homicide? Or for that matter, the serial killer involved in these 'Pedophile Priest Murders'?"

"Again, I am not at liberty to say, Counselor. I would imagine that we will be looking into that matter very shortly after I meet again with the Chicago Police Department and their investigators."

Gleason continued to push his case, as if to make a grand revelation. "Would it be accurate to say, Ms. Laurent, that when an arrest has been made in a related murder case, that the insurance company can postpone the related life insurance claims until the homicide case has been tried in a court of law? When an establishment of guilt has been found regarding the alleged killer?" Gleason kept inquiring. He was verbally making his assumptions to Olivia as though he were standing before a grand jury in a court of law.

"That would be accurate."

"And if the alleged murderer were found not guilty in that homicide, the insurance company can approve the insurance claim and pay the proceeds to the beneficiary, correct?"

"Yes, Mr. Gleason...that would be correct," as Olivia was beginning to grow weary and impatient of Gleason's questions.

"Let's imagine, if you will, that your company acquires a private detective, and that your investigator uncovers evidence which would make you believe that the beneficiary of these life insurance policies did *not* perpetrate the murders of these former priests. Would that evidence, or any lack thereof, incline your company to approve these insurance claims?"

"Well, probably, eh...yes...it would."

"Even before this murder case is tried in court?"

"Yes. Once we have definite evidence that could indicate that the beneficiary was not the perpetrator to these murders, we would automatically approve the life insurance claim. Even if only some of the evidence is circumstantial on the part of the Archdiocese, we would be within our rights to approve or deny these claims regardless of the suspicions of the Chicago P.D.," she explained.

"I see," said the Chicago counselor said. "And of course, any evidence that you would uncover, you are not obligated to share this evidence with the Chicago P.D., correct?"

"No, we are not," she answered. "Where are you going with all of this, Mr. Gleason?" Olivia was starting to get angry. She was beginning to count to ten under breath as she was thinking of initiating this old attorney's exit, and then possibly, throwing this old son-of-a-bitch out of her thirty-sixth-floor window.

"We suspect that there are other parties involved in these homicides that may be trying to 'frame' the Archdiocese and specifically, Monsignor Kilbane as the perpetrator of these murders. I believe that there is not enough evidence to make any such conclusions," Gleason explained.

He just sat there in front of her desk, reiterating his point.

"Ms. Laurent, as you have said, if a private investigator were hired by your company, and no additional evidence is uncovered in a homicide case such as this, you could use this lack of evidence to approve the insurance claim. Correct?" Olivia was silent, thinking again about her answer. The old man only smiled, opened his briefcase, and withdrew a large white envelope and placed it on Olivia's desk.

"I'm sure the contents of this will persuade you to hire a private investigator and conclude that there is a lack of evidence in these murders. I trust this envelope will assist you in formulating the correct decision, Ms. Laurent. Now if you'll excuse me, I must get back on the road. There is a heavy rain storm coming in tonight, and I need to drive back to Chicago. Have a good day, Ms. Laurent."

Attorney James Gleason then rose from his chair and quickly exited Olivia's office, leaving the envelope on her desk. After he left, Olivia opened the large tightly sealed envelope. It contained five bundles of tightly banned, one hundred-dollar bills, with $10,000 bans around each bundle. The old attorney had left $50,000 on her desk in new, crisp, unmarked bills.

She was obviously being bribed, to close out and approve these life insurance policy claims made by the Archdiocese of Chicago. The Chicago attorney obviously intended to make sure that there was enough money available to the Archdiocese as a result of these murders so that there could be civil claims made against these funds in a future liability lawsuit. Gleason wanted to make certain that her insurance company approved and closed out these multi-million-dollar life insurance claims, without going through the Chicago Police Department or their investigations. She sat there at her desk, speechless, not knowing what she should do.

Olivia was now in a quandary: Should she disclose this 'visit' and this 'envelope' to Detective Dorian and the Chicago P.D. and assist him in these

187

murder investigations? Or should she take matters into her own hands, and hire a private investigator and conduct her own investigations? Should she keep the money? Or should she turn it over to the police? After several long, nervous moments, she hurriedly took the large envelope and placed it inside of her bottom desk drawer.

"Cindy," she called her assistant over the telephone.

"Yes, boss," she replied.

"Could you get me some information on the nearest Comerica Bank branch please?"

"Ok, sure," Cindy replied, not understanding her boss's request.

"Thank you," replied Olivia, knowing that keeping that kind of excessive cash was not safe in her office.

'Gleason' exited out of the elevator and walked quickly outside to the adjacent parking lot of the Renaissance Center. After he got into his car, he quickly unbuckled his pants and deflated the 'stomach cushion' which he was wearing underneath his suit. He then removed his skull cap costume, rubbed off his facial props and his fake 'Irish nose' which he used as part of his disguise. He then quickly wiped off his makeup with the wet towelettes he had kept hidden underneath the seat of his rented Ford Escape. The imposter then began driving onto Jefferson Avenue and entered the Ford Expressway, speeding west towards Chicago. The actor gazed at his review mirror and smiled.

'Brother Ezekiel' had successfully accomplished his assigned task.

CHAPTER TWENTY-TWO

All the families were gathered in the parking lot of Holy Family Church, as the yellow school bus pulled up to the long line of school age boys, ready to board for summer camp. It was a beautiful, hot July morning in 1969, as the boys were loading up their duffle bags for their two-week camping experience at the CYO (Catholic Youth Organization) camp. It was a three-hour bus ride to the shores of Green Bay, Wisconsin, where the children endeavored in camping, fishing, archery, orienteering, hiking, swimming and other summer activities. Johnny Fortuna and his best friend, Bobby O'Donnell were meeting up that summer morning, and the fourth-grade boys couldn't be more excited.

"Hey Johnny, did you pack your model rockets?" Bobby eagerly asked as he saw his best friend lined up to board the long, yellow school bus.

"Of course!" he excitedly answered. Bobby then closely approached Johnny as he stood in line, making him feel his back pockets for the pocket knife and some new fishing tackle he decided to bring along.

The boys boarded the school bus and sat next to each other towards the back, while the other boys filled up the rest of the empty seats. Johnny's mother was anxiously standing beneath the school bus windows, wiping her eyes with a handkerchief as she sadly said good bye to her son.

"Okay gentlemen, lets' settle down," Father Matt exclaimed as he was the last to board the bus, along with some other teenage camp counselors. Father Matthew McDougall was a popular young priest in his late twenties, and the young boys at Holy Family School were quite fond of him. The children at Holy Family referred to him as being one of the "cooler" priests in school. After taking attendance of all the boys who signed up for summer camp that muggy, July morning, Fr. Matt motioned the bus driver to begin their journey.

"What's up, Father?" Johnny asked in his normal cocky voice.

"Glad to see you made it aboard, young man!" Fr. Matt excitedly said, as he individually greeted each of the prospective campers on the bus.

"Hopefully the two of you will be on your best behavior and we won't be shipping either one of you back to Chicago."

"Not a chance, Padre," Bobby responded in his usual snarky tone of voice.

As the boys settled down in their seats, Fr. Matt started some activities to keep the boys occupied throughout the bus ride, playing such travel riding games like "Name that Capital", "Spot the License Plate" and other games. They began singing "Ninety-Nine Bottles of Beer" and various other school bus songs. Fr. Matt was always very engaging with the children and was well respected within the Holy Family community. He had just been ordained a couple of years ago from Mundelein Seminary, and was teaching the fourth-grade class at Holy Family Grade School. He was happy to serve at a Catholic Church within the Chicagoland area, being a native of the Logan Square neighborhood.

As the children arrived at the Green Bay campground, the campers lined up according to their different cabins that they were assigned to. There were ten white, rustic cabins, with bunk beds that could accommodate ten to twelve children per cabin. Nearby was a large latrine, with bathrooms and showers located in the middle of campground and was within proximity of the ten sleeping cabins. There was also a cafeteria, or "mess hall", where everyone met for breakfasts, lunches and dinners. Several other buildings which hosted arts and crafts, music, a gym and other activities were also located nearby. Towards the very end of the campground was an archery range, where the boys would be taking archery classes.

Johnny and Bobby were assigned to Cabin Seven, and they both grabbed their duffle bags and selected the bunk beds located at the far end of the cabin. Bobby took the top bunk, and Johnny grabbed the bottom. They both excitedly unpacked their gear and clothing and settled themselves in to their new home away from home for the next two weeks.

Each cabin was assigned two camp counselors. Cabin Seven was assigned a college aged camp counselor named "Dean" and Father Matt. Dean was a long-haired college student in his early twenties and was excited to plan the various daily activities for the boys. There were many college students during that time who took summer jobs as camp counselors for the CYO organization that summer.

The summer of 1969 was an exciting summer indeed, with the astronauts walking on the moon, the Woodstock music festival going on, Chicago Cubs baseball and the Beatles were still popular. The young fourth graders at that time were beginning to put down their baseball cards and comic books, and starting to discover girls, fast cars, rock and roll, and of course, Playboy magazines. Their first night in cabin seven was uneventful, as the boys stayed up for some scary ghost stories, told by Father Matt, with accompanying sound effects by Dean and the others.

Everyone knew the drill. If they had to go to the bathroom in the middle of the night, quietly got up and walked over to the latrine without slamming the front door and waking everyone up in the cabin. The bathroom located outside of the cabin was approximately 200 yards away, and had several toilets, sinks, and open hot showers where the boys were required to shower in the morning.

That first morning, Father Matt woke up the boys at 7:00am, and made sure all of them had their toiletries before walking single file to the latrine. Some of the boys made comments that they thought it was unusual that Father Matt felt it necessary to supervise them while they all are taking showers. He would stand by the shower stalls and watch each one of the boys

191

lather up. Perhaps, many thought, he was making sure none of them were 'horsing around', as some of them would throw bars of soap and snap towels at one another while Fr. Matt wasn't looking.

Each morning, Father Matt played a game with the boys. He had them finish their showers and wrap themselves tightly with their towels around their waists. He would then have them line up, and sprint back to the cabin with their hands on their heads, wearing only their towels. If their towels fell off during the foot race, they had to finish the race without wearing them. In order keep the boys from getting homesick, there weren't any telephones available for the young boys to call their parents at the camp. The telephones were in the clinic and the offices next to the mess hall, and unless it was an emergency, the boys weren't allowed to call home. Everyone took naps after lunch for an hour in the afternoon, and that was when the boys could write letters home.

After the third day at camp, young Johnny was starting to feel homesick. He wrote his mother everyday while he was at camp and told Mrs. Fortuna about all their fun camping activities. On one occasion, he wrote her about their daily towel sprinting activities every morning. Johnny's mother failed to find the humor in these naked foot races and tried to contact the CYO camp office to communicate her displeasure. She was assured by the CYO supervisor that these races were a camp tradition and were supervised by all the camp counselors in "good fun."

One evening, in the middle of the night, Bobby was awakened by one of the boys sleeping on the top bunk adjacent to his. His name was Stephan, and he was crying, while burying his face against his pillow.

"What's wrong Stephan? Did you have a bad dream?" Bobby innocently asked.

"No."

"Are you okay?" he insisted.

"No," he answered.

Just then, Father Matt quietly walked into the cabin, and ordered both boys to fall back asleep without making any more noise. He then walked up to Stephan's top bunk and tried to comfort him, letting him know that everything was going to "be okay".

The next several nights, Bobby noticed that there were several other boys who had ventured out to use the latrine in the middle of the night, and a few of them would come back fairly upset when they arrived back in their bunk beds.

The following day, Johnny approached Bobby while they were at the archery range.

"Bobby, do you still have your knife?" he asked his friend.

"Yeah, why?"

"Someone has been hiding in the stalls and making the kids play 'Doctors' with him in the middle of the night when they get up to go to the bathroom. Joey just told me," Johnny said.

"Maybe it's a Boogey Man," Bobby laughed out loud.

"No! Seriously Bobby! Someone is out there! Every night!"

"Okay, so you want to go out and stab them?" Bobby asked.

"No. But maybe we should check it out tonight," Johnny suggested.

The boys both agreed that they would venture out in the middle of the night that evening and keep watch at the latrine. Around 2:00am, the two boys grabbed their pocket knife snuck out of Cabin Seven to the outside latrine. The latrine was dark and there were no lights on. They waited behind the bushes, as they watched one of the boys from another cabin, get up to go to the bathroom.

Several minutes passed, until they both heard some crying and some screaming coming from inside of the latrine. The two boys rushed into the latrine and turned the lights on. A man with a mask, wearing only a tee shirt and boxer shorts, ran out of the back entrance. A young boy, standing over the bathroom stall with his pants down, was crying profusely.

"What happened?" Bobby asked the boy.

"That man tried to shove something inside of me while I was peeing," the boy said while crying between breathes. Neither of the boys got a good look at the man when he quickly ran out of the latrine.

Johnny and Bobby walked the distraught little boy back to Cabin Five where he was staying, then snuck back to their beds and their cabin. The next morning, Johnny and Bobby mentioned something to Father Matt about seeing a 'boogey man' attacking a boy in the latrine the night before. Father Matt dismissed the incident, saying that it was probably one of the camp counselors playing a 'scary ghost game' with the boys from another cabin.

There were several more instances that occurred after that evening with different boys in their cabins, but Johnny and Bobby just dismissed it as part of their "ghost story" camp games. On the final evening of camp, Bobby had to get up to go to the bathroom. He got down from his bunk, and grabbed his pocket knife, just in case. It was about 2:00am. Bobby walked alone to the latrine, where the lights had been shut off and it was dark.

As he removed his pajamas and stood over the urinal, someone covered his mouth from behind. Before he could turn around, he felt someone pushing his head up against the tiled wall. Bobby, still grasping his pocket knife, thrust it into the leg of the attacker. There was a loud scream, and Bobby quickly pulled up his pajamas and ran back to his cabin. As he tried to wake up Dean to tell him of the incident, he noticed that Father Matt was not there in his bed. Grabbing a flash-light, Dean and Bobby ventured out back to the latrine to investigate. There wasn't any sign of anyone or anything, anywhere around the outdoor bathrooms or showers.

"Where is Father Matt?" Bobby demanded to know.

"Matt has trouble sleeping and is probably reading his book over at the mess hall," Dean replied.

They walked around the camp looking for the intruder but found no sign of him anywhere.

Bobby returned to his bunk by 4:00am but was too wound up and upset to fall back asleep.

That final morning, all the boys lined up to board the school bus, which was taking them back to Chicago. Father Matt was supervising the trip back home and was walking with a slight limp.

When one of the boys asked him about it, he mentioned that he had pulled a thigh muscle from all the camp activities the day before. All the campers filled the empty seats of the bus, and they began their journey back to the parking lot of Holy Family School, where all their parents were waiting.

As Father Matt was standing in the middle of the aisle of the school bus, playing different games with the other campers, Johnny noticed something on Father Matt's right pant leg, as he was wearing his long pants on an unusually hot, scorching summer day. He told Bobby about it, and they both looked at each other in horror.

Father Matt's right thigh was bleeding.

That following September of 1969, when the boys returned to Holy Family School to start the school year, everyone was surprised to learn that Father Matt had not returned to teach at their school. The only explanation given to the parents and children was that Father Matt had been transferred to teach at another Catholic grade school on the far south side of Chicago, where he was badly needed. It wasn't until over thirty years later, when all the rumors were confirmed that several boys at the CYO camp were attacked and sexually molested during that summer of 1969. A hand full of parents had complained to the Archdiocese of Chicago at the time about the inappropriate camp episodes, and after an internal investigation were told by the Archdiocese that the perpetrator of these "incidents" had been punished.

But no one at Holy Family School ever made mention of Father Matthew McDougall again.

CHAPTER TWENTY-THREE

A white, silver haired man in a newly acquired rental car sat in the parking lot of Rush Medical Hospital on West Harrison Street. It was a warm, wet Tuesday afternoon, and the severe morning thunderstorms had left large puddles of water scattered across the hospital parking lot. The man, wearing a black shirt and white collar, had been sitting in his Avis, blue Chevy Impala with stolen license plates for almost an hour, situating himself in his new, clergy uniform before entering the medical facility. He was carefully applying his makeup, putting on a 'skull cap' to cover his grey hair and to accompany his ornate disguise.

The imposter gazed at his rear-view mirror and complimented himself at how distinguished and authentic he looked on that day. He had purchased his new priest ensemble from the internet last week and was busy fine-tuning his white clergy collar and dusting off his black, short sleeve shirt. He put on his dark Ray-Ban sunglasses and hoped that his wearing them on a cloudy day wouldn't seem too obvious. Grabbing his dark raincoat from the back seat, he exited his car. The stranger was careful to make sure that the contents in his raincoat didn't fall out of his coat pocket, as he casually walked through the revolving front doors and towards the hospital information desk.

"I'm Monsignor Joseph Kilbane, and I'm here to visit Matthew McDougall. Could you give me his room number please?" he asked the nice old lady at the reception desk.

The volunteer senior receptionist was all too eager to assist the priest, who had approached her at the front desk. She immediately noticed how distinguished the older cleric looked, even though he was wearing his dark sunglasses on a cloudy, rainy Chicago day.

As he was signing the guest register, she immediately noticed a shiny, gold ring with a red cross that he was wearing on his right hand, and in her mind, automatically confirmed that he was a Man of God.

"Did the sun finally come out this afternoon, Father?" she asked the friendly looking pastor.

"Eh... yes, it will," he nervously said. "These are prescription sunglasses."

"I have that very same problem, Father. I always forget my glasses at home, and I often have to wear my prescription sunglasses," the old volunteer replied.

The 'Monsignor' quickly took off his sun glasses and anxiously, put on his wire rimmed eyewear that he was so famous for wearing.

"What parish are you with?" she eagerly asked, as he was adjusting his spectacles.

"Holy Name Cathedral," the distinguished priest quickly replied, growing impatient with all this idle chatter.

"Could you give me his room number please?" he eagerly asked her again.

"Oh yes...Room 821, Bed A," she politely replied. "Are you here to give him communion?"

"I'm here for his confession and last rites," he annoyingly replied, wondering why this old women was asking him all these rapid-fire questions.

The older receptionist began thinking to herself, how wonderful it was that an Archdiocesan parish priest would come from Holy Name Cathedral to the West Loop hospital for a dying Catholic's confession and last rites. He must have been called from the dying patient's family, she thought to herself, specifically requesting the presence of an Archdiocesan clergy.

Mr. Matthew McDougall was a dying patient, with late stage four lung cancer. He had been receiving experimental chemotherapy treatments and had been in the hospital for over two weeks. The former smoker's body was ridden with needles and chemicals, and most of the nurses within the hospital ward on the eighth floor did not expect him to live past the end of the week.

McDougall was weak and was in and out of consciousness, as the cancer ward nurses continued to monitor his lack of progress. His only nephew and living relative, Raymond McDougall, was told that the sickly man would remain on hospice and made comfortable for as long as possible. His uncle did not have long to live, he was told. But the nephew was not aware of the diocesan priest's surprise visit to his uncle's bedside.

Mr. McDougall was a 77-year old former priest, who was formerly employed as a high school English teacher at Roberto Clemente High School on North Western Avenue for almost twenty-five years. Mr. McDougall was very active with the young teenagers at the high school and was very involved in couching their junior and varsity baseball teams. He was a very well-liked popular teacher, who never had any 'formal' documented problems or reported issues with the Chicago Public School Board.

McDougall's background when he was hired as a teacher, was never thoroughly checked by the school board or the high school's principal back in 1985. Had Matt McDougall's background been properly investigated, the various child molestation accusations that he was accused of while an associate pastor at various Chicago parishes would have possibly, come to light. But Cardinal Bernardo, who was Cardinal Brody's successor after his death in 1983, pursued his CPS connections to ensure that the former Fr. McDougall's employment was all but guaranteed at the Chicago high school.

Cardinal Bernardo forced McDougall to resign from the priesthood back in 1985, and as part of his 'deal', would not be prosecuted or charged for any of his various pedophile crimes. His Eminence procured the former priest's public school employment, while assisting him in his resignation and signing all the necessary life insurance documents. McDougall, as part of this agreement, was forced into intense therapy, in order to reassure His Eminence and the Archdiocese of Chicago that McDougall was no longer a "threat" to young children.

When Matthew McDougall started teaching at the high school, he developed a strong friendship with a Mr. James Hennig, who had been the high school's principal for many, many years. Mr. Hennig was also a former seminarian and had a solid connection with Cardinal Bernardo and the Chicago Archdiocese at the time.

McDougall was clean and incident free for many years, until one young teenager discovered the varsity baseball coach one afternoon, masturbating in a custodian's utility closet in the boy's locker room while the other young boys were taking showers after practice. The incident was reported to the school's principal the next day, and although he denied it, was severely reprimanded by the principal in 1992. Because of their strong friendship, Hennig never reported the incident.

Tommy Griseta, one of the young baseball players on the varsity team who had recently been benched, accused McDougall in 1995 of forcing him to perform oral sex one evening after a night game in the coach's office. Again, the incident was investigated thoroughly by Mr. Hennig, the school's principal. Because of Tommy's repeated school suspensions for other matters, the student's integrity was questioned, and the accusation was discounted and dismissed. There had been other incidents of inappropriate behavior that was frequently noticed and reported by other students as well, including the groping of some young boys in the locker room after baseball practice. When McDougall finally retired in 2009, the rumors of his being a "pervert" were quite rampant within the local Chicago community. But thanks to his strong relationship with the principal during his years at the school, no definitive charges were ever filed with either the Chicago Police Department or the Chicago Public School Board.

There wasn't any doubt that McDougall was a closet homosexual and pedophile. He managed to hide his penchant for perverted, deviant sex with young boys well during his later years in retirement. Matthew McDougall lived alone, in a comfortable townhouse in Westchester. Except for a very large library of child pornography, which he kept in a locked safe in his basement, he lived a normal life.

He would often take vacations to South Korea, Hong Kong, Vietnam, and other exotic destinations to the Orient every summer. He would enlist the services of very young, inexpensive 'male guides' to support him and assist him in his travels. The very young teenagers would accompany McDougall in his sight-seeing adventures and attended to his other 'personal' needs while he traveled abroad.

"Monsignor Kilbane" took the elevator to the eighth floor of the hospital and walked past the nurse's station toward the designated patient's room. He hoped he would find McDougall there alone in his hospital room and without a roommate, as he was told this over the phone yesterday when he inquired with the hospital. He walked slowly down the hallway, noticing that there were no cameras or other security devices monitoring the safety of its patients. The only security was the ward nurse's station nearby. He also noticed that the hospital room was adjacent to the fire door, opening to the emergency stairwell leading to an exit out of the building.

As he entered Room 821, he noticed the older, balding man, sleeping and almost comatose. The old man had several tubes and IV bottles protruding from his body, and he was heavily sedated. The heart monitor machine was beeping quietly, as the graphs of his heart rate were being properly displayed on the green screen.

The priest found an empty chair next to the bed and took out his small bible and rosary. He wrapped the rosary beads around the old patient's hands, and then started reciting the Lord's Prayer. He continued praying as one of the floor nurses entered the room.

"Good Afternoon, Father," the young, blonde haired nurse said to the priest.

"Good Afternoon," he replied, still holding his left hand over the patient's arm while reciting his prayers. He was looking in the other direction when the nurse entered the room and tried to keep from making direct eye contact and displaying his face to the nurse.

"I'm here to give him his last rites," he continued to tell the young nurse, while he was looking down, reading his bible. The young nurse took the patient's vitals and his blood pressure from the harness already strapped to his right arm.

"Don't let me interrupt you, Father," she sweetly said. "Would you like me to close the curtains and the door?"

"Yes, please."

The young nurse finished charting the patient, then obeyed his request and closed the door to the dying old man's hospital room. She thought that it was unusual that the priest was looking towards the wall and wasn't making eye contact with the patient while praying and administering the patient's last rites. 'Monsignor Kilbane' continued to pray with the old man for several minutes, as he watched the patient breath.

"Fr. Matthew McDougall?" the priest quietly called out to the dying patient. "Do you know who I am?"

McDougall, barely responsive, looked over to the direction of the priest, trying to focus on who was calling him by his ordained name.

"Do you know who I am?" 'Kilbane' asked again.

The old, dying patient, opening his eyes, tried to focus on the priest. The patient only shook his head, trying desperately to move his lips.

"I am your death angel," the imposter replied.

The 'priest' then removed a small bottle of holy water from his coat pocket. 'Kilbane' pulled down the bed covers of the patient, then sprinkled the holy water on the old man while saying the executioner's ritual prayer from the secret society:

"Fr. McDougall," he started, "I pray to the Lord Jesus, that you may be forgiven for the many sins and abuses, torment and suffering, that you have caused God's children in your quest to fulfill your deviant transgressions. You have fallen victim to Satan's desires and demands, and you have caused an amount of great suffering to the many innocent children whom you have exploited against the Lord and his holy covenants. As a Catholic priest and a soldier of God, you have taken sacred vows and sworn to them in the Lord's name. We now offer your tainted soul to the Virgin Mary, that you may be cleansed in the Kingdom of Heaven. We beseech thee, oh Lord, that you may be forgiven and accepted again into the Paradise of our Almighty Father, in the name of the Rose Crucifix."

As was the sacred tradition of the Rose Crucifix, each victim of the secret society was blessed, when possible, with holy water, and then prayed over by their executioner. Each fatality, in order to be accepted by the Kingdom of Heaven at the time of their death, is then adorned with a long stemmed, red rose.

The red rose symbolizes the offering of that victim's soul to the Virgin Mary, to exonerate them and offer them back to the Kingdom of Heaven.

Each secret society execution can only be performed using a sharp knife, as no other murder weapon can be used when expiring the victim. The knife and cutting of the victim's torso symbolize Azrael, the Angel of Death, who gouges out the tainted souls of his victims before offering their bodies back to the Lord. This method is also in tradition with the secret society's ancient 15th century rituals, with its execution procedures following the medieval laws of the Society of the Rose Crucifix.

'Monsignor Kilbane' then took out a long-stemmed red rose, which he had wrapped in his raincoat, and placed it on McDougall's chest.

"May Jesus grant you mercy, Father McDougall."

'Monsignor Kilbane' then put on a pair of plastic gloves, which he had folded in his pants pocket. He then withdrew a long, sharp, butcher's knife from the pocket of his raincoat, and quickly, thrust the knife into McDougall's neck. Blood started to spring out everywhere like a fountain onto the patient's face, chest and onto his bed. He then, took a pillow and covered the ex-priest's face and mouth, as he began to loudly gag, fighting for air while he struggled to breath. He then inserted the knife several times into McDougall's abdomen, stabbing him across his torso many times, making sure that he didn't pierce his heart.

Blood was spurting out like a jet spring across his hospital bed, as the red fluid from his numerous knife wounds began forming a pool of blood onto the hospital floor. The killer was careful to make sure none of the blood had splattered onto his newly acquired clergy uniform. 'Monsignor Kilbane' then swiftly stood up from his chair, and immediately left the hospital room.

He quickly turned left down the hallway and rapidly entered the emergency stairwell, running down the eight floors of stairs without anyone questioning his hasty decent. As he removed his rubber gloves while approaching the exit door on the first floor, he noticed that it directly opened to the parking lot outside.

Without anyone noticing or questioning him, he casually put on his rain coat and hurriedly walked towards his Chevy Impala rental car in the parking lot.

But in all his haste while leaving the hospital room, the secret society's killer had made a critical mistake. 'Kilbane' nervously forgot to retrieve the serrated knife, which he inadvertently left inserted into McDougall's abdomen.

A few minutes went by before the heart monitor alarm went off, alerting the nurse's station of the sudden stoppage of McDougall's heart. As the blonde nurse entered the room, she gasped as she saw all the blood splattered everywhere across the old patient's body, walls and floor. The long knife was still inserted in the patient, with a red rose carefully placed on top of him.

She quickly alerted the nurse's station, and several nurses and doctors ran into McDougall's room. They were trying in vain to stop the bleeding, noticing the numerous, deep knife wounds which were dispersed across the patient's torso and around his neck. Several nurses began to ask for more assistance, as two more nurses were trying in vain to stop all the horrendous, excessive bleeding. After several minutes of frantic first aid and lifesaving efforts, the patient had bled to death, suffering from the massive bleeding from all his knife wounds. Another doctor looked at the clock and pronounced McDougall dead. The sharp knife, which was still inserted into the ex-priest's abdomen, was removed as a bloody sheet from the hospital bed was pulled across the former Fr. McDougall's ashen white face. It was exactly 3:33pm.

As the disguised Monsignor Kilbane started his rental car and exited the parking lot, he peered into his rear-view mirror, verifying that no one was following him.

The disguised priest smiled with pride, immediately removing his white collar. He then quickly removed his skull cap and used a moist cloth to take off his makeup at the adjacent Ashland Avenue traffic light.

'Brother Barabbas' was amused and began laughing to himself, knowing he had done the Lord's work.

All in the name of the Rose Crucifix.

CHAPTER TWENTY-FOUR

ANOTHER MURDER

My stomach was starting to gurgle with hunger pains, and I was contemplating whether I should run out and grab a sandwich on that late Tuesday afternoon. I was too busy to eat lunch earlier that day, and I looked at the wall clock in my office. It was almost 4:00pm...too late for lunch, and too early for dinner, I thought to myself. I had put on my suit jacket and was about to walk out of my office when my desk phone started ringing loudly.

"Detective Dorian," I answered, thinking that my next phone call should just be a freaky fast delivery from Jimmy John's.

"Phil? It's Tommy Morton...we've got another dead priest."

I suddenly felt my body go numb, and I could feel my heart pounding out of my chest. My mind was swirling with confusion, and I was beginning to wonder if this nightmare was ever going to end.

"What? Where? What happened?"

"Rush Hospital in the West Loop. Just got the call. The victim was a dying cancer patient. Somebody just walked into his room and stabbed the shit out of him."

"Huh? No nurses? No security? What the hell?" I loudly reacted.

I sat back down at my desk, as the reality of another pedophile priest murder on my watch was becoming too much for me to bear.

"When?" I asked him.

"About a half hour ago...same killer, same red rose," he blurted out.

205

"Oh shit," I said out loud, as a thousand different thoughts and questions started going through my head. There was a long silence on the phone as the two of us were speechless, trying to get our heads around how and why this could have happened.

"I'm running out to Rush right now and I'll meet you there. Expect a party," as he abruptly hung up the phone.

Maybe it was because I hadn't eaten that afternoon, as I wasn't sure why I was starting to feel so nauseous. I sat there at my desk and buried my head in my hands. My brain was beginning to pound. It was an insurmountable amount of pain that started with my temples and continued to worsen as each moment ticked by. It was an extreme nausea, and it felt like another one of my punishing migraine headaches. My skull was feeling like someone had taken a sledgehammer and began hitting both sides of my brain.

I grabbed a bottle of Advil in my desk drawer and walked over to the water cooler in the precinct kitchen on the other side of the office. I just stood there for a moment, waiting for the pain and the queasy feeling to subside. The stress of these 'Pedophile Priest Murders' and the strain of a serial killer on the loose was becoming totally unbearable. All this anxiety was beginning to take a physical toll on me, as I stood there for several moments, all alone in the precinct kitchen. I kept shaking my head in disbelief.

I did not want to go to this crime scene. With three homicides and three dead ex-priests in less than a month, I knew that all hell was going to break lose in Chicago. I could see it coming down the road. The pressure on the Chicago P.D. to solve these murders, the media publicity, and the anxiety of these homicides was going to turn my life into a living hell. The burden to solve these serial killings on the department will be the kind of pressure we haven't seen since the "Tylenol Murders" back in September 1982.

I felt defeated. I felt discouraged. I physically felt pain. I wanted to walk back into my office and lock the door, shut off the lights and pull the phone cord off the wall. I just wanted to hide. I wanted to sit at my desk, all alone in the dark, and pretend that none of this was happening.

Grabbing my car keys, I walked outside in the warm rain and into my Crown Vic police car. I put both my hands on the steering wheel and closed my eyes for a moment, taking a long, deep breath.

"*Dear God, please give me strength,*" I prayed to myself out loud, and then turned on the sirens.

The parking lot of the Rush Medical Hospital on West Harrison Street was filled with Chicago Police Cars, as I pulled up as close as I could to the front door. There were already several policemen talking and interviewing everyone in the lobby and within the reception area. I noticed a policeman with a notepad in his hand, speaking with an older lady on the couch near the window, while several other detectives were speaking with other hospital staff. It was a though the whole hospital had broken loose and was on high alert and seemed like every single copper in Chicago was at the scene of the crime.

Tommy Morton saw me walking through the revolving door and greeted me.

"This isn't good, Philly," he immediately said.

"What's going on? What do we have here?" I immediately started rifling off some questions to Tommy, questions that I knew I wasn't going to like the answers to.

"We've got a dead stabbing victim up on the eighth floor. His name is Matthew McDougall, a 77-year-old Chicago ex-priest from Westchester. He was a dying lung cancer patient. The head nurse up in the cancer ward said the old man only had days to live," Tommy reported.

"A dying cancer patient, with only days to live, gets stabbed and fileted in broad daylight up in the eighth floor in the cancer ward? This just doesn't make any sense."

I was immediately confused, trying to get my head around this whole murder scene, with all its cops and investigators walking around.

"Seems like this killer is getting ballsy. Someone dressed as a priest, registered at the front desk as 'Monsignor Joseph Kilbane.' The receptionist at the information desk got a good look at him," as Tommy started looking at his notes.

"About 5 feet, ten inches tall, heavier build, older, middle aged man, bald with wire rimmed glasses. She says he was very friendly," Morton recapped.

"Monsignor Kilbane? Are you kidding?" I said out loud.

"Is the wicked Monsignor brazen enough to show up at a hospital and kill a pedophile priest in broad daylight now?" I asked Tommy.

"I don't know," he replied. "It doesn't add up."

"The killer was pretty sloppy too. He left his knife next to the red rose, still inserted in the victim."

"We have a knife this time?" I asked out loud. "Sounds like the killer is getting more generous with the evidence."

"Any witnesses?" I asked.

"A few nurses noticed the Monsignor, who first entered the hospital wearing dark sunglasses, and then was walking around the eighth ward holding a rain coat over his left arm. Another one of the nurses observed the priest praying and administering the patient's late rites before closing door in his room. She thought it was unusual that the priest didn't seem focused while praying over the patient. Several minutes later, the heart monitor went off and she saw the patient, mutilated and blood was everywhere. She's pretty shaken up right now," Tommy said.

I looked around, and recognized several investigators from several other districts, interviewing and talking amongst themselves. I noticed a few FBI agents walking around as well.

"Who else is on this case?" I stupidly asked.

"Everybody, Phil. It looks like this isn't just your case anymore."

I looked around and immediately noticed my buddy, Detective Paul Russo, talking to a few FBI agents and another Chicago policeman when he made eye contact with me. He only nodded his head at me for a moment, and then after a few minutes, excused himself from the other agents that he was conversing with. He then motioned Commander Callahan, and they both walked over towards my direction.

"We need your homicide files," Russo immediately said in a cold, heartless voice.

I immediately looked at the Commander, who was suspiciously glaring at me as though I were the killer. By the expression on his face, I immediately knew what his next directive was going to be.

"Turn over all of your files on these 'Pedophile Priest Murders' to Intelligence. You're done."

I looked him, shocked and confused.

"What?"

"You heard me. You're off this case," the Commander repeated, while Russo was giving me that condescending smirk of his.

"Sir, why are you pulling me off? I'm starting to make some progress and I'm...," I tried to plead, knowing it would get me nowhere.

"Seriously?" Paul Russo interrupted, "You haven't done shit, Dorian. You haven't gotten anywhere on this case," he interjected, knowing that my 'traitor boss' would back him up.

"We've got a serial killer running around Chicago, killing and stabbing ex-priests, while you're sleeping at your desk and eating goddamn sandwiches," the Commander fired off at me in a loud, callous voice.

Commander Callahan had probably just gotten his ass chewed out by the Superintendent, and I was trying very hard not to take his comments personally. I could tell that Callahan, along with the rest of the 'Top-Brass', were already taking heat from the 'Ivory Tower' to solve these murders and to get this serial killer off the streets. I expected him to lay into me for this murder as well, not that it was my fault. But because of all the heat and pressure that everyone in the Chicago

Police Department was now feeling, every person was going to be on edge. For whatever reason, the Superintendent wanted their 'Star Detectives' working on this case, which meant Russo and his 'Intel Boys' at the Twenty-First.

"The Mayor is pissed, and he wants this psycho killer off the goddamn streets," Russo exclaimed.

"Our Intel Unit has a good rapport with the Feds, and they'll work better with our boys on this serial killer investigation," Russo interjected.

I shook my head, without saying another word. I simply acknowledged Commander Callahan and Russo, and walked away, alone towards the revolving door. Detective Morton made eye contact with me, as if to say, "I'll catch you later", then walked over to the other side of the hospital lobby to talk with another one of the detectives.

At that moment, it felt as though a '500-pound gorilla' had been lifted off my shoulders. There was a part of me that just wanted to run out of that hospital, drive over to the nearest watering hole and celebrate. These 'Pedophile Priest Murders' were no longer my problem.

But then I stopped myself for a second and just stood there, looking at all the yellow crime scene tape across the hospital lobby and all the activity going on from everyone at the Chicago P.D.

I'm a policeman, I'm a detective, and I'm a damned good one. I said to myself.

Why should I let these arrogant bastards push me off this investigation? I just couldn't walk away from all of this. Not now, not yet...not without a fight. I just wasn't wired that way. I felt obligated to see these murder investigations through, one way or the other.

I then noticed several more police cars pulling into the hospital parking lot along with a black, unmarked SUV with blue sirens on. Within minutes, Mayor Ron Leibowitz exited the vehicle, along with several of his security body guards and some of the Chicago 'Top Brass'. He walked right past me through the revolving doors, along with Superintendent Ryan, and was approached by several other commanders and sergeants who began informing the Mayor regarding the status of this investigation.

I could hear the Mayor talking loudly, almost screaming, to the Superintendent;

"Why hasn't this bastard been taken off the streets?" I overheard him say.

At that point, I decided to make a gutsy decision, and it was probably the riskiest judgement call I had ever made in my career.

I walked over to the Superintendent and the Mayor and introduced myself.

"Good Afternoon, Mr. Mayor, I'm Detective Dorian," as he graciously shook my hand, while Superintendent Ryan stood there, surprised by my direct, forceful approach.

"I'm the head detective working on these "Pedophile Priest Murders," I began to say, as the Mayor gave me that welcoming look in his eyes that I've often seen on televised newscasts.

"Really?" he exclaimed, "Let's talk."

The three of us walked over to one of the couches near the farthest part of the hospital lobby, and I began to brief the Mayor and the Superintendent regarding everything I had discovered regarding these murders. I explained all the facts in this case, and expressed my thoughts and suspicions concerning the Archdiocese of Chicago, mob-boss Little Tony DiMatteo, the life insurance claims and of course, Monsignor Kilbane. We sat there and talked together for over thirty minutes, as I noticed Russo and Commander Callahan, giving me dirty looks the whole time from the other side of the lobby.

"So where do we go from here, Detective," the Mayor eagerly asked.

"We're cross checking all of the ex-priests within the Chicagoland area for the last fifty years, and we're close to getting some DNA crime scene results from the last murder scene. Seeing that this serial killer got sloppy today, there should be plenty of incriminating evidence here at the hospital," I answered.

211

"I'm sure we can lift some prints, some DNA and other proof from the crime scene upstairs," I continued, trying my best to enlighten the Mayor. I observed Commander Callahan from the corner of my eye, coldly glaring at me from a distance. He looked as though he was ready to make me another murder victim.

"We have witnesses now, which didn't have at the other crime scenes," I described. "We probably have him on some security cameras here as well. I'm sure we can get a description on the killer and ID him," I boldly predicted.

The Mayor looked at the Superintendent, and then Ryan called over Commander Callahan.

"Commander," Superintendent Ryan began, "Keep Detective Dorian on, and have him work with the Intel Unit on this case. We need all the heads we can get."

Commander Callahan looked shocked, as he locked his eyes into mine for several seconds.

"But I thought you wanted the Intel Unit to...."

"I know what I said, Commander. We need Dorian here to stay involved with Intel," the Superintendent replied.

The Mayor then looked sternly at the Commander, letting him verbally know that he wasn't interested in playing 'Copper Politics' with either him or anyone else within the department.

"I want this serial killer off the streets, before every Chicago Catholic Church goes into panic mode," said the Mayor.

"We don't need this right now. We've got our hands full with all these gang-bangers and drug dealers killing each other on the South Side. We don't need this in our city," Leibowitz continued, looking at all of the policemen and detectives that were standing nearby looking at us. The Mayor then looked at me, dead square in the eyes:

"Catch this bastard."

CHAPTER TWENTY- FIVE

The frigid March winds were cold and blistery one evening that previous spring, as each of the brothers of this sacred order were assembling for their monthly meeting. The Knights of the Society of the Rose Crucifix always assembled on the Third Thursday of each month, and there were important issues on the agenda that needed discussion at this monthly assembly.

Each brother knight, secretly and discretely, entered the abandoned brownstone church on West Division Street, following their normal procedure. As was their entry ritual, each brother had a designated time to enter the old church building for the sake of secrecy. Each knight had his own key to enter the door, then walked into the vestibule to adorn their red, pointed masks without disclosing their real identities. As was their tradition of attendance, every brother knight adorned their formal black tuxedos, red hooded masks and their gold, red cross rings.

At exactly 6:00pm on that gusty spring evening, Brother Jeramiah was the first designated knight to enter building. He unlocked the door with his special key, adorned his mask, and was the first to sit at the long wooden table located in the middle of the old, stained glass church. At 6:15pm, Brother Aaron entered the abandoned brownstone structure, using his special, designated entry key. At 6:30pm, Brother Barabbas arrived in his Cadillac SUV, parked it along Ashland Avenue, and then entered the sacred hall. Each brother knight was given an assigned time to enter the building and adorn his mask, so that the secrecy of each brother knight's identity was specially protected and kept

213

sacred. By 8:00pm, Brother Ezekiel, the Grand Knight, was the last to arrive.

The meeting came to order at 8:07pm, with the Grand Knight Ezekiel leading the assembly with the Pledge of Allegiance and an opening prayer.
Afterwards, he called his fellow brothers to the agenda at hand.

"Brother Knights, as you are aware, we have a new brother to welcome into our spiritual, holy order, Brother Barabbas," he proclaimed. All the knights then stood up and applauded their new member, as Barabbas stood silently to the ovation.

The prior month's minutes and old business was discussed and settled, then the Grand Knight directed the meeting:

"With a new member in our order, our great fraternity of twelve is now complete, and we may now do the Lord's work in upholding His sacred sacraments. It is our duty, to advocate the sacred decrees of our Holy Father and to prosecute those individuals who have broken these blessed commandments. Do have we any new business to bring forth before this sacred society?"

There were several minutes of silence, until Brother Tobiah requested the attention of his fraternal brothers.

"My brothers, we have a situation which I believe merit's the attention of this society. May I address the table of twelve, oh worthy Grand Knight?" Tobiah requested in a deep raspy voice.

"Permission granted," he replied.

"As you all may recall, I have brought to the attention of this holy brotherhood the dilemma of a former priest, Father John Marquardt. As previously mentioned, I have discussed his great and many abuses and sins of his past to all of you in prior meetings. You have all recommended that, instead of taking direct action that we as a holy society dutifully pray over his tainted soul. I do believe that now is the time to take such a special action, because of the current circumstances which are now before us," he continued.

"What current circumstances are those, Brother Tobiah?" asked the Grand Knight.

"It has come to my attention, from a very reliable source, that the Archdiocese of Chicago is interested in eradicating some of its former pedophile priests for the life insurance money," Tobiah exclaimed.

All the brothers looked at each other, not understanding the full context of Brother Tobiah's statement. There was a long silence at the table, as if all the brother knights were speechless.

"Specifically, the Administrative Chief of Staff to the Cardinal, Monsignor Joseph Kilbane, is in need of, shall we call him, a 'hired hit man'," he continued.

"The Archdiocese is looking for a 'hired assassin'?" asked Brother Zebedee.

"Yes, Brother Zebedee. Apparently, the Archdiocese is cash poor and looking to 'cash out' on the life insurance policies that were taken years ago on the lives of these former pedophile priests."

Everyone at the long, mahogany table turned their masked heads to each other in amazement, all of them struggling to understand the total 'breadth' of his statement.

"Continue on, Brother Tobiah," demanded the Grand Knight. Brother Ezekiel had immediately recognized the deep, raspy voice behind the red hood.

"Monsignor Kilbane has approached 'someone of great power' within the underworld to assist him in acquiring and securing a 'contract for hire' on these defrocked priests. Apparently, the cash position of the Archdiocese has become so bad that they are now considering selling off and liquidating churches and other valuable real estate at discounted prices to fulfill the civil and legal settlements of these pedophile lawsuits that have been brought against the Archdiocese of Chicago."

More silence at the table of twelve knights, as the Grand Knight asked for more discussion of this matter.

"What are you suggesting, Brother Tobiah?" asked Brother Adam, not quite understanding what his fellow knight was suggesting.

Tobiah, without hesitating, finally put it out there:

"What better way to eradicate these sick monsters, these violators of their sacred vows, than to abolish them and take them out, and to create blame on the Archdiocese of Chicago? To frame and put the culpability squarely on the front door of the Cardinal himself?" he explained in his usual deep, raspy voice.

Everyone looked at one another again, wondering how this murderous scheme would work and how it would benefit their sacred society.

"You are suggesting that we, as the knights of this sacred society, become the 'hit men' for the Archdiocese?" inquired Brother Abel.

"Exactly."

There was more stillness at the table for several long minutes, until Brother Jeremiah broke this silence.

"Why should we enrich the Archdiocese of Chicago, and assist them in collecting the life insurance proceeds of these defrocked and disgraced former priests? We all have a great distain for the Archdiocese, and the methods by which they allowed these deviant sexual predators to continue their ministries. Why should we help them?" he protested.

"We are not helping them," Tobiah answered. "We are burying them."

"How so?" asked Brother Adam.

"The Chicago P.D. will investigate these 'redemptions', and when the word gets out that Kilbane was scheming a "death-for-hire" plot on these ex-pedophile priests, he and the Archdiocese will become the primary suspects in these homicides," Tobiah gleefully plotted.

The Grand Knight was unusually silent throughout this dialog. It was the practice of the brother knights of the Society of the Rose Crucifix to never use the word 'murder' before its other members. Because the victims' tainted souls were being saved from the depths of purgatory, the word 'redemption' is often used and interchanged.

"How much are these life insurance policies?" asked Brother Jacob.

"Each policy is between one to five million dollars, whatever Cardinals Brody and Bernardo were able to secure on these ex-priests at the time of their resignation," Tobiah answered.

As members of the Society of the Rose Crucifix, the brother knights had been plotting and planning a means to begin the elimination and demise of these pedophile ex-priests for a very long time. They have prayed together and looked for guidance in their manifest, to right the moral wrongs which these former clerics have inflicted on God's children for so many, many years.

This situation was now a golden opportunity, suggested Brother Tobiah, to begin the eradication of all those who had ever preyed and sexually abused any of the Lord's beloved little children. As brothers of this 'holy' secret society, this circumstance allowed them to consider taking out several ex-priests and quite possibly, framing the Archdiocese of Chicago in the process. If the "secret society" could pull it off, all the brothers thought, it would be a brilliant scheme.

"Whom will we choose as our first candidate?" asked Brother Adam.

"I wish to put forth the name of the former Father John Marquardt. He personally abused myself and many of my friends as a child within our community," Brother Tobiah immediately put forth to the table of red-hooded members.

The Grand Knight immediately interceded.

"Brother Tobiah, as you know, it is a majority vote of this Society that decides the fate of these tainted servants of the Lord. You must put forth a motion before this membership."

After several minutes of silence around the long, mahogany table of red hooded brothers, a motion was put forth.

"My fellow brothers," Brother Tobiah began, "I make a motion to save and redeem the tainted soul of the former Father John Marquardt."

It was the accepted terminology of the Society of the Rose Crucifix to use the exact words of "save and redeem their tainted souls" rather than the words of "destroy and murder" its victims.

The Grand Knight then looked around the table.

"Is there a second on this motion?"

Brother Cain, who was more than familiar with Fr. Marquardt, immediately seconded the motion before the table. The Grand Knight then continued to request a vote on the motion before the fraternal table of brother knights.

"All those in favor of the salvation and redemption of the soul of the former Father John Marquardt, please affirm or deny the motion before this table when your name is called," he requested.

"Brother Able?" the Grand Knight began.

"Aye," he answered

"Brother Jedidiah,"

"Aye."

"Brother Reuben"

"Aye," the hooded brother replied.

The Grand Knight went around the whole table of twelve seated brother knights, requesting each to affirm or deny the action put forth before the board. Each brother's assumed name was recited, and each Knight of the Rose Crucifix affirmed the motion. It was unanimous.

The Grand Knight then requested one of the brother knights at the table to volunteer his services in assisting in their victim's salvation. Brother Ezekiel was more than excited to solicit a volunteer for this duty. After a few long minutes, one of the brothers responded.

"May I, oh worthy Grand Knight, be the deliverer of the tainted soul of this broken servant of God, Father John Marquardt. May I be the deliverer and the executioner of his emaciated heart, to our Almighty Father, and bestow the red rose of our great society, the name of our Blessed Virgin Mother," immediately volunteered Brother Cain, reading from the formal book of the secret society's scriptures.

Called the Executioner's Acceptance, this scripted verse has been handed down through the centuries to the brother knights of the Society of the Rose Crucifix. This is a formal vow, recited by the accepting brother, or executioner, to carry out the secret society's manifest upon those whom the knights of this secret society wish to 'redeem' or bring to 'salvation'.

"We accept your commitment, Brother Cain, to deliver the red rose of Our Blessed Mother and send the tainted soul of Fr. John Marquardt, to the Kingdom of Heaven, oh great Brother Cain," replied the Grand Knight.

The table of hooded brothers then began to applaud, knowing that the successful carrying of this 'motion of salvation' and intercession was in the capable hands of their respected Brother Cain.

"You shall carry out this motion in this upcoming month of our Blessed Virgin Mary, or the month of May," ordered the Grand Knight.

As he pounded his wooden gavel on the table to proclaim this final motion of redemption, the brother knights all then applauded again, offering their support to their respected Brother Cain. After several minutes of conversations between themselves, another suggestion was put forth before the table.

"My Brother Knights," began Brother Barabbas. "How will we designate our next candidates to be chosen for 'salvation', and when will these act of 'redemption' be carried out? We have a limited window of time before we can choose and continue these sacred orders."

"Brother Barabbas, "as Brother Ebenezer began, "you are not familiar with the means and methods of whom we choose for redemption. We, as a Society of the Rose Crucifix, select the order and candidates in accordance to the names of our great servants of the Bible, and the times in which we can carry out these sacred 'redemptions'," he explained.

"We will meet again very soon to choose our next redemption candidate," proclaimed Grand Knight Ezekiel, hinting that another pedophile ex-priest would be chosen sooner rather than later.

There was no other business to discuss before the board of brother knights at that time, and the motion to adjourn was accepted. With that, Brother Abel supervised the exit of each hooded brother, as they all departed the old, brownstone church, one by one.

Brother Cain exited the antiquated building and walked over to his parked car on Ashland Avenue. He was both excited and elated to be chosen to execute the 'reclamation' of the former Father Marquardt's tainted soul within the next two months. He knew, with his extensive police background, that he was more than qualified to carry out his 'society' orders and not have the Chicago Police Department immediately suspect him in this potential homicide. He was more than capable to 'execute his orders' professionally and will begin planning his secret society mandate within the next two months.

He was doing this for many reasons, he thought to himself. For all the abused victims of those demented servants of God, for all those children that had been victimized so many years ago.

For all the young boys whose innocent souls this sexual deviant had stolen away, for all those children that were sexually molested for so many years...he was carrying out his orders for them.

But most of all, 'Brother Cain' was doing this for one very important reason:

To avenge the memory of his best friend.

CHAPTER TWENTY-SIX

The lights of all the magnificent skyscrapers of Chicago brightly flickered and illuminated the sky, an inviting backdrop for all the city stargazers to look up and enjoy the show. My shoes had gotten thoroughly soaked from walking through all the rain puddles of the hospital parking lot, as I was exiting Rush Medical Hospital that evening.

It was late...almost eleven o'clock, and we had spent several hours going through the crime scene at the hospital up on the eighth floor. Both myself and Detective Tommy Morton had interviewed most of the nurses, doctors and staff that been working in the cancer unit of that ward. We were able to secure copies of the security cameras that had captured the images of Monsignor Kilbane walking through the hospital lobby and into the elevator going to the eighth floor that afternoon. We were also able to obtain a significant amount of evidence from the crime scene, as our CSI unit had acquired the killer's murder weapon and of course, the long-stemmed red rose. I was hoping there would be some DNA evidence that we could possibly, make a definite match to the murderer and the hospital victim. Morton was working with the IT guys downstairs, and they were all going over the security camera footage posted in the hospital parking lot. They were running a check on some of the license plate numbers that had entered and exited the hospital at the time of the murder.

All of this seemed to implicate Monsignor Joseph Kilbane as the alleged murderer and killer, the only person that I had suspected all along. He was on one of the security cameras, exiting the parking lot in a blue, late model Chevy Impala with an Illinois license plate number "V46-1038" traced back to a vehicle registered to the Archdiocese of Chicago. We now had more than enough evidence to arrest Monsignor Kilbane and charge him with the murder of Matthew McDougall. We had sent a squad car over to his Lincoln Park townhome to pick him up earlier that evening, and he was probably locked up at the Twenty-Fifth District over on Grand Avenue until his arraignment in the morning.

It was as though Kilbane, the second most powerful cleric in Chicago, had been gift wrapped and delivered to the Chicago Police Department, covered with blue ribbons and a pretty little bow. He had conveniently fallen right into our laps as the murder suspect. All we had to do was arrest him, finger print him, take his 'formal portrait' and lock him up on a first-degree murder charge.

But my detective instincts were over reacting that evening. This was all too perfect...and far too easy. Something just didn't feel right with all of this.

I noticed Tommy Morton was still outside, standing next to his cop car parked diagonally in a handicapped parking space and having a cigarette.

"I thought you quit," I exclaimed as began walking towards him. I remembered Tommy being a three-pack-a-day cigarette smoker and was very excited for him when he announced to everyone that he had quit smoking several years ago.

"These pedophile priest murders have pushed me back to the whiskey and cigarettes," he said disappointedly, taking a final drag from his Marlboro Light, then flicking it onto the wet, asphalt pavement. "Now, I'm goddamn chain smoking again."

I was standing right in front of the Seventeenth District detective and just glared at him, as he was exhaling the cigarette smoke from his nostrils. Morton looked at me intently, and he could see there was something on my mind.

"What's up, Philly?"

"I don't know, Tommy. I just don't know," I replied, shaking my head several times and wishing that I had taken up smoking.

"Are you thinking what I'm thinking?" Tommy casually mentioned.

I looked at him again and nodded my head. Detective Morton and I had worked together on several homicide cases over the years, and we always had a good working relationship. He was an easy-going but very detailed, street-smart detective. Tommy always seemed to have my back on any case that we had ever worked together. We had a mutual respect, and we seemed to work, almost in tandem, as he was able to pick up the pieces of any case where I had left off. Unlike a lot of detectives in the Chicago P.D., Morton didn't let his ego, or his ambition get in the way to doing his job.

"How did this serial murder case suddenly get so easy?" I asked him, point blank.

"I've been racking my head for almost a month, trying to get a decent break in these Pedophile Priest Murders. I could not even get a decent DNA reading on a cigarette butt that we had recovered at the last crime scene...you know, that Senopoli murder case. Now we have another 'pedophile priest murder', which was committed in the middle of the day, complete with eye-witness descriptions and full action videos."

"Maybe I'm tired and just over-reacting," I continued ranting. "But I don't understand how these serial murders suddenly became this easy."

"I get it, Phil. I was thinking the same thing. I'm confused as to why Kilbane would so brazenly show up at a hospital in the middle of the day and stab his victim in a hospital cancer ward, knowing that he was in full view of all the hospital security cameras? Why would he kill a cancer patient that probably only had days' to live? He's either very ballsy, or maybe, just fucking stupid," Tommy said, as he started fidgeting with his lighter, wondering whether he should light up another cigarette.

"Stupid?" I replied. "That isn't a word I would ever use to describe Kilbane."

I stood there for a few seconds, almost embarrassed to say to next thought that was going through my head.

"Maybe," I said out loud, "it really *wasn't* him."

Detective Morton just glared at me, furrowing his eyebrows. He was probably thinking that I wasn't lucid, and I should probably be wearing an asylum straight jacket and locked up at the Loyola Mental Ward. He then started shaking his head, deciding to have that other cigarette after all, and lit it up. He took a deep, long drag, allowing the smoke to slowly exhale from his nostrils as he was pondering my last statement.

"Now I know you're losing it, Phil. How could it *not* be Kilbane? We have eye witnesses and camera video shots."

"Kilbane is not this stupid. And I don't think he's this bold. Nobody goes into a public hospital and commits a murder in plain sight in the middle of the day unless they wanted to get caught. That doesn't sound like anyone at the Chicago Archdiocese or, Monsignor Kilbane. My sixth sense in jumping out of my head right now, and something is telling me that the priest in those security videos isn't Kilbane."

"Wanna know what I think?" as he finished his half-smoked cigarette and flicked onto the parking lot.

"I think Kilbane has a death wish and is ready to take one for the team. He's figuring that maybe, he'll do life at Menard and regularly 'touch his toes' as the prison chaplain for the next thirty or so years. Maybe for him, doing time might be a better option...you know, with all the stress and pressure he's feeling at the Archdiocese," Tommy speculated.

"You're referring to all these abused child victim lawsuits going on?" I verified.

"Yeah, maybe this is Kilbane's way of checking out."

I thought about it for a moment, but I just couldn't picture the Monsignor trading in his opulent office digs at the Archdiocese, his lavish Lincoln Park townhouse, and all his power and prestige, for a 6 x 8 'luxury hotel suite' at the Menard Correctional Center.

"That doesn't sound like Kilbane. He's a hard-nosed, old-school, son-of-a-bitch from Bridgeport. His balls are made of steel, and I can't see him taking a hit for anyone, least of all the Cardinal."

"I don't understand you, Phil. Why are you having doubts? You've got him on all the security cameras. Everyone at the hospital has I-D'd him, and the vehicle plates register to the Archdiocese. A collar is a collar, man. Don't question it!"

"Like I said, this is all too easy."

We both stood there, alone and late at night in the brightly lit parking lot of Rush Medical Hospital. We were both silent for several long minutes, second guessing ourselves, wondering whether this murder was all a set-up.

I suddenly noticed a television news camera truck leaving the other side of the parking lot. It was a WDRV-8 news van, and it looked like it was about to exit onto Ashland Avenue. It abruptly stopped at the exit. The reverse lights went on and suddenly, the white van started backing up and sped over towards our direction.

"Don't look now, Philly, but your buddy is coming over here."

"Wonderful," I sarcastically said out loud.

The white news truck with the "WDRV Channel 8" logo pulled up alongside Tommy's squad car, and my favorite news reporter jumped out of the passenger side, wearing that usual shit-smile of his.

"Isn't it past your bedtime?" I asked Chaz Rizzo and he casually approached us. He was wearing a beige London Fog rain coat, covering his custom designed, black pin-striped Hugo Boss suit.

"I was about to ask you guys the same thing. This is time and a half for you guys, right?"

Tommy was noticeably tired, and I could tell he wasn't in the mood to answer a thousand questions from the media or least of all, Chaz Rizzo.

"Lieutenant Columbo called. He wants his raincoat back," Tommy wryly said, trying to tell Rizzo, in a very nice way, to get lost. Detective Morton had several run-ins with Rizzo on other homicide investigations, and often made his feelings very clear that he had no use for him. After all the stresses and dealings with the "Ivory Tower", Superintendent Ryan and the Mayor that day, I was worn out too. I was not in the mood for one of Rizzo's bantering 'cat-and-mouse' conversations.

"Why are you still here?" I asked him.

"We were doing a live feed for the Ten O'clock broadcast, and we just wrapped everything up," Rizzo replied, as he asked Tommy for a light while putting a cigarette in his mouth.

"You gotta' be happy, Riz. All of this serial killer crap is keeping you guys gainfully employed, right?" I said, trying very hard to be nice to my 'sometimes-friend-sometimes asshole' news reporter.

Rizzo just lit up his cigarette and took a long deep drag, blowing smoke circles off into the warm, moon struck night. It had been raining on and off all day, and the thick, muggy dampness of the air made the summer twilight that evening almost unbearable.

"Did you guys go over and pick up Kilbane yet?"

"We sent a squad car over to Lincoln Park to pick him up this afternoon," I slowly replied, wondering why the hell I was even answering any of his questions.

Rizzo just kept sucking on his cigarette, as the engine of the news truck was still idling. I was hoping that his camera man, who was also his driver, would just pull Rizzo back inside and leave. But Chaz kept standing there...silent, just smoking his cigarette. He kept staring off at all the bustling cars and traffic driving along Ashland Avenue.

Something just wasn't right with Rizzo. I could tell something was on his mind. Maybe, with all the bantering that he and I had done over the years, I was starting to get into the head of my favorite nemesis.

"What's on your mind, Chaz?" I was starting to sound like we were friends.

He just quietly looked at me. It was as though he had mental telepathy, and his eyes attentively locked into mine.

"This just isn't adding up, guys," he replied.

Somehow, I knew he was thinking the same thing that I was.

"How so?" Tommy asked.

He looked at Detective Morton point blank, probably thinking he wasn't the sharpest pencil in the box.

"I've got a stack of Benny's that says Kilbane didn't do this. He's way too smart to just show up at a hospital ward in the middle of the day and start stabbing somebody. It doesn't make any sense."

"Maybe the Archdiocese is getting hard up for the insurance money...maybe they're getting desperate," Tommy suggested.

"Desperate enough to do this? Why didn't he just drop off his driver's license at the front desk before going upstairs and stabbing the shit out of that old priest? Why stab a terminal cancer patient with only days to live?" Rizzo asked.

"Do you guys really think he's that stupid? Or that desperate? It just doesn't make any sense to me."

"Phil was just saying the same thing." Tommy just looked at me directly, now realizing that I wasn't the only one losing my mind.

"But you've been leaning hard on Kilbane since the very beginning, Phil. You should be happy now that we can "collar" him on this murder and maybe, the other two murders as well," Morton said.

I only shook my head in silence, watching Chaz Rizzo maneuver his cigarette as though it were a Cuban cigar.

"Don't get me wrong guys," I slowly replied. "I have no love whatsoever for Monsignor Kilbane. If he did this, he belongs in the deepest, darkest halls of Hell, just for the way he cut up and filleted those victims. But I'm not interested in locking up the wrong guy for a crime he didn't commit."

"Hey guys, we've got a collar now," exclaimed Tommy. "We've got a solved murder and maybe, we just took the 'Pedophile Priest Murderer' off the streets. Kilbane is obviously a 'whack-job' with anger issues against pedophiles. I say let's go over to O'Callaghan's on Hubbard Street and celebrate," he proclaimed.

I could tell that Tommy Morton had about as much energy as I did. After a hard day's work of interviewing hospital personnel and investigating these recent homicides, I knew he was full of shit. Tommy probably didn't have the stamina to hold up a beer bottle, let alone go off drinking and partying at some 'gin mill' on a week night.

"You guys go ahead," I told Tommy and Rizzo, knowing full well that Detective Morton would never be caught dead sitting at the same bar with Channel Eight's most famous news reporter.

"I'm exhausted. I'll meet you at the Twenty-Fifth in the morning, Tom," I said, knowing that we would have Monsignor Kilbane all to ourselves tomorrow in lock-up.

"I'm right behind you, Phil...good night." Detective Morton jumped in his squad car and beat me to the parking lot exit.

I casually walked a few feet away towards my Crown Victoria, got in and started the ignition. I waved to Rizzo, who was still standing outside of his news truck, finishing his cigarette. He nodded and locked his eyes again with mine, still displaying that worried look on his face. He seemed to be in a trance.

We both knew that the "Pedophile Priest Murderer" was still out there on the streets.

CHAPTER TWENTY-SEVEN

The early daybreak traffic was heavy that morning, as I was making a turn on Grand Avenue over to the Twenty-Fifth Police District. I had just acquired my Dunkin' Donuts large coffee, cream and sugar at the drive thru, with my usual toasted sesame seed bagel, extra cream cheese. I was maneuvering my police squad car with 'three hands', using two of them to keep my coffee from spilling onto my lap while negotiating a left-hand turn onto the precinct parking lot. I had switched over lately to Dunkin' Donuts from Starbucks for my early morning routine, realizing that I couldn't afford it anymore on my meager detective's salary. Since numbers weren't my strong suit, it took me several years to figure out that I could buy a half dozen jelly donuts for the same price as one Starbucks venti, extra wet, low fat cappuccino with a double of shot of caramel macchiato.

I walked into the Twenty-Fifth District and was greeted by Desk Sergeant Donald Ettinger, who was expecting both myself and Detective Morton that morning to interview and interrogate Monsignor Joseph Kilbane. He was picked up last night at his Lincoln Park luxury townhouse and had spent the night in lockup until his plea hearing later that morning. I was fully expecting him to have his attorney on hand when we arrived.

"Hey Philly," I could hear Tommy Morton walking in behind me as I was checking in with the front desk. I put the bagel in my mouth while I was shaking Tommy's hand, and temporarily maneuvered my breakfast onto the desk sergeant's front desk.

"Dunkin' Donuts and bagels, I see, huh' Philly," I was totally expecting him to make one of his 'when are you gonna join Weight Watchers' comments as he was walking through the front precinct door.

"You otta' switch to coffee and cigarettes... breakfast of champions, you know," he said, flicking his cigarette butt out the front door.

"Yeah, right Tommy."

"Where's our boy?" he eagerly asked.

"Still in lock up, I'm sure. We won't be able to talk to him until his 'Prince of Darkness' attorney shows up, and I'll bet he's still not here."

We had an eight o'clock appointment with the desk sergeant and Kilbane's attorney along with his client, and I fully expected the upscale, Monadnock Building, criminal attorney to be late for our early morning interview.

"Kilbane and his attorney are in the interview room, waiting for you two," Sergeant Ettinger announced to my surprise.

"His attorney is here already? I'm shocked," as I smiled, still trying to finish my sesame seed bagel.

"At $650 dollars an hour, I'm sure the Archdiocese expects him to be here on time, especially if their Chief of Staff is doing a 'sleep over' here in lock-up" the Sergeant replied.

We both followed the desk sergeant over to the interrogation room, which I immediately noticed, was fully monitored with several cameras mounted on each corner of the interview area.

"What? Are we making movies now?" I immediately asked the Sergeant.

"The Ivory Tower just had us install these cameras. Apparently, there have been too many prisoner 'rough ups' that have been getting the P.D.

230

into too many lawsuits and a lot of bad media publicity lately," he replied.

"That's too bad," Morton replied.

"We've got a 'luxury hotel suit' downstairs, if you guys ever need to use it," the Sergeant suggested, referring to the basement 'cage' that was used to 'interrogate' high risk prisoners, without any cameras or witnesses.

"Thanks, Sarg," I replied. "We'll keep that in mind."

The desk sergeant unlocked the door and opened the interview room, where the Monsignor and his well-dressed attorney were waiting. Kilbane was wearing an orange jump suit and had been stripped of his clothing and gold crucifix, which he had always blatantly displayed as if it were some sort of holstered weapon. He looked pretty beat up, and was unshaven, dirty and tired. The Monsignor looked, as though he hadn't slept. It was probably on account of his trying to sleep on those hard, uncomfortable cots, and having to share his extravagant new digs with 'Bubba' and a few of his other new roommates.

His appearance contrasted with his overpriced attorney, David Herzog, wearing a black, pin-striped Ermenegildo Zegna suit with several gold rings and an oversized, diamond studded Rolex watch. His expensive Creed cologne was overbearing, as his morning scent took over the interrogation room. The strong smell reminded me of being in some sort of sleazy, sordid French whorehouse.

"Well, well, look who's back for a visit?" I managed to say, knowing that I was going to thoroughly enjoy the next fun-filled hour with our newest, high profile prisoner.

"Good morning Detectives," David managed to say, as he stood up to shake our hands. The Monsignor was silent, and sat there motionless, letting his attorney do all the talking.

"As you both are aware, my client did not commit this murder," he began his volley.

"We've got your boy on video cameras entering the hospital and the cancer ward, and several of the hospital staff have I-D'd him in the surveillance tapes and witnessed him going into the patient's hospital room. He also left us a present at the crime scene," Detective Morton began.

"Sorry, Counselor. This time, your boy 'ain't walkin'," I said, still holding my soon-to-be cold Dunkin' Donuts coffee.

The high-end Monadnock attorney started throwing around that cocky smile of his, probably thinking his client was going to 'dance out of here' the same way he did after his prior DUI arrest. Even though I had a feeling in my gut that Kilbane wasn't the killer, I was not about to let him walk out of here again the same way he did two weeks ago.

"We've asked to see the security videos photographs from Rush Hospital, detectives. It's going to be difficult to keep him here under arrest, with his being elsewhere other than at the hospital yesterday afternoon."

"Humor us, Counselor. Where was your client yesterday, between 3:00 and 3:30pm?"

"He was at the Archdiocese, working as usual. His 'admin' can attest to it."

"Unless he has video security cameras proving he was there, that's going to be a tough sell, Counselor. I've met his administrative assistant there at the Archdiocese, and her word or anyone else's at the diocese office isn't going to be enough to convince us or the plea hearing judge to believe he was anywhere else," I sternly replied.

232

"He's not going to 'alibi out' this time," Tommy said, as he had already convinced himself that Kilbane was the one and only "Pedophile Murderer".

"We've also got his blue Chevy Malibu along with the license plates, registered to the Archdiocese," I casually mentioned.

"Those license plates were stolen off of a similar vehicle, parked at the Cardinal's mansion," Herzog replied.

I looked over at Tommy. He had 'poured over' the surveillance tapes at the hospital yesterday and had ran those "V46-1038" Illinois license plates several times, registering to the Chicago Archdiocese.

"Did anyone report those plates stolen?" Detective Morton asked.

"No, Detectives. It wasn't discovered until last night after Monsignor Kilbane was arrested. The car had been sitting in the parking lot and hadn't been driven by anyone at the mansion for a few days. No one noticed the missing plates until after my client was picked up," David argued.

"Besides, my client regularly drives a black, Cadillac CTS, not a blue Chevy Malibu."

"Really? And your client would never switch cars before driving over to the hospital and stabbing the shit out of some terminal cancer patient? Do you think that argument is really going to work?" Tommy replied.

"We've already talked to the State's Attorney's office. They're going to ask the judge to hold your boy here, without bail," I stated, looking directly at Kilbane.

"Why?" the Monsignor angrily responded, "I didn't kill anybody!" His attorney was grasping his client's hand, trying to silently tell him not to talk. I looked at Kilbane and his short, over-priced attorney and decided to throw them both a curve ball.

"Okay, Father Joe. I want to show you that I'm a reasonable, God-fearing Catholic. How about if you tell us why you were at that restaurant two weeks ago having that meeting with Little Tony with a suit case full of cash?" I said as the Monsignor glared at me in his orange jump suit.

"Seriously, Monsignor. Tell us what the hell you were doing with fifty large in cash, having dinner with Tony DiMatteo at the Trattoria Pagliacci two weeks ago, and I'll go back to the DA's office and convince him to talk to the judge about getting you released on bail," I repeated my offer again to the prisoner. He just sat there, speechless. David only looked at me, wondering if I was serious.

"I will have to talk to my client about your offer."

"There is nothing to talk about," I angrily replied. "We've got you boy on Candid Camera at the hospital before and after the murder yesterday. If he wants to go home and sleep in his own bed tonight, he's gotta' give us Little Tony."

Monsignor Kilbane only sat there silently, and his face was expressionless.

"You see, Counselor, I know why your client was having dinner with Little Tony that night. He was trying to pay him off for a 'murder for hire' proposition that he figured the DiMatteo Family had already executed. When he realized that Tony wasn't interested, or for whatever reason, decided not to commit the murder or accept his money, your client decided to take out these pedophile ex-priests himself," I exclaimed.

"It's pretty well known around the Chicago Archdiocese that the Monsignor, here, isn't very fond of these retired pedophile ex-priests who were forced to resign and now, have these high-priced insurance policies on their heads," I stated even though, I knew deep down in my gut, that Kilbane probably wasn't the murderer.

"We know your client isn't going to 'rat-out' his grade school buddy. The 'Rules of Bridgeport' just don't work that way, Counselor."

The two of them only sat there, silent. I knew that, even if we had him on a 'YouTube' video as 'Jack the Ripper', Kilbane was not about to turn in his Mafia 'pallie', whom he was trying to use to solicit a murder. We all knew that Kilbane just didn't "roll" that way.

"There's a lot of holes in your story and this investigation, Detective. Monsignor Kilbane isn't the 'Pedophile Priest Murderer'" he loudly protested, knowing that he couldn't offer up any more excuses for his client.

"Counselor, if he isn't the 'Pedophile Priest Murderer', he is definitely the 'Pedophile Priest Insurance Collector'. Your client here, hasn't wasted any time submitting the insurance claims on these murdered ex-priests. So, we can all agree that there is a motive, especially with all of these child molestation lawsuits being filed against the Archdiocese."

"There is no law against filing an insurance claim, Detective."

"Yeah, but...come on, Counselor. These damn priests were still warm in their graves when the Monsignor here, submitted the paperwork to collect the insurance money. You're not going to be able to dispute that. There is definitely a motive here, Mr. Herzog."

The attorney and his client sat there, totally speechless.

"We're looking forward to having fun at the plea hearing and criminal arraignment this morning, boys," Detective Morton gloated, as we both stood up from the interview table.

"We'll see you both in court, Gentlemen," I said, drinking what was left inside of my styrofoam Dunkin' Donuts coffee cup and leaving the interrogation room.

Kilbane's plea hearing and criminal arraignment was scheduled for ten o'clock that morning, but I knew there wasn't going to be any surprises. The Cook County Prosecutors' Office was under a lot of pressure, along with the Chicago P.D., to make an arrest, *any arrest*, on these Pedophile Priest Murders. The way I figured it, it was in the best interest of everyone in Chicago to keep Kilbane locked up at Cook County Jail on South California, until we all figured out who the *real* Pedophile Priest Murderer was.

Tommy Morton agreed to hang out at the courthouse over at Twenty Sixth and California for Kilbane's plea hearing, in case he needed to testify. I knew it was going to be a total 'media zoo' over there, and I wasn't interested in being a part of that. Regardless of what the hospital witnesses and video tapes disclosed regarding this homicide case, my investigative intuition was telling me otherwise. As I returned to my squad car, my inner voice was screaming at me, deep down inside.

The 'Pedophile Priest Murderer' was still out there, making plans for his next victim.

CHAPTER TWENTY-EIGHT

It was probably around 11:30 that morning when my stomach started making noises, and I began thinking about lunch. I had made a huge pork roast in the 'crock pot' the night before and had enough leftovers to tie me over for the next few days. I had brown-bagged my lunch that day, so I had walked into the precinct cafeteria and grabbed my food out of the refrigerator, along with a Diet Coke. My mind was so embossed in these pedophile priest murders that I could hardly wrap my head around anything else.

The arraignment in court that morning went as expected. Monsignor Kilbane was being held without bail, as the DA's office easily linked the video and security cameras at Rush Medical Hospital to Kilbane, casually walking into the hospital and committing the gruesome murder.

But something was said at Kilbane's interrogation that I just couldn't get out of my head. It was on my mind all morning. Those stolen Illinois license plates, the "V46-1038" plates that were registered to the Archdiocese of Chicago, matched the same plates with the same car description on the parking lot security cameras. I sent a squad car over to the Cardinal's mansion to pick up the blue Chevy Impala which had been sitting in their lot, and indeed, the parked Impala was without a license plate. We impounded the car, and CSI was going through the vehicle for prints and other evidence.

What if the blue Chevy Impala wasn't the same car in the surveillance tapes? What if another, similar car with those stolen plates was used? A rental car perhaps?

I started calling all the car rental agencies in the Chicagoland area and the airports, asking for any records involving the rental of a 'late model blue Chevy Impala' during the last seventy-two hours. After some hard digging and spending most of the afternoon on the phone, three hits came back. One rental was from Avis Rental Car, the other two rentals were from Enterprise Car Rental. Of those three car rentals, one was a female in her late fifties, a psychiatrist from Rochester, New York, who had returned the car yesterday morning. The other car rental was to an older retired couple from Sarasota, Florida, who still had the rented car until tomorrow.

That left a 59-year-old male, by the name of Lawrence Bartell, who resided at 5208 North Narragansett in Chicago. He returned a blue Chevy Impala late last night to the Avis rental office at O'Hare Airport. I had the young lady at Avis scan and email the contract directly to my computer. The first question in my mind, was why would a local resident need a rental car?

Upon further investigation, I had discovered that the car, which was only used for one day, was paid for in cash, and used for a little over 24 hours. I acquired the mobile telephone number which was used on the rental contract, but when I called the number, was disconnected. I had looked at the contract and noticed that a driver's license was used as the required identification. I ran the driver's license through the Secretary of State and verified the name. I also checked with Avis to see if the car had been re-rented again or was still on the rental lot at the O'Hare garage. She called me back and verified that the car was still in the parking garage and hadn't been rented. Since it had just been returned the night before and had not been cleaned out yet, I called Tommy and asked him to run over there and impound the car. I wanted CSI to run some prints and get whatever other evidence was inside of the vehicle. I then asked Tommy to meet me over at 5208 North Narragansett.

As I approached the front entrance of the yellow brick bungalow, Tommy went in the back yard to keep an eye on the back door. When I rang the front door bell, I heard some loud cluttering noises. I then heard Tommy yell out "Chicago Police" and I ran towards the back yard with my gun drawn.

Tommy had already began chasing the suspect down the back alley and, even though he was now a heavy smoker, was able to easily catch and apprehend the suspect about a half block down the back way. He must have had something to hide, as he was not interested in answering the door or our questions. We handcuffed the suspect and brought him down to the Sixteenth District.

Bartell, was a taller man in his late fifty's, with gray, receding hair and was wearing dark horn-rimmed glasses. He was very silent in the squad car and, at first, said very little when we sat him down in the interrogation room. As I was studying the suspect, I imagined him on the security tapes, and noticed he had the same body type and build as Monsignor Kilbane. While I was sitting with the suspect, I noticed an unusual ring that he was wearing on his right hand. It looked very familiar, and I couldn't remember where I had seen it before.

"That looks pretty expensive," I said, drawing the suspect's attention to his right hand. "Where did you get that ring?" It was shiny and gold, with a red cross design clad in very small rubies. He didn't say much, other than he had 'received it as a gift'.

"Why did you run when I knocked on the front door?" I asked him. Bartell sat there silent for several moments, as if to think long and hard about his answer.

"I've been very behind on my child support payments, and I thought you guys had come over to take me into custody. I can't afford to miss any more days of work," Bartell replied.

"This has nothing to do with child support. We wanted to ask you a few questions regarding your rental car from Avis. We noticed that it was used for only a day and was returned late last evening. Why did you need a rental car?" I asked.

"My car was in the shop, and I needed it to go to work," he replied.

"We talked to the Avis employee who rented you the car, and she said you were very specific as to the type and kind of car you were interested in renting that day. Why a blue Chevy Impala?" I inquired.

"I wasn't specific. That happened to be the only car that was available," he quickly denied.

"Well, it just so happens that the same make and model of that car is the same car that was driven and used by a murder suspect in a hospital homicide yesterday. That same car was displaying a stolen license plate. Do you know anything about it?"

Bartell protested, "I don't know anything about any murder. I needed a rental car to go to work yesterday. That's all," he said loudly.

"What happened to your vehicle?"

"It was in the body shop, and the driver's side door was getting fixed from an accident I was in last week. He needed to keep the car in the shop until today."

"He didn't have a loaner car to give you?" I asked him.

"No, the rental car is covered under my insurance."

"Do you have the name of the body shop?" I politely asked.

Bartell stumbled for several long seconds, until he pulled out his wallet.

"I thought I had his card in my wallet," as he kept fumbling.

"What's the name of the shop and where is it?"

"Arcadia Body Shop, on West Irving Park," he replied.

"I need the name of your employer and his number. We need to verify your whereabouts yesterday afternoon too," I said.

Bartell then gave me his employer's information. He said he worked at M & A Machining Shop on

Belmont and Laramie as a die and machine operator. He reluctantly answered a few more specific questions about his job description and work hours. I then decided to hold him in lockup for a little while until I could verify his employer and body shop information. I needed to check out his story. I figured that, if his alibi was true, and the body shop could confirm the accident and his car repair, that Bartell was going to be a dead end and I would release him later that evening.

I called his employer and left him a message to call me back, as he was out of the office and was "not available". It was after 5:00pm, and when I called the body shop, it had already closed. I then left a message on the company's voice mail. As I was sitting at my desk making these phone calls, I couldn't get that guy's ring out of my head. I had seen it before, but where?

As I was at my computer trying to do some other cross checking and trying to verify his employment, my desk phone rang. It was Commander Callahan.

"Dorian, get downstairs to lock up. NOW!" he yelled as he abruptly hung up the phone. I was confused. I ran downstairs with some other officers and detectives to check on the jail cell where we were keeping Bartell.

The prisoner was laying on the prison cot of the jail cell and was totally unresponsive. It looked as though he had been convulsing and had vomit all over himself and on the prison floor. It first looked as though he had been choking. One of the patrolman was trying to administer CPR while another was calling EMS, telling them to get over to the district station right away. His eyes were wide open as if to have that "death stare", as he was lying on his back without a heartbeat or any other vital signs.

When the Chicago Fire EMS truck arrived, they tried in vain to revive him. The attending paramedic had estimated that he had already been dead for several minutes or more before the attending officer had noticed on the monitor that he was not moving.

'What happened to him?" I demanded to know from the paramedic.

"Not sure, but it looks like he's been poisoned," he replied. "He's dead. We can't revive him."

What the hell just happened? He couldn't have been in his jail cell for more than a few hours. He requested the attending officer for a glass of water earlier, but other than that, nothing unusual. Several other paramedics arrived at the Sixteenth District, and Commander Callahan was speaking with the one of the Chicago Fire Department Deputy Chiefs.

"Did you remove all of the suspects possessions and inventory them before locking him up?" the Deputy Chief asked me.

"Well...yeah. I had one of the patrol officers remove his belongings, his belt and shoe laces," I replied, still dazed and confused about what had actually happened.

"We're going over the surveillance tapes now, but nothing unusual happened, other than his receiving a glass of water," another officer stated.

The CSI investigators arrived and were taking pictures of the crime scene, as I walked over the cell monitoring station and tried to get some answers. Several of the officers and investigators were going over the surveillance tapes, and it was verified that no one else had entered the suspect's prison cell. They were looking at the specific tape frames, watching and inventorying all the suspect's actions and physical movements over the last few hours.

After receiving a glass of water, Bartell turned his back away from the camera, and reached into his pocket. It looked as though he had put something in his mouth before drinking from the styrofoam cup. He then walked over to his cot and laid down, and after several long minutes, started convulsing.

"He obviously had something in his pocket," observed one of the investigators.

"Didn't you guys empty the prisoner's pockets? Didn't you guys inventory them with all of his other possessions before lockup?" the Commander loudly interrogated the attending female policeman.

"We did. We made him empty his pockets. He had some loosely wrapped cough drops which he could keep because he said he had a 'sore throat'.

"Sore throat my ass!" I angrily replied. "Those throat lozenges were probably arsenic pills."

For whatever reason, Bartell felt it imperative to take a poison pill and 'check out' rather than face any consequences of whatever crime he had committed or was guilty of. But I just didn't understand it. We didn't lean very hard on him, and if his alibis and his employer had corroborated, we probably would have immediately released him. Why would he panic and kill himself?

As Bartell's dead body was removed by the coroner in a black body bag, several other detectives began working on his story. It turned out later that, Bartell's late model Cadillac SUV was never in a car accident and had been parked on the street on North Narragansett for several days, even receiving a couple of parking tickets.

He had been terminated by his employer over a month ago, and the dead suspect had recently been unemployed. The only thing that did check out was that he hadn't paid child support in over a year to his ex-wife and two young children, with whom he had a very estranged relationship with. I kept turning over the facts of this recent suicide over in my head, and I began believing more and more, that Kilbane had nothing to do with any of these murders. There was something or someone much, much bigger out there, and it was something that I just couldn't understand.

I walked downstairs over to the evidence room where there was an attending officer and asked to see the dead prisoner's belongings. It was still sealed in a manila envelope. I unsealed it and opened the contents on a nearby desk. There was Bartell's wallet, which had $67.00 dollars in small bills inside, and .87 cents in some loose change. There was also a weathered silver Burberry watch with a blue dial and some scratches on the crystal, several keys with a "Nashville" keychain, and the gold ring with the ruby encrusted red cross. I picked up the ring and studied it for several minutes. I knew I had seen this ring somewhere before, and it looked familiar.

I then did something that I had never done before. While the attending evidence officer wasn't looking, I took the ring from the evidence bag and put it in my pocket. I acquired a new manila envelope and then 'sealed' it, returning the contents back to the attending clerk. My 'sixth sense' was screaming inside of me again, as I abruptly exited the evidence room. I was desperate, and I had a suspicious feeling.

My gut was telling me that this expensive gold ring had a connection to these "Pedophile Priest Murders".

CHAPTER TWENTY-NINE

The rush-hour traffic on Harlem and Belmont Avenues was horrendous that morning, as I was on my way to pay a good friend a visit. The sun was blatantly in my eyes as I was fumbling with my sunglasses and trying to maneuver my squad car. That was a monumental task, between the double-parked cars and the 'stop and go' buses which continued to slow down the north bound stream of traffic.

Arezzo Jewelry was an established jewelry store on North Harlem Avenue, and my old high school friend, Michael Arezzo had owned and managed the store for many years. I had called him and asked him to make time for me earlier that morning, as I needed his jewelry expertise.

We had both gone to Holy Cross High School in River Grove, and we remained good friends after we graduated and periodically talked whenever I was in the neighborhood. Although we had lost touch lately after my messy divorce, Michael was always there to rescue me in the past when I was in dire straits. He always assisted me when I needed a fast, last minute 'Christmas gift' on Christmas Eve or a discounted Lladro statute (which my ex-wife collected) whenever I was in the 'doghouse', which I often visited during our twenty-five years of marital bliss.

I hadn't had much need for jewelry since my grueling divorce, and I hadn't seen or talked to Michael since our thirtieth high school reunion a few years ago. After parking my squad car on the east side of the street, I made my way to the front entrance of his elaborate jewelry store. I was buzzed in, and I waited several minutes before Michael came out of the back room.

"Philip!" he exclaimed my name, as if he was excited to see me. His eyes and line of sight went immediately towards my forty-four-inch waist line.

"Hello Michael." We shook hands and immediately hugged one another, as my large, oversized stomach got to closely rub up next to his.

"We're on 'Dunkin' Donut' diets, I see," as he smiled. He seemed to be as embarrassed as I was about our over-sized waistlines. Michael was a tall, good looking Italian who only seemed to look better with age. Except for his visible over-indulgence for pasta, and with a few distinguished greys, he looked almost the same as he did in high school.

"How's Jeanne?" I asked, noticing that his wife and full-time salesperson was not behind the counter.

"She's great," he replied. "You're here to buy an engagement ring for your new girlfriend?" he presumptuously asked, knowing full well that I was there for anything but that.

"I wish, Mikie, but no...no girlfriend yet."

"I see. You'll have to work on that before the next reunion," he kiddingly commented, fumbling with his reading glasses tied around his neck and the jeweler's eye-piece that he regularly kept in his shirt pocket.

"Not in any rush," I disclaimed, hoping to dispel any immediate rumors.

Michael then brought me into the back room, and immediately offered me an espresso coffee, which I eagerly accepted. We both sat down at his desk and exchanged pleasantries as we were enjoying our jolts of caffeine. We were making small talk and catching up on 'Holy Cross' gossip, talking about all our old classmates of the all-boys school that we attended together. There were so many guys that we ran into over the years but had lost track of since our high school graduation.

Arezzo was grooming his son, Vincent, to take over the business. He was complaining that he didn't have the time anymore to enjoy a decent vacation or any time off, since he was open seven days a week. Michael mentioned that his business was booming and was getting new customers every day.

After finishing our espressos, I reached into my coat pocket and pulled out the plastic sandwich bag that contained the gold and ruby clad ring with the bejeweled red cross.

"Michael, have you ever seen one of these before?"

He grasped the ring from my hand and immediately put on his jewelers eyepiece. He gazed at it for a long period of time, as he fumbled with the jewelry piece, concentrating on the stamp markings on the back of the ring that couldn't be seen with the naked eye.

"Where did you get this ring?" he asked, with a concerned, shock look on his face.

I stared at him for a few seconds, and just coldly replied, "Police business."

He continued to stare at the ring with his eyepiece, as the look of amazement never left his face.

"I haven't seen one of these rings in many, many years," he slowly said, still trying to make out the internal stampings.

"I had a customer once, many years ago, who wanted to duplicate one of these rings, and couldn't get it done because there was someone who had a design patent on it," he said.

"Design patent?"

"Well yeah, it's kind of like someone trying to duplicate a Rolex watch. They have a design patent on it, and you must go to the original designer if you want to order that watch. The same applies to this ring," he explained.

After a few more minutes of studying the gold object, Michael exclaimed loudly,

"Here it is. There is a very small stamp on the inside of the ring. You can only see it with the eyepiece. It's stamped with a design of a rose and the letters 'SRC'."

"SRC? What is that? Someone's initials?" I asked.

Michael immediately put the ring down on his desk and went into another room where he had some reference materials. He started fumbling through several books on gold jewelry patents and was focused on researching those stamped initials and design. After a twenty minutes of fumbling and researching, he came back to his desk with an open book in his hand and started to make a phone call.

"What's up, Mikie?"

"Hold on, Phil. I need to make this call."

He was calling a downtown jewelry store at 376 South Wabash in Chicago and was on hold for several minutes until the owner and manager, David Feinstein of George Feinstein & Sons Fine Jewelry came on the line. Michael Arezzo was making small talk with him for a few moments, then asked him about the 'gold, 18 carat bejeweled ruby red cross ring.'

"What do you know about this ring, David? It has the initials 'SRC' and the design of a rose stamped on the inside. From what I recall and what I've found, you guys are the only ones in Chicago who are authorized to stamp out and fabricate this ring," he said.

There was a very long silence on the phone.

"David? Are you there?" More silent moments.

"David?"

"Excuse me, Michael...I have a customer here. Let me call you back."

CLICK!

I could hear the party on the other line loudly terminate the phone call. Michael just stared at me with a shocked look on his face.

"That was weird," he said. He continued to fumble with the ring, periodically trying to make out the 'SRC' stamped letters inside along with the rose design.

"Why do you think he cut you off?"

"I don't know. I haven't seen or talked to David Feinstein in a few years. They have an established jewelry store on South Wabash, and it's been around over one hundred years or more. David is, like, the fourth generation to run and take over the business," he explained.

"Really?"

"I'm pretty sure these guys are the only ones authorized to fabricate and manufacture these rings. You can't just buy one. You must go through them and get special permission before you can buy a ring like this. And they'll charge you good money to fabricate one of these rings."

"What is a ring like this worth?" I decided to ask.

"Seriously? They're priceless. Says here in the book that there are only a limited number of rings at any one time in any area. The rubies are especially imported from Italy and is an ancient design from back in the Renaissance period in Florence. It says here when the owner of the ring dies, the ring must be destroyed or buried with its owner when he passes away. Says here that the design belongs to some 'fraternal order,'" Michael explained.

"What fraternal order?"

"I don't know. Only says a 'fraternal order'. It would make sense though. I remember my customer a long time ago having a really hard time getting anyone to give any him information on fabricating this ring, let alone buying one."

"What does Feinstein have to do with this?"

"I know they're the fabricators. At least that's the rumor on the streets. I've heard it mentioned at a few jewelry shows that they're the only ones authorized by this 'fraternal order' to fabricate and sell these rings. But they are very exclusive," Michael explained.

He then gave the ring back to me, after returning it in the plastic sandwich bag.

"Where did you get this ring?" he was pushing me for an answer.

"Police business," I replied again.

"Come on, Phil! We go back too far. Tell me where you got this, or the next time you come in here looking for a last-minute gift on Christmas Eve, I'll throw you out!" he was joking, and I knew he wasn't serious.

We were both smiling at his joke, as I eagerly asked him, "Are you jammed up here? Can you leave for a few hours?"

"Sure. My son is here. He can run things for a while. Why?" I looked at him intently. "Let's take a ride and pay Mr. Feinstein a visit."

Michael was all too eager to leave his store. He must have thought we were auditioning for 'Dragnet', as he excitedly jumped into the passenger side of my squad car. The traffic on I-290 was light, and in less than twenty minutes, we were double parking my Crown Vic in front of 376 South Wabash in the Chicago Loop downtown. Arezzo pressed the buzzer button, and we then walked up the three flights of stairs of the very old, antiquated three story building. He was explaining to me all along how old and established the Feinstein jewelry store was, with a deep-rooted, established clientele that spanned several generations, mostly from the North Shore of Chicago and its high-end suburbs.

After walking up the stairs, there was another glass door, which we needed to be buzzed into. One of the sales associates, not knowing who we were, automatically buzzed us inside, probably against her boss's wishes as he was tending to another customer.

As we walked into the store, David Feinstein gave Michael one of those shocked, 'what the fuck are you doing here' looks as we waited for the store owner to finish with his customer. Feinstein was a bald, good looking young man wearing a crisp white shirt and tie, diamond cufflinks and several rings on his fingers. He was also displaying a glittering, over-sized gold watch and several diamond bracelets on each wrist. He was probably exhibiting several hundred thousand dollars' worth of jewelry on both hands. I said to myself in a loud whisper that I hoped he didn't go around in public wearing all that damn, expensive jewelry. Michael began chuckling, as I'm sure he had heard me.

"I'll be right with you, Michael," he immediately said, as he was ringing up his customer who obviously, had a lot of money to spend.

After twenty minutes or so, David Feinstein approached Michael and gave him a handshake and a man-hug, trying to pretend that he was happy to see him. Mike introduced me only as his friend, Phil, and asked if we could meet him in private.

"I'm sorry you both came all the way down here, but I'm really jammed up. Could we all get together at another time?" he politely asked us, getting ready to blow us off for another customer.

At that moment, I started getting irritated and I pulled out my police star, properly introducing myself.

"I'm Detective Philip Dorian from the Chicago Police Department at the Sixteenth District. Could we have a word with you please?"

Feinstein only looked at me with a blank stare, as he was momentarily speechless.

"I need to call my lawyer," he then said immediately.

"I wouldn't do that if I were you," I said very nicely, leaning over his jewelry counter and getting as close as I could to his face. I was starting to get extremely aggravated with this asshole.

"Because if that's how you're going to play this, I will handcuff and arrest you in front of all of your high-class, North Shore, 'hoity-toity' customers here and totally fucking embarrass you in your own jewelry store. Then we can all go to Jefferson Park and have a nice little party with your lawyer at my precinct. Now does doesn't that sound like fun?" I sternly exclaimed, making sure he understood every syllable that was coming out of my mouth.

"Now I don't think you would like that now, would you, Mr. Feinstein?" as I was giving him my Cheshire cat grin that I only saved for criminal interrogations.

Feinstein looked at the both of us, knowing that we were serious. He only said 'follow me' as he walked from behind the jewelry display case and towards the back room.

It was an old, dark, dingy room clad with several large safes, a small kitchenette and an old dining table that looked like it had come with the dilapidated old building.

"What can I do for you gentlemen?" he eagerly asked, anxious to get rid of us.

"What do you know about this?" as I pulled out the plastic sandwich bag with the priceless gold, red crossed ring.

He glared at it quickly and pretended he didn't know anything about it.

"Nothing. I've never seen this before," shaking his head.

Michael Arezzo just started laughing, as he looked over at me, hoping I wouldn't arrest him right there on the spot. I only glared at Feinstein, giving him one of my "don't mess with me" dirty looks that I usually saved for drug dealers and south side gang bangers.

"Now why are you lying to us, Mr. Feinstein? We know that you're the only one in Chicago authorized to fabricate this ring for some fraternal order, God only knows who." I had my 'Barney Miller' face on, trying to politely talk nice to him.

"Let's all play nice in the sandbox, here. Cooperate and tell me whatever it is that you know about this ring."

He looked at me again, knowing that I was ready to mess up his pretty boy face if he kept talking smart.

"Honestly Detective, I don't know much. Our family has been fabricating these rings for years, ever since my grandfather owned this store over one hundred years ago. All I know is that once in a very great while, we get a written purchase order in a sealed envelope dropped off at our mailbox, requesting the fabrication of this 'SRC' ring...that's what we call it. We're told not to ask any questions. Someone anony-mously comes in to inspect it, picks it up and leaves us with an envelope full of cash and walks away. It's usually a very quick, very clean transaction," he stated.

"How much cash do you usually receive?"

He looked at me nervously, probably thinking I was really a federal agent from the Treasury Department. He only shook his head.

"Come on, David," Michael pleaded. "He's not going to report you. We all know its unclaimed cash. Just tell him the truth."

David Feinstein looked at me and held up five fingers.

"Five thousand bucks?" I asked. Feinstein only shook his head.

"$50,000?" exclaimed Arezzo, raising his eyebrows.

Feinstein nodded. "That's our fee which includes our being very discrete about any information regarding this ring," said Feinstein.

"What does the 'SRC' stand for?" I eagerly asked. Feinstein only looked at me again, anxious to end our little back room party. There were several long moments of silence, as Feinstein was contemplating his answer.

"If I tell you," he hesitated, "will you both promise to immediately leave and to never come into my store again? Never asking me anymore questions about this ring?" he requested.

"Deal," Michael immediately said, knowing that I would never agree to such silly, foolish terms.

I gave Michael the dirtiest of looks, which included my furrowed eyebrows.

Feinstein then got up and pulled out a blank sheet of white paper out of one of his computer printers. He scribbled something down for a few moments while standing in front of one of his many safes. He then folded it and stuffed it into a plain white envelope from his adjacent desk. I got the impression he was handing us the security codes from the Pentagon for the 'red button' and the nuclear warhead missiles. Feinstein then sealed it and passed it over to Arezzo.

"Could you both leave now? Please? "

I glared at Michael Arezzo, not liking the way we were being manhandled out the door. I was ready to get up and handcuff this little son-of-a-bitch, rather than expose ourselves to his backroom, jewelry store drama. Michael only grasped my arm, preventing me from doing something that would have probably gotten me on the six o'clock news.

"Thank you, David," he said, as he steered me towards the exit and outside of the jewelry store.

We walked down the three flights of stairs without saying a word to each other until we were outside, standing on the sidewalk in front of my double-parked squad car.

"Now that was fun," Michael smiled, still holding the sealed envelope.

I only looked at him and shook my head, as he opened the freshly sealed envelope with his index finger. He read the white sheet of paper and then looked at me, totally perplexed. He then crumbled it up and tossed it into a nearby open garbage can. Arezzo started walking towards the passenger side of my squad car, as he was suddenly very anxious to get back to his jewelry store. I only stood there, staring at Michael.

"What does it say?" I asked as I bent down over the open garbage can to retrieve the crumbled-up piece of paper.

"This guy is full of shit. Let's get out of here," he said, knowing that this little downtown trip was a total waste of our time. I got the immediate impression that he didn't want me to read the note.

I opened the crumpled-up note and read what it said. A crude drawing of a rose with the 'SRC' initials were hastily scribbled on the memo, along with the three words for which it stood for:

Society Rose Crucifix.

CHAPTER THIRTY

The sunrise of that early morning made it necessary for Olivia to pull down her sun visor and reach for her sunglasses, as she set the cruise control of her almost new, white BMW. She had left her condo in downtown Detroit early that morning and was making her way towards Chicago on interstate I-94. Olivia was well equipped for the long, five-hour drive, with her Starbucks, extra wet cappuccino and a few bottles of cold water on the front seat of her car. Her cell phone was programmed into her hands-free audio display as it began to ring first thing that morning. It was Cindy from her office.

"Hey Cindy," she immediately answered, while continuing west on I-94 past the Parma 130 exit.

"Hey Olivia. What's your ETA to Chicago?"

"I've probably got another four hours ahead of me. Miss me already?"

"Of course. Your hotel reservations at the Sheridan are all set for this week," Cindy said. "I will text you with the address and the confirmation info."

"Thanks Cindy. You're the best." Olivia often wondered where she would be in her life without her responsible administrative assistant.

"Think you'll need a whole week in Chicago to settle these claims? Or are you going to do some 'Windy City' partying too?" She could tell that there was a slight tone of jealousy in her administrative assistant's voice.

"Hopefully. You know Chicago is a beautiful city in the summertime," Olivia replied.

Her drive to Chicago that early morning was really, a multi-faceted journey. Since her unexpected visit from the Chicago attorney yesterday, and along with his 'unusual gift', Olivia figured that she needed to get more involved with these Chicago homicide investigations. She just didn't want to hire a strange private investigator to look over the shoulders of the Chicago Police Department and aimlessly go along with their conclusions. And she certainly didn't want to get into the FBI's way or any other of the federal and state agencies that were involved with this case.

But after Gleason's visit, she felt that she needed to personally get involved. There were some large insurance claims at stake here. With wrongful death lawsuits being filed, she didn't want to expose her company to any additional liabilities down the road, especially from the Archdiocese of Chicago. She was also afraid to make the wrong call, and she felt that she needed to be 'more involved' in this extensive criminal investigation, one way or the other.

And yes, of course, there was one more reason for this long, five-hour drive. Detective Philip Dorian. She had not heard from him since their 'business' dinner date a week ago, and she had finally left him a message yesterday. He was obviously too busy to return her call. She had gotten the impression from his desk sergeant that Phillip was 'knee-deep in shit' regarding these "Pedophile Priest Murders," and probably didn't have the time to call her back.

Phillip Dorian made quite an indelible impression on her the last time she was in town. He was handsome, easy-going, and extremely kind and respectful to her on that last evening they had spent together at the restaurant and the Chicago River Walk. Although that evening had started out with platonic intentions in discussing the progress of these investigations, she couldn't seem get him out of her mind. They had spent several hours discussing their personal lives, and she got the impression that he was still quite tainted from his divorce. She hoped she could penetrate through his 'emotional brick wall', as he seemed to have a latent distrust for women. She hoped that maybe, she could be a part of his life, even though he was an intense Chicago Blackhawks hockey fan.

I have no use for Chicago Blackhawks, she jokingly thought. She imagined herself with Phillip at a Detroit-Chicago hockey game, sitting at rink-side seats at the United Center, wearing her Red Wings jersey and Phil with his Blackhawks attire. What fun it would be, she thought to herself, to potentially share her life with someone who would look beyond her brains and beauty and to show her how to laugh, love and have fun again. Her life seemed to be so bland and boring lately, drinking with her girlfriends on Thursday nights and going on occasional, 'nowhere' dates with men whose only interest was a one-night stand.

Phillip Dorian seemed so different. They seemed to have so many interests in common, besides being intense hockey fans. He seemed to be very empathetic and had a sense of humor that she hadn't seen in a very long time. Phil was a gentleman who didn't take himself too seriously and displayed quite a bit of class on that brief night that they shared together. Olivia was hoping, deep down inside, that their personal chemistry could to lead to something more.

Olivia balanced the steering wheel with her knee while she opened a bottle of water, as she continued to drive westbound towards Chicago.

I was leaving the 'Jeweler's Row' section of South Wabash Street and was making my way back to towards the Eisenhower Expressway. I had to drop off Michael Arezzo back to his jewelry store on North Harlem Avenue, and was hoping there wasn't a significant amount of traffic. Michael was totally silent since leaving Feinstein's jewelry store and hadn't said too much on our way back. He was staring off into traffic, as if he were in a psychological trance.

"Mikie, are you okay?" I asked.

"I'm fine, Phil." Several long minutes continued to pass while he continued to remain silent.

"What's on your mind," I eagerly asked.

"Nothing...everything is fine."

"Really?" I asked him, knowing full well that he was handing me a line of crap.

"How do you feel about grabbing lunch?" I asked him, looking at my watch and realizing that I was way overdue.

"Okay..." he said slowly, "Dei Edoardo's is open for lunch in Oak Park. It's right on Lake Street after the Harlem Exit."

"Got it."

I realized throughout the car ride that his Wheels were turning and there was something on his mind. I thought maybe, some Italian food and an early afternoon glass of wine might loosen his tongue, especially if it had something to do with that 'red cross' ring. I parked my Crown Vic near a handicapped parking space in front of the Lake Street restaurant and we were both seated. We ordered a bottle of Pinot Noir, hoping that at the very least, I could get Michael out of his silent funk. He was well into his second glass of wine, when he finally started to confide his thoughts.

"I have a confession to make, Phil."

"If you're looking for a priest, you're in the wrong place," I joked.

"I have seen that ring many times before, and it has been bringing back some memories about my

258

Nonno in Italy that I haven't remembered in a very long time."

"Really?" I was rather surprised at his revelation.

"My grandfather in Italy had a ring just like that. He wore it all the time and never took it off," he confessed.

He took another long drink of his red wine and continued. "Our family is from a town not far from Lucca in Italy, a medieval town called Barga. I often visited my grandparents there when I was a kid and spent several summers there with them. I always admired that ruby red cross ring, and I asked him several times if he would ever let me have that ring when he passed on. He always joked and said that "the ring would be buried with him when he was gone". But I never understood why. During the summer of 1989, I spent that last summer with my grandparents. My Nonno was quite sick then, so I wanted to spend as much time as I could with him." He took another long swallow, as our pasta entrée's began to arrive.

"I've heard of that fraternal organization before. They were called the 'Societa' Crocifisso Della Rosa', and my Nonno was one of them back in our town of Barga. They were originally referred to as the 'Assassins of the Pope' or the 'Assassini per Il Papa', and they were a covert organization created by the Vatican some five hundred years ago. They had played a big part in the anti-fascist, anti-Mussolini movement in Italy during World War Two."

"When I asked my Nonno about where the ring was from, he explained that the ring was part of a fraternal order of the Vatican and that he was an honorary knight. He explained that he was part of a holy, privileged secret society that was created by the Pope, to 'take out' anyone who had 'broken the holy orders of the Catholic Church'. He actually considered himself a 'Holy Soldier of Christ.'"

"During World War II, " he continued, "Pope Pius XII and the Vatican were considered neutral during that terrible war, but it was in the Vatican's best interests to covertly, eliminate as many of the influential Fascists in Italy as possible, and especially, Mussolini. His fraternal organization was one of the underground groups that helped capture and assassinate him and his girlfriend when they were trying to escape from Italy over into Switzerland," he explained.

"And your grandfather was part of this order?"

"Yes. It's a very clandestine group that's been around Italy since the fifteenth century. They were created in Florence by Pope Clement VII, from what I remember being told. They have always been a very secretive group of hired assassins who directly have worked for the Vatican for centuries to destroy any and all of the Pope's enemies."

"Really?" as I was becoming so intrigued with his explanation, I was almost starting to lose my appetite.

"They're a very secretive organization. So secretive, they don't even know each other's real identities or membership. They all wear red hoods to cover their faces at meetings and use ancient, biblical names to refer to each other. And they are very skilled, highly trained killers," Arezzo explained.

"How do you know all of this?" I asked him.

"My Nonno explained all of this to me the last summer that I was with him, as he was practically on his deathbed. It was as though he was making his confession to me before he died," as Arezzo poured himself another glass of wine.

"The 'SRC' is a very secretive group, but I always thought they only existed in Italy. It seems that they've spread across Europe and now, North America over the last fifty years or so. From what I was told, they have always received their orders from the Pope," he explained. Michael then looked at me intently, as if he wished to get confrontational.

"So, tell me Phillip, where *did* you get that ring?" Michael asked me for the third time.

"I 'borrowed' it from the precinct evidence room. It belonged to a suspect who took a poison pill and committed suicide in our district. We were questioning him regarding a 'rental car' that may have been used in the stabbing murder of that ex-priest at Rush Hospital the other day. I only took it because I had seen this ring somewhere before and had a feeling it had something to do with these homicides."

"But I heard on the news that an arrest was made on those murders," he replied.

"Well, there has been. But there are still too many loose ends, and I'm not sure that we've arrested the right guy," I explained to Michael, after he assured me that we could speak confidentially.

"What else do you know?"

"I don't know anything about them here in the United States. But the 'Society of the Rose Crucifix', according to my grandfather, targeted homosexuals, gays, pedophiles, and even abortionists, those doctors who routinely performed illegal abortions in Italy. There were several pedophile priests who were mysteriously murdered back in the 50's and '60's, according to my grandfather. They targeted anyone who went against the Vatican and the doctrines of the Catholic Church."

We started to make a dent on our lunch entrees', as my linguini with stuffed mussels was starting to get cold. I was trying to devour all this new information, wondering where and how I was going to verify all of this.

"Have you noticed that all of these "Pedophile Priest Murders" were all brutal stabbings?" Michael asked.

"Yes."

"That's because, according to what I was told, the serrated knife was the only suitable instrument used to cleanse the souls of these demons, according to the Catholic Church. Its' victims are all possessed by the devil, and the knife is the only way to release the evil from their souls so that they can properly die and enter the afterlife," he explained, taking another bite of his now cold gnocchi.

"They are all well trained butchers, who definitely know how to wield a knife."

I was speechless, as I was only able to say the word "Wow," under my breath.

"It's no wonder we originally thought these were Mafia hits," I replied.

Michael started laughing. "The Mafia?" as he took another sip of his wine.

"These psychos make the Mafia look like a little league soccer team. These guys are all shrewd, intelligent, religious zealots who carefully plan and butcher their victims, all in the name of God."

"And this has all been going on in Italy?"

"Yes, for the last five hundred years. But I had never heard of them being here in the United States, let alone in Chicago until I started inquiring about that ring several years ago," Michael was talking with his mouth full.

When I asked him who the person was who was looking to duplicate the ring recently, Michael explained, "I was the one inquiring about trying to duplicate that ring here in the city. I couldn't find one in Florence or anywhere else when I was in Italy. That's

262

when I found out you had to be a part of a 'fraternal organization' to get one. When I finally realized who they were, I put two and two together and dropped it. According to my Grandfather, these psycho-bastards are dangerous."

"Holy Shit!" I said out loud, as I was using my bread to clean off my plate.

"So, I take it you never got your Grandfather's ring?" I tried to joke.

"No. According to his will, he requested that the ring be buried with him back in Barga."

"What do you know about the long-stemmed red rose that the killers leave at the crime scene?" Arezzo thought about it for a minute.

"From what I remember, roses are the most consecrated and the most holy flower of the Catholic Church, and has always been used to venerate Mary, the Virgin Mother of Jesus," he explained.

"The red rose is not just a token of love but symbolizes courage and the power to uphold the Lord's most holy commandments. My parents and my grandparents venerated the Virgin Mother and had a holy statute of her in our living room. There was always a lighted candle and freshly cut red roses beneath the statute. Whenever my mother went to church, she always had fresh red roses with her and placed them at the foot of the holy Virgin Mary."

"But why a red rose? I thought a white rose is the symbol of innocence and purity," I asked.

"A white rose does symbolize innocence and purity. But for those who have greatly sinned and broken the Lord's Holy Commandments, the red rose symbolizes hope for all those sinners to return to Jesus and the Virgin Mother Mary, and to be accepted again into the Kingdom of Heaven."

"How do you know all of this," I suspiciously asked.

"I stayed awake in religion class," he joked as he was referring to our classes at Holy Cross High School. He was smiling and seemed to be in a lighter mood as he was finishing his gnocchi.

We finished our lunch and I let Arezzo pick up the tab. We left Dei Edoardo's Italian Restaurant, and I dropped Michael off back at his jewelry store. But a very sick feeling started to overwhelm me. What if Feinstein is more connected to this organization then he claimed to be, and he put the word out that the Chicago P.D. has one of these rare, 'SRC' rings? What if this 'Society of the Rose Cross' is looking to get their ring back, seeing that I have it in my possession and Feinstein informed them of that? Would my life be in danger? I needed to run back to my office and try to do some heavy research. I had a sick feeling these religious psychos might be looking for that ring. But I also realized something that afternoon that scared the living shit out of me:

There's a religious cult of serial killers, right here in Chicago.

CHAPTER THIRTY-ONE

I pulled into the parking lot of the Sixteenth District in a daze that afternoon, as though my Crown Victoria squad car had driven itself. I sat in the parking lot for several long minutes, fumbling with the 'SRC' ring that I had carefully wrapped in a plastic sandwich bag. The inside of my squad car seemed to be the only form of peace and solace that I could find during that time, as I put both of my hands on the steering wheel and said a quick prayer to myself. I was praying that my biggest fears and recent revelations regarding a 'secret society of killers' and these 'Pedophile Priest Murders' were completely wrong.

I walked into my police district and back to my office. I wasn't at my desk more than five minutes when my desk phone rang.

"Phil? It's Tommy."

"What's the word, Tommy?"

"Kilbane bonded out this morning."

"What?"

I was so involved in researching that 'SRC' ring over the last few days and thinking about who the real murderers could be, that I had not given much thought about Kilbane 'rotting' in his jail cell.

"How did that happen, Tommy?"

"Apparently, when that suspect committed suicide at your district, his attorney convinced the judge that there was a possibility that the suspect on those hospital videos may not have been Kilbane. David

Herzog had the judge review the tapes with him and played up the 'stolen license plate' theory. We also got the DNA evidence back from the crime lab. The DNA didn't match up with Kilbane's. He was also able to convince the judge that Kilbane wasn't a flight threat," Detective Morton explained. I was speechless as I thought about the situation for several long seconds.

"Did anyone bring up the possibility that Kilbane might be safer in jail than free on bail?"

"I guess not. He posted a one-million-dollar bail bond," Morton replied.

I thought to myself for a moment, that maybe the Archdiocese was already spending their life insurance proceeds before the claims were even approved. I knew that with Kilbane free on bond, and with the seed of doubt planted into the head of a judge and a potential jury, that the pressure to catch the real killer, or 'killers' was right back on our shoulders again.

I was truly concerned for Kilbane's safety. If my theory of the Monsignor soliciting a hit man for the murder of these pedophile priests was correct, I figured Little Tony might have something to say about it. We had a squad car watching and following DiMatteo around for several days now, and they were routinely reporting back to us. Except for Little Tony 'going to confession' that morning at Holy Name Cathedral, there was no unusual activity going on with DiMatteo's undertakings. But with our department putting the heat on both Kilbane and Little Tony, I had a funny feeling in my gut that 'something was going to crack'.

If you put a pot of water on a stove and turn the gas on high, the water is eventually going to boil. We were turning up the heat on Kilbane and DiMatteo, and I knew something was about to happen. I figured by now that Kilbane had nothing to do with any of these 'Pedophile Priest Murders'. But I knew he was guilty of soliciting a homicide. I wanted either him or Little Tony to 'fess up' and possibly rat each other out and admit to the Archdiocese's evil intentions.

That's a long shot...good luck with that one, I thought to myself. The 'Bridgeport Fraternity' didn't work that way, and I didn't expect either the Monsignor or 'the Capo' to be making any police confessions anytime soon. Which now supported my assumption that perhaps, Kilbane was far safer in a Chicago jail cell than at the Cardinal's mansion. If Little Tony was even a little suspicious or worried about the Monsignor 'singing to the coppers', he may want to do something about that. Something very radical and drastic.

It was almost five o'clock that afternoon when there was a knock on my office door. As I looked up from my computer screen, I could immediately see who it was, and my heart rate started beating out of my chest. Even my hands were beginning to perspire.

"You like surprising me, don't you?" I exclaimed as I excitedly stood up from my desk and opened the door for her. She smiled as I gave her a quick peck on the cheek as she looked and smelled incredible.

Olivia was wearing a tight pair of blue jeans and a white blouse, with a stylish blue windbreaker that gave me the impression that she was ready to go to a ball game or do some hard drinking at a local watering hole. We exchanged pleasantries and she quickly sat down in front of my desk. I noticed that she didn't bring her usual briefcase along, and I got the immediate impression that this casual meeting was more for play than for business.

"You don't return my calls, Detective. You must very busy *catching your man...*" she said in a sultry tone of voice. Her expression sounded more like a rehearsed Greta Garbo line from an old 'Mata Hari' movie.

"I've been pretty busy, Olivia. It's such a nice surprise to see you here. What brings you to Chicago?" I asked, wondering if her casual appearance meant that she was interested in more play and less work. For some reason, I couldn't take my eyes off her, as she probably knew I was a sucker for a hot, beautiful brunette in a tight pair of blue jeans.

"I haven't heard from you or gotten an update on these 'Pedophile Murders', and I'm getting some pressure to close out these insurance claims one way or the other. So, my office sent me down here to see if I could be of any help in this investigation."

"Any help?" I innocently asked.

"Well, yeah...you know...some help," she repeated as she gave me a wink. "Would you rather have me helping you on the case? Or some old, fat, stuffy private investigator that was hired by the Great Lakes Insurance Company?"

"Well...if you put it that way..." I was still in shock, seeing Olivia in my office again.

"Great. So what time are you off, Detective?"

"Well, I have a few things here to wrap up and..."

"What is this rumor I hear about Chicago Style Pizza? Do you people actually think that your pizza is much better than ours?"

"Well...to tell you the truth, I haven't had Detroit pizza, so I really don't have anything to compare it to," I joked. "Now mind you, I've never met a pizza that I didn't like, so I would be a very biased judge. But having New York pizza, I can definitely say that Chicago pizza is better..."

"New York? Are you kidding? Blaaaaah. Total kaka!" she exclaimed as she sat herself on the chair in front of my desk and made her pizza and food critique. She was crossing those gorgeous legs, all wrapped up in those very sexy blue jeans and a black pair of Zanotti shoes, bouncing her right leg on her left knee while making her statement.

268

"Hmmm....sounds like somebody wants some pizza." I observed.

"Take your best shot, Detective. Where can a hungry girl get a great pizza in this town?"

I thought about it for several moments and a small, quaint pizzeria on the north side came immediately into my mind. I threw a few papers into my small brief case and packed up for the evening. Seems that I have a 'business' pizza date with a beautiful, insurance executive.

We pulled up on Wrightwood Avenue to a small, quaint pizzeria which was well known in Ravenswood. Spacca Roma was a popular pizzeria with a wood burning oven and hand tossed, Roman style pizza with a discrete dough recipe direct from Italy. It was usually crowded almost every night there, as it was almost five-thirty when we were seated. We had a lively conversation on the way over, as she is talking about her job, her friends and her healthy lifestyle.

"You do realize, Phil. I will need an extra hour at the gym for this pizza tomorrow."

"It will be well worth it. The pizza coming out of this wood burning oven is to die for. I promise you, the dough will melt in your mouth," I assured her.

We ordered a couple of Peroni Italian beers, and the waitress brought over some freshly baked bread and some baked garlic, chopped into a small dish of virgin olive oil mixed with some parmesan cheese.

"So, Phil...what's new with this investigation?" she began to inquire. I started to give her a progress report on all three of the 'Pedophile Priest Murders', along with the suspect's sudden suicide at our district. I also told her about some of the evidence that we encountered pointing to Kilbane as the murder suspect during our Rush Hospital investigation. It had probably taken almost thirty minutes to brief her on all the current and discovered facts in these homicide cases.

The waitress brought over another cold Italian beer along with our pizzas, which were individually baked with green peppers, olives, onions and pepperoni. They looked and smelled heavenly. As we were both devouring our first slices, I continued to tell her about the evidence that I had 'borrowed' from the evidence room the other day. I reached into my suitcoat pocket and pulled out the plastic sandwich bag with its contents.

The expression on Olivia's face totally changed. "Oh my God," she exclaimed in a loud decibel, as I took the ring out of the plastic bag and passed it across the table.

"I've seen this ring before," she said. "I had a visit from an attorney from Chicago yesterday, who was representing the Marquardt family, looking for information on the life insurance claim that was filed by the Chicago Archdiocese," Olivia explained. "He was inquiring about the claim status, as his client's family estate had intentions of filing a wrongful death lawsuit against the Archdiocese. I noticed that he was wearing a ring exactly like this one."

I looked at her, giving her my 'furrowed eyebrow' look. "Why didn't you tell me? Why didn't you call me yesterday?"

"I did, Phil. You were out of the office and you never returned my call."

She was right. I saw that she had left me a telephone message, but I didn't have a chance to call her back.

"What else did he say?" as she passed James Gleason's business card over to me across the table.

"That's all he really said. He had driven all to way to Detroit to try to get some information on the insurance claim investigation."

"Really?" I replied, reaching for another piece of pizza. Something didn't sound right.

"This guy, a Chicago attorney, drives five hours to Detroit from Chicago just to ask you a few questions regarding these 'Pedophile Priest Murder' life insurance claims? And that's it?"

"That's it," she replied.

"Why didn't he just call you?"

"Probably because he knew I wouldn't have taken his call," she eagerly answered.

"And he was wearing a ring like this?"

"Yes, he was."

I was devouring my pizza and contemplating her explanation of this 'Gleason' character and his Detroit visit to her office. She had given me an accurate description of the older man and the dialog that was discussed. I pulled out my cell phone and 'Googled' the attorney James Gleason's name and address. There were several 'Gleason's' that were attorneys in downtown Chicago, but none matching the exact name or address displayed on the business card.

"There is no such attorney's name or address matching this card, Olivia. Did you try searching his name on the internet?"

"I didn't have a chance. When I didn't hear from you, I started planning my trip to Chicago."

I silently looked at her for a moment. My sixth sense was talking to me again, and I just couldn't understand what it was saying. Why wouldn't Olivia do more investigating from her company office, rather than rush over here from Detroit?

"And you say you've seen this ring before?"

"Yes, Phil. Gleason was wearing a ring just like this. I recognize it."

I immediately realized that Olivia probably received an official visit from a member of a 'Society of the Rose Crucifix'. My mind was going into a thousand different directions, and I just didn't know what to make out of any of them. Was Olivia sincere? Was she being honest with me? Was she telling me the truth? Was there another connection here between Olivia and this 'SRC' ring?

I asked her several more questions regarding 'Gleason' as to his appearance, what he looked like and what he was wearing. As I was rifling off my questions, I could tell that Olivia was starting to get irritated.

"Phil, I didn't come here to get interrogated by the police," she said defensively, as she was taking the last sip of her Peroni beer.

"Okay, I'll dial it back. But I insist that you come down to the precinct and file a police report with me tomorrow morning, so that we can put all of this down on record for our investigation. This is quite a break, you know."

"Yes, Detective Dorian."

"And I will need you to write up an accurate description of this 'Gleason' character."

"Yes, Detective Dorian."

"And I will also need you to give me an accurate description of the ring that he was wearing."

"Yes, Detective Dorian."

She was smiling, as the waitress brought over another cold one. I suddenly felt something rubbing up against my leg. Olivia was glaring at me with those sultry brown eyes, and she was rubbing her shoeless bare foot up against my right thigh. It was taking all my psychological strength to keep myself from getting very, very excited.

Lots of strength….lots and lots of strength. I started thinking about the investigation. I started thinking about my Roman style pizza. I started thinking about Chicago Cubs baseball. None of that was working.

"Do you always rub your bare feet up against the legs of Chicago Coppers?" I asked, trying to keep my voice from quivering.

"Only the ones I'm attracted to," she mischievously replied. "You know Detective…"

"You're not going to call me 'Phil' anymore?" I asked.

"Yes, Phil," as she continued to rub her bare foot up against my leg and in my crotch. "You promised me on my last visit that you were going to take me to Navy Pier."

"Navy Pier? Now?" I replied.

"Well yes…it is a beautiful night. What better way to get to know each other than from high up in the sky overlooking this beautiful city? Besides, I've always wanted to go up on that Ferris Wheel."

She stopped and pressed her foot up hard. "You're not afraid of heights, are you?"

I almost answered her in a falsetto voice. "No," as I shook my head and lied.

Great. There I was at Spacca Roma Pizzeria, trying to finish my pizza and beer with her bare foot rubbing hard between my legs. I was trying to figure out how the hell I was going to gracefully get up from the table and drive us over to Navy Pier without embarrassing the hell out of myself.

I suddenly grabbed her bare foot.

"You're going to have to stop doing that," still holding her left foot, "before I make a scene and we both find out how ticklish you are."

"You wouldn't dare," she playfully replied.

"Try me."

There I was, with a beautiful, classy brunette from Detroit, making a hard pass at me while I was trying like hell to ignore her advances. My sixth sense was talking to me again, and I knew that ignoring her was going to be a very difficult task.

She smiled at me with those alluring brown eyes as she withdrew her foot. This woman is absolutely, drop-dead gorgeous. I could tell she was teasing me, to see how I would react to her advances. There was a part of me that just wanted to jump over the table and make incredible love to her...there on the floor, right in the middle of the pizzeria. But I knew I had to control myself, realizing that I wasn't eighteen years old anymore. I had to be a responsible adult. I had to be a gentleman. I had to try like hell to control myself.

We both finished our pizza and beers, allowing myself to calm down as I paid the waitress. We then got into her white, BMW as she handed me the keys allowing me to drive, and we made our way to Navy Pier. I figured we would go on the Ferris Wheel and I would show her the City of Chicago from high up in the air...without looking down.

I immediately knew she would be taking me up to 'Cloud Nine'.

Chapter Thirty-Two

The administrative assistant had been waiting in her late model Cadillac at 26th and California Streets for almost an hour as she was expecting Monsignor Kilbane to be released from the Cook County Corrections Center. It was almost eleven o'clock that morning, as Kilbane had his administrative assistant, Laura Palella to pick him up, as he was just released on bond earlier in court that morning. She had just finished her Dunkin' Donuts coffee and bagel in her car and was waiting for the desk clerks to finish up and complete the paperwork.

"Hello Laura," he excitedly said as he appeared out of the front door of the corrections center and opened the passenger side of her car.

"Thanks for coming to pick me up," he said, still adjusting his black, short sleeve shirt and white collar from when he was picked up several evenings before. He had hastily changed out of his orange prison jumpsuit and into his street clothes as they were finishing up his tentative release on bail.

"I'm not going to miss those orange pajamas at all," he joked, as he put on his seatbelt.

"We're glad you're out of there, Father," she graciously said. "We're all sorry you had to go through all of this," Ms. Palella apologized, as if any of this was her fault.

"Me too," he said, knowing that as soon as he returned to his office that his first appointment was going to be with the Cardinal.

"Has Cardinal Markowitz been briefed on any of this?" he asked, knowing that he was asking his administrative assistant a very stupid question.

"Oh, yes," she answered. "The Cardinal would like to see you immediately."

Ms. Palella negotiated the traffic on Cermak Road as the Monsignor was very quiet during most of the car ride back to the State Street mansion. There really wasn't much to talk about, as he did not want to enlighten his assistant on any more information other than what she had already heard on the news or read in the newspapers.

Kilbane was worried. He was concerned as to what the Cardinal had to say about all of this. He did not brief the Cardinal about any of these investigations or the questioning directed towards him by Detective Dorian. He kept the Cardinal in the dark, figuring that he had all of this under control.

It was just after twelve o'clock, as the Monsignor was back at his office, reviewing his telephone messages and other immediate matters at hand when there was at a knock on his already opened door. Kilbane didn't even have to look up from his desk, as he knew immediately that it was the Cardinal.

"Good afternoon, Your Eminence."

"Good afternoon, Monsignor," Cardinal Markowitz replied, in an almost sarcastic tone of voice.

The Cardinal immediate closed Kilbane's office door behind him as he made himself comfortable at the chair in front of the Monsignor's desk. The Cardinal obviously, was not in a good mood.

"I trust you had a pleasant stay on your vacation, Father?" the Cardinal said in a snarky tone of voice. Kilbane knew immediately that the tone of this very personal meeting between himself and Markowitz was not going to be a very pleasant one. He only looked at the Cardinal with a blank, speechless stare.

"What I would like to know, Father, is why? Why would you be stupid enough to try and solicit a 'murder for hire' scheme with Little Tony, of *all* people?"

"Your Eminence, I can explain..."

"Explain what? Do you have any idea what you have exposed this Archdiocese to? A 'murder for hire' plot to eliminate any and all prior pedophile ex-priests for the insurance money? How stupid are you?"

"Your Eminence, I was trying to..."

"Shut up, Joe!" the Cardinal said as he loudly pounded his open hand on the Monsignor's desk. Kilbane only looked at the Cardinal, as he rose from his office chair and began pacing the Monsignor's office, back and forth.

"I would rather put a 'For Sale' sign up in front of Holy Name Cathedral than risk the good name and reputation of this Archdiocese on a 'Murder for Hire' scheme with the Chicago Mafia. My telephone has been ringing non-stop from the Vatican, wondering what kind of goddamned scheme we have going on here in Chicago," the Cardinal angrily replied.

Apparently, the word of this so-called 'scheme' was leaked to the media, and of course, Channel 8's star Mafia reporter, Chaz Rizzo was all over it. He went on the air and 'hypothesized' publicly on his Eyewitness News broadcast that there was a relationship between the Cardinal's Chief of Staff and Chicago's 'Capo dei Capi', and that there was a connection with the murder of the former Fr. McDougall at Rush Hospital and the Monsignor's proposed, murderous scheme.

"Do you have any idea what kind of bad press we are getting right now? As if we don't have enough to worry about. It's bad enough that these pedophile priests and all of their torrid horror stories concerning their victims hitting the press, and now, we have this too to worry about too."

"But your Eminence, I…"

"Shut up, Joe!" The Cardinal loudly interrupted, while glaring at the Monsignor.

"I only bailed you out of jail so that I could have the pleasure of bitch-slapping you myself, instead of letting those animals over at Cook County Jail do it. What the hell were you thinking, Joe?" the Cardinal screamed, knowing full well what the Monsignor was really trying to do.

"I was thinking of the precarious financial position of our Archdiocese," Kilbane managed to say.

"Really? And hiring one of Little Tony's hit men was the best you could do? We've got several vacant schools that we've closed down that we can't seem to get rid of, and you think 'knocking off' some old priests are a good solution?" The volume of the Cardinals' voice was starting to come down by a few decibels. "You should have at least discussed all of this with me first, Joe."

"This was a confidential meeting between two very old friends, Your Eminence. It happened before Christmas and I certainly didn't ever think that this was going to be front page news."

"Look Joe…Little Tony is the most powerful crime boss in the city. That guy can't fart sideways without the Chicago coppers knowing about it. You should know this," Markowitz replied, in a normal tone of voice.

"It was a very private meeting, Your Eminence, and I had no idea this would be broadcasted all over town."

"Well, somebody publicized it. Did you ever think that maybe Little Tony was wearing a wire?"

"On that night? No way!" Kilbane replied.

"Somebody said something, Joe. You know better than this. You know you have to be careful when you're meeting up with somebody like DiMatteo," the Cardinal reasoned.

"Well," Markowitz continued, "It doesn't matter now. Our attorneys have pretty much convinced the judge that it wasn't you on those security cameras over at Rush the other day. David Herzog has pretty much assured me that he can aggressively defend this murder wrap. Apparently, the DNA on the murder weapon doesn't match yours."

The two of them seemed to calm down as the Cardinal sat back in his chair.

"But I can't have you here right now, Joe."

"What?"

"You heard me. You're going on 'sabbatical'."

"What 'sabbatical'?"

"I'm going to have our office put out a press release today that you will home and in town on sabbatical, studying, teaching and praying, of course. I've arranged for you to be an adjunct professor over at Loyola University. You can teach some religion classes there until all of this blows over," the Cardinal announced. Kilbane only sat at his chair, speechless.

"Why are you getting rid of me?"

"I'm not asking you to resign, Joe. I'm just telling you that you need to be out of here and keep a very low profile for a while until all this 'blows over'. The State Attorney's Office needs to drop these murder charges against you. Our attorneys' will be working overtime to not only clear your name, but the name of this Archdiocese as well. But for now, you can't be here."

Monsignor Kilbane continued to sit there, wondering how he could convince the Cardinal to keep him involved with the daily affairs of the Archdiocese of Chicago. There was no doubt in anyone's mind that Kilbane was always the 'man in charge' at the Archdiocese. To suddenly relinquish all this power, even for a short period of time, was a huge detriment to the Monsignor's ego and reputation. Kilbane only sat there, in silence.

The Cardinal, as if to read his mind, retorted, "You could always go back to the 'Ritz Carleton' over at Twenty-Sixth and California, if you like." Markowitz was referring to the Cook County Corrections Center.

"No, thanks."

"Then I think teaching a few religion classes over at Loyola is a better option, wouldn't you agree, Father?"

Kilbane silently nodded his head. He knew that the Cardinal was making a decision that was probably in the best interests of the Archdiocese of Chicago. There was enough bad press floating around, and the Cardinal didn't need to be answering to the media or the Chicago Police anymore until this 'Pedophile Priest Murderer' was caught and these horrendous homicide cases have been solved.

The Monsignor rose from behind his desk and approached the Cardinal. He genuflected, kissed his ring, and thanked him for all his help and support during these very difficult times. Cardinal Markowitz gave him a very firm embrace, a longer than normal hug, before leaving his office. There seemed to be a sense of finality in the way the Cardinal held him, that gave the Monsignor the latent sense that he wasn't coming back.

It was almost eight o'clock that evening, and it was dark in the adjacent parking garage as Monsignor Kilbane was walking out of the Cardinal's mansion, carrying several boxes in his hand. As he was walking towards his car, he noticed a black Mercedes limousine sitting at the edge of the parking garage with the engine running and the lights on. He said a silent prayer to himself, as he only hoped it wasn't whom he thought it was.

The long black car moved closer in the direction where the Monsignor's Cadillac was parked, as Kilbane started loading the boxes into the trunk of his car. As the limousine pulled up behind Kilbane's Cadillac, the rear window of the long, black car rolled down.

"Get in, Joe," was all the familiar voice said.

Monsignor Kilbane knew immediately that it was Little Tony and hesitated for several long moments. The crime boss was able to 'decoy' the Chicago Police surveillance car that had been following him over the last several days and had discretely arrived at the Cardinal's mansion without being noticed.

"Get in here, Joe. Now!" Little Tony loudly demanded, as he was ready to order the driver and his other henchmen to physically force him into the car.

The Monsignor closed the trunk of his automobile and reluctantly, entered the passenger side of the Mercedes. Bringing along only his black briefcase, Kilbane entered the limousine. He then heard the car doors immediately lock as the car swiftly sped away. Going at a very high rate of speed, the Mercedes first traveled southbound on State Street, and then continued onto the Dan Ryan Expressway.

Over the next day, several people tried to contact the Monsignor and were unable to reach him, as his cell phone had been suddenly disconnected. Two days later, his cleaning lady arrived at Kilbane's luxury townhouse in Lincoln Park, only to notice that the Monsignor's dog had not been let out of the house for a few days. There was waste and animal excrement everywhere. In the following three days, no one had seen or heard from Kilbane, and a missing person's report was finally filed by the Archdiocese of Chicago with the Chicago Police Department. Chaz Rizzo reported it as the lead news story on WDIV Eyewitness News that the Monsignor was a 'missing person' who had quite possibly, jumped bail.

No one had seen him, as if he had just simply disappeared.

The Most Reverend Monsignor Joseph Francis Kilbane was never seen or heard from again.

CHAPTER THIRTY-THREE

The warm spring April air seemed to dance around the city, as every person in Chicago at the time seemed to have spring fever. It had been a very long, cold winter, as if everyone believed the warm alluring breezes of spring would never come. Tulips were sprouting everywhere along West Division Street, as the brother knights of the Society of the Rose Crucifix were slowly arriving for their monthly assembly at the old, brownstone church.

Each of the brother knights entered the antiquated building one by one, in the order of their assigned times of entry. Brother Jeramiah was the first knight to enter building at exactly 6:00pm on that warm spring evening. He unlocked the door with his special key and adorned his mask. At 6:15pm, so too, did Brother Aaron, followed by Brother Barabbas at 6:30pm. Each brother knight, as was the ritual, entered the old church at their assigned times and privately, adorned their masks. At 8:00pm, Brother Ezekiel, the Grand Knight arrived.

The meeting came to order at 8:08pm, with the Grand Knight Ezekiel leading the assembly with the Pledge of Allegiance and an opening prayer. Afterwards, he called his fellow brothers to the agenda at hand.

There were some important matters to discuss, as the Grand Knight Ezekiel led the assembly of red hooded brothers. The prior month's minutes and old business was discussed and settled, then the Grand Knight directed the meeting:

"Brother Knights, as you remember, Brother Cain has been designated to save and redeem the tainted soul of the former Father John Marquardt at out last meeting," the Grand Knight reminded the assembly.

"We ask our brother to apprise us of his progress regarding this endeavor," he said.

Brother Cain then began to discuss Marquardt's residing address, his volunteer work at Lurie Children's Hospital, and his other habits and daily routine. He then went into detail as to the proposed date, time and point of 'reclamation and deliverance', which everyone agreed should be performed in the month of May, the month of the Virgin Blessed Mother. All twelve of the attending knights agreed to Brother Cain's proposal for Marquardt's 'redemption'.

"Brother Knights," continued the Grand Knight. "We have another candidate which has been suggested by another one of our brothers."

At that point, Brother Rueben asked for the floor, as all the red hooded knights proceeded to listen.

"Brother Knights, I propose the reclamation and deliverance of the soul of the former Fr. Lucas Senopoli," he declared in the form of a motion, as he continued to describe in detail, the various abuses and sexual deviances that were committed by the former priest in his stint as the Dean of Students and Principal at St. Peter Chanel and Notre Dame High Schools. After a brief discussion, the Grand Knight went around the whole table of twelve. He then requested each to affirm or deny the action put forth before the board. Each brother's assumed name was recited, and each Knight of the Rose Crucifix affirmed the motion. Again, it was unanimous.

The Grand Knight then requested one of the brother knights at the table to volunteer his services in assisting in their victim's salvation. After several minutes of silence, one of the brothers responded.

"May I, oh worthy Grand Knight, be the deliverer of the tainted soul of this broken servant of God, Father Lucas Senopoli. May I be the deliverer and the executioner of his emaciated heart, to our Almighty Father, and bestow the red rose of our great society, in the name of our Blessed Virgin Mother," immediately volunteered Brother Able, reading from the formal book of the secret society's scriptures.

"We accept your commitment, Brother Able, to deliver the red rose of Our Blessed Mother and send the tainted soul of Fr. Lucas Senopoli, to the Kingdom of Heaven, oh great Brother Able," replied the Grand Knight.

The table of hooded brothers then began to applaud, knowing that the successful carrying of this 'motion of salvation' and intercession was in the capable hands of their respected Brother Able.

"You shall carry out this motion in this upcoming month of our Blessed Virgin Mary, or the month of May," again ordered the Grand Knight.

"We will meet again very soon to choose our next redemption candidate," proclaimed Grand Knight Ezekiel, hinting that another pedophile ex-priest would again be chosen.

There was no other business to discuss before the board of brother knights at that time, and the motion to adjourn was accepted. With that, Brother Aaron supervised the exit of each hooded brother, as they all departed the old, brownstone church, one by one.

It was now Brother Able's turn to bring this pedophile ex-priest to 'redemption', as he exited the antiquated brown stone church and walked over to his parked car on West Division Avenue. He was excited to be chosen and began plotting his Senopoli's 'deliverance' in his mind, as Brother Able had been one of Senopoli's many sexual victims.

He remembered being a young freshman in Notre Dame High School in early 1980's, when Senopoli caught him and another friend smoking in the boy's bathroom. He was brought into the Principal's office and forced to strip down, as the deviant priest whipped him repeatedly on his bare buttocks with his 'rider's crop'.

After his friend was excused, he was physically forced and 'bullied' into performing oral sex on the priest. Several pictures were taken of him naked by Senopoli and proudly placed in his 'red album'. He was traumatized for many years over the incident and had been in a significant amount of therapy sessions for a long period of time. Because his parents were devout Catholics, he was ashamed to tell them, and never brought forth any significant legal charges against the sexual predator. He foolishly believed that it was in his own best interests, to forget the whole incident. Brother Able always broke into a cold sweat and would have anxiety attacks every time he remembered that horrible experience in his head.

That is until he became a Brother Knight of the Society pf the Rose Crucifix. Since adorning the red hooded mask and the red cross ruby ring, he felt a sense of rescue and salvation. He now felt the inner strength he had needed within himself, after being so mortified and degraded to that low level at such an early age.

He could now think about his revenge against the deviant former priest. He thought about the torrid details, of what kind of serrated knife he should use, and where the point of 'redemption' should take place. After all these many, many years, Brother Able could now take reprisal on the man who threatened to psychologically destroy his young life. He could now physically inflict his intense hatred for being forced by that sexual monster to perform that shameful act of homosexuality. He couldn't wait to grip that serrated blade and insert it deeply into Senopoli, cutting and butchering his disgustingly hideous body and dismembering him. He vividly thought about how hard he could thrust his vengeance into him with every powerful stroke of that sharp, serrated blade.

He pulled down his visor while sitting in traffic and gazed at his own image in the mirror. He studied and stared into his dark brown eyes and smiled to himself, knowing that he now had the intense look of a very long-awaited retribution.

Brother Able tried to control his excitement, as he continued to weave through the traffic of the Eisenhower Expressway.

He now looked forward to the 'redemption' of Fr. Lucas Senopoli.

CHAPTER THIRTY-FOUR

FERRIS WHEEL

It was still light outside as I parked Olivia's car in the covered parking lot of Navy Pier that evening. She allowed me to drive her car, as she didn't know her way around Chicago, and wanted to relax on the passenger side while I took the responsibility of driving around the city. We had quite a lively discussion, talking about each other's past lives and interests.

"You still have a wall," she finally said, as I was gently parking her car in the open parking space of the garage.

"Who are you talking about?"

"You. Phillip Dorian...yes, you," she said.

"You're not over your ex-wife, and you think every other woman is out to hurt and destroy you. Now you have a twelve-inch, brick wall surrounding yourself. You don't trust anyone, and you certainly don't trust women."

I looked at her for a moment, confused as to whether she was more interested in fighting with me or making love to me.

"Really? Tell me, 'Dr. Laura', how did you come to that assessment?"

"I can just tell. You're very guarded. You're jaded," she explained as she exited the passenger side of her car. She grasped my arm as we were both finding our way out of the parking garage and outside towards the pier. I thought about her assessment for a moment, realizing that I had to be very careful with my answer.

"It's been a long, slow, emotional recovery, Olivia. It's one thing when your spouse of many years wants to divorce you. That's bad enough. But when you come to the realization that the person you once loved with all your heart and soul is trying to destroy you, then that's devastating. It takes a very long time to get over that. But I suppose you're right. I probably do have a wall."

"And you haven't been in another relationship since your divorce?"

"No. To be honest with you, I've had no interest. Between my daughter and my granddaughter, plus all the demands of this job, I've had neither the desire, the time nor the ambition to pursue another relationship."

"And you're not lonely?" she replied.

"I didn't say that. It's just that if I had a choice between getting emotionally decimated again and being alone, I would rather stay home alone with my yellow lab, Ginger. At least I know she won't hurt me."

Olivia grasped my arm even tighter as we walked along the busy sidewalk of Navy Pier, observing all the boats parked alongside of the mile-long pier. It was fun to 'people watch' everyone there at each of the many varied food and vending stands.

"Like I said," she repeated, as she surprisingly kissed me on the cheek as we were walking arm-in-arm.

"You have a wall."

I looked at her and smiled. I then realized that I was walking around Navy Pier with a beautiful, brown-eyed, dark haired sledge hammer.

We approached the Ferris Wheel and I paid our admission, then found an open seat together on the amusement ride. We were strapped in, with a steel bar stretched across our waists in case we both had the crazy idea to jump. The Ferris Wheel then began to slowly turn, as Olivia cuddled as close as she could next to me, her arm still grasping mine and holding my perspiring hand.

"Phil? You're not getting nervous, are you?"

"Oh, no." I said, trying not to look down. "I'm fine."

Olivia started to giggle, as she admired the beauty of all the landmark buildings and all lit up skyscrapers dashing their magnificent lights across Lake Michigan. The water seemed to be as still as glass on that warm summer evening, and it provided a mirror image of the beautiful city which it so accurately adorned. I pointed out the 'Sears Tower' and the John Hancock Buildings, along with the Prudential Building and the Museum Campus, right alongside Soldier Field. The lights of Wrigley Field on the north side of town were brightly shining across the sky, as the Chicago Cubs were playing a summer night game.

"You are so lucky to live in such a beautiful city," she proclaimed, realizing that I had a very stiff neck from not looking downward.

"Indeed," I managed to say, as I was counting the slow revolutions of the Ferris Wheel in my head.

"Phil? Why are you so nervous? We're only two hundred feet in the air. If this strap breaks or this steel bar comes lose, we will only fall ...oh, maybe, eight stories down. It will be a quick death. We probably won't feel a thing. It's not like jumping out of an airplane without a parachute or anything, so what are you worried about?"

My hands started to drench with perspiration as my face started to sweat with anxiety. I needed to remind myself to forcefully throw this woman directly into Lake Michigan as soon as I got off this damned Ferris Wheel.

"Come on, Phil. You're not *really* nervous, are you?"

"No, Olivia...I am *not* nervous," as I silently said the Lord's Prayer to myself.

"Oh, good. You wouldn't want me to believe that I'm riding on a Ferris Wheel with some wimpy Chicago detective who catches ferocious bad guys but is afraid of heights, now would you?"

I started counting to ten, as I was on my third 'Our Father' and was reciting the entire Holy Rosary in my head.

"Eh.... no." I managed to say.

"Phil...are you religious?"

"Yes."

"Do you go to church?"

"Yes."

"Oh good. I do too. So, when this chair breaks off and falls eight stories to the ground, we'll both go straight to heaven together. Won't that be cool?"

A long silence and more 'Hail Mary's'.

"Do you want me to start rocking, back and forth? C'mon, Phil…wouldn't that be fun?"

"No," I said loudly.

"Are you sure? This ride is kind of slow…"

"No," I said again.

I'm going to choke this woman, if I ever survive this Ferris Wheel ride.

Olivia started laughing like a teenaged school girl at my expense. I only smiled and looked across straight ahead, as I was getting the words of the 'Lord's Prayer' all mixed up and jumbled in my head.

I practically jumped off the Ferris Wheel and kissed the holy, sacred ground of Navy Pier when the ride was over with. Olivia started laughing, keeping her very calm and cool demeanor. She obviously wasn't afraid of heights and wasn't fazed at all at being two hundred feet off the ground. She smiled as she grasped my arm again, as we walked towards the concrete walkway of the pier.

"Do you like ice cream?" she asked.

"Of course, who doesn't?" I replied.

"Good. Let's find some ice cream. I'll buy." I figured since she terrorized me some two hundred feet in the air, her buying me ice cream was the very least she could do.

We walked around Navy Pier, looking intently for an ice cream stand until we found one, not far away from Harry Carey's outdoor restaurant. They seemed to have a varied list of flavors, and I was excited to discover that they had my favorite.

"I'll have the strawberry swirl," she asked the young girl taking our order.

"Banana, please."

She had a surprised look on her face.

"Banana? Who the hell likes banana ice cream?" she remarked.

"I do. It's the best, most delicious ice cream in the whole world. If you're looking for a way into my heart, banana ice cream will do it."

"Got it," as she giggled and gave me another kiss on the cheek. She paid for our goodies and we discovered a wooden bench near the water. We were gazing at the many crowds of people walking around the pier and silently both enjoying the water, the atmosphere, and the warm summer breezes of the Chicago lakefront.

"So how long are you here for, Olivia?"

"Probably a week or so. Hopefully you'll have these 'Pedophile Priest Murders' solved by then."

"From your lips to God's ears," I replied, as I was taking several delicious licks of my banana ice cream cone. At that point, I wasn't sure if I wanted to be disturbed until my brief encounter with ice cream heaven was over with.

We finished our ice cream cones and started walking towards her car in the parking lot. I noticed it was past ten o'clock on a weeknight, and I realized that I needed to be at the precinct very early the next morning. She opened her white BMW 328i and unlocked the passenger door, allowing me inside. Since she insisted on driving, I figured she was going to drive us to her hotel room at the Chicago Sheridan Hotel, a short distance away.

Tonight, could be my lucky night, I thought to myself, as I leaned my head back and closed my eyes. I figured I would relax for a few minutes for the short car ride to her hotel.

It was probably thirty minutes later, when Olivia was nudging me to wake up. She had been standing on the other side of the car with the passenger car door open, trying to wake me up from my evening snooze.

"Do you always snore when you sleep?" She was laughing while trying to wake me up.

"I'm sorry," I apologized, as I was trying to get my bearings straight. We were in the parking lot of the

Sixteenth District where my squad car was parked, and it was almost eleven o'clock.

So much for getting lucky, I thought to myself. I shook the sleep from my eyes and proceeded to exit her car, while she stood there holding the car door open. I must have been snoring so loudly, she got spooked and probably changed her mind about bringing me to her hotel room.

"Good night, Phil," she said. I was figuring on a customary kiss on the cheek.

She then wrapped her arms around my neck, and proceeded to kiss me with those luscious, strawberry flavored lips of hers. I was totally overwhelmed, as I couldn't remember ever being kissed so intently. It had been such a long time, and she tasted wonderful.

"We have a murderer to catch, Detective," she smiled, giving me more small, sweet little kisses on my face and my neck. She then walked around to the driver's side of her BMW.

"I will see you in the morning. Sweet dreams," as she winked her eye and blew me a kiss.

Within seconds, she whisked away from the police district parking lot and left me only standing there, wondering what had just happened that evening.

I couldn't remember the last time I had enjoyed myself so much on a date. I was struggling to keep myself from floating up in the air. Olivia Laurent was an incredibly beautiful, smart, classy lady. It was taking all my emotional strength to keep myself from chasing after her in my squad car, pulling her over and making incredible love to her right then and there.

This all seemed too good to be true, I thought to myself, and my sixth sense started talking to me again. Why was Olivia being so nice to me? Why was she here in Chicago? What was she hiding? Was she being sincere? I started to ask myself a thousand more questions, as I was having such a difficult time getting myself to open and trust another human being, let alone her. She was right, I thought to myself. I was jaded. I disappointedly, got into my squad car and proceeded to drive onto North Milwaukee Avenue.

At that moment, I only wished for a 'do-over' and repeat our wonderful evening together.

CHAPTER THIRTY-FIVE

KILBANE IS MISSING

I could barely open my eyes that early morning as I got out of bed, trying to wake up and get myself ready for work. I put on my black bathrobe and made myself a cup of coffee, as Ginger was all too eager to be taken outside for her morning walk. I grabbed her leash and my cup of coffee and took the elevator from my fourth-floor loft to the outside exit. It was only five o'clock in the morning, and my building in the West Loop was desolate on that early warm, sunny morning.

After bringing my yellow Labrador back inside, I showered, shaved, and ruffled through my closet to find a white shirt that was clean enough to wear that day. As I was getting dressed, I kept thinking about Olivia.

Our evening the night before was amazing. Even though it didn't end up in an 'intimate way', it was still a great evening. She was so casual, yet so classy. She was easy to talk to, easy to get along with, and had an incredible sense of humor. She was smart enough to engage in any topical conversation but was astute enough to know when it was appropriate to voice her personal opinions. She must have realized how broken I was inside...over my ex-wife, my divorce, my failures, and my life. She immediately realized that I had a thick, concrete wall wrapped all around myself and my emotions.

I maneuvered around the early daybreak traffic that morning on North Milwaukee Avenue, making my usual stop at Dunkin' Donuts for my large coffee and toasted bagel. As I entered my office, I noticed that there was more than the usual activity going on at the precinct. A few of the other detectives were scurrying about, as there seemed to be way too much activity going on at 7:30am. As I sat down at my desk, you would have never guessed who came strolling in with his unlit cigarette.

"Hey Philly," he said, dressed impeccably in one of his new, black pinstriped suits.

"What's up, Riz." I figured I better devour as much of my bagel as I could, before this reporter gives me an upset stomach.

"Hey did you hear? The Archdiocese just filed a missing person's report on Kilbane?" Rizzo proclaimed.

"What? Are you kidding?" as I put down my still warm and toasted sesame seed bagel. 'Didn't he just 'bond out' of court the other day?" I replied, trying to get my head around this.

"Yep. A million bucks too. He hasn't been seen or heard from since the other night. Just heard it over the police blotter," Rizzo said.

As Chaz Rizzo walked over to the precinct kitchen to get a cup of that undrinkable Mrs. Folgers coffee, I picked up the desk phone and called Tommy's cell.

"I just heard," he picked up the phone, without even saying 'Hello'.

"Who's going to the Cardinal's Mansion?" I asked.

"I'll leave here in a few minutes. I will meet you there," Tommy directed.

At that moment, Chaz Rizzo returned to my desk and started making himself comfortable with his precinct coffee and unlit cigarette.

"Ok, Carl Bernstein, what's your take on all of this?" I asked the famous, crime fighting, sleuth news reporter.

Rizzo just smiled as I offered him half of my sesame seed bagel.

"I think Little Tony took him on a 'fishing trip.' Bet the farm, Philly."

"How do you even know that Little Tony is involved? We've had him on twenty-four-hour surveillance," I naively asked.

"C'mon, Phil. That don't mean nothin'," he said, as his Chicago south side accent was more prevalent that morning.

"He probably 'decoyed' you guys and grabbed him. It would only make sense. DiMatteo got to the Monsignor before he 'ratted him out' on the 'murder for hire' scheme."

"I figured something was going to happen, Riz. I just knew it. I've been saying all along that Kilbane was safer in jail than on the streets, and it certainly didn't take him long," I observed.

"The Archdiocese had put out a press release the other day, announcing Kilbane's 'sabbatical'. He was going to be a professor at Loyola for a while," Rizzo said with his mouth full.

"Obviously, Little Tony had other ideas." I picked up the phone again and called Tommy.

"Hey Tommy, changed my mind on the Cardinal's Mansion. Why don't you guys go ahead and let me know what's going on. I think we're going to pay a visit to Little Tony," I announced.

"That's a better idea, Phil. I'll come along. Meet you there at South Ashland," Tommy replied.

Rizzo was finishing up his coffee and then figured he better shove off. "Gotta run, Philly. Have a date at the Cardinal's mansion," figuring that the missing Monsignor was going to be his lead story at six o'clock.

"See you around, Chaz," I said, as I grabbed my star and my gun from my desk drawer.

"Oh, by the way, Rizzo. Don't turn this into another 'Mafia hit' story, please? All we have is a missing employee from the Archdiocese," I was trying to get Rizzo to 'dial it down' until we had more facts on the case.

"A missing employee from the Archdiocese? Who happens to be the most powerful priest in Chicago, after Cardinal Markowitz? Who plots a 'murder for hire' scheme with 'The Boys', goes on 'Candid' Camera' before murdering a priest, then jumps bail?" Rizzo sarcastically repeated the facts of this case. He then started laughing. "I think you're trying to get me fired, Philly."

"Only in my wildest dreams," I sarcastically replied.

As I pulled my squad car into the parking lot of the DiMatteo Tomato Company, Tommy Morton was already there waiting for me. We both got out our cars and looked around the area before entering the building. I developed a habit of looking around for surveillance cameras whenever I pulled into a strange parking lot.

"Wave to the cameras, "I mentioned to Detective Morton, as we walked around the parking lot. There was an unmarked squad car already parked on the southwest corner of the lot, and I walked over to the black unmarked car. I figured I would ask our guy a few questions.

Patrolman Mike DiNatale had been following DiMatteo around for the last two weeks, keeping a detailed account of when and where Little Tony was going and whatever his activities had been. I asked him to give me a detailed report over the last seventy-two hours, and he casually mentioned that DiMatteo was basically either at work or going home.

"It's been a pretty boring stack-out," DiNatale said, drinking his coffee.

"Any chance he may have ditched you, or taken a decoy vehicle and gone elsewhere?" I asked.

"How? He only has two cars...his Maserati and his Mercedes Limousine, and we've had both cars staked out and accounted for."

"Any chance he might have slipped away from you?"

"No way, Phil. We've been watching him 24/7. He's hasn't gone anywhere or done anything unusual," he said.

Tommy and I just looked at each other and shook our heads. I picked my cell phone and called my precinct office.

"Have one of the detectives over at the mansion check for any surveillance or security cameras for any businesses in the area and see if we can access the tapes. We've got to have a shot of Kilbane leaving his office sometime Tuesday evening," I instructed.

"Thanks Mike," I casually mentioned to the patrolman.

"How long do you want to stake out this guy?" he asked.

"Not much longer. I'll let you know. Kilbane's gotta turn up somewhere," Detective Morton replied.

We both walked into the DiMatteo Tomato plant and flashed our stars to his warehouse manager, who directed us to Tony's office up on the second floor. When we walked in, his dark-haired secretary was already expecting us in the reception room.

"Mr. DiMatteo will be right with you," she mentioned.

Tommy and I waited for probably twenty minutes or more, as we were both offered espressos and whatever other stale goodies he had laying around at his over expansive, multi-million-dollar warehouse building. We were both expecting DiMatteo to be in one of his cocky moods, so I was rather shocked when he finally appeared out of his office, shaking our hands.

"Good Morning, Detectives," as he was very pleasant.

"Morning, Tony," I replied, figuring he probably already knew why we were there.

"Have you guys ever seen my warehouse?" he eagerly asked. We both looked at each other and mentioned that we hadn't. We were then given the 'nickel tour' around his processing plant, his truck warehouse, and all his expansive offices. As we were going around the plant, he brought us into a large office.

"Have you gentlemen ever met my Controller?" he asked, as a large, heavy set man rose up from behind his desk.

"This is Sal Marrocco," he introduced us, as he shook both of our hands. As we were exchanging pleasantries, I noticed a shiny, ruby red cross gold ring that he was wearing on his right hand, and my mind started racing and my hands began to perspire. I pulled my notebook and took down his name, making sure I noted the ruby, red cross, gold ring that he was wearing. As we were leaving his office, I casually said something to the Controller.

"I like your ring," as I pointed it out to his attention, trying to gage his reaction.

"Thanks. My wife got it for me last Christmas," he replied, in a very deep, raspy voice.

"Do you happen to know where she purchased it?"

"I don't know, but I'll ask her. Probably some expensive jewelry store downtown," he said.

We then followed DiMatteo and Marrocco into the adjacent conference room, which had a long, expansive mahogany table and several chairs surrounding it. The room was dimly lit, and had several, large framed photographs of Frank Sinatra and the other Rat Pack images that I would normally expect to see in any Italo-American business office. We both sat down, while Tony walked over to his espresso bar at the corner of the room and made himself an espresso.

"We may need you to get us some information on that ring, if you don't mind," I replied, going back to Marrocco's red crossed, gold ring.

"Why?" Marrocco asked.

"We had a prison cell suicide the other day, and the victim was wearing the same kind of ring," I replied.

"There must be a thousand rings like this one, Detective. I'm sure you can run out and buy one yourself," Marrocco answered. At that moment, Tony started getting a little testy, as we were all sitting around his conference room table.

"Excuse me, Detective? I bring you around my shop and you guys start asking my controller questions? What kind of fucking shit is this?" DiMatteo exclaimed.

"It's alright, Tony," as Marrocco tried to calm down his boss. "Why are you gentlemen here?" as he pointed his directive towards us.

"Don't know if you guys heard, but Monsignor Kilbane went missing the other night, and was wondering if either of you knew anything about it?" Detective Morton asked.

Little Tony DiMatteo started laughing. "Are you guys fucking serious? You got a guy outside following me around like a lost puppy dog, staked out in my

301

parking lot and at my fucking house for the last two weeks, and you guys wanna know if 'I know where Kilbane is'?" Marrocco and the 'Capo' both looked at each other and started laughing.

"The last we heard, Monsignor Kilbane was in Cook County Jail for murder," Marrocco replied.

"That was the case, but he bonded out Tuesday morning and disappeared the same night," Detective Morton replied.

"Can't help you with that, Detectives," Marrocco replied, as I realized that Sal Marrocco was really the 'Consigliere' to the DiMatteo Family. I had never dealt with Marrocco before, but I remembered what I had heard about him several years ago. He's a very educated, very street smart, very shrewd attorney who poses as the company 'Controller' for Tony DiMatteo's operations. The 'Capo' would never do or say anything without his Consigliere's permission.

"Why don't you ask your copper downstairs in the parking lot, Dorian? He knows where I was."

"We already did, Tony."

"Then what the hell do you want from us? Do you want us to tell you something juicy, like he's swimming at the bottom of Lake Michigan with a pair of cement shoes? Come on, Dorian," Tony smirked.

"Just thought you might want to volunteer some information. When was the last time you talked to him?" Morton asked.

'I went to confession after mass a week ago over at Holy Name Cathedral, and he was there. But you guys already know this," Tony replied in his normal, cocky tone of voice.

"If you really went to Holy Name to confess your sins, Tony, you'd probably still be there in the confessional right now," I observed.

DiMatteo glared at the two of us, rendering the dirtiest of looks. "I went to mass and I said a few prayers. I confessed a few of my sins to Fr. Joe, and I left. Not that it's any of your damn business what I do in church, Dorian."

"What did you two talk about?"

"Where?"

"In the confessional," I boldly asked.

"Really?" Tony surprisingly replied.

"Let's see...I said, 'Bless me Father, for I have sinned. I've rubbed out five assholes from my receivable list, slept with three prostitutes and cracked around my wife six times since my last confession,'" Tony sarcastically answered.

"What the hell kind of question is that, Dorian? I gotta tell you what I say in the goddamn confessional too?" Tony starting to get really aggravated.

"I think you both better leave, Detectives," Marrocco suggested, as everyone rose from the conference table.

We got up, and exited the conference room, as the Consigliere graciously showed us where the exit door was. As we were leaving, Tony mentioned something about asking our 'stake-out' patrolman downstairs in the parking lot if he needed to use the bathroom or wanted any coffee.

I spent the rest of the day in my office, working on any additional leads and information regarding the Kilbane disappearance. There were several businesses on State Street adjacent to the Cardinal's Mansion that had security cameras, but none of them picked up any activity in the mansion parking lot. There was one business that had a security camera directly aimed in the same direction as the cardinal's mansion but wasn't working at the time. There were no witnesses or accounts from anyone who may have seen what happened to the Monsignor after everyone left work that Tuesday evening.

It was about 5:30pm when I received another visitor. It was Detective Paul Russo from the Intelligence Unit. I had been avoiding him lately, since over stepping him and Commander Callahan at Rush Hospital after the McDougall murder, and he had left me several messages.

"You've been dodging me, Dorian," he said as he entered my office. He knew I was blowing him off.

"I figured with Kilbane in jail, you might have some bigger fish to fry," I replied, not really looking forward to talking to him since his trying to muscle in on these 'Pedophile Murder' investigations.

"What happened to Kilbane," he asked as he sat at the chair in front of my desk.

"Looks like he either jumped bail or went on vacation, compliments of DiMatteo Travel," I replied.

"Have you traced any surveillance tapes or interviewed any witnesses?"

"There have been none. The cameras surrounding the mansion when Kilbane left work either didn't have a clear shot or weren't working Tuesday night," I replied.

He sat there for a minute, mulling over the information. The way Russo was asking the questions, I couldn't tell if he was genuinely interested in helping me resolve this case or if he was on a fishing expedition.

"What does DiMatteo have to say?"

"He's 'alibied out'. We've had a tail on him for the last few weeks," I replied, fidgeting with my adjustable pencil.

"Interesting. Think Little Tony knows something?" he asked.

"Definitely. He probably rubbed him out himself, thinking he was going to sing," I said.

"And his cell phone? Credit cards?"

"Cell phone is dead. We haven't put a trace on his credit cards yet."

"I'll have my unit try to tag his cards and see if we have any hits," he casually replied.

I was pretty occupied with everything going on at that moment and wasn't really paying a lot of attention to Russo or what he was saying. I figured he was trying to get his own update on this 'Missing Monsignor' case to report back to his superiors, or maybe he was just being nosey.

"Let's stay in touch," he casually said, then got up and began to leave my office. As he offered to shake my hand, I noticed something that shook me to the core, as if a bolt of lightning had suddenly impaled my whole body. This time, I took a good look at his right hand and knew immediately what he was wearing.

It was an 18-karat gold, ruby, red-crossed ring.

CHAPTER THIRTY-SIX

A FINAL REDEMPTION

It was a warm summer evening when the Brother Knights of the Society of the Rose Crucifix gathered at the old, brownstone church on West Division Street. As was their usual ritual, each brother knight arrived at their designated times, wearing their red hooded masks and black tuxedos. It was after eight thirty that evening, and the monthly meeting was late in starting its assembly. Eleven of the gathered brother knights were sitting at the long mahogany table within the vacant church, waiting for two of their remaining brothers to arrive so that the gathering could begin.

Their Grand Knight, Brother Ezekiel, and another member, Brother Barabbas, had still not arrived. Brother Aaron, who was the First Vice President and considered second in command, verbally took attendance and then seized control of their monthly meeting. He called the assembly to order at 8:34pm. Before calling his fellow brothers to the agenda at hand, Brother Aaron led them in the Pledge of Allegiance and the opening prayer.

"My Brother Knights, as you are aware, we have successfully accomplished the objectives at hand during the past month of our Blessed Mother Mary, in the accomplishment of the redemption and salvation of the souls of our previous designated candidates. The tainted souls of Fathers John Marquardt, Lucas Senopoli, and Matthew McDougall have been successfully rescued and exonerated into the kingdom of Heaven," Brother Aaron proclaimed, as the other brothers stood up and applauded.

"Congratulations are in order to Brother Cain, Brother Abel and Brother Barabbas in successfully redeeming their souls."

The two brother knights accepted the handshakes and words of praise and acclamation from each of the brothers there at the meeting, even though all the knights at hand were privately concerned regarding the whereabouts of their two missing brothers, Barabbas and Ezekiel.

As was the procedure of the Society of the Rose Crucifix, after two absences, arrangements are made for the remaining brothers to replace those missing members with new ones, retiring their secret society names and ruby red cross rings. Each brother has taken an oath to never reveal their identities, to each other or to the rest of the world. The missing brothers can only be retired or removed from the secret society through the act of death or suicide and must have their ruby red cross rings either destroyed or buried with them at the time of their deaths. This has been the sacred tradition of the Society of the Rose Crucifix since the fifteenth century, as the holy order of secret assassins to His Holiness in Rome.

The prior month's minutes and old business was discussed and settled, then the Acting Grand Knight, Brother Aaron, directed the meeting:

"Brother Knights, we must continue to do the Lord's work in upholding His sacred sacraments. It is our duty, to advocate the sacred decrees of our Holy Father and to prosecute those individuals who have broken these blessed commandments. Do have we any new business to bring forth before this sacred society?"

There were several minutes of silence, until Brother Jebediah, requested the attention of his fraternal brothers.

"Oh, worthy Grand Knight, in keeping with the order of redemption and salvation which we have designated to the prior past souls that we have previously mentioned, I wish to bring forth the name of the tainted soul of another fallen ex-priest."

"May I discretely address the table of this sacred society, oh worthy Grand Knight?" Jebediah requested.

"Permission granted," Brother Aaron replied.

Unlike the previous requests for redemption, Brother Jebediah withdrew a piece of paper which he had folded in his tuxedo jacket, containing the name of the next ex-priest to be selected for 'redemption'. Because of Brother Jebediah's prior past relationship with this ex-priest, and because of this ex-priest's extreme sinful acts against his victims, he exercised the option of non-verbally proposing the name of this candidate. By doing so, Jebediah was expressing his belief that the soul of this ex-priest was beyond redemption and should only be treated as an unholy servant of Satan.

"My dearest Brother Knights," Jebediah addressed the other hooded members, "I have chosen to non-verbally propose the name of this fallen ex-priest because I do not believe that his tainted soul can ever be saved or redeemed into the gates of Heaven."

The piece of paper was passed around the table, as each knight read the name of the candidate. The acting Grand Knight Brother Aaron then inquired of Jebediah, "Why do you believe this, Brother?"

Brother Jebediah then elaborated. "This former ex-priest has molested and raped my youngest sister during the last twenty years and pushed her into destroying her life. He has since left the priesthood, never showing any remorse or responsibility for his aberrant actions, against my sister or any other of his molested victims," Jebediah stated.

"My beloved sister was found dead several months ago, becoming a homeless prostitute and drug addict. I believe that the deviant actions of this ex-priest against my sister were responsible for destroying her life, and I do not believe he is worthy of the redemption and salvation of his soul."

"Were there other molested victims?" Brother Zebadiah asked.

"Yes. There were many other molested victims, and he was never brought to justice. He was later hired as a high school teacher after leaving his ministry and continued to rape and molest other young girls."

The Acting Grand Knight studied the name of the proposed ex-priest, realizing that his first name was a continuation of the pattern of biblical candidates which the secret society has previously chosen to follow.

"Brother Jebediah, do you sincerely believe that this former priest was responsible for the death of your beloved sister?"

"I do, oh worthy Grand Knight. She was in therapy for many years and she shared his continued sexual abuses and childhood molestations to her various counselors and psychologists since high school. Although she was in intense therapy, with all the medications that she was prescribed, her extreme depression could never be controlled. Her doctors all stated that her alcohol and drug abuse was a direct result of this diabolical priests' despicable actions."

"My fellow brothers," Brother Aaron began, "I make a motion that we eradicate the tainted soul of this unspoken servant of Satan."

The Acting Grand Knight then looked around the table.

"Is there a second on this motion?"

Brother Rueben immediately seconded the motion before the table. The Acting Grand Knight then continued to request a vote on the motion before the fraternal table of brother knights.

"All those in favor of the salvation and redemption of this unspoken deviant, this unmentioned servant of the devil, please affirm or deny the motion before this table when your name is called," he requested.

"Brother Able?" the Acting Grand Knight began.

"Aye," he answered

"Brother Cain,"

"Aye."

"Brother Joachim"

"Aye," the hooded brother replied.

The Acting Grand Knight went around the whole table of the ten seated brother knights, requesting each to affirm or deny the action put forth before the board. Each brother's assumed name was recited, and each Knight of the Rose Crucifix affirmed the motion. Of course, it was unanimous.

The Acting Grand Knight then requested one of the brother knights at the table to volunteer his services in assisting in their proposed sentencing. After a several long minutes, one of the brothers responded.

"May I, oh worthy Grand Knight, be the deliverer of the tainted soul of this deviant servant of God, into the deepest, darkest halls of purgatory. May I be the deliverer and the executioner of his emaciated tainted heart, and bestow the red rose of our great society, the name of our Blessed Virgin Mother," again volunteered Brother Cain, who was successful in his previous redemption. He was reading from the Executioner's Acceptance, variating the words of this formal vow to deliver this pedophile's 'tainted soul' into the darkest domains of Hell.

"We accept your commitment, Brother Cain, to deliver the red rose of Our Blessed Mother and send the tainted soul of this unspoken servant of Satan, into the 'darkest domains of Hell', oh great Brother Cain," replied the Acting Grand Knight.

The table of hooded brothers then began to applaud, knowing that the successful carrying of this 'motion of execution' and intercession was in the capable hands of their respected Brother Cain.

"You shall carry out this motion immediately," ordered the Acting Grand Knight.

As he pounded his wooden gavel on the table to proclaim this final motion of redemption, the brother knights all then applauded, offering to again, pledge their support to their respected Brother Cain.

Since there was no other business to discuss before the board of brother knights at that time, the motion to adjourn was accepted. With that, Brother Abel supervised the exit of each hooded brother, as they all departed the old, brownstone church, one by one.

Brother Jebediah exited the antiquated building and walked over to his car, which was parked several blocks down West Division Street. He was both excited and relieved that his personal revenge against the man who inadvertently, killed his little sister would finally be carried out. He had heard great things about Brother Cain. Jebediah had even heard rumors that Brother Cain was a respected member of the Chicago Police Department and was more than familiar with all the facets of murder and executions. He figured that, with Brother Cain's rumored police background and recent skill as an executioner, that he was more than qualified to carry out the personal revenge that he so desperately needed to bring closure to his youngest sister's death.

For all the young little girls whose innocent souls this sexual predator had stolen away, for all those innocent little children that this sick, pedophile priest sexually molested for so many years, Jebediah now knew that the Lord's revenge was at hand. He looked up at the starry, summer sky as he unlocked the car door of his Lexus.

He knew that the untimely death of his little sister would finally be avenged.

CHAPTER THIRTY-SEVEN

It was close to seven o'clock in the evening as I was wrapping things up at my office. It had been a very exhausting day. I was thinking about the two individuals that were coincidentally wearing the same ring that day and kept wondering if there was a connection, so I decided to give my friend at Arezzo Jewelry another call.

"Michael, its Phil."

"Hey Phillip, what's the good word?"

"Quick question, Mike. Is there a possibility that someone else in the city might be fabricating those gold, ruby red crossed rings? Perhaps another jeweler in Chicago somewhere?"

Michael Arezzo thought for a moment.

"The same exact, identical, gold ruby red crossed rings?" he asked.

"Yes, the same identical ring. Could someone else be fabricating them?"

"No. There's no way," he replied. "There's a patented design on those rings with a specific die cast. Even if they were knock offs, they still wouldn't be the exact same ring."

"What if I told you I encountered two people with the exact, identical, same gold, ruby, red crossed rings today? Two rings that looked to be authentic and identical...the same rings as the one from the suicide victim?"

There was another moment of silence.

"Michael?" No answer.

"Michael, are you there?"

"Yes," he finally responded, after several moments of dead silence.

"What do you think," as I pushed him for an answer.

There was a long pause.

"I would say you have a big problem on your hands," he finally replied.

I stood there next to my desk with my keys in my hand as I hung up the phone. My hands started to perspire, and I was practically in a trance. I was trying to mentally make the connection between the Consigliere of the DiMatteo Family and a veteran Chicago Cop from the Intelligence Unit at the Twenty-First District, and why they would be wearing the same identical ring, a ring that's supposedly associated with this 'Society of the Rose Crucifix'.

I had gone on the internet earlier that day but found little information about the secret society other than the details Michael Arezzo I had given me. According to the internet, they were disbanded in Italy over one hundred years ago. The internet makes no mention of any modern-day secret society referring to that same name, especially a 'secret society' in Chicago.

I started walking out to the parking lot towards my squad car when my cell phone rang.

"Hello?"

"Good evening Detective. Did you catch any bad guys today?" It was Olivia, and I smiled to myself at the sound of her voice.

"Yep. As a matter of fact, all the bad guys are lined up and marching into the 'paddy wagon' as we speak," I played along.

"How are you? I thought you were coming in to fill out a report?" I eagerly asked.

"Yeah, I know. I was working from my hotel room today, trying to put out a few fires over the phone and on line. I can't even go out of town anymore," she casually replied. She obviously didn't put a lot of importance in filing a statement for my investigation.

"How do you feel about beaches, picnics and Lake Michigan?" Olivia inquired.

"I like all three. Why?"

"Do you know where Northwestern University is?" she asked.

"Of course, on North Sheridan Road."

"There's a secluded picnic area off the rocks there, on a bluff right on Lake Michigan. How about meeting me there tonight? I'll bring the food. You bring the wine and a blanket."

At that moment, I realized there wasn't another person in the whole world that I would have rather spent a warm, Chicago summer evening with than her, with a bottle of wine and a blanket on the beach. I didn't have to think about my response for very long.

"Sure. Is eight o'clock okay?"

"Yep. See you there, Detective."

I ran home and threw on some Bermuda shorts and one of my blue, Hawaiian shirts. I grabbed a bottle of my favorite wine from my personal inventory within my kitchen cupboard and ran out the door. I drove as quickly as I could over to Northwestern University, right off Sheridan Road. It was almost 8:30 by the time I fought all the evening traffic and got there. Olivia was already sitting on one of the benches overlooking Lake Michigan near the beach house, eagerly waiting for me with her very large, wicker picnic basket.

"Hey Phil," as her planted a warm, welcoming kiss on my lips. She could taste her strawberry lip gloss.

"Hey Olivia, I'm sorry I'm late. I went home to change first."

"Did you steel that picnic basket from Yogi Bear?" I joked, noting its large size.

She smiled and nodded her head, noting that she was so glad to see me that early evening. She was wearing a dark pair of shorts with a casual white, mid-drift blouse which exposed her pierced belly ring, and a pair of summer sandals. Her hair was up in a ponytail and was wearing a dark pair of Ray Ban sunglasses. She appeared as though she were going to a Beach Boys concert at Ravinia and looked amazing.

We walked together through the university campus, across the adjacent parking lot and the sandy beach over the grassy bluff. It was a beautiful location, sitting high upon the lake with the large rocks sitting below. I unfolded our blanket, laid it across the grass in front of the lake and helped her unpack our picnic goodies. I could tell she had spent a lot of time shopping and preparing for our evening excursion. Olivia said she had even purchased the large, "Yogi Bear" wicker basket for this special occasion. We started munching on an antipasto tray, some chips and some other treats. We began making ourselves comfortable as I opened a bottle of Belle Glos Pinot Noir.

We exchanged some more pleasantries, discussing each other's day and I told her the events that I was encountering regarding this investigation. She had a casual way about her that was completely disarming. I felt totally comfortable with her, and she was very easy to talk to. She told me about her educational background and how she put herself through law school while working part time as an insurance adjuster. Olivia mentioned that she was part Italian as well, as her mother was from Rome and her father was French Canadian, born in Montreal.

"Well, we have something in common."

'Really?" she asked.

"My paternal grandfather's name was Vincenzo Doriano, from northern Italy. He changed his name and dropped the 'o' when he immigrated here as a young man in the 1930's," I explained.

"Back then, everyone wanted to blend in."

She smiled and looked pleased, noting that we both had some Italian blood running through our veins.

I told her about all my fraternity activities at Central Michigan University after graduating from Holy Cross High School in River Grove.

"Did you always want to be a cop?" she asked.

"Yes, since I was a kid. Used to play 'cops and robbers' with all the other kids in the neighborhood where I grew up in Elmwood Park," I explained while still enjoying my sandwich.

"Got a Law Enforcement degree from Central Michigan University. I was accepted into law school several years ago, but my ex-wife had other ideas."

"That's too bad, you would make a great lawyer," she observed.

"Well, I'm almost fifty years old now, so it's a little late for me."

I sat back on the blanket and closed my eyes, as the warm wind from the lake seemed to massage and relax my over stressed body with each gust of air.

"So, Ms. Laurent? Tell me again. Why isn't there a ring on your finger?" I eagerly asked her yet again, after a few minutes of enjoyable silence. I knew I was being nosey.

"I was engaged twice, but never made it to the altar. I lost interest in the 'married with children' and the 'white picket fence' scenarios. I realized I was getting more satisfaction from my career, my friends and my family than from all of my broken relationships."

"Have there been many?" I asked, knowing I should have been minding my own business.

"Enough to know that 'my perfect man' probably isn't out there, and that I'm probably better off alone," she replied.

"Hmmm...that sounds pretty cold. Aren't you lonely?" I asked, enjoying the turkey, ham and cheese submarine sandwich she had eagerly purchased from Jimmy John's.

"Not really. I have my friends that I typically go out with, and of course, I have my family as well. Until the right person comes along, I'm not interested in 'dating around' anymore."

"I can't believe that after all of this time, you haven't found a suitable beau," I replied.

"Believe it or not, I haven't. Maybe I'm just too picky," she replied, as she was really enjoying her glass of wine.

"My compliments on the wine, Detective."

"Thanks. I've always enjoyed this Belle Glos brand. And by the way, if you call me 'Detective' one more time, I will arrest you," I said, winking my eye.

"On what charge, Detective?" as she smiled and kissed me...a wet and luscious kiss well placed on my mouth. Her kisses tasted wonderful, as the sweet smell of her perfume mixed well with the Lake Michigan air.

We both sat there on the blanket, watching all the sailboats crossing Lake Michigan and the younger students playing and frolicking on the sandy beach below. It was a warm evening, and the wind from the urban lake felt pleasing, and mixed very nicely with bright sun setting across campus.

She then took my half empty glass of Pinot Noir, placed it on the grass, and she started repeatedly kissing me again...on my cheeks, on my face, and on my neck. I was starting to get extremely excited as we fell onto the blanket, while I held her beneath me and returned the favor. Her well-toned, petite body next to my five-foot, ten-inch frame felt wonderful, as I continued to kiss her across her neck, placing kisses on where ever her skin was exposed. I started kissing her around her stomach and her well placed navel ring. I unbuttoned several buttons of her white blouse and placed more strategic kisses around her black bra, which were covering her well-endowed, tanned breasts.

"Phil? The Evanston Police are going to arrest us," she laughed, as my head was promptly buried in her chest.

"Not to worry," I explained between kisses. "The police extend professional courtesies between departments," I jokingly clarified.

We continued to kiss and embrace each other for what seemed like hours, as the darkened sky encircled the glistening Chicago lights along the Lake Michigan shoreline. The stars were bright and abundant, as they moved and danced across the urban, Midwestern sky. It was just past eleven o'clock when we both agreed that we should probably continue our 'mash and grab' session at another location, somewhere other than in a public place.

We rolled up the blanket and packed up our
basket and proceeded to walk back to our cars. We then
held hands and began singing together, like two little
children in grade school.

We were laughing and singing practically every
stupid, corny song that came into our heads. We were
both having a great time, enjoying that warm, summer
evening and each other.

"Phil? You realize that you can't sing. You know
this, right?" she mentioned.

"We can't all sing like Sinatra," I laughed,
kissing her on the cheek while walking towards our
cars.

She opened the trunk of her car and began
loading her over-sized wicker basket into the back of
her BMW.

"You're going to follow me, right?" she eagerly
asked, as we both knew without mention that we were
going back to her hotel room.

I only nodded my head and followed her back to
the Sheridan Hotel on West Wacker Drive. We couldn't
have been in her hotel room more than five seconds
before she assaulted me, unbuttoning my shirt as I
eagerly undid her blouse and black bra. We were wildly
undressing each other like two high school teenagers.
She stood there naked, showing off her unbelievably,
well-shaped body. Her abdomen looked like an athlete's
chiseled six-pack, as if she spent all her spare time
doing sit-ups and core exercises. Her breasts were
perfectly shaped, as her rosy nipples seemed to
protrude with every kiss that I implanted on her chest.
She was suntanned and very well-toned, as I placed
wet, long kisses along every inch of her curvaceous
body.

We continued our love making for what seemed
like hours. The curtains of her 28th floor hotel room
remained wide open the whole time, overlooking the
River North and all the amazing skyscrapers lined up
and down along the Lake Michigan shoreline. It had
been years since I had made love to a woman, especially
a beautiful woman like Olivia, and it felt wonderful.

We fell asleep in each other's arms that night, hoping that the morning sunrise would never come.

As I closed my eyes, I could feel that solid, concrete wall crumbling down.

CHAPTER THIRTY-EIGHT

I managed to slip out of Olivia's Sheridan Hotel Suite very early that morning without waking her up and grabbed a cup of coffee near the concierge's front desk. I ran home and showered, and I was at my desk by seven that morning. I probably wasn't sitting there at my desk no more than ten seconds before Commander Callahan was knocking at my office door.

"Good morning, Dorian," as he made himself comfortable on the old wooden chair in front of my desk.

"What's your progress on these 'Pedophile Priest Murders'?" Callahan calmly asked. I was surprised that he was even approaching me after the way I stepped around him at Rush Hospital.

"Detective Morton and I have made a considerable amount of progress," I stated, touching up briefly on some of the evidence points that we uncovered. Because of the amount of time Morton and I had been putting into these serial homicides, Callahan put in for Detective Morton's transfer into our district from the Seventeenth.

"Well, first, I owe you an apology, Dorian. I leaned way too hard on you when you had suspicions regarding Kilbane and these murders. It looks like he was the murderer all along."

"Still not sure, Commander. He's gone missing now since being released on bail, and I'm not sure how all of this relates to these homicides," I casually mentioned. I didn't want to completely brief him because I only had an unconfirmed hunch on some of the facts of these serial murders. I then asked Commander Callahan a personal question, not knowing how he would respond.

"Commander, how well do you know Detective Russo?"

"Fairly well. I've worked with him for several years in solving many homicides and some other difficult cases. He's a very good police officer, and an excellent detective. He manages to get a lot done and solve a lot of murders, along with his Intelligence Unit at the Twenty-First District. Why are you asking me this, Dorian?"

"He's been no help to us on these homicides, and we've received no assistance from either himself or the Twenty-First."

"They've been pretty jammed up, with all the 'bangers' and 'dealers' going down," he replied.

"Perhaps, Commander. But there have been several 'intel requests' which I've made to his unit that he has never responded to," I pointed out to him. "It's almost as if he's trying to stall this case. And as soon as Kilbane was picked up on murder charges, he has pretty much assumed that the 'Pedophile Priest Murderer' is now off the streets. I'm not convinced that he is."

I was in dire need of some real coffee that morning, as I didn't have time to make my Dunkin' Donuts run. That was probably the reason why I was beginning to slur my speech in front of the Commander. I then decided to make a request of Callahan, knowing that it will probably get me into more trouble.

"I would like to put a 'tail' on DiMatteo's Controller, Sal Marrocco," I eagerly asked.

"Why? We've had a 'tail' on DiMatteo, and that's turned up nothing. Patrolman DiNatale has been watching 'The Capo' for almost two weeks now, and we've got nothing to show for it. What do you think you're going to find on his controller?"

"I've got a substantial lead, and I'm not at liberty to say what it is." I did not want to tell him my thoughts and suspicions regarding those 'SRC' rings that both he and Russo are wearing, and how they may be related to the ruby *red crossed* gold ring the suicide victim was wearing while he was in lock-up.

"Well, I can't justify any more surveillance on this case, Detective. As far as I'm concerned, Kilbane needs to turn up and take the rap on these murders," he said.

When he said that, I knew that asking to put a 'tail' on Detective Paul Russo was going to be completely out of the question. Besides, I didn't want to tip off the Commander of my suspicions, as I had a gut feeling that he was far closer to Russo than he was letting me know.

'*Be careful of what you say, and who you say it to,*' has always been a cardinal rule of mine, and it's helped me survive being a cop in the Chicago Police Department. I've always been very leery of trusting anyone, especially within the department. If I would have told Callahan what my real suspicions and theories were regarding these homicides, he would have put me back on the streets, wearing my 'blues' and writing up parking tickets.

This 'secret society' theory, Arezzo's history lesson, along with these 'SRC' rings floating around, has made me believe that there was more than one killer out there, and Kilbane wasn't one of them. The Monsignor should have stayed put at Twenty-Sixth and California, as he was far safer there. I had a gut feeling that Little Tony took his grade-school buddy on a 'one-way trip to parts unknown'.

If there anyone can make anybody disappear without a trace, it's Little Tony DiMatteo. He's done it before. I was sure 'The Capo' was getting nervous about Kilbane getting leaned on by us, that we supposedly had him on surveillance tape over at the hospital, and that we were pushing him hard and heavy about his 'Murder for Hire' scheme. He wanted the Monsignor out of the way for good.

"Keep me apprised, Detective," were Callahan's last words, as he got up and left my office.

The rest of that morning was rather uneventful, as I continued to try to track down information regarding this 'secret society', and to pull out as much information as I could from the internet, our department library and other outside sources. It was almost noon when I decided to call up my favorite insurance executive.

"Good morning," she managed to exclaim as she had gotten up rather late that morning. "You snuck out of here early, I see."

"Some of us have to work and make a living," I replied.

We continued to make small talk, flirting with each other and talking about our prior evening's favorite events. We decided to make dinner plans later that evening over at the 'Bella Luna' restaurant on Grand Avenue. We met up around six o'clock later that evening, and of course, had a wonderful time.

During the next several days, Olivia and I continued to see each other, as we were both getting to know each better. We were starting to develop a very close, personal relationship, and I thoroughly enjoyed spending time with her. Between all the 'wining and dining' and the deep, personal conversations we were enjoying, my 'solid, concrete wall' had totally disintegrated.

We went to a Chicago Cubs game on Friday night, as they were playing the Milwaukee Brewers. The Cubs won 6-5 in extra innings. We spent that wonderful night together, and every evening thereafter, talking and making love for hours on end. I finally asked her to give up her hotel suite and bring her things over to my place, as long as she was staying in Chicago. Olivia didn't seem to be in any hurry to return to her executive job position at the Great Lakes Life Insurance Company in Detroit, and she spent a considerable amount of time working from her lap top and calling into her office. During that time, she managed to turn my living room into her 'home away from home' office, and had papers, documents, and file folders scattered everywhere.

"I'm sorry I've trashed your living room," she apologized a few times, but I really didn't mind. It was nice to come home to someone other than my yellow lab Ginger, and it was great having her around.

Another benefit of having Olivia around was that she was an amazing cook. She had made my favorite Italian dish, pappardelle con sugo di manzo for me one evening, and I thought I had died and gone to heaven. I really was enjoying coming home to a wonderful, home cooked meal on the nights that we weren't going out and enjoying the Chicago summer. Most every night, we went on the rooftop of my building after dinner, with two glasses and with a bottle of wine. We had long, intimate conversations and stared at the evening stars, enjoying the various phases of the bright, summer moon.

But there was one thing that I couldn't get out of my mind. I had asked her several times to come into my office and give me an 'official statement' on that 'Attorney James Gleason' visit that she had received at her office in Detroit.

She promised to do so, but other things always came up for her. She seemed to never find the time to follow through with my request. She was always too busy, or on other days, claimed that she had just completely forgotten about it. Olivia was giving me the impression that she was stalling, as she was continuously making excuses. It was almost as if she didn't want to go on record.

I decided not to push it with her, as we were getting along so well and having such a wonderful time with her being here in Chicago. I wrote up a memo in the incident report and put it in my investigation files, thinking that I would review it with her later whenever she decided to come in and give me her statement.

During all of time I was spending with Olivia, I came to realize that she was extremely religious. She was a devout Catholic, and she often fell asleep at night holding a red beaded rosary in her hands. She explained that her mother had given it to her a long time ago, and often prayed the rosary whenever she could. So, when Sunday morning came around, Olivia wanted to go to early morning mass.

I took her to eight o'clock mass at Assumption Church located on Illinois and Franklin Streets on that

Sunday. The old, small Catholic Church was established and attended by St. Francis Xavier Cabrini in the late nineteenth century and had a lot of old history surrounding the quaint, marble church.

We arrived there early Sunday morning, and we were both following along with the morning service. During the whole time in church, my mind was wondering. I kept thinking about the 'Pedophile Priest Murders', and the three ex-priests had been brutally murdered and killed on my watch. I was still trying to make the 'secret society' connection in my head, and how all of this pointed away from Kilbane as the murderer. There had been three murders so far, and I kept thinking that, if numbers and religion were a relevant part of this case, that perhaps, another execution of an ex-priest might be in the making.

My mind kept wondering off, as the priest was saying the early morning mass. He then walked from the front of the white, marble altar to the podium off to the left side of the church to begin reading the gospel.

"A reading of the gospel according to John," he proclaimed, as everyone in the almost crowded church crossed themselves to listen to his reading.

'The gospel according to John' I repeated to myself, remembering that our first 'Pedophile Priest' murder victim was the former Fr. John Marquardt.

'The gospel according to John' I said to myself again, trying to recall the names of the other murder victims, the former Fr. Lucas Senopoli, and the former Fr. Matthew McDougall.

'The gospel according to John' I said to myself again, not paying any attention to whatever bible scripture the priest was reading. I said it to myself again...and again...and again.

Suddenly, it hit me like a ton of bricks, as if some miraculous, outside influence had suddenly impaled my whole body. A thousand different thoughts began running through my mind.

'Holy Shit"I verbally said out loud, as a startled Olivia gave me the dirtiest of looks in the middle of mass. The other parishioners next to us must have heard me as well, as they also seemed startled. They were probably thinking that I was having some divine intervention in church.

"Olivia, I have to leave. I need to make an important phone call and it can't wait. I'll call you later," as I immediately excused myself. She had a startled look on her face, as I ran out of the church's front entrance on Illinois Street and proceeded to find a nearby Starbucks. I needed to immediately contact Detective Tommy Morton, who was my loyal partner, and the only one I could trust in these 'Pedophile Priest Murders'.

"Tommy...its Phil. We need to talk." He was still groggy, as he was trying to wake up while answering his cellular phone.

"Phil? Don't you ever sleep? It's Sunday," he remarked.

"Can you meet me at Starbucks? ASAP...I need to talk to you face to face," not trusting the cell towers or the possibility that my cell phone calls might be monitored.

"Well...yeah...okay...I guess." I gave him the place and time of where I was at, and I then texted Olivia, profusely apologizing for my hurried, sudden departure from church.

I wasn't sure if I wanted to share whatever was on my mind regarding these 'Pedophile Priest Murders' with her just yet. I needed to talk to Detective Morton, just to make sure that I wasn't losing my mind.

Morton strolled into the Starbucks in the West Loop on the corner of West Madison and Morgan Streets, no less than twenty minutes later. He had his 'bedhead' hairdo and was wearing an ugly Jimmy Buffet tee shirt and his red pajama bottoms. I quickly ordered him a 'Caffé Americano' coffee, knowing that he wasn't going to be very appreciative of getting him out of bed early on a Sunday morning.

"This better be good, Phil," he immediately remarked, without even giving me a 'good morning' greeting.

"Tommy, who were the four evangelists who wrote the gospels in the Bible?" I eagerly asked.

He looked at me with a dazed stare for a few long seconds.

"You got me out of bed early on a Sunday morning to ask me that?" he asked.

"Tommy, hear me out. Again, who were the four evangelists who wrote the gospels in the bible?" I asked him again.

Tommy grew up in the Logan Square neighborhood and I remembered him mentioning that he also had an extensive Catholic school education, graduating from St. Patrick High School.

He thought about it for a moment, trying to remember what little he had learned in grade school or in catechism class.

"Let's see...there was John, Luke, Matthew and Mark, right?" He was naming them off using his four fingers and seemed puzzled, not sure if he had rendered the correct answer.

"That's right Tom. Now, what were the first names of the murder victims?"

He looked at me for several long seconds as he was trying to get some well needed caffeine into his body. Suddenly, I could see the transformation on his face.

"Oh my God," he managed to say. He looked at me, his blue eyes were as big as saucers.

"So, you're thinking there will be another 'Pedophile Priest Murder' victim, and his first name will be 'Mark'?"

"Exactly."

Tommy took a long sip of his black, Caffé Americano coffee, which wasn't any more special or flavorful than the same coffee at McDonald's, but only three dollars more. He was deep in thought, putting together the 'SRC' ring theory and the 'secret society' information that I had told him about earlier that week.

"Phil, you're assuming there will be another murder victim. I'm not sure that's going to happen, especially now that Kilbane has checked out and is missing."

"Tommy, the Number Four is a significant number in Christianity and in the Bible. If these supposed 'assassins' of the Pope are hell bent on eliminating ex-priests, then I think there's a pattern here. The fact that these guys have first names that correspond to the biblical evangelists is a noteworthy pattern." I explained.

"Assuming there is going to be another murder. The Number Three' is a significant number too," Tommy said, referring to the Holy Trinity. "If Kilbane really is the murderer, we're wasting our time."

"I think we need to get some decent 'intel information' here and find out all the names and whereabouts of any and all ex-priests with the first name of 'Mark' or any name like it in the Chicagoland area. Then we put some surveillance on that person or persons, and see if we can prove up this pattern," I hypothesized. "We also need to put a tag on Russo. I've got big money that says he's somehow connected to all of this, along with DiMatteo's Consigliere."

"Who? Marrocco?" he verified.

"Yes."

"You obviously know very little about the Mafia. You can pass on Marrocco," Tommy said.

"Why?"

"Crime Family Consiglieri's don't do murders. They advise. They consult. They don't kill. We don't need to waste any time on Marrocco," he reasoned.

"But Tommy, Sal Marrocco wears an 'SRC' ring," I said.

"That doesn't mean he's personally killing anyone. Maybe he's just a part of this 'secret society' acting as their consigliere as well," Morton said, taking another sip of his over-priced coffee.

"We can't pick him up for questioning. He will then know that we're on to him," Tommy said.

Several long, quiet minutes ticked by, as Detective Tommy Morton sat there in the middle of Starbucks, wearing his ugly Jimmy Buffett tee shirt, looking as though he were having a 'divine intervention'.

"What if Marrocco is the real guy who instigated these murders?" Tommy asked.

"What do you mean?"

"Who do you think informed these guys about Kilbane's plan to hire out a DiMatteo hit man to perform these murders? I'm willing to bet that it was Sal Marrocco who let the 'cat out of the bag'."

At that moment, Tommy Morton, with the help of 'Jimmy Buffett' and his undrinkable coffee, put it all together.

"Little Tony, who probably tells his Consigliere everything, told Marrocco about Kilbane's idea, and Marrocco in turn, informed the 'Society of the Rose Crucifix' about it. It was Marrocco who gave the 'SRC' the green light to kill off these pedophile ex-priests. In this way, this 'secret society' takes out all of these 'holy pedophiles' and puts the blame squarely on the Archdiocese," Tommy explained.

"And seeing that the Archdiocese supported and hid these 'pedophile priests' from the public for so many years, this 'secret society' now has an old axe to grind with the Cardinal. With the Chicago Archdiocese as the beneficiaries of these high dollar life insurance policies, they would now have the perfect motive to execute these old ex-priests," I reasoned out loud.

We both nodded our heads, realizing that our theoretical hypothesis was not farfetched. It all seemed to make perfect sense. Little Tony must have mentioned his conversation with Kilbane last Christmas to his family Consigliere, who in turn, informed his 'Mickey Mouse Club' society of killers. With these life insurance policies lingering around, they now have an excuse to execute these pedophile ex-priests, putting the blame squarely on Kilbane and the Archdiocese.

I felt like I had just finished a very difficult, 1000-piece puzzle and had finally inserted the very last puzzle piece. Tommy and I just looked at each other, nodding our heads that early Sunday morning in the middle of Starbucks.

We both then realized that there was one more 'Pedophile Priest Murder' just waiting to happen.

And we had to get there first.

CHAPTER THIRTY-NINE

LITTLE VERONICA

The parking lot of Resurrection Hospital in Chicago was nearly packed with cars as Fr. Mark Ryan searched for a parking space for his new 1979 Chevrolet Monte Carlo. His parents had just purchased the car for him after his graduation from the seminary and didn't want to get the car nicked or scratched in the parking lot. He was looking for a remote parking space away from the other cars.

His mother and father were very proud of him, as he had just been assigned as the associate pastor for St. Charles Parish in Jefferson Park. He was all too eager to impress his pastor after his recent graduation from Sacred Heart Seminary that previous spring in 1979. Fr. Mark wanted to go above and beyond his normal, pastoral job duties at the Jefferson Park church. He had spent several previous summers doing volunteer work for the Catholic missions in Sudan, Chad and Ethiopia and was very happy to be home again in Chicago. Fr. Mark was all too eager to enjoy the summer in his first obligation as a Catholic priest, doing local pastoral work in his new assignment with the Archdiocese of Chicago.

He had been asked by his pastor, Fr. Thomas O'Shea, to anoint an eight-year-old little girl who had just had her appendix removed. Her family did a lot of volunteer work at St. Charles Parish, and wanted their daughter to be anointed and given Holy Communion that morning. She was a third grader at the catholic grade school there and had just made her First Communion that previous spring.

Little Veronica DiCarlo had been in the hospital for four days. She was a cute, rambunctious little girl with dark curly brown hair and big brown eyes the size of saucers. She was slowly recovering from her appendix operation, as her appendix had burst while she was playing at recess last week. The third grader was very fortunate that Sister Marianne was attentive enough to immediately drive her to the Resurrection Hospital emergency room, rather than waste precious minutes waiting for an ambulance. She was up and alert that morning and was coloring in her Disney coloring book when Fr. Mark entered her room in the children's ward on the fourth floor.

"Good morning Veronica," Fr. Mark said as he entered her room. He noticed immediately that the other hospital bed next to hers was vacant.

"Good morning, Father Mark," she excitedly said. She was very familiar with the young handsome priest, who would periodically assist the grade school nuns and in teaching religion and gym classes at the St. Charles grade school. Veronica's heart would skip a beat every time she saw Fr. Mark and had confided to her other girlfriends that she had quite a crush on him.

"How are they treating you here, Veronica?"

"Just great, Father. I just had pancakes for breakfast with French toast and syrup. I get ice cream every night with chocolate chip cookies too. I'm never going home," she excitedly exclaimed, as she continued to color a Daisy Duck page from her coloring book with her crayons.

"How are you feeling? You look fine," the young priest observed.

"I feel great. The doctors said if I'm better they will send me home tomorrow. But I don't want to go home. I like it here."

Fr. Ryan started to laugh. "I think your mom and dad would rather you come home and be with your brothers and sisters. Besides, you don't want to get too far behind on your school work."

It was late October of that school year in 1979, and the teachers had sent over some homework for her to finish and complete before she returned to class. Veronica was the youngest of six children, and with her mother and father both working full time, depended on her older siblings to watch over her until her parents returned home from work. The eight-year-old was responsible for doing her chores around the house for her five dollar per week allowance, as was happy to be able to skip out on those responsibilities while she recovered in the hospital.

The little girl excitedly told the young priest of her hospital experiences, with all the doctors and nurses fussing over her since her operation. As the youngest child of a large family, little Veronica always felt ignored. She didn't receive the same kind of attention that her older siblings received in her devoutly Catholic family and was always excited when Fr. Mark was 'nice to her.'

After he exchanged more pleasantries with the little girl, he put on his white stole and closed the curtains around her hospital bed. He withdrew a bottle of holy water, a black beaded rosary and a small bible from his small black brief case and began praying over the eight-year-old. He said several prayers from his small bible and gave the little girl communion, helping her say her prayers of thanks.

As Fr. Mark Ryan prayed, his mind would frequently go elsewhere. Fr. Mark was aware of the dark, obscure demons that were hidden deep within his soul. As a newly ordained priest, he often struggled with the 'celibacy vow' that he had taken as a young seminarian. He had regularly taken advantage of the young Sudanese and Ethiopian girls while he was a missionary, never having to answer to anyone regarding his deviant sexual behavior. He often prayed for strength, as he intensely struggled to control his aberrant, pedophile urges.

Fr. Mark gave the eight-year-old little girl the black rosary as a gift, showing her how to pray and recite the different prayers associated with each bead. He explained the sacred mysteries that were associated with the rosary, and how to recite them.

He then suddenly, asked little Veronica to show him her operation scars, as he withdrew the bed sheets off her. The little girl was all too eager to do so, as he placed his hands over her operation bandages, anointing them with holy water.

As the little girl was looking on, he withdrew a small flask of baby oil from his black bag and began rubbing the little girl's body. He explained to her that it was 'holy oil' and began rubbing the oil up and down her young body, putting his hand on her genitals and placing extra oil on her 'private parts.' The little girl didn't know what was going on and was startled by the priest's continued fondling beneath her hospital gown.

"You know, Veronica, you must never speak to anyone about this holy oil that I am rubbing on you. This is a special oil from Jesus and will heal you much faster than the medicines and the special bandages the doctors put on you."

"Yes, Father," replied the little girl, as she was all too eager to comply with the young priest.

"Do you remember what I told you in religion class? They do nail little girls to the cross too when they break special secrets with the priests. You do remember, right?"

"Oh yes, Father Mark. I don't want to be nailed on the cross like Jesus did."

Fr. Mark continued to rub oil and fondle the young girl, until he heard one of the nurses enter her hospital room. He quickly withdrew his hands and covered her with the bed sheet, as the nurse opened the curtains.

"Is everything okay here," the older nurse asked, looking suspiciously at the young priest.

"Oh yes. Father Mark was just blessing my operation," Veronica said.

The nurse looked at the little girl and removed the bed sheet that was covering her. She immediately noticed the excessive amount of baby oil covering the young girl's body.

"What is going on here?" the nurse demanded.

"I was just anointing her, and Veronica here has just received Holy Communion, right?" as the little girl nodded with agreement.

The older nurse glared at the young priest, as he was removing his holy stole and depositing his small bible back into his black bag. She became immediately suspicious, as Fr. Mark Ryan bade his 'farewells' and hastily left the hospital children's ward. 'Nurse Linda', which the little girl called her and oversaw the children's ward, began asking questions to Veronica as to what had just happened after the priest exited her room.

"Nothing," she continued to say, afraid of being 'nailed to the cross like Jesus' if she mentioned anything to anyone about what had just happened. Convinced that something inappropriate had occurred, she placed a call to St. Charles Parish and mentioned something to Veronica's parents when they came to visit their daughter later that evening.

Pastor O'Shea immediately dismissed the report from the hospital, as he knew that his newly ordained young priest 'was very well liked' within St. Charles's Parish and that the incident would be quickly forgotten. The third-grader's parents, knowing that their youngest child had a propensity to 'exaggerate' the truth, figured that the 'holy oil' used by Fr. Mark was all a part of his anointing ritual in spiritually healing their littlest girl. They figured that the nurse was obviously overreacting.

Veronica DiCarlo continued to attend St. Charles's School, along with her siblings, and graduated from the eighth grade in 1985. Throughout her grade school years, she was asked periodically to visit Father Ryan at St. Charles's rectory after school. He told her that her appendix scar needed to be 'blessed' so that the intense pain would never come back, and the young priest continued to cover the girl with 'holy oil'. He would fondle her and then eventually, began repeatedly raping her. She was continuously reminded not to say anything to anyone, as she did not want to be 'nailed to the cross like Jesus', the same cross as the one on her black rosary.

Veronica cherished that black beaded rosary Fr. Mark had given her at the hospital as a little girl, and often carried it with her. Because Veronica was neglected so often at home, she appreciated the attention she received from Father Mark, and didn't suspect there was anything wrong with the priest's behavior until she started attending Mother Guerin High School in River Grove. She described her experiences to her counselor, Sister Magdalena, who eventually, reported the incidents to the Archdiocese of Chicago.

One of the Archdiocesan priests came to the high school to interview the sixteen-year-old Veronica. By then, she was barely passing her classes and her erratic school behavior was becoming quite dubious. By the time she was a senior in high school, she was a full-blown drug addict. She had spent several weeks in alcohol rehabilitation and had been suspended several times for her problematic conduct and excessive absences. The counselor had many sessions and meetings with the troubled young girl during and after school, and Sister 'Lena' would always remember the black rosary that Veronica always carried with her and would often wear around her neck. It took all the nun's power, intense praying and influence to convince the other Sisters of St. Mary to graduate Veronica from Mother Guerin High School in 1989.

Fr. Mark Ryan was often reprimanded by the Archdiocese of Chicago and was placed in 'intense therapy' several times, until he was forced to resign from his pastoral duties in 1992. He continued to teach at several parochial high schools in the Chicagoland area until his recent retirement. He never took responsibility for his many young rape victims, or for the psychological and emotional damage that he had inflicted on them. Little girls like Veronica DiCarlo, whom he had been sexually molested and abused at a very early age, forever damaging and mutilating their young, impressable souls.

That is, until one day a several months ago, when he received an anonymous phone call. It was from an irate, angry man with a deep, low voice. He threatened and cursed the pedophile ex-priest over the phone, explaining that the 'deepest depths of Hell would be too good for him', promising revenge and inflicting a 'slow, bloody, miserable death' very soon.

Veronica DiCarlo, at age 45, became an alcoholic and a drug addict. She had been married, divorced and discarded several times. Veronica had several abortions and had been in and out of drug and alcohol rehab continuously throughout her life. She was literally disowned by her close knit, Italian-Catholic family. As a means of survival, she had become a prostitute and had an extensive rap sheet with the Chicago Police. Veronica often traded her body and sexual favors for food, for heroin, for alcohol and cocaine. She often slept in cardboard boxes and in flop houses, hanging out in seedy neighborhoods far away from her childhood home in Jefferson Park.

One day, she was found dead behind an abandoned warehouse in an open field on South Stoney Island and 93rd Streets. Veronica had apparently died of a drug overdose and had been dead for several days. When the Chicago P.D. found her infested, partially decomposed body, she was gripping something tightly in her right hand:

It was a black rosary.

CHAPTER FORTY

"If you didn't want to go to church, all you had to do was say it."

"I'm sorry, Olivia. I just had a thought regarding these murder investigations come to my head and I had to talk to my partner about it. I become overwhelmed," I replied, as I knew I had it coming.

"I don't appreciate being abandoned in the middle of mass, Phil. Whatever you got into your head could have waited until after church."

Olivia was right. I didn't need to run out of that church in the middle of mass that morning. I was totally apologetic that Sunday morning as I arrived back at the loft, knowing that she would be irate and waiting for me. But these "Pedophile Priest Murders" had been overruling my life, and the thought of these serial killers still out there was completely consuming me. I knew I couldn't trust anyone with any additional information on this case, and I had to be careful who I trusted and given any information to. At that point, I knew I could only trust Tommy Morton in my department.

I wanted so much to trust Olivia with updates on this case. But...my sixth sense was screaming at me again. I didn't quite understand her apprehensiveness in not filing a police report and going on record with the 'Attorney James Gleason' visit. There was something inside of me that was holding me back, and I decided to listen to my intuition. I knew that if I continued to share my information with Morton, the two of us could 'put our heads together', assemble the facts of this case together and solve it. But at this point, I just couldn't completely trust Olivia with everything.

Not just yet.

I walked over to Olivia while she was standing in the kitchen, and I put my arms around her waist from behind as she was cutting up the garlic and onions. She was cooking, preparing to make her traditional 'Sunday Sauce' for our afternoon dinner.

"You know, I hear you're supposed to make love before Sunday afternoon spaghetti sauce," I whispered in her ear, knowing that I could interest her in working up our appetite.

"You know I'm pissed. Why are you doing this?" as I continued to place small kisses and love bites along the back of her neck, her ears, and her soft, sensuous skin which smelled absolutely wonderful. As I continued to strategically place my kisses along the front of her neck and breasts, she dropped the knife, which incredibly stuck into the hardwood floor. It missed my foot within inches.

She started to laugh. "You should be careful, Detective. Never approach a women with a knife from behind," as we both laughed, and proceeded to my bedroom late Sunday morning.

The early morning traffic was heavy that early Monday, as I was making a left-hand turn onto my favorite Dunkin' Donuts for my large coffee and my usual sesame seed bagel. After merging back onto North Milwaukee Avenue traffic, my mind was consumed with the status of these "Pedophile Priest Murders" and my discussion with Tommy that previous morning.

But I was also thinking about Olivia. We had spent a wonderful Sunday together, as it was her final day in Chicago. I found myself getting extremely attached to her, as we had been spending the last several days together. She had to leave my place late last evening to drive back to Detroit. She promised to drive back in the following Friday night to spend the next weekend together. I offered to fly to Detroit and visit her, but we both realized that it wasn't possible if I was working on these outstanding murder cases.

I was very hesitant to use the 'L' word and had to force myself to keep from saying it in front of her. I wanted so much to tell her what I was feeling. Olivia was so easy to talk to, and we spent most of our time laughing and joking together, at just about everything we talked about. I couldn't remember the last time I had felt so comfortable with someone, who had the intellect and patience to understand me and get to know me.

Olivia was kind and easy-going, and she was willing to help me work through all my emotional shortcomings. She knew from the very beginning of how broken and emotionally scarred I was, but she was enduring and tolerant. She made me feel special, and she made me feel like I was the most wonderful man in the whole world. That 'solid, concrete wall' around my heart was now completely torn down, and I was scared to death.

But her stalling and pushing me off when I asked her to come into the precinct to file a police report, still bothered me. I just couldn't get it out of my head.

I walked into my precinct and over to Detective Tommy Morton's office, which was adjacent to mine, and sat at his front chair. I was consuming my goodies from the donut shop, while he was eyeing a pack of Marlboro Lights sitting on top of his desk, just waiting to be smoked.

"How many cigarettes are you up to now?" I ignorantly asked, realizing that Detective Morton almost always had a cigarette in his mouth.

"I can't wait to solve these friggin' murders, Phil. This 'three-pack-a-day' routine is getting too damn expensive."

"Yeah, okay, Tommy," I joked. "Blame it on the 'Pedophile Priest Murders'. Go ahead and kill yourself smoking cigarettes." I made myself comfortable in front of his desk with my cream cheese bagel and coffee.

"I saw Oprah on a Weight Watchers commercial last night. They're running a summer special this month," he mentioned. "If you lose weight and can fit into a Speedo bathing suit, the first fifty pounds are free," he joked back, taking another shot at my waistline.

I sat in front of his desk, and we were both silent as he was on his computer screen, trying to find information on any and all the ex-priests in the Chicagoland area over the last fifty years.

"I called Intel again over at the Twenty-First. They promised me a comprehensive list this afternoon," Morton said.

"You didn't specifically limit the list to all those named 'Mark', did you?"

"Of course not. I figured Russo is probably watching us like a hawk if he knows something, and he's probably eye-balling everything that's coming out of his precinct regarding this investigation."

"Good."

Detective Morton continued to search the internet and make notes on his notepad, trying to find more online evidence. He noticed me only sitting there speechless. He knew something was on my mind.

"How are things with your new girlfriend?"

"Olivia? Just fine," I answered.

Tommy stopped what he was doing and looked at me. We had gotten to be very close friends over the last few weeks, and I mentioned that I had started dating Olivia. At first, he didn't say much about it. But for whatever reason that morning, he could see something that was on my mind.

"Phil...aren't you nervous dating someone who has a conflict of interest in these serial murders?"

"What do you mean," I stupidly asked, even though I knew exactly what he was talking about.

"Come on, Phil. She's the one holding the purse strings for these insurance claims for the Archdiocese. How much are we up to now, with the death of three priests? Fifteen million or more?"

"I haven't told her much, Tommy. I've only given her some tidbits of information which she has inquired about. I've been giving her just enough information to keep her company from hiring an independent private investigator and getting in the way of these homicide cases," I replied.

"And what makes you think she hasn't done that already, Phil?"

"If she has, she hasn't informed me about it."

"Could that be the reason why she's spending so much time in Chicago? To perform her own investigation and keep track of her own private investigators?"

Tommy had a point. I was so involved in trying to solve these 'Pedophile Priest Murders', I never thought that she could have very well hired her own investigators, using my loft as her remote office. She could have quite possibly, been conducting her own private investigation on behalf of the life insurance company. She could have been working on this case behind my back in my own living room, never mentioning a single word about it.

"I would be careful if I were you, Phil. Until these cases are solved, I would keep her at arm's length."

Now my 'sixth sense' was yelling at me again. Could this be related to why she didn't want to file a police report regarding her 'miscellaneous visit' from Gleason'? Who could quite possibly be a member of this 'SRC Secret Society'? Was she hiding something?

"Tommy, do you have any connections at the Detroit Police Department?" I asked.

"Yeah, sure," he thought. "As a matter of fact, I have an old fraternity brother, who is a detective on the force there."

"Find out whatever information you can get on Olivia Laurent. Have someone do a thorough 'run-up' on her and see what comes up. Have one of their detectives look into her financial records as well," I asked.

"Okay, Phil. Let me make some phone calls."

I left Tommy's adjacent office, totally befuddled and confused. Was it quite possible that Olivia was using me to get additional information on these outstanding life insurance claims? If she was, what was in it for her? My mind was racing in a million different directions.

That afternoon, Tommy Morton knocked on my office door, with several pieces of paper in his hand.

"Phil, I've got that information you requested." I was dreading what Tommy had found.

"From the records that were pulled by the Detroit Police Department, your girlfriend is clean, for starters."

"Well...that's good, right?"

"Yes, except now my suspicions are turning over in my head. The AG's office did some financial checking,

344

corresponding her filed tax returns with various broker investment accounts. One thing came, that…well….maybe it's nothing."

"What is it, Tommy?"

"She just recently opened up a safe deposit box at Comerica Bank."

"So?"

"She opened up the safe deposit box on the same day that she told you about her "Gleason" visit."

I had previously mentioned Olivia's personal visit from 'Gleason' in Detroit that prior week to Tommy. I looked at my calendar, pinpointing the exact date, and which Comerica Bank branch she had opened the safe deposit box at. It was indeed the same day.

"Why is this unusual to you?" I was trying very hard to give her the benefit of the doubt.

"Really Phil? Come on. She gets a visit from some suspicious character, who says he's a lawyer from Chicago representing one of the victim's families. His business name and address don't check out, and he happens to be wearing an 'SRC' ring. On that very same day, she opens a safe deposit box. Then on the very next day, she's in Chicago, snooping around this investigation." I thought long and hard about what Tommy was saying.

"Doesn't all of this make you suspicious?" he asked again, driving his point home.

"Maybe she had a lot of jewelry that she needed to deposit. Maybe she just decided to get a safe deposit box for other reasons," as I was looking for a reasonable, alternative explanation. I didn't want to believe the worst.

"Or…maybe this Gleason character gave her something that she didn't want to keep in her office.

Did she ever come in to give you a statement on this guy's visit in Detroit?" Tommy asked.

"No. I asked her to come in a few times, but she couldn't make it in. She's been very busy," I replied, trying to make up more excuses for her.

"Or...she doesn't want to go on the record." Tommy suggested.

I sat there for several minutes in silence, trying to digest all this new information. I realized that perhaps, Olivia wasn't being one hundred percent honest with me, and that there was a possibility that she had hired her own private investigators to research these homicides and insurance claims.

I decided to make a few more phone calls and talked to one of the detectives at the Twenty-First District who was on Paul Russo's team. His name was Detective Max Palanti, and we had once worked together on a homicide case before. He was also extremely loyal to Russo, so I had to be very careful how I phrased my questions. I figured that if there was another private investigator involved on these 'Pedophile Priest Murders," Detective Palanti at Intel would know about it.

"Hey Max, its Phil Dorian from the Sixteenth," I replied when he answered the phone.

"Phil, what's up? I hear you're 'knee deep' into these 'Pedophile Priest Murders,'" he mentioned. I figured by that point, the whole Chicago Police Department probably knew about my being the lead investigator on these homicide cases.

We then talked and exchanged a few pleasantries, catching each other up on our personal lives. I ended up spending longer on the telephone talking with Palanti than I wanted to, remembering what a 'Chatty Cathy' he was.

"Max, have you been getting any inquiries from the Great Lakes Insurance Company regarding these homicides?" I inquired.

"Are you kidding? We've been getting phone calls every day...especially from their claims department and their own private investigator," he answered.

"Do you remember their names?" I asked.

"Yes, I've got her card right her," as he stumbled through his desk while still holding the telephone.

"Here it is...her name is Olivia Laurent, and she's from the life insurance company." At that moment, I felt my heart drop down to my stomach.

"Who else has been inquiring?"

"Besides the FBI and the media, some other private investigator named Michael Lemanski. His office is in the South Loop. Apparently, he was hired by this woman to investigate the validity of these claims and especially, Monsignor Kilbane's possible involvement."

Just beautiful, I thought to myself. Olivia had hired an outside private investigator while she was here in Chicago and never mentioned a word about it. That was all I needed to hear.

None of this was sounding good concerning the women who had so valiantly, destroyed and crumbled that concrete wall that was surrounding my previously broken heart. At that moment, I was in complete and total emotional pain, and I was physically sick to my stomach. I realized that I could never completely trust this woman. She was probably hiding other information from me regarding this case and Lord knows what else.

I calmly walked into the men's room from my office, walked into a bathroom stall and I physically threw up. I was standing over the toilet, just puking my guts out. Tommy came into the men's bathroom several minutes later.

"Phil, are you okay?"

"Yeah, Tom. I'm alright. Must have gotten some spoiled cream cheese on my bagel this morning." I was trying to make excuses, but Tommy knew better.

"Take the rest of the day off, Phil. I'll cover for you. I'll call you with anything else that I find out."

"Thanks Tommy," as I grabbed my gun and suitcoat and walked out of the district.

As I sat in my Crown Vic that afternoon in the parking lot of the precinct office. My head was dizzy, and my stomach was still queasy and in knots. There was a part of me that wanted to drive five hours down I-94, straight over to Olivia's Detroit office and just choke the living shit out of her. I felt like I had been used. I felt like I was completely deceived and our whole time together was just a lie. I just sat in my car with both hands on the steering wheel for several long, quiet minutes. It seemed like my squad car was the only place where I could find any peace and quiet and put in a quick prayer.

I prayed for understanding. I prayed for patience, and I prayed for strength. I didn't want to believe that the woman that I had completely opened myself up to was conducting her own murder investigation behind my back, and never thought to mention any of this to me. And why the safe deposit box? On the same day as her visit from Gleason? What the hell was she hiding?

I knew I had to play it cool from here on out. I knew I had to keep quiet and not let Olivia know what I know. I had to play my cards close to my chest. From that day forward, I had a new name:

Cool Hand Luke.

CHAPTER FORTY-ONE

When I got to my office the next morning, there were several files sitting on my desk. Tommy Morton had called me the night before, letting me know that he had finally received the information we had requested from Intel regarding the list of ex-priests in Chicago. He had gone through the extensive list and located the specific information regarding ex-priests with the first names of Mark, or a derivative thereof. The four files on my desk were the names of the former priests Mark Decker, Marc Ugolini, Marcus Gillian, and Mark Ryan. I read through the files extensively, as Morton had done a great job doing an extensive background check on each former priest.

Mark Decker, 53 years old, had resigned from the priesthood in 2009, and was now currently married with children and living in Highland Park. He currently works as an executive banker for Bank of America in the city.

Marc Ugolini had resigned from the Archdiocese in 1995 and was now 67 years old and currently living in Naples, Florida. He is currently a widower and had worked as a financial planner for a Chicago Loop consulting firm before his recent retirement.

Marcus Gillian, 71, left the Joliet Diocese in 1999 and worked as a cost accountant for a manufacturing company in Geneva, Illinois for many years. Gillian was married and divorced twice, and is currently retired and living in Scottsdale, Arizona.

Mark Ryan, 70 years old, who left the Archdiocese of Chicago in 1992, was a former high school English and Religion teacher at both Montini High School in Lombard and Driscoll High Schools in Addison before his retirement four years ago. He is currently living in a townhome in the Sauganash neighborhood on the north side of Chicago and does extensive volunteer work at a handicapped children's home in Ravenswood. His file states that he currently unmarried and lives alone.

None of the files included any formal charges, arrests or accusations of any sexual deviant behavior by any of the former priests. Two of the four former priests now lived and retired out of state, while one former priest was currently married with children. I concluded that those circumstances precluded three of them from being likely candidates for the 'secret society'.

By process of elimination, Mark Ryan was the only likely candidate who could possibly, fit the profile. It was a long shot, but I convinced Commander Callahan to give me a few patrolmen to start the surveillance of Ryan, who lived at 6014 N. Kilpatrick in the north end of Chicago. We had put an unmarked car in front of his house, and another car to follow Ryan, his daily whereabouts and his routine. He seemed to enjoy going to the local gym early every morning, and except for doing a few daily errands, didn't often leave his house.

I also did something on my own that afternoon that probably would have gotten me in trouble, had my Commander been aware of my inquiries. I called Detective Max Palanti at the Twenty-First District and asked him to meet me at a local Starbucks nearby. I asked him if there was a possibility of talking to him in confidence regarding these 'Pedophile Priest Murders' and the current status of this case. I mentioned my suspicions regarding his boss, Detective Sergeant Paul Russo and inquired about the possibility of tracking his whereabouts daily.

"There's no way you're going to be able to 'put a tail' on him without his knowledge," Palanti mentioned.

"Russo is pretty well connected in the Chicago P.D., and will eventually find out about any inquiries or surveillance you may be putting on him."

"Doesn't he have his own squad car which he uses on a daily basis?" I asked. "Maybe we could put a GPS tracking device on it."

"There already is. All the squad cars in the Twenty-First have GPS devices on them, and the desk sergeant can pretty much trace where all the police squad cars are. Besides, if Russo was going to do something unlawful, illegal, or something very stupid, he's not going to do it using a Chicago P.D. squad car," he reasoned.

"So, do I have to start 'tagging' this guy myself?" I asked, knowing that this was really a silly question.

"Either that or hire your own surveillance team on the 'down low', without the Chicago P.D. knowing about it. But even if you do, Russo is way too smart to allow himself to be followed. He looks for that shit. He's a pretty sharp, careful guy, Phil," the detective remarked of his boss. This conversation only left me even more frustrated.

"Can you at least let me know if you see or hear of anything that's suspicious concerning Russo and his actions? I've got a sick feeling that Russo knows more than what he's letting on regarding these murders," I requested.

"Will do, Phil," he said. Palanti then gave me his 'scouts honor' that he would be discrete regarding my suspicions and our conversation.

We began the surveillance of the former Fr. Mark Ryan, hoping that within the next several days, the 'secret society' would try to get to him. I also decided to spend a few nights following and putting surveillance on Russo, using my personal car, a late model blue Ford Escape. I figured Tommy and I could take turns and keep an eye on this guy, hoping we could find some clues.

I also decided to do some digging on Sal Marrocco, the family consigliere. I researched all the police records and information that was available on him. He was a married man, with three grown college age children, and a long-time resident of Burr Ridge, Illinois. He had no priors, no violations, and no arrest record of any kind. Not even a speeding ticket.

The only thing that was unusual about Marrocco was that he liked to accumulate a lot of parking tickets. One would think that a powerful, mobbed up guy like Marrocco, who likes to stay under the radar, could at least make sure his car was legitimately parked.

Typical wise guy, I thought to myself. Marrocco probably thinks he's too much of a *spaccone* or a big shot to feed the 'green box' and get a parking receipt. He probably waited until he accumulated enough of them, and then got them fixed or adjusted by whoever his police connection was in getting these parking violations abated. I decided to look up the specific details of those parking tickets, license plate numbers, addresses and dates. He had accumulated over twenty parking tickets over the last six months, some of them sporadically to different addresses downtown.

But I thought it was unusual that six of those parking tickets were issued at the same West Division Street address. When checking the dates of those violations, I noticed something even more unusual. Those parking tickets seemed to always be issued on the third Thursday of each month. Very unusual, I thought to myself. I decided to take a ride over to the area of where the parking violations were regularly issued, around the West Division and Ashland Avenue areas.

In looking around the area, there wasn't anything that I thought was unusual. There was a dry cleaner on the corner, a Mexican taco joint, an auto repair shop on Ashland Avenue, a small pizzeria facing West Division and an abandoned old, brownstone church on the corner. The church had an old, very antiquated sign in front of it. "Calvary M.B. Baptist Church' was all it said, and the church looked like it hadn't been occupied in years. There were a few broken stained-glass windows, and one of the windows was boarded up on the side of the old, antiquated building.

Something came over me, and I had a hunch. I knocked on a few of the neighbors surrounding the old building. One old man, who didn't want to give me his name at first, said that he thought the building was rented out 'once a month', and saw various, well dressed guys going into the building.

"Does this usually happen on the third Thursday of each month?" I asked the old man.

"Eh...yes, I think so. Come to think of it, you're right. The third Thursday of each month, a bunch of well-dressed guys, looks like they're wearing tuxedos, meet there for a few hours once a month at night," the old man recalled. He then told me his name was 'Gus', and said he didn't want me 'to write nuttin' down.'

"Anything else unusual, Gus?" I asked him.

"Well, yeah, if you think this is unusual..."

"What?"

"Well, it's kinda' weird. They don't all go inside at once, ya' know. I noticed 'dem one night...that only one guy, well dressed, looks like he's wearin' a tuxedo goes, into 'da church, and then, after a little bit, another one goes in, one at a time. They never all go in at once, ya' know. And then after a few hours, one by one, they's all leave," Gus recounted, in a very thick Chicago accent.

"Guys in tuxedos, going into the old church late at night, one at a time?" I repeated.

"Well, yeah...I don't know if you think that's weird or not. But it seems like 'des guys are very careful about how they enter and leave 'da building," said the old man.

"Thanks Gus. If you think of anything else or notice anything, please give me a call," as I gave him my card.

I realized by looking at my calendar that we were in the second week of June, and that the third Thursday of the month was coming up next week. I noted it in my calendar that I needed to return there next week and stake this place out.

The next evening, Tommy and I decided to do some surveillance on Detective Paul Russo. He lived in a red bricked bungalow in the Logan Square area on 3431 West Lyndale Street. I knew that just following him around wasn't going to do us a whole lot of good or get us a significant amount of information. I realized that we needed to search his home but knew getting a search warrant from a judge would alert him to our suspicions. We needed more evidence, even if it wouldn't be admissible on its own. We needed more information that would tie him directly to this 'secret society'.

We waited for him to leave his house, which was approximately 8:00 o'clock. Tommy Morton followed Russo in his unmarked car, while I broke into his house using the back door. I had one of those lock picking kits that the locksmiths use, which easily works on older and over-the-counter hardware store locks. When I got inside, I looked around his house, spending about five to ten minutes in each room, until I got to his bedroom upstairs. Going through his bedroom, I found several serrated knives in the upper left-hand drawer of his dresser. I took pictures of them on my iPhone and looked around and took some other photos of some other items which I thought were important. Remembering my conversation with 'Gus the neighbor' the night before, I decided to go through his wardrobe closet. There, I found all the information that I needed:

Hanging in a Nordstrom garment bag was a black tuxedo with an attached white plastic sack. Inside the sack was a folded red cover which looked like a red, Klu-Klux-Klan mask, with holes cut out for the eyes. Upon further inspection, I found even more direct evidence: Attached to his tuxedo label, was his 'secret society' name tag, still pinned to his tuxedo jacket.

Bingo...the Las Vegas jackpot machine was spinning triple-sevens, with all the bells and whistles going off loudly in my head.

I took some more pictures, then decided to 'high-tail it' out of there before Russo returned home. I called Morton and told him of what I found. I met him at the nearby coffee shop not far away and discussed my investigation results with him.

All we needed now was to connect him to the next, planned execution.

I had arrived home late that night and only had some pasta leftovers that Olivia had made over the weekend for dinner. I was literally standing in front of the microwave in my underwear when my cell phone loudly rang.

"What's up, stranger? I haven't heard from you in a while."

"Sorry...I just got home," noticing that it was already past eleven o'clock. I was still happy to hear Olivia's voice over the phone, even though I had some reservations.

"Is Chicago still a safe place under your watch, Detective?" she playfully asked.

"Well, we haven't got our man yet if that's what you're referring to. Still following leads," I replied. I decided earlier that I was not going to be very forthright with any information regarding the 'Pedophile Priest Murders'.

We exchanged a few pleasantries and talked about each other's day, as I tried to leave out as much information as possible regarding the investigations. I tried to change the subject several times, talking about the day's current events while CNN was blaring loudly in the background.

"What's wrong, Phil? You sound distant."

"Oh, nothing honey. I'm just tired. It's been a very long day." Olivia probably picked up on my apprehensiveness over the telephone, but she decided not to push it.

"Are we still on for Friday night? Can I stay at your place again?" she asked.

"Of course," I replied, feeling as though I didn't have any choice.

"Great. We'll talk before I get into town. I can't wait to see you. Ciao!" as she blew me a kiss over the phone.

As I ended the phone call, I realized the quandary I was in. I had to be the greatest actor in the world, hiding my feelings, my reservations, my disappointment and my anger towards Olivia. I realized that I couldn't trust her, and I wasn't sure I wanted to continue our relationship anymore. Not until I could, at the very least, get some straight answers out of her. I've never been an actor, and hiding my feelings has never been one of my stronger personality traits.

Maybe after Friday night, I'll be nominated for an Academy Award.

CHAPTER FORTY-TWO

THE LAST SUPPER

The traffic on Grand Avenue was backed up to North Milwaukee Avenue, as I was maneuvering my squad car going west bound to Bella Luna Ristorante that Friday evening. Olivia had called me on her drive into Chicago and was running late. Rather than meeting her at my loft, we agreed to get together at the restaurant, as she had left her office in Detroit late that afternoon and was still on the road.

I had stayed behind and worked late at the precinct. There were some additional files and paperwork that I needed to catch up on. Although it was Friday, I was in no hurry to go home, and I wasn't that excited about getting together with Olivia. To be honest, I was very apprehensive about getting together and seeing her that evening. My emotions had run the gambit for the last couple of days, from missing her and our intense relationship, to disappointment, anger and betrayal. The possibility of her withholding information and conceivably, going behind my back and around me in these Pedophile Priest Murder investigations irritated the hell out of me.

I found parking at the hot dog stand across the street on the corner of Grand and Noble Streets, and noticed Olivia's white BMW with Michigan license plates, parked directly across from the restaurant. I was wearing a new Brooks Brothers dark tweed sport coat that evening, which I had picked up a few days ago after work.

It seemed that all the stress of these homicide investigations had produced at least one good result: I had lost some weight. I was down a few sizes all the way around, and dating Olivia lately gave me a good excuse to run out and buy some better fitting, more fashionable clothing. I strolled into the checker clothed Italian restaurant, noticing Olivia sitting towards the back of the cute little 'trattoria'. The dim lights and the soft, crooning music seemed to provide an excellent backdrop as I made my grand entrance.

"Hey baby!" Olivia exclaimed as she got up from the table, giving me a warm, wet kiss and a long, intense hug. As I smiled and kissed her back, I could hear Frank Sinatra's "Witchcraft" song playing softly in the background.

How appropriate, I thought to myself.

"It's so nice to see you again. I love your sports coat."

"Thanks. Just picked it up the other day," I replied.

"The dark tweed looks good on you. You're looking more and more dapper every day, Mr. Dorian," she said, flattering me with endearing compliments.

I didn't know what to believe anymore. I was questioning her sincerity, her honesty and her integrity, as I was totally conflicted. There was a part of me that wanted to forget whatever I had heard or found out from the Detroit Police Department, and to just make incredible love to her right there in the middle of the restaurant.

She was wearing a smart, dark gray Burberry jacket, with a dark red blouse, short gray skirt and black, high heeled shoes. Her wavy, curly shoulder length hair complimented soft red lipstick, as she was wearing very light makeup. Olivia had a natural beauty, as her dark olive skin made her look so much younger than her years. From a distance, she could have passed for Jennifer Lopez's double, with her soft brown eyes and sexy smile. She looked and smelled totally amazing.

"I missed you," she said, as we received our wine glasses of Pinot Noir. I looked at her and smiled, as I was trying so very hard keep my disappointment and my anger under wraps.

We continued to make small talk, as she told me her activities for the week and the various problems going on in her office. We talked about her family and her friends, as I reciprocated, trying to keep up with the conversation. She looked at me intently at times, as if she knew something was awry.

We continued to converse as our dinner entrées arrived, and I nervously tried to keep our table discussion from lagging. I was doing my very best to keep my ill feelings under wraps, but I could tell Olivia was getting suspicious. As I was taking the last bite of my veal scaloppini, she finally confronted me:

"Phil, you're not yourself tonight. What's wrong?"

"Nothing, honey. Everything is fine," I denied.

"No, Phil. I know you a lot better than you think, and you have been very cold and distant all night. What's going on?"

I tried not to look up, as I knew my anger would be written all over my face.

"Is it this investigation? Is there something going on? What's going on with these 'Pedophile Priest Murders?'" she pressed.

I couldn't hold it in any longer.

"I don't know, Olivia. Why don't you ask Detective Palanti over at Intel? I'm sure he can give you an update," I angrily replied.

Olivia's expression turned three shades of white, as she suddenly had that shocked look on her face.

"Why didn't you tell me you were working directly with another CPD detective on these claims?

Why didn't you tell me you had hired a private investigator last week?"

"Phil, these life insurance claims are my job. I didn't want to tell you because I didn't want to get in the way of your investigations. Besides, I don't owe you any explanation regarding anything concerning my job or how I do it," she defensively replied.

"Really? Is that why you hired this P.I...what's his name? Michael Lemanski? You hire a private investigator behind my back and you say nothing? Here, we have been trying to get Intel at the Twenty-First to get us information on these investigations and Palanti is feeding info to your guy instead. And then you say you don't 'owe me an explanation'?"

My anger started to build up, and then I exploded. "You and I have gotten so close, and you stayed at my place and set up shop in my living room. You were working in my house and behind my back on this investigation, and you said absolutely nothing."

"I didn't want to get in your way, Phil. And yes, I do NOT owe you an explanation!"

"Really Olivia? You couldn't be honest and tell me what you were up to? And besides, I asked you to come into my district office and fill out a police report on this 'Gleason visit' that you received at your office in Detroit. I asked you several times, and each time you made up an excuse. Why Olivia? Did you not want to go on record? Did this visit really happen? What else do you know, Olivia?" I started to press her hard, and I could tell she was getting aggravated as the steam started to come out of her eyes. Her expression was turning into total anger.

"I owe you nothing Phillip, and yes, I really *did* get a visit from 'Gleason', and the reason I told you about it was to assist you in your investigation. I've told you everything, Phil. I've told you the truth," she insisted, her voice starting to get louder and louder.

"You've told me everything, Olivia? Really?"

"Yes...really," as her eyes were starting to well up.

"Then why would you open a Comerica Bank safe deposit box on the same day as this 'Gleason' visit? What was so important that you had to open up a box on that day and then come to Chicago the very next day?" I was asking her hard-hitting questions, and I wasn't holding back.

She looked at me in total shock as she began to explode.

"How would you know about a safe deposit box? You've been investigating me?" she started yelling.

"You son-of-a-bitch! Boy, once a detective, always a fucking detective, huh, Phil? " She started to throw her napkin on the table as she got up and grabbed her car keys and her purse.

"What was so important that you needed a safe deposit box on that day, Olivia?" I interrogated, as though she were sitting in my holding room at the precinct and being examined by a room full of coppers.

"That's none of your damn business, Detective!"

"Then maybe I should ask the Cook County D.A's office to get a subpoena and make it my business, Olivia. You obviously have something to hide. Something that needed to be put into a safe deposit box right away!"

"Fuck you, Phil," as she angrily started to walk out of the restaurant. It looked as though she was in a foot race for the door. I decided to run after her, which maybe wasn't the smartest move. I was chasing after her in the middle of the restaurant, yelling at her with more questions.

"Why are you leaving Olivia, if you have nothing to hide? Why are you running away?" I yelled out at her, as we were getting the attention of the other restaurant patrons. She angrily looked towards me as she approached and unlocked her BMW, opening her car door.

"You'll always be a detective, Phil. No matter what I say or do. You'll always be suspicious. Why can't you love and accept someone for who they are? Why can't you accept reality for a change, instead of looking at every woman as though we all have an angle? The whole world is out to fuck you, right, Phil?" she said as she was starting to cry.

"I cared so much about you, Phil! I was looking so forward to having you in my life," she loudly sobbed.

She started crying profusely, standing next to her car with her door wide open. As I stood in front of the restaurant door, I could see her tears streaming down her face.

"For your information," she began to yell back, "I had some gold jewelry which I had been keeping in my purse for several weeks' now...expensive jewelry that my mother had given me. I didn't feel comfortable walking around with $20,000 worth of gold and diamonds in my purse or keeping them at home."

As the tears were running down her face, I seriously thought about tackling her down in the middle of Grand Avenue and putting an end to this whole argument. I wanted to apologize. I was starting to feel terrible, remorseful and so goddamned guilty.

"Come back inside, Olivia. Stop running away. Let's talk about this."

"No, dammit! I care about you so much. Put that down in your damned report and in your damn subpoena, Detective Dorian!" as she got into her expensive, high end BMW and put the car in drive.

I approached her car and knocked on her passenger side window, yelling back, "Why are you running away, Olivia? Come back inside!"

"Go to Hell!" she yelled back.

She pulled out as fast as she could onto the busy boulevard, pushing down on her accelerator and loudly screeching the tires of her car. She almost collided into another car, trying to run away from me in front of the restaurant as fast as she could. I stood there for several minutes, watching her car go west bound on Grand Avenue. Her BMW taillights were getting smaller and smaller, as she drove further and further away.

If Olivia was telling me the truth, then why was she getting so angry and running away when I was asking her questions? Why was she so defensive? Because I found out about her safe deposit box? What was she hiding from me? What was Olivia not telling me?

I kept turning the events of our dinner date over and over in my head, trying to make heads or tails out of all that had just happened. I was frozen in front of 1372 West Grand Avenue, as if I couldn't move. I was so conflicted and upset, and now I was feeling emotions that I hadn't felt in a very long time.

I paid the bill and went home that evening. I tried to call and text Olivia that night and several times the following Saturday morning, but she didn't respond. By the way her Apple iPhone was immediately responding, I could tell that she had blocked my phone calls and texts.

Olivia made me feel as though I didn't have a right to be investigative and suspicious. If she would have come into the precinct and filled out that police report, I would have had no reason to be so apprehensive and distrustful. I was angry that she had flipped and pointed the blame and her anger towards me. I was hoping we would talk again whenever she cooled off. But unfortunately, that never happened, and

I was left feeling the very thing that I hoped I would never emotionally, ever feel again.

I was feeling pain.

CHAPTER FORTY-THREE

THE FOURTH EVANGELIST

It was still dark outside as Mark Ryan arrived at 5:00am at the Sauganash Fitness Center for his morning workout routine. Ryan was very religious about getting in his fitness routine every morning. At the age of 70 years old, he was still quite fit and trim. He usually spends an hour doing cardio exercises on the Precor elliptical machine and then another thirty minutes power walking on the treadmill. Afterwards, he did over hundred crunch exercises and some light weights before the end of his two-hour morning regimen.

On that morning, his routine was no different. He spent two hours doing his normal workout, then returned to the men's locker room. There were only a few people working out that early morning at the gym, and the locker room was void of other people. Ryan removed his workout clothes and walked toward the adjacent shower room, where there were several private shower stalls.

An older man, dressed in gray sweatpants and a black tee shirt, sunglasses and black baseball cap, entered the men's locker room of the Sauganash Fitness Center, carrying a gym bag. He walked around the locker room, making sure there was no one else there, except noticing that Ryan was taking a shower in the shower stall. The man then removed all his clothing and placed them in a locker. He then put on a pair of elastic, surgical gloves. Being naked and holding only a knife and a red rose, he placed the flower on the floor next to the shower stall. The locker room intruder then approached the lone gentleman while he was taking a hot shower.

As the hot water was continuing to lather the former priest, the intruder opened his shower stall door and placed his hand over Ryan's mouth from behind, closing the shower door behind him. He then quickly inserting a sharp serrated knife deep into his throat. Blood began squirting everywhere inside the stall, covering the glass stall door which seemed to be the only witness to this gruesome murder as the killer said a quick prayer.

"May Jesus have mercy on your soul, Father Ryan,"

The murderer began to continuously stab Ryan's torso from behind, while blood was splattering everywhere along the shower floor and onto its white, ceramic tiled walls.

With the shower door still closed and the water still running, the naked intruder stood under the hot water for a few seconds, washing Ryan's blood off his body. After blessing the body, he grabbed his knife and exited the shower, placing the red rose on top of Ryan's wet, lifeless body. He then quickly walked back to towards his locker.

As the killer hastily dried off and was throwing his clothes back on, another older man came into the men's locker room of the Sauganash Fitness Center and walked towards his locker. The stranger had already worked out and was proceeding to get undressed to take a shower in the adjacent shower room. The intruder looked in the other direction, making sure the man didn't get a good look at him, then proceeded to quickly leave. Wearing his cap and sunglasses, he then hurriedly exited the Sauganash Fitness Center, and casually drove away in a black, older model Ford Explorer.

It was barely 7:30 when I had arrived at my office. I didn't even have time to take a sip of my Dunkin' Donuts coffee before my cell phone starting ringing. It was Tommy.

"Phil...Ryan was murdered."

"What?"

"Yeah, Phil, Mark Ryan was just found dead at the Sauganash Fitness Center. Somebody walked into the men's locker room and stabbed him while he was taking a shower."

"How in the hell did they get to Ryan? We had fucking surveillance on him."

"Don't know Phil. Just got a phone call from the Twentieth District. They had an unmarked cop car in the parking lot of the Fitness Center. They saw Ryan walk in at 5:00am, and they found him stabbed to death around 7:15 in the shower stall."

"I'll be right there."

I jumped into my squad car and raced over to the 3140 West Peterson address of the Fitness Center, approaching what would be now the fourth "Pedophile Priest Murder" in six weeks. I imagined it was going to be a friggin' zoo out there with the media, the police, the politicians and the 'Ivory Tower'.

As I arrived at the parking lot in Sauganash, there was crime tape blocking off the Fitness Center entrance and Chicago patrol cars everywhere. There was even a helicopter circling the area high above, and it looked like 'Vietnam' with detectives and patrolman ubiquitously around the area. I was afraid to approach the front door as I was bombarded with reporters inquiring about the victim and the crime scene. Tommy Morton was the first one to approach me.

"The Superintendent wants to see us," he said, as he was holding a cigarette with one hand and his pack of Marlboro Lights in the other.

"Wonderful, just can't friggin' wait," I replied.

We walked past the front desk and into the men's locker room where the shower area was taped off. The body of a naked older man was laying in the shower stall. His throat had been slit and he had several stab wounds across his torso. His blood had been slowly draining towards the middle of the shower room, and there were blood stains splattered everywhere around the shower cubicle. Because the murder took place in the shower area of the locker room, I expected to find more blood around the murder scene than I did. It was as though the murderer had time to 'wash off' the body before placing his signature red rose on the former priest.

Superintendent Ryan was already fielding questions from the press when I approached him and Commander Callahan, standing near the front desk.

"Why haven't we solved these murders?" demanded the Superintendent.

"We have a lot of clues and some evidence. We had this victim under surveillance. We predicted he was the next victim."

"Then how in the hell did he end up murdered?"

"We don't know. We had a squad car parked in front of the victims' house, and a 'tail' on him 24/7," I replied. I felt foolish trying to explain to the Superintendent that we predicted the next "Pedophile Priest Murder" victim.

"Let me get this straight, Dorian. You figured out that this guy was the next victim, and with police surveillance, you still couldn't stop his murder?"

"Apparently not, Superintendent," I replied, knowing that I would now probably feel the wrath of his temper.

"How did you know this former priest was the next victim, and what other evidence do you have," he asked me point blank asked me.

I looked at Commander Callahan, knowing that I would have to limit my answer to his questions, not wanting to disclose any information that I had on Detective Russo at the Twenty-First District.

"We believe it's more than one killer, and they're part of a religious cult," I tried to explain.

The Superintendent looked at Callahan at myself, with that surprisingly shocked look on his face.

"There is a lot of information that Detective Morton and I have uncovered, and we are not at liberty to explain our theories on this just yet."

"Well, when are we going to hear your 'crime symposium' on these 'Pedophile Priest Murders', Detective," Callahan was starting to explode. "I can't believe that you predicted the murder of this victim, and yet you were unable to stop it."

At that moment, Detective Russo showed up at the crime scene, and elbowed his way between the other patrolman and the media reporters and shook hands with all of us standing in a circle in the middle of the fitness center near the front desk.

"We have another victim, I see," was all Russo said.

"Yes," I replied. I was gazing very closely at Russo, as he looked like he was a little disheveled. I noticed right away that his hair was wet, as though he didn't have time to dry it off.

"Did you go out for your usual run, Paul?" I cleverly asked.

"Yes. I just finished my run on the lakefront when I heard about this murder. I got dressed and ran over here right away."

My sixth sense was talking to me again, and it hadn't even had its Dunkin' Donuts coffee.

"This murder took place in the shower stall," I said directly to Russo. He tried to look surprised, but I was seeing right through it.

We continued to discuss the details of the crime scene. Tommy confirmed that there were no security cameras either in the building or in the parking lot, which I thought was unusual. He had talked to the Recreation Director, a Ms. Justine Lishamer, who said that the park district didn't have the funds budgeted for such security allowances, as the clientele were mostly senior citizens in the area.

I interviewed the patrolman in the squad car, who was supposedly 'tailing' Ryan, but said he didn't see anything unusual. He couldn't even tell me which cars had gone in or out of the parking lot that morning, which made me believe that the copper in charge of watching Ryan must have fallen asleep.

Commander Callahan approached me in private, when the others were not within earshot of our conversation.

"Dorian do you and Morton know what the hell you're doing?" he point blank asked, as he motioned Tommy over to our huddle.

"Trust me, Commander. We were onto this one. I have a feeling the patrolman in charge of surveilling Ryan fell asleep in the parking lot, otherwise, we would have caught the killer," I explained.

"We have a witness who thinks they saw a black, older model Ford Explorer leave the parking lot just before the body was discovered," Morton said.

Thankfully someone was awake, I thought to myself.

"I'm getting some shit from the Superintendent. I need a report on this case on my desk by tomorrow morning. I hope it will be as enlightening as you say it will be," Callahan sternly ordered, trying very hard to keep his temper under wraps.

We both looked at the Commander and nodded our heads in unison, knowing that we had our marching orders in hand.

We interviewed a few of the other employees of the Fitness Center and took some notes, but the whole time my eye was on Russo. He was standing around, talking to a few patrolman and trying to look busy. As he was walking back to his squad car, I decided to catch up with him.

"Paul, have you got a minute?"

"Sure," he uncomfortably answered, as he opened his squad car door.

I opened the passenger door and sat with him in his car. By that time, his salt and pepper hair had dried off and looked disheveled.

"Where were you this morning, Detective?" I asked him, point blank.

"I told you, Dorian. I was finishing my run on the lakefront."

"How far did you run?"

"About four miles, up to Belmont Harbor and back."

"How long did it take you?" I inquired.

"About 32 minutes."

"Do you run with a running watch?" I asked.

"Well yeah, sure.

"Where is it?" I asked.

Detective Russo pulled out his Nike running watch from his glove box. Knowing the habits of most dedicated joggers, they usually have their running watches close at hand, especially competitive runners like Russo.

"Can you show me your running time from this morning?" Most running watches not only have exact split times from their runs but have GPS capabilities as well.

Russo started fidgeting with his black running watch, pressing some of the buttons and looking for his morning distance time.

"That's funny," he exclaimed. "My time must have gotten erased."

I looked at him suspiciously, and I knew in my mind that I had him.

He started getting defensive. "Why all the questions, Dorian?"

"Is there someone who can verify your whereabouts this morning?"

"Where are you going with this, Dorian?" he demanded, while raising his voice.

I just looked at him, as I placed my hand next to my gun holster. I wanted to call over Morton and have him help me arrest him right there on the spot, but I knew I didn't have enough to hold him. Besides, I didn't want to blow up my theory and have this whole case explode in my face.

I just glared at him for about over a minute, and I wanted to let him know that I was now holding the cards to solving these murder cases. I also noticed that he was wearing his 'SRC' red-cross ring on his right hand while it was on the steering wheel. Russo started looking nervous with my questioning.

"Detective Russo, who were the four evangelists in the Bible?" I asked him.

He had a shocked look on his face at first, pretending he didn't know what I was talking about. But then, he began to smirk as he was nodding his head. He knew exactly where I was going with my questions, and a cool look of confidence came over his face. I could tell by the look in his eyes, that he knew I was onto him, and that his 'out for a run' story wasn't going to hold up.

"You can't prove a goddamn thing, Dorian," he laughed, as the look on his face turned from jovial to evil and satanic.

His response was almost cocky, as if he truly believed that he could never be caught or accused of any murder. He truly believed he was a professional, and that he never made any mistakes. He knew that I didn't have any concrete evidence against him, and that there was no way I could make any murder charge against him stick on that morning.

I gave him my Cheshire cat grin, as my right hand was still covering my holstered gun. As I began to exit his car, I initially didn't say another word. But I continued to study him for another minute or so, waiting for him to say something else incriminating.

"Make sure your running watch is working next time you're out for a run, Russo," I advised him as I was closing his passenger car door. I was doing everything in my power to keep myself from lunging at him right then and there. I then gave him my final words as he was turning on the ignition.

"And by the way...watch your back, 'Brother Cain'."

Russo only looked at me and smiled. He didn't even look shocked, only shaking his head in amusement. He then stepped on the accelerator and peeled his squad car out of the fitness center parking lot.

At that moment, I knew it was only a matter of time.

CHAPTER FORTY-FOUR

The summer sun was beginning to linger past five o'clock, as the warm extended evenings began to push back the late June sunsets. I had been sitting in my car for almost an hour, drinking a diet Coke and eating a Jimmy John's ham and cheese sub. I was parked about a half a block away from the old, brownstone church on West Division Street, trying to do more surveillance on any activity going on there.

After four "Pedophile Priest Murders", we didn't have any conclusive DNA evidence to match up to any of the suspects in these homicides. Kilbane's DNA and Bartell's DNA samples were a negative at all the crime scenes, and I neglected to steal anything from Russo's house (like a toothbrush or a comb) for DNA testing at the crime labs. Russo's personal vehicle was a late model Ford Mustang, not an older model Ford Explorer, so all my bets were running high that he would show up at this meeting at this old church on Division Street.

It was the third Thursday of the month, and according to the neighborhood witnesses, the abandoned building was used once a month by a 'bunch of guys wearing tuxedos', going in and out one at a time. I had a funny feeling after my unofficial 'search' of Russo's house that this was the place where the 'secret society' or the Society of the Rose Crucifix has their monthly meeting. The plan was that I was going to wait for Russo to show up, and Tommy Morton and I were going to confront him then. Morton was on another stack-out on another case in the district, so he agreed to come here as soon as he could.

It was just past 6:00pm, when I noticed one guy, dressed in a tuxedo, enter the abandoned church, using a key to enter the building. At 6:15pm, another guy, also dressed in a tuxedo, entered the building. Same routine at 6:30, 6:45 and 7:00. Using my high-power Minolta camera lens, I took pictures of everyone entering the abandoned church. It seemed that they were entering the building one at a time, every fifteen minutes.

I checked my watch and I called Tommy. It was almost 7:15pm, and he still hadn't showed up to assist me in this surveillance. I tried calling and texting him. His only response was that he was on his way. Another well-dressed guy in a penguin suit showed up to open the old door, again using his own key. At that point, I counted nine guys who had individually entered the abandoned church, but so far, no Russo. Tommy Morton still hadn't showed up to assist me.

I had researched that there were 'supposedly' at least twelve individuals, plus their grand knight, which totaled thirteen individuals that were a part of this secret society. I presumed that their entrance pattern would continue until at least eight o'clock.

I looked at my watch again. It was 7:35pm, and still, no Tommy.

At 7:45pm, I noticed Paul Russo walking along the south side of West Division Street towards the abandoned church. He was wearing his tuxedo, of course and was carefully looking around to see if he was being followed. I was nervous approaching him by myself, but I figured that I had no other choice. I got out of my car at that point and waited for him to insert his key into the front door of the old church.

"Russo!" I yelled out, as I quickly ran towards him before he entered the church.

"Need to bring you in to answer some questions," I officially said.

He must have recognized me immediately, as he quickly unlocked the door and entered inside. At that point, I called for back-up, hoping there would be some other squad cars in the area.

I knocked hard on the front door of the building, which was dead-bolted and locked, of course. I could hear a lot of commotion going on inside, as I continued to knock and announced that I was a 'Chicago P.D.' and demanded that they 'open up'.

Two squad cars had then showed up on West Division Street, and another squad car on South Ashland Avenue to give me the backup that I needed. At that point, I decided to shoot out the locks on the front door and enter the building, with my Glock revolver cocked and loaded.

As I entered the building, I was jumped by two individuals wearing red masks, with one putting his arm around my neck while the other grabbed my gun. They must have known that there were other squad cars behind me, and they quickly pulled me towards the east side of the church.

From what I could tell, there were at least six or seven red hooded men wearing black tuxedos standing in front of me, demanding to know who I was.

"Detective Dorian, Chicago P.D.' was all I managed to say, as another hooded 'knight began to confront me, holding a large knife. My arms and hands were held and pulled behind my back as I suddenly felt an excoriating pain spurn deeply into my stomach. As I looked down, the hooded member managed to pump the knife into my abdomen two or three times, as the blood started to spew out of my shirt and jacket. I lost my breath and I could no longer breathe, as I collapsed onto the floor. The knife still in my stomach, and there was blood gushing everywhere. The pain was excruciating, and I must have fell unconscious.

That was the last thing I remember.

CHAPTER FORTY-FIVE

"We are being invaded" Brother Rueben yelled out, as Brother Cain and Brother Abel dropped the fallen police detective onto the floor. The 'secret society' had an 'escape drill' which was part of their ritual code.

"Circondare" loudly exclaimed Brother Aaron, which was the society code word for 'encircle and self-destruct.' It was part of their society code that if the Society of the Rose Crucifix were ever invaded unexpectedly by an outsider, that the stranger would be immediately stabbed and destroyed.

As was part of their ritual, all the brother knights then formed a circle around the marble alter, holding each other's had and saying the Lord's prayer out loud. The knights that were encircled around the altar were Brothers Jebediah, Cain, Abel, Jacob, Zebedee, Jeramiah, Aaron, Adam, Rueben and Ebenezer. Another prayer in Latin was quickly said as the Chicago Police began entering the church with their guns drawn.

"May the Lord have mercy on our souls," exclaimed Brother Jacob, as he had earlier grabbed the three sticks of dynamite that were taped underneath the altar. He pulled out his lighter, lit up the three sticks of explosives and threw them into the middle of the church.

"Wait...stop," yelled one of the patrolman, as a large explosion suddenly occurred. Flames began to combust and surround the inner structure of the church building as it quickly detonated the inner wooden beams and structures.

The other policemen began to retreat outside, as several firetrucks from the Chicago Fire Department began to arrive. At that point, Detective Tommy Morton showed up at the scene of the fire and looked around for his partner.

"Has anyone seen Dorian?" he asked several firefighters and other policeman that were nearby. He tried calling his partner several times, but there was no answer.

For some odd reason, Morton must have figured out that his partner was inside of the old abandoned church at the time of the explosion. Without hesitation, he ran into the burning church, looking for Dorian.

As the flames were engulfing the already burnt structure, Morton looked around the front of the vestibule and on the east side of that church. At that point, he saw a man lying on the marble floor, with a knife sticking out of his stomach, surrounded in a pool of blood. He quickly called the assistance of another firefighter, who was helping the other firefighter in trying to put out the blaze. The two of them then managed to drag out Dorian, whose body seemed lifeless as he was being carried out and onto an awaiting stretcher. He was then placed on a gurney and quickly loaded onto and Chicago EMS Truck, while a paramedic began working on his vitals and administering oxygen.

"How does he look?" Morton asked one of the paramedics.

"Not good. He has a faint pulse and has lost a lot of blood." Dorian had apparently been stabbed several times in the abdomen and was fighting for his life.

Morton and a few other policeman went to assist the other paramedics and began pulling bodies out of the burning building. By that time, the news trucks began showing up at the scene. Chaz Rizzo ran out of the news truck and approached Tommy Morton.

"Where's Dorian?"

"He was in the building when it exploded. He was cut up pretty good," he managed to say, trying hard not to get emotional.

'They're taking him over to the hospital now."

Rizzo swallowed hard as he tried to collect his composure, then called the news cameras over while trying to get additional information from the other fire chiefs and police that were there.

Several bodies started being recovered from the fire scene, as the building was so inflamed that it was impossible for all the firemen to assess how many more people were inside. It wasn't until several hours later, well past midnight, that the firemen and EMT's were able to re-enter the building.

It was well after 2:00am when the flames were completely extinguished, and a crime scene tape had been circled around the burnt down structure. Three bodies were immediately recovered but were pronounced dead on arrival at the hospital. Four more bodies were pulled from the burning building but died at the scene from their burn injuries. The final three bodies were not immediately recovered until all the burning debris was removed the next morning. Those three bodies had been charred beyond recognition and were surrounding the front of the church around the now destroyed, marble altar. There were ten fatalities in all, with one injured policemen in critical condition.

Chaz Rizzo began his nightly news feed for Channel Eight Eyewitness news for the ten o'clock broadcast and began reporting on the church explosion and the number of fatalities inside. He began getting emotional when he announced the name of the injured police detective:

"Detective Phillip Dorian, a twenty-five-year veteran of the Chicago Police Department in the Sixteenth District, had been critically injured, enduring several stab wounds by the alleged assailants before being rescued from the burning structure. He has been taken to Rush Medical Hospital," he emotionally announced.

He then wiped the tears from his eyes as he tried to complete his newscast:

"Detective Dorian is in very critical condition, and is fighting for his life," he ended.

"This is Chaz Rizzo, live at West Division and Ashland Avenues, Eyewitness News."

Rizzo then walked over to his news truck and tearfully, lit up a cigarette. He wiped his eyes, as he awaited the news of the medical condition of his detective friend from Rush Medical Hospital.

The waiting room of Rush Medical Hospital was filled with police and detectives from the Sixteenth District, as Superintendent Ryan showed up along with a few of the 'Ivory Tower' top brass. Commander Callahan met the Superintendent at the door and gave him a briefing of what had happened and Dorian's condition.

"He's fighting for his life, Superintendent. He's endured several deep stab wounds to his abdomen, and there has been serious damage to his intestines, his stomach and his spleen."

"How does it look," Ryan asked.

"It's not good," the Commander replied.

At point, several other people from the media started walking into the waiting room of the Rush Hospital emergency department and began asking questions about Dorian's condition before the other patrolman started to throw them out.

Chaz Rizzo was one of the throng of reporters, as he approached Tommy Morton.

"How is he, Tommy? Any word?"

"He's been in surgery for the last three hours. The doctors are trying to repair the damage to his intestines and his stomach. The doctors said it looked pretty bad."

"What else are the doctors saying?"

Tommy looked at Rizzo, as he started getting emotional.

"They're giving him a less than fifty percent chance of survival. Way too much internal damage."

Tommy was wiping the tears from his eyes as Rizzo gave him a long, hard hug.

"We gotta stay positive," Rizzo said. "Dorian is a strong guy. He'll pull through."

The emergency room was still filled with throngs of policeman and Dorians' daughter, who was being comforted by the other detectives and their families. It wasn't until 2:00am before one of the doctors emerged from the surgery room.

"We were able to repair the internal damage to his intestine and his stomach. We had to remove his appendix and gall bladder, but we were able to save his spleen. It looks hopeful." Dr. Fanelli said, the head surgeon in charge.

"He will be using a bag for a while, but his condition is improving."

The words 'Thank God' and sighs of relief around the room were in order. Those words were practically said in unison by the forty or more people gathered in the emergency waiting room for the update on Dorian's condition.

Everyone seemed to be feeling better, but no one was more relieved than Chaz Rizzo. Although he always had a rocky relationship with the Detective at best, he respected and greatly admired Phil Dorian. He was a good cop, and a good man, thought to himself. He had been sitting in the corner of the waiting room, his head buried in his hand, as if to be in deep prayer. When the doctor emerged from surgery, he immediately hugged Tommy Morton and began to cry, a sound of both thankfulness and relief.

"Thank god," he exclaimed to Morton. He then grabbed a cigarette from his coat pocket and went outside to smoke off his stress and worry.

Sal Marrocco was at his Burr Ridge home watching the 10:00 o'clock news. He was trying to calm himself down with a glass of wine when he saw the Chaz Rizzo broadcast on Channel 8 Eyewitness News.

The Consigliere was visibly shaken. He had abruptly returned home that evening, after he had tried to make his way to the old abandoned, brownstone church. He was running late to that meeting when he approached the West Division address at 8:00pm and noticed all the police cars parked in front of the old church building.

He knew of the policy that was practiced by the SRC membership when a stranger infiltrated the 'secret society'. He was aware of the 'Circondare' procedure, knowing that they would have to self-destruct and destroy their secret organization.

As he watched the news broadcast, he said a quick prayer to himself. He now realized that all his remaining fraternity brothers had been killed and destroyed in the church explosion.

Marrocco was extremely upset and emotional about the loss of his brother knights, although he did not personally know any of them. Everyone wore red masks and concealed their identities. He never had a chance to develop any friendships or attachments to any of these men, yet he was still visibly upset and stunned. He never got to know any of these hooded members and fellow comrades. Marrocco only knew, because of their common mission and manifest, that there was no need or necessity to ever develop any personal attachments or comradery with any of the members of their ancient fraternity. It was as though each member stoically served the discrete organization as expendable soldiers, and their membership was another means to a justifiable end. With the ten members perishing in the church explosion, he knew everyone was gone.

He thought about their valuable rings and hoped that each member's precious 'SRC' ring had been either destroyed in the fire, or would be buried with its deceased members, as was their 'secret society' tradition. Because the rings were 18 karat Italian gold, these were more susceptible to being destroyed and probably melted in the explosion, Marrocco figured.

'Brother Tobiah' was now the only surviving member of the Society of the Rose Crucifix.

The Consigliere finished his glass of wine and tearfully, shut off the television.

"We shall return," he said to himself.

CHAPTER FORTY-SIX

HOCKEY GAME

I felt uncomfortable sitting in a wheelchair, as I was being processed by the nurses and staff at Rush Medical Hospital for my release. It had been two months and three operations later after that grizzly church fire that almost cost me my life. My stomach has been literally destroyed by the knife wounds, and I was so tired of wearing that bag until my stomach had fully healed. I was told I would have to wear the bag for a few more weeks until my stomach and intestines had fully healed.

I owed at tremendous debt to Tommy Morton for pulling me out of that building before it exploded, as I was told. I didn't remember much after confronting Russo and the hooded brother knights. That night was still a huge blur in my mind.

Morton was standing by the revolving door as the nurses put the finishing touches on my release. A nurse greeted him as he walked over to me while I was still sitting in my wheelchair, and we shook hands and he gave me a brief hug. I called him to pick me up and bring me home earlier that morning, as no one else was available.

"So glad you're feeling better," he exclaimed.

"Thanks for coming, Tommy. I hear I owe you my life."

"Buy me a coffee, Dorian. Otherwise, you owe me nothing," he valiantly replied.

Morton was always a modest guy, and his lack of ego and easy demeanor was something that I always admired about him. As I was signing my release documents, another nurse approached me from the pharmacy.

"You need to take one pill a day for pain," she said, as she handed me a filled prescription of acetaminophen. "If you're still in a lot of pain after one pill, give us a call."

It was a vile with at least 20 pills. I knew that getting addicted to these opioids would be an easy thing for me to do with all the other aches and pains I was feeling from this injury.

Morton helped me get into the car and I was more than grateful for the ride home. We made some small talk about his wife and kids, and he decided to ask me some personal questions.

"Have you heard from your 'insurance executive' girlfriend lately?" he asked.

"No. We had a fallout a couple of days before the explosion and I haven't heard from her at all."

"She had to have heard about your injuries and the explosion fatalities all the way from Detroit. It was national news for a while. She didn't even try to contact you?"

"Nope. Not even a 'Get-Well' text." The disappointment in my voice was more than apparent.

"Well, I'm sure she was using you for information regarding those homicides, so you're far better off."

The traffic was light that afternoon as he was driving me to my loft in the West Loop. We began discussing some 'Ivory Tower' politics before I started to ask some specific questions regarding the church explosion and the "Pedophile Priest Murder' case.

"So how many victims were in that explosion, again?" I asked, although I was told and read about it in the media several times.

"Chicago Fire and EMS recovered ten bodies, including Paul Russo's. Most of the victims were charred beyond recognition and had to have their dental records sent to the morgue before making a positive ID on the rest of them," Morton replied.

"Ten bodies?"

"Yeah, ten of them. Some of them were still wearing tuxedos and name tags with their biblical names on them, and some of the burn victims were burnt beyond recognition. We had a hell of a time figuring out their identities. Thank God for dental records," he replied.

I began counting the number in my head, and the number 'ten' didn't make any sense. From what I had researched, the Society of the Rose Crucifix consisted of twelve members plus the Grand Knight, which was modeled after Jesus and His Twelve Apostles.

"Was Marrocco one of the victims?"

"No. He was interviewed by the Twenty-First District after the fire, and Intel figured they didn't have enough evidence to hold him accountable or to bring any charges against him. He denied being a member and 'alibied' out on the same date and time of the explosion."

With the suicide of Bartell at our district lockup, I figured there were two more 'SRC' members that were not a part of that fire. If Marrocco was an SRC member, that meant that there was still one missing and outstanding.

With the death of four pedophile priests and the church explosion, 'Ivory Tower', along with the rest of Chicago's politicians and media pretty much declared these homicide cases closed. But with one unaccountable member of the 'SRC' still out there, I wasn't buying it. To finally conclude that the 'SRC' was finally dead and destroyed was still a hard sell for me.

I was ordered by Commander Callahan to stay home and relax for the remaining part of that week, but I was restless and bored by the third day I was home. There was only so many walks and playing 'fetch' with Ginger that I could do during the day, so I decided to go back to work at the precinct later that week.

The day I had arrived back to work, there were 'Welcome Back Phil' signs and balloons surrounding my desk in my office, along with a small chocolate cake and several of my favorite Dunkin' Donuts eclairs and jelly donuts. I had lost over fifty pounds and was down to a thirty-two waist while I was in the hospital. Eating all of those decadent goodies would still be very difficult for me, as I was still wearing a bag.

Several precinct workers and patrolmen came into my office to congratulate me, giving me their good wishes on my healthy recovery. Even Commander Callahan come into my office to welcome me back to work, as he gave me an emotional embrace. It felt great to be missed and appreciated by everyone there in the Sixteenth District, which was something I wasn't feeling much of while these 'Pedophile Priest Murders' were being investigated.

I later received a visit later that morning from my favorite news reporter. He was speechless at first, as he entered my office, only giving me an intense embrace when he immediately saw me. There were tears in his eyes as he seemed to be grateful to see me well and back at work.

"Should we get a room?" I joked, as I was finding it difficult to pull away from his powerful bear hug.

"Shut up, Philly! It's so great to see you again," Chaz Rizzo said, as he invited himself into my office and made himself comfortable.

"We're so glad you're feeling better," he exclaimed, as his comments and well wishes sounded totally genuine. He then began to tell me of the number of well-wishers at the Channel Eight news station that were praying for my speedy recovery from the stabbing injury.

"Congratulations on solving the 'Pedophile Priest Murders," as he popped an unlit Marlboro Light cigarette into his mouth.

"How do you figure?"

"Come on Philly. You did some great detective work out there, tracing those parking tickets and all, and figuring out that 'secret society' cult that was going on in that abandoned church. I was almost positive there was only one serial killer doing these murders," Chaz explained.

'I'm impressed, Philly. For an old detective, you've still got it," he jokingly exclaimed, shaking my hand at the same time.

"Looks like you're going to have to start scrounging elsewhere for your news reports, Riz. Hopefully, we won't be having anymore 'Pedophile Priest Murders' anymore."

"Yeah, Philly. Thanks to you and Morton, the 'pedophile priest' community can start breathing easier again, now that the society of 'sick, psycho-bastards' has been destroyed."

The way Rizzo had made that statement just didn't make me feel very triumphant or victorious. I felt empty and unrewarded. I felt unbelievably hapless.

Chaz Rizzo's statement made me feel remorseful and sympathetic towards the Brother Knights of the Society of the Rose Crucifix. This was an ancient brotherhood of men, who were trained as killers and executioners, supposedly 'appointed by God' to deliver justice for those many young, helpless victims of the Catholic Church. They stood on behalf of the many young children, whose young lives had been ruined by these sexual deviants, who had been able to escape justice for so many years, thanks to institutions like the

Archdiocese of Chicago, the Vatican and perhaps, the entire Roman Catholic Church.

Maybe, these 'SRC' brothers, as demented as they were, had the right idea. These were the brother knights, who felt it was their obligation to deliver and bring justice to those many sexual deviants, who hid behind the vestments of their priesthood. To bring reckoning to those servants of the Church, those pedophiles who preached the gospel to their flocks at holy mass, then raped and sodomized their helpless young victims when no one was looking.

For all those pedophile ex-priests, now living comfortable lives while their young victims grew up to a cruel, unsympathetic world, the 'SRC' stood for the defense of those poor, innocent children. Those grown-up victims who have now turned to drugs, alcohol and very often, suicide to ease their pain. All the lawsuits, all the publicity, all the shame directed towards those sexual deviants, can never replace the stolen innocence that was taken from these young children for so many, many years.

For several long moments, I thought to myself, these gallant knights of the Rose Crucifix were the executioners and the deliverers of their own brand of justice. These 'brothers' put themselves in charge of carrying out formal 'death sentences' on behalf of those young victims whose lives have been forever ruined by the trusted servants of the Roman Catholic Church.

With all the shocking injustices of a hypocritical Vatican, the dioceses of the world now have a fraternity of red hooded men whom they must now answer to. Their fraternity was an ancient society of brothers, created to deliver righteousness on behalf of the church's many innocent victims. Theirs was a brotherhood of men, exuding a form of indictment against those sick, sexual deviants who have hidden behind the Lord's altar, within the hallowed halls of the church's sacristy, for way too long.

Perhaps, I thought to myself, the destruction of this 'secret society' in Chicago may *not* have been such a good thing.

"Phil? Are you alright?" as I must have drifted off into a trance.

"Oh, yes, I'm okay." I was having a lot of trouble concentrating and staying focused lately.

"Good, I came by to drop these off to you and your partner. Just a little token of our appreciation at the news station," he said, as he placed four Chicago Blackhawks tickets to next month's opening hockey game against the Detroit Red Wings.

"For what? Being a pain in my ass?" I joked.

"Consider these tickets a gift from a grateful station, Detective. Besides, I hear the Blackhawks have put together a great team this year, so the opening game will be a good one."

The Channel Eight Eyewitness News crew had season box tickets to all the Chicago sports teams, and it was a great way to get the Chicago coppers to 'play nice' with the news media. Seems like the nicer we were to their reporters, the more tickets we were 'comped' to Chicago sports events and games.

"Thank you, Chaz," as I gave him a hug. "You were a huge help," I replied.

He made that girlish giggle that still got on my nerves and walked out of my office, with that unlit cigarette still in his mouth.

I called Tommy and let him know that he had a hot date with his wife at the United Center next month on October 4th. Not having a significant other anymore, I invited my seven-year-old granddaughter, Brianna, to come along to the hockey game. She said that she would check her schedule and let me know.

That early fall weather could not have been more perfect, as my granddaughter was dropped off in front of United Center on that warm autumn evening. The crowds of hockey fans that were lined up at Gate Three were overflowing onto Madison Street. I tightly grasped little Brianna's hand as we entered the famed, United Center with all its revered statutes of hockey and basketball heroes.

"Ever been to a hockey game before?" I asked her, already knowing the answer to my question.

"No, I've been too busy with homework and dancing recitals to bother with hockey games," she replied, using her normal 'seven-year-old going on twenty-nine' tone of voice.

"Well, you're in for a treat," I said, as we made our way through the throngs of people and up to our lower box seats. Our tickets said we were in Section 117, just five rows away from front glass near the goalie net. With the proximity of the Chicago Blackhawks players in their designated benches near the penalty box, I could tell that even my sophisticated little granddaughter was impressed. Tommy Morton and his wife, Clara, were already waiting for us at our designated chairs.

"You know, maybe your buddy Rizzo isn't such a bad guy after all," Tommy mentioned, even though I could tell he still had a sliver of contempt for the pushy news reporter.

"It pays to be nice sometimes," I smiled, as I was enjoying the interaction between Clara and my little Brianna.

We were all enjoying the hockey game, up through the third period, when I decided to get up and appease my granddaughter, who had been bugging me the whole time for 'cheesy French fries'. Tommy and I both needed a beer as well. Seeing that we hadn't had dinner that night, I decided to go to the concession stand and see what kind of food was available.

I walked up to the concession stand and stood in line for about five minutes, when I heard a familiar voice calling my name from behind me.

"Hello, Phil." It was Olivia.

I must have had a shocked look on my face, and I was momentarily, speechless. She was wearing a Detroit Red Wings white and red jersey and a red hat displaying the traditional Red Wings logo in front of it. She had on a pair of tight blue jeans and her dark, brown hair was in a pony-tail. Of course, she looked amazing.

"How are you feeling," she managed to say, as I was still at a loss for words. "I heard you were injured."

"Eh...yes, I was. Stab wound in the gut, no big deal," as I tried to make light of it.

She looked at me intently, her eyes starting to well up with tears as I was having difficulty responding. My heart was beating out of my chest, and my hands were starting to perspire.

"Surprised to see you here, of all places," I mentioned.

"I'm in town on business. I'm just here with an associate from my company," as she pointed to her seating area not very far from mine.

I placed myself out of the concession line and walked over towards the other end of the hallway, as I had a distinct feeling that an intense conversation between us was going to develop.

"I tried to call you," I bluntly said. "You blocked my calls."

"I know. I'm sorry. I was hurt," she managed to say, as I noticed her eyes welling up even more.

"Then you heard that the 'Pedophile Priest Murder' cases have been solved?"

"Yes, I did," she managed to say. "Congratulations...a job well done." A few more silent moments.

"So now, your office can finally settle these life insurance claims for the Archdiocese, correct?" I inquired.

"We have a few for more details to resolve, but that's how it's looking."

There were a few more silent minutes, as we continued to awkwardly stare at each other and make conversation.

"When did you get out of the hospital?"

"Last month, Olivia. Were you going to call me?" I asked, knowing that I was now walking into an emotional hornet's nest. I'm sure she denoted a tone of anger in my voice.

"I wanted to, Phil...believe me, I did. I wanted to contact you when I came into town the other day. I was just so afraid of how you would react. You've been on my mind."

"I see," as there were more awkward moments.

"Who are you here with?" she inquired.

"My granddaughter, Brianna, Tommy and his wife. I should be getting back to them. They're going to wonder what happened to me." She continued to look at me intently, only now there even were tears streaming down her face.

"Can I call you tomorrow? Maybe we can have lunch?" she inquired.

"I'm still pretty jammed up, Olivia. I was off work for quite a while, and I still have a ton of paperwork that I'm trying to catch up on."

"I understand," she replied.

I was about to walk away when she tightly grasped my hand and placed a wet kiss on my right cheek. By now, her face was completely drenched with her tears streaming down her face. She was acting as though she didn't want to let me go.

"Phil?" I looked at her, trying hard not to respond.

"I love you," she managed to say. I went into shock.

Her mascara was running, and she was wiping her moistened face with her left hand. At that moment, she looked like she was struggling not to have an emotional breakdown.

I just stared at her, as I was totally stunned. She had never said that to me before. For that moment, I was without words. I wanted to tell her that I loved her back. I wanted to tell her how much I had missed her and how hurt I was. I wanted to apologize for the way it all ended at the restaurant. I wanted to make love to her right there at the United Center and pretend that nothing had ever happened.

But then, my sixth sense, my 'voice of reason' started talking. I thought about the way she had run out of that restaurant last summer, and how she blocked my phone calls and never contacted me. Olivia knew I was involved in that fatal church fire, and she knew that I had been injured and barely escaped that fire explosion with my life. It was in social media, the national evening news broadcasts and in all the major newspapers. My hospital room was filled with get well cards, flowers, and get well wishes from almost every police department across the country and almost every politician in Chicago.

And yet, I didn't hear from her. Not a phone call. Not a text. Not a get-well card. Nothing.

While she was in Chicago, she stayed at my house and worked on her insurance claims and met up with other Chicago P.D. detectives behind my back. She even hired a private investigator to work around me on the 'Pedophile Priest Murders'. She opened a safe deposit box on the same day as her 'visit' from an alleged 'SRC' member, posing as a Chicago attorney. I never did subpoena or verify the contents of that box, and it was probably better that I didn't know.

And then finally, when I asked and inquired about her covert activities, she made me feel as though it was none of my business. She had successfully crumbled that concrete wall that took me years to construct around my already broken heart...only for her to break it all over again.

I looked at her intently and shook my head. I silently let her know that she wasn't excused for her actions, for walking out of my life that night at the restaurant, and for hurting me the way she did.

"I see how you love me," I coldly replied.

I then pulled my hand away from her, now trying to physically run away from the emotional prison she was trying so hard to lock me back into again.

As I was recovering in the hospital from my injuries and my broken heart, I promised myself that I would never fall so hard, so quick, for someone so lethal and so self-serving...ever again. Olivia obviously had her own agenda, and whatever it was, I wanted no part of it. I took one long last look at her, emblazing her image into my memory.

"Have a great life, Olivia," I loudly said.

And then, I walked away.

CHAPTER FORTY-SEVEN

The hot, setting sun began to dip under the clouds as the calm blue water appeared to be a sheet of glass on that early evening. The calendar said November, but the Caribbean sun never let the temperature get below eighty degrees. A man wearing a white fedora hat, a pair of white shorts and a blue Hawaiian shirt sat on the beach in a comfortable lounge chair, enjoying his Manhattan under a grass hut overlooking the Atlantic Ocean. The sunsets of the remote island of Labadee were breath taking, the man thought to himself, as he took another long swallow from his alcoholic beverage.

The white, untouched sands of the island beaches were pristine, surrounding the large white, blue clay shingled villa sitting at the foothills of the remote island. The retired gentleman had been renting the 4,175 square foot mansion for the last several months and was relieved that he was able to finally close on the opulent villa for the negotiated purchase price of $1.7 million yesterday. The traveler had spent the last few days settling into his newly owned home, which he now had the pleasure to enjoy.

A Haitian servant approached the man in the lounge chair, inquiring about anything else he may need before retiring. He had just enjoyed a beach front dinner and was quietly digesting his food while enjoying the island sunset. This was his normal evening routine.

"Is there anything else you may need, Signor Joe?"

"No, Javier. I'm fine, thank you. See you in the morning."

Joseph Kilbane fumbled with his sunglasses and smiled to himself. He was recapping the activities of the last several months in his mind as he was able to finally, relax and enjoy his permanent vacation.

He was thankful to Little Tony DiMatteo, who was able to drive him to the South Bend Regional Airport on the night he disappeared. He boarded a private jet to embark on the three-hour flight to Miami International Airport, where DiMatteo had connections. Dressed as a regular layman, he boarded another private Cessna 210 with his brief case carrying over $50,000 in cash to Port-au-Prince Airport in Haiti. After a four-hour layover, and using his fake American passport, he boarded a yacht at the Haitian harbor to transport him to the island two hours away. The large Sea Ray Sundancer, which was owned by a DiMatteo 'family friend', was a comfortable means of transportation to his new home on the island of Labadee.

Since the events of Chicago and the fire destruction of the brown stone church on West Division Street, the Great Lakes Life Insurance Company had no choice but to pay the life insurance claims of the former priests John Marquardt, Lucas Senopoli, Matthew McDougall, and Mark Ryan, totaling over twenty million dollars, made payable to the Archdiocese of Chicago.

When the money was finally wire transferred to the Archdiocese, Monsignor Giacomo Fusciardi, the Vatican Special Diplomat to the Pope, paid an unusual visit to the Chicago Cardinal. There was an unsecured, outstanding debt to the Vatican that needed repayment. The Holy See and the Vatican Curia had called in the outstanding loan payable to the Vatican for the amount totaling $35 million dollars, plus interest. These funds had been borrowed by Cardinal Markowitz several years ago to meet some the legal obligations of the child molestation lawsuits that had been piling up against the Archdiocese.

After some intense negotiations, Cardinal Markowitz settled with the Institute for Works of

Religion (IWR), commonly referred to as the Vatican Bank, for the total sum of the insurance proceeds plus an additional ten, or $30 million dollars.

Understanding that the Archdiocese of Chicago was on the brink of bankruptcy, the Vatican was very agreeable to settle for a nominal amount of that unsecured, uncollateralized loan.

The Vatican Curia was also happy to pay off Kilbane and Little Tony DiMatteo. The two had very specific, damaging information regarding the former Cardinal Jose Maria Buonsante's handling of various pedophile priests' scandals in Caracas, Venezuela before going to Rome. The Monsignor threatened to go public several times to the Holy See, which would have been a public relations nightmare for the Pope and the Vatican Curia.

Since the Vatican Bank's financial transactions are discrete, the 'IWR' forwarded twenty million to a Swiss bank account, under the name of Salvatore Aldo Marrocco, the DiMatteo Family Consigliere. Of that amount, ten million was transferred to a Cayman Islands bank account under the name of Joseph Francis O'Leary, his mother's maiden name and now, his legal alias.

DiMatteo then arranged to have two million of those proceeds cashed in and sent, via private boat, to Joseph Kilbane. A Haitian driver had delivered a large black satchel earlier that week to the former Monsignor, to secure the closing purchase of his large mansion and for his own living expenses on the island. He knew that, even though he had to split the settlement proceeds with the Vatican and Little Tony, Kilbane still had enough money to secure his comfortable retirement for the rest of his life on that private island.

A tanned, dark haired, beautiful women brought him over another Manhattan. She had gone back to the villa to change out of her bathing suit and was wearing a casual pair of white Capri pants and a red, sexy, mid-drift tee shirt, which exposed her pierced belly button.

"Hey, honey," she exclaimed, as she kissed Kilbane on the lips. They had just shared a wonderful, ocean front dinner together and was finally feeling relaxed. She arrived by boat that morning after her long, grueling flight, which originated from Detroit's Metro Airport on the prior day.

"Hey, Olivia. You didn't you get yourself a drink?"

"No, baby. I've had enough alcohol for one day."

Olivia Laurent had spent most of the day relaxing with Kilbane on the desolate island, laying on the beach. She had been enjoying the warm, ocean water and the mansion pool nearby. She watched the sun slowly set, along with her priest-boyfriend, with whom she had an intense, romantic relationship with for the *last two years*.

She laid down on the lounge chair after adjusting her seat and placed another kiss on Kilbane's cheek.

"This is such a wonderful life," as she looked towards the setting sun, grasping his hand.

As the sunset had finally settled over the secluded island, Kilbane glanced over to Olivia and smiled. He then gazed over the clear, blue Atlantic Ocean and took another long sip of his drink. Fidgeting with his ruby, red cross ring, the former Monsignor proudly smiled to himself.

At long last, 'Brother Ezekiel' now had it made.

ACKNOWLEDGEMENTS

My thanks to the many people who helped, assisted and inspired me in writing and completing this novel:

To John Scott Aiello, a wonderful friend whose many high school stories and recollections were a huge inspiration.

To Lori Munoz, Michael Spilotro of Arezzo Jewelry, George Shea of AMI Group, and Officer Sergeant James Ciannella of the Chicago Police Department 18th District for all their proofreading and technical advice. Their editing and story suggestions were of great assistance.

To Erich Vokral of Allwebco Designs, for his book cover designs on this book and the 'Of Bread & Wine' novel.

To my daughter Gianna Potempa, and my son-in-law, Pete Potempa, for their formatting and marketing skills, and for all of their help and patience with me.

To my classmates in my writing workshop, for all their recommendations and constructive comments.

To my three sons, Roberto, Matteo and Stefano, whose names I have periodically inserted in my writing. A reminder to always work hard, dream big, and to never give up on your goals, no matter how big or small.

And to Ginette Piagentini, for her story advice and her help with editing. My thanks to her for being my captive audience and tolerating my 3:00am writing sessions.

Her support, her encouragement and her love have been nothing short of amazing.

Made in the USA
Middletown, DE
31 January 2019